The Secrets of Don Pedro Miguel

Frank P. Araujo

The Secrets of Don Pedro Miguel

Frank P. Araujo

Quartet Global

Seattle

Published by Quartet Global
Seattle, WA
Contact: quartetglobal@gmail.com

This is a work of fiction.

Cover Painting by permission of Ruth Coelho
Cover design by M. Anne Sweet
Author photo by Frank P. Araujo

ISBN-13: 978-0-9840-493-5-6 (Trade Paper)

This work of fiction
is written in part
to the memory of my son
and in part
to the loving friends and relatives
who were there for me
during that time of loss and separation

.

ACKNOWLEDGMENTS

This book couldn't have happened without input, inspiration and good vibes from A."P"A., M.E.S.; Cat, Roberto, Ruth, Anne and, of course, Red.

.

Oh what a tangled web we weave.
When first we practise to deceive!

Sir Walter Scott, *(1771 - 1832)*
Marmion, Canto vi. Stanza 17

PART ONE

The manuscript
Albergue El Palacio, San Luisita, Sonora, Mexico
11:58 PM, Saturday, March 21, 1970

Alter reading the manuscript. Santos Villalobos glanced across the table at tall, lanky Matt Spyner. Matt's intense blue eyes behind round brass wire rim glasses bored into Santos.

"So, what do you think?" Matt said.

"Damn good, Matt. But it ain't anthropology."

"Whadda mean, 'ain't anthropology?' "

"The Academics won't buy this," Santos said. "They want nose counts, verifiable models, populations studies– shit like that. This is art."

"You're wrong," Matt said.

"How many people have seen this work?"

"Besides you, Ed Singer and my girlfriend."

"What did the great Professor Singer say?"

Matt looked away, then said,

"He told me to do it over a-fucking-gain."

"Go public with what you've found, man. Share it."

"Go public? Whadda mean?"

Santos tapped the manuscript in front of him.

"Matt. This is a jewel, a Star of..."

"That's my life's work, man, not a dime-store dangle-bangle."

"And, it's good," Santos said. "It's just not anthropology."

Matt leaned on his fists on the table, then spoke,

"This is what real anthropology should be– the journey into alternative reality– science in its purest form! It's not the same old crap about friendly natives living in happy little villages."

"No argument," Santos said. "This is a goldmine. People are starving for this viewpoint."

Matt exploded. "This isn't just some hophead's acid trip. This is reality—the reality beyond reality."

"This can also be a money tree, Matt."

"Money tree?" Matt said.

"You got it all, man," Santos said. "The academic credentials to buy acceptability, the Noble Savage perspective and the whole

1

hallucinogenic experience. People will lap this up like tom cats slurping cream."

"Fuck that!" Matt shouted.

Snatching up the manuscript, he yelled, "I'd burn this work before I'd prostitute it."

"Hey," Santos said. "Easy does it."

Shaking the manuscript at Santos, Matt stumbled to the sink, seized a can of lighter fluid, a box of kitchen matches. "I'll fucking do it!"

Santos jumped up, grabbed onto the manuscript.

"Don't go all goofy on me, man," he said.

Dropping the fluid and matches, Matt gripped the manuscript.

His red face turned pale.

His hand went to his head.

Blood gushed out of his nose.

"You're bleeding," Santos said. "All that dope's hit you like a hammer!"

Matt stumbled back knocking over a chair, then crumpled to the floor where he lay still, clutching the manuscript to his chest.

Santos leaned over him, looked into his dilated, dull eyes. Easing the manuscript from Matt's hands, Santos took it to the table.

He stopped, thumbed through the manuscript, then glanced at the door.

Looking around, he spotted a ragged phone book near some newspapers next to the bed.

Tearing off the manuscript's title page, Santos ripped up the phone book, arranged the pages with some newspaper making sure the pile was about the same size as the manuscript.

He poured lighter fluid on the papers, lit the pile, watched it burn. While the pages burned to ashes, Santos charred the edges of the manuscript title page, then dropped it on top of the burnt residue.

Snatching up an aluminum binder from the night stand, Santos jammed the manuscript inside, darted a quick glance back at the unconscious Matt on the floor, then slipped out the door.

Santos popped down the stairs, paused at the bottom.

The front desk was deserted. The tiny lobby empty.

Zipping up his black leather jacket, Santos stepped out, hurried down the street.

Lights from shop windows sliced the dark along the empty street. Gripping the binder tight to his chest, Santos stepped around the corner.

A man popped out of the alley, seized Santos's shoulder, pushed him up against the wall of the building.

"Where you off to, amigo?" the man said.

In the dim light, Santos saw a tall dark-skinned man with a hook nose. He shined a flash light into Santos's face.

"What you're doing out here this time of night?" he said.

"Who in the hell wants to know?"

The man whipped out an identification billfold. "Lt. Manuel Ortega, *Policia Nacional*, wants to know."

He shined his light on Santos's hand. "Where'd you get this blood, Amigo?"

"What blood?"

"Here on your hands."

Santos gasped, noticing the blood for the first time.

Manuel reached behind his back for his handcuffs.

"Let's take a little walk to the police station for a friendly chat."

Santos struck out with the edge of the aluminum binder catching the policeman in the throat. He loosened his grip, stumbled back, choking.

Santos ran.

~*~*~

Matt came to with a jerk. He touched his face, stared at his bloody hands, then at the blood spotted chair on the floor.

Santos was gone.

Then, seeing the matches, the lighter fluid, the pile of ashes, Matt moaned,

"Oh God, no!"

He crawled to the pile, then stared down at the ashes beneath the charred title page.

Holding his hands to his head, he sobbed banging his head on the floor. Then, looking back at the pile of ashes, he stumbled to his feet, pulled out a canvas bag from the old wardrobe. Jerking open the chest of drawers, he snatched out clothes, threw them into the bag.

He found his passport.

He retrieved an envelope full of pesos and dollars taped behind the kitchen drawer. Stuffing these into the bag, he zipped it up, then lumbered to the door.

He paused, glanced back at the pile of ashes, then stalked down the hall leaving the door ajar.

~*~*~

La semana santa
Plaza Central, San Luisita, Sonora, Mexico
Next day, 6:47 AM, Sunday, March 22, 1970

Palm Sunday, the first day of Holy Week in San Luisita broke cloudy with a threat of rain. Panchito Gonzales looked over the crowd of people from the rural areas mixed with the townsfolk gathered in front of the church in the Plaza Central.

Dressed in new white pants, new white shirt, new red bandana, new *huaraches*, Panchito shivered, gripped the palm branch in the cold morning breeze. From the rear of the crowd, he stared at the blessed image of Saint Luisa that had been placed in front of the church's door the night before. The votive candles surrounding the statue flickered, snapping in the light wind.

Sunrise!

The church doors opened. The white vestments of the altar attendants shone ghost-like against the priest's red chasuble and stole. They floated out the doorway to take up positions in front of the statue.

When the first rays of sunlight lit the cross at the top of the steeple, m e m b e r s o f the band, in bright red uniforms adorned with gold braid, raised their instruments, rent the morning air with a tinny blast of trumpets sparked by the thump of a large bass drum. At that moment, the priest blessed the statue with drops of holy water from the aspergillum and aspersorium held the altar boys.

Panchito crossed himself, kissed his thumb when the priest walked in front of the crowd spraying them with holy water.

4

~*~*~

Same day, 9:15 AM, Friday

Two blocks from the plaza on the second floor of the hotel, Maria Consuela heard the band music. She resented not being there. She loved carrying flowers in the procession, the sounds, smells, joys of *La Semana Santa*. Selecting a key from her jangling ring, she stepped to the first door, then stopped.

The door was ajar.

She rapped on the doorjamb.

"Permission to come in?"

No answer. She swung the door open, stepped in.

The overturned chair caught her eye. She saw the pile of ashes. Bending down, she looked at the stains on the chair.

This is blood!

She didn't want blood. She wasn't afraid of blood but blood meant police. She didn't like police. Retreating, she closed the door, then trotted downstairs to tell the manager.

Let him call the authorities.

~*~*~

Later, same day, 11:14 AM, Friday

Entering the room on the second floor, Captain Dagoberto Ramirez Palacios took a small cigar from his pocket, lit it, then tip-toed through the scattered debris in the hotel room.

"This room reeks of *yerba*," he said. "What's your read, Luis?"

Lt. Jose Luis Guzman, Ramirez's adjutant snapping photographs, looked at his colleague of many years, then said,

"Blood, a pile of ashes, and this, a dried hallucinogenic mushroom. That's it."

"Just blood?"

"The maid says the Gringo who stayed here was kind of weird."

5

"Great," Ramirez said, "We're up to our asses in coyotes, drug smugglers and now blood and a missing weird Gringo."

Raising the camera, Guzman snapped another shot.

"Can't tell yet whose blood it is but we found a baggie of marijuana," he said.

"Anything else?"

"No," Luis said. "He must have eaten the roaches."

"Well, there goes our big drug case," Ramirez said. "Send the blood samples to the capital. We want to keep our friends in the US happy."

"Think any of this connects to the *coyotes* and drug traffic here?" Guzman said.

Everything in Mexico now connects to the drug traffic."

A young policeman came into the room, saluted, then spoke,

"*Mi capitán*, a delivery boy just found a body over by the barbershop."

Ramirez, weary, his head throbbing, flicked cigar ash into the palm of his hand.

"I hope you got more film," he said to Guzman. "This could be a long day."

~*~*~

A crowd had gathered when the two senior policemen arrived. Ramirez and Guzman returned the salute of a young officer guarding a man's body sprawled near the side of the barbershop.

Guzman bent over the body.

"Anything been touched?" he said.

"No, sir," the officer said. "The kid found him just as I was coming around the corner on my way to the Albergue."

"We're lucky," Guzman said. "The rats haven't picked his wallet."

Guzman took the ID badge wallet from the dead man's hand.

"Whores and the Holy Mother!" he said, then held the ID up to Ramirez.

"Oh shit," Ramirez said, "A *Nacional*!

"Not just a *Nacional*, Captain. It's Manuel. Colonel Ortega's son."

"This is truly not good, Luis," Ramirez said.

He stepped back, paused at the edge of the building, looked back at Guzman.

"This affirms my answer to your earlier question, Jose Luis."

"Remind me," Guzman said.

"Everything in Mexico connects to the the drug traffic," the Captain said.

~*~*~

Honeymoon interrupted
Cabo De San Lucas, Baja California, Mexico
Two days later, 6:03 AM, Tuesday, March 24, 1970

The jingle of the phone startled Pepe from his deep sleep. He glared at the phone on the table outside the bedroom on the patio table. Slipping on a pair of loose-fitting white cotton pants, he padded out to answer the ringing. Looking back inside at the blond woman in the bed, he smiled remembering the love-making the night before. He picked up the receiver, slid the door shut.

"*Bueno,*" he said. "This had better be important."

"Gilberto Sanchez speaks. I'm sorry to disturb you on your honeymoon."

"Gallo, you dog. What are you doing calling me so early in the morning, *hermano?*"

"Bad news. Manolito's been killed."

Pepe, lowering the phone in his hand as if in a dream, sank into a chair, returned the phone to his ear.

"When?" he said.

"We just got the word last night. He was checking out a smuggling operation in Santa Luisita. The local police found his body Sunday morning and called us. I checked it out before I called you."

Pepe couldn't speak, move. He blinked, choked for breath.

"Are you still there, Pepe?"

"Give me a moment, Gallo..."

"Take your time."

Pepe stared through the window glass at his wife asleep on the bed.

He gazed over the balcony at the sea, breathed deep, blinked again and again.

He was back, his voice hard.

"What happened?"

"It's not clear. They think he choked to death after being struck in the throat. There were traces of someone's blood on his clothes, but his pistol was holstered."

"You're saying it wasn't his blood?"

"It doesn't look like it but they're checking it out."

"Are you on top of it?"

"You know I'm on top of it."

"What about the locals?"

"Captain Ramirez-- a straight shooter. He's been with us every step of the way. No back doors from that end. This was strictly an outside job."

"Any ideas who?"

"No, but bet your ass, we'll turn it every way we can until we come up with answers."

Pepe caught his breath, gritted his teeth.

"Have you called my mother?" he said.

"I called you first, *hermano*."

A long silence followed before Gallo's emotional broken voice came back on.

"Pepe. I can't say..., can't tell you how sorry, sorry..."

Pepe cradled the phone. He stood, leaned on the balcony, staring out at the sea. He let his eyes wander over the immensity of the water, tracing its stretch toward the horizon.

The sea, the sea.

Wash the present painful thoughts from my mind.

Immense, deep, limitless, profound, eternal, unending ... all these things, feelings ... they wash away– in time.

Someone had taken his brother from him– less than a week before, his brother had stood beside him when he married.

His brother. The kid brother he told where the priest kept the keys to the wine cupboard when they were altar boys.

He turned back to the window, stared again at the woman asleep in the bed. Her bare white back spoke to him of great love, tenderness. He remembered her softness, the feel of her body next to his, her blue eyes, her blond hair. He remembered her kissing his brother's cheek, Manolito's shyness at the attention of a beautiful woman.

She would understand why they would have to cut this magic time short.

There was work to do.

~*~*~

True confessions
Lola Santiago's Apartment, West Los Angeles, CA
11:38 AM, Friday, Mar 27, 1970

Santos Villalobos watched Lola Santiago standing at the window. A drizzling rain tapped on the iron gratings covering the windows of the shops and stores around the neighborhood.

Lola raised her voice in full volume Spanish-accented English,

"How could you be so fucking stupid?"

Glaring at Santos sitting on the couch, she strode around the room, waving her arms.

"Things just happened too fast," Santos said.

"You killed a cop."

"It was an accident."

"Do you think those Mexican cops give a shit if it was an accident?"

Santos shrugged. Lola paced back to the window.

Outside, a passing car made squishy sounds in the light rain that hung in the air.

"You're sure no one saw you?" she said.

"Absolutely."

"Meet anybody earlier who'd remember you?"

"Only a cleaning lady. She didn't give me a second look."

"How about when you went out with this guy?"

Santos looked at her tight blouse, the well-formed breasts, the long, silky mane of black hair.

"We ate at a little taqueria," Santos said. "We were in his little world. He talked in Spanish; I listened."

"Anyone else see you?"

"Anyone that saw us would think I was just another Mexican."

Lola came over to the couch, sat beside him. She lay her hand on his leg.

"Why'd you get involved?"

"He'd done this work, experienced it first hand, living with this shaman, taking peyote, mushrooms and drinking lotsa tequila. Then he wrote this paper..." Santos said. "...A fucking masterpiece!"

"He married?" Lola said.

"A girl friend, an archaeologist. They're not into psychoanalytic things."

"Where was she?" Lola said.

Santos glanced at her, her clothes fit her figure, tight, provoking.

"Back in the States," he said. "This guy, Matt said they were on the outs– he was bitter about it."

Lola folded her arms over her breasts, a shiny gold Guadalupana medal between her breasts reflected the light.

"What about this manuscript?" she said.

Santos stared a moment at the medal, his eyes dropping again to her breasts.

"He wrote it as a thesis, then showed it to Edgar Singer, the big authority on Southwest indigenous cultures. Manny Barber– my major professor and Singer were grad students together at Columbia. Manny suggested I call on Singer to recommend possible field sites. Singer gave me this guy's name and location along with several others. No way he'd know if I called on him or not."

"What happened then?"

"After we ate, we went back to his place to blow some weed. I was fascinated with what this guy was saying. He showed me the manuscript. It was a gold mine-- coulda gotten published as it was..."

"What did he say to that?"

Santos sighed, turned his face toward the floor.

"This is where it gets crapped."

He recounted the details of the angry encounter, his initial fright, recovery and taking the manuscript.

She sat close to him, hands folded in her lap.

"Didn't you call for help?" she said.

"Thought about it," Santos said. "Then, looking at the manuscript...I saw possibilities."

"What kind of possibilities?"

"Big ones. I'd stumbled on a piece of work that could be my ticket out of town."

She snatched her hand from his leg. Her voice rose in pitch, volume.

"So you stole a fucking collection of ramblings and going-ons about drug tripping, and exposed your ass to criminal charges?"

"When I saw he wasn't dead, it came to me what to do," Santos said. "He was stoned, went down, cracked his head. I knew when he'd come to, he wouldn't remember shit. So, I burned the phone book and newspapers..."

"You should have called the cops and covered your ass," Lola said.

"...so that when this *pendejo* would wake up, he'd see a pile of ashes and figure he'd burnt it up like he was threatening to."

"What are you going to do now?" she said.

"I'm going to read it again till I can make it into something that I know will sell. That stupid shit– he didn't know what he had."

He looked over at her, his large eyes fixed on hers.

"Well, I do," he said. "And I intend to make it do just what I want."

"And what's that?"

"We're on the edge of a big scene involving drugs altering consciousness. Aldous Huxley's written about the visionary experience, people are experimenting with hallucinogens, marijuana's mainstream for younger middle and upper class Euro-Americans. People go giddy gah-gah about the spirit world, reincarnation alternative dimensions of reality and Native American arcane knowledge. This book has it all and will lay it out for them."

"If you publish this, this guy's ghost will always be there."

"I don't believe in ghosts, Lola."

"Goddam it, put this in a book and this guy'll have your ass in court for stealing, plagiarism, copyright infringement, for... pure asshole stupidity!"

"He told me there was only one copy of the manuscript. Singer won't remember the details. I know academics– when he started to read it and it got freaky, he chucked it."

"He'd still know."

Santos's eyes were shining.

"A good lawyer like your cousin Cassie'd shred him in court and he'll know that."

"But the guy who wrote it would know it too."

Santos raised his voice.

"How in the fuck is he going to prove it?"

"There's the girl friend," Lola said.

She stepped to the window again.

"This guy can tie you to that dead cop."

"How? There's only circumstantial evidence I was ever there, let alone anything that could associate me with that cop."

Lola stopped talking. After a moment of silence, she said,

"You've really thought this thing through, haven't you?"

"Your damn right I have."

"But, you'll have to change it."

"I already know how I'm going to do it."

"How will Barber and all those other guys at the University react?"

"I'll publish it before I show it to Barber. Once it's in print, it's got legs, momentum. Academics are always impressed by the printed page."

"So, you're not just looking at this as a dissertation?"

Santos snorted, then said,

"When this is published, the bucks will fly in. If the ivy-covered halls don't want it in their libraries, I'll console myself with the money."

"You think it's that good?"

He raised his eyes, sought hers.

"I don't fucking *think* so," he said. "I fucking *know* so."

Her voice became husky, taut.

"Then, I guess you'd better do it," she said.

~*~*~

Meeting of the minds
Over Sonora, Mexico
Four days later, 6:47 AM. Tuesday, March 31, 1970

Ivo Drako looked through the oval porthole at the jet's shadow slipping through cotton-ball clouds over the arid Mexican landscape. The jet dipped a wing in rapid descent toward a green spot splashed between two hills. A winding river on the brown-gray earth came into view cutting through a high range of mountains to the east.

The quick correction to the straight-in approach jostled Drako from his thoughts. The morning sun reflecting off the window flash-blinded him. He flinched, feeling the shudder of the wheel carriage lowering. Donning a pair of sunglasses, he spoke in Russian to the three big men on the craft with him,

"*Uzhe zharko kak voroty ada vnisu*, already hot as the hubs of hell down there."

On the ground, the jet rolled to the end of the strip, then swung back towards three parked limousines where unsmiling men, in dark suits, wearing dark sunglasses, stood motionless.

The jet stopped, its engine whined died down. Drako saw the flight attendant pop open the door, uncoil the built-in accommodation ladder, then scramble down to set a metal footstool at the bottom.

Pulling a handkerchief from his pocket, Drako wiped his forehead. One of the men picked up a briefcase. The other two stood, adjusted their light clothing.

"*Poshlii!* Let's go!" Drako said, then led them down from the plane.

A big Mexican without sunglasses in a dark blue silk suit stepped forward, greeted Drako in English.

"Welcome to Hacienda el Aguila, Sr. Drako," he said. "I hope you had a pleasant flight."

"How can you wear a suit in this heat, Mauricio?" Drako said.

"This is the cool time of the day," Mauricio said. "The air conditioner in the Cadillac is already going, Sir."

Mauricio held open the car door. The four men crawled into the rear plush leather seats of the limo. Mauricio took the jumper seat facing them.

"How's the family, Mauricio?" Drako said.

"Very well, sir," the big man said. "Thank you for asking."

"And, Luis?"

"Thank you, Sir. Sr. Alban is quite well."

Drako settled back, glanced out the window. Seeing the closed compound in front of them with two armed guards at the gate, he spoke in Russian to the three men,

"Relax. We're all friends here."

Inside the compound, the driver pulled into a circular driveway leading up to a large three storey house. At the steps, two more armed man stepped forward, opened the car doors. Drako and his companions followed Mauricio into the house.

The door opened into an ornate patio. There, a short Indian woman with piercing light yellow-hazel eyes, long gray hair braided into a queue down her back waited for them.

Bright red and green embroidery trimmed the neck, sleeves and hem of her knee length white cotton dress. A thin headband of the same red and green around her forehead dangled down the back of her braided queue. She wore no jewelry, no adornments.

"*Hola,* Doña Luz," Drako spoke in Spanish. "It's good to see you again."

She motioned them to follow her through the patio, filled with flowers, fountains, statues, into the center of the house.

"This little woman was Luis's nanny," Drako whispered in Russian. "She still watches over him."

A short, dark-skinned man dressed in cream-colored slacks, a red and white flowered silk shirt under thick, curly black hair and a neat moustache strode out to greet them.

"Ivo," he said. "Welcome back to Mexico."

Drako embraced him, kissed him three times on his cheeks.

"Good to see you, Lucho."

Luis "Lucero" Alban laughed, wiped his cheeks.

"You Slavs and your kissing. We Mexicans save our kisses for the pretty girls."

Drako made introductions. "This is Sergei Potapov from Moscow, Sasha Markovsky from Leningrad and Daniel Litzov from Minsk."

Lucero greeted them in Russian. All showed surprise, stared back at Drako, who stood enjoying the scene with a wide smirk.

"Lucho was with the Cubans for years and spent six months in the Soviet Union."

Lucero held up his hand.

"Enough small talk, friends. Come in, Fuchs, our other partner is waiting."

Lucero led them through a large room out to an awning covered patio where a table had been set.

At the head of the table a small, thin man sat in a padded arm chair, his hands resting on a gold headed cane. His bodyguard, a big man in a light blue silk suit hovering at the elbow of the older man helped him rise. Fuchs, called *The Old Zorro,* extended his hand to Drako.

"Ivo. Good to see you in good health."

Drako embraced the old man, kissed his hand.

"You look well for a guy pushing 80, Jacobo. These are my associates from Russia and Belarus. Comrades, Jacobo Fuchs."

"Gentlemen," Lucero said, "let's sit. In Mexico we never let a guest leave without a full stomach."

Fuchs took the head of the table, his body guard to his right.

Lucero motioned to the chairs arranged at the table. After taking the seat at the other end of the table, he signaled the servants to serve, Mauricio sitting next to him.

Casting a glance at Fuchs, Potapov leaned over to Markovsky, whispered in Russian,

"So, that's the old Jew?"

Fuchs's eyes flashed, he snapped back at them in Russian.

"Yes, I'm the old Jew. I landed here in Vera Cruz in the 30s, one step ahead of the Nazis."

Litzov split his face in a wide grin. "I'm a Jew too, *gospodin* Fuchs."

Fuchs blinked, then his face cracked into a smile. He cackled,

"And a fox as well."

Lucero burst out laughing.

"Very good, Jacobo! *Litzov,* 'Fox!' in Russian"

Shooting an assuring glance at his three companions as a parade of servers placed plates of food on the table, Drako served himself, then his friends with deliberate, sweeping gestures.

"This is some of the best food you can get in Mexico. The locals add more sauces to make it more piquant, but I'm sure you'll be pleased."

During the meal, Markovsky, Potapov, Litzov exchanged small talk with Fuchs, Drako, Lucero. When dessert, *flan*, thick with caramel syrup, was served, Lucero spoke.

"Let's go into the other room and be a bit more relaxed. I have an excellent collection of vodka and other choices."

~*~*~

Transactions
Hacienda El Aguila,
Later, same day, Tuesday

Fuchs's bodyguard helped him to his feet. Lucero led the way back into the big room where overstuffed leather chairs were arranged around an oval table. Fuchs ambled over to a high-backed, elegantly carved chair at the head of the table where he sat, his bodyguard taking up position at his back. Arms crossed, he looked steady-- very lethal.

Drako admired lethal-looking men. He needed men like that.

Seated in a chair against a wall, a thin man in a gray suit waited, legs crossed holding a square black leather case on his lap.

When Drako along with the Russians claimed their seats, Lucero sat at the other end facing Fuchs, Mauricio standing at his right hand. Drako, in the middle had to look both directions to keep his eye on them.

"As the Gringos say," Lucero said, "Let's get down to brass tacks."

Fuchs looked over at the Russians.

"What are you going to do for us?" he said.

"We have a problem with excess cash," Drako said in English. "They have a problem with excess product. They can provide all the raw opium we can take and take all our excess cash."

Servants arrived with the drinks. When they had gone, Lucero waved his hand.

"We've got the cash," he said, "and we can meet reasonable prices– but product has to be top grade."

Markovsky popped open his briefcase, took out an inch square brick of a molasses colored substance wrapped in plastic.

"If you got the greenbacks, then we got the dope," he said.

"They're still getting raw opium out of Afghanistan and Kirghizia," Drako broke in. "I picked this sample at random from their stock."

At Lucero's signal, the thin, gray suited man, stepped forward. He set his black leather case on the table, opened it then set out three capped beakers.

Drako watched the attendant slice three thin samples from the opium brick. Uncapping the beakers, he dropped a slice into each of the glass containers.

One beaker turned a violet color.

A few seconds later, the second emitted fumes and an astringent smell.

Then, the third concoction burst into bubbles.

The chemist turned to Lucero, eyes wide, nodded with approval, then said, "¡*Muy impresionante!*"

Lucero snapped his fingers. Mauricio stepped forward, opened an aluminum briefcase on the table, revealing packed rows of greenbacks.

"I can absorb all the hard currency you can tender through my bank," Litzov said, "Our fishing fleets make regular stops here and are not searched by the US Coast Guard. We have several places in the West Indies where we can drop off product if the chase gets hot."

Lucero nodded. Mauricio, his bodyguard picked up a cedar humidor box, opened it. Plucking out a cigar, Mauricio sliced off the tip, handed it to Lucero then lit it with a long wooden match. Lucero took a deep drag, then blew smoke toward the ceiling.

"I like it," he said.

Fuchs addressed Litzov: "How can you move cash through a government accounting system?"

"The Soviet government has granted charters to certain banks to transact currency outside of the Secretariat of the Treasury," Litzov said.

" 'Certain banks?' " Fuchs said.

"Several high ranking party members maintain private accounts in these banks. When the Secretariat audits our books it's only to determine that debits balance credits."

Lucero waved his cigar. "So, not all transactions are scrutinized?" he said.

Litzov paused.

"May I have a cigar?" Litzov said.

"Of course," Lucero said. "Forgive me for being a poor host."

Mauricio brought the cedar humidor box over to the Russian banker. Selecting a cigar, Litzov rolled it between his fingers, smelled it.

"Cuban," he said. "Hand-rolled."

Mauricio snipped the end, held out the large match. Litzov sat back, took a long draw, exhaled the smoke.

"Excellent, Sr. Alban. Most excellent."

Litzov paused, then said, "The substance of our international transactions lies outside the interest of the Ministry. All transactions are done in the Soviet Union, but we do negotiate business with designated limited partner banks as long as they are not connected with any country in the NATO alliance."

His hands resting on his cane Fuchs looked over at Lucero, closed his eyes, nodded.

Lucero clapped his hands together.

"Then, we're agreed," he said.

Drako leaned over to his three companions, spoke to them in Russian in a low voice,

"What do you think?"

"Looks good to me," Potapov said.

"Sasha?"

Markovsky was staring at Doña Luz standing in the corner, arms folded over her chest.

"That woman gives me the creeps," he said.

"How so?" Drako said.

"She looks like a witch."

"She is a witch," Litzov said.

Leading their guests to the door, Lucero whispered to Drako.

"We need to talk."

Drako glanced back at Fuchs who like his name stood watching them, a fox eyeing a pair of roosters strutting among the hens.

~*~*~

Courtesy call
Palacio Municipal, San Luisita, Sonora, Mexico
Same day, 11:40 AM, Tuesday, March 31, 1970

Pepe Ortega parked his rental car in the plaza, then got out. His tailored blue wool suit was urban but his plain high polished black western boots were rural.

Watching the people milling around the early morning open air market at the end of the plaza, he warmed to the color of their clothes, the sharp sounds of Indian women's voices calling their wares. He smelled the mix of produce, spices, fresh-cut meat–all emerging from men in white peasant clothing, women in bright flowered dresses.

The smell of fresh tortillas reminded him that he had not eaten since the night before but ignoring the pangs he made his way to the Municipal building.

Inside, he stepped through an opaque-windowed door where an intense young woman in a dark uniform sat behind a polished wooden counter. The dark brown hair rolled into a bun pinched tight at the back of her head, the ovoid glasses gave her face a tight-lipped cat-like appearance. At the sound of the door opening, she looked up from her work.

"Can I help you?" she said.

"I'm Asuncion Ortega. I hope Captain Ramirez can spare a colleague a few moments."

"You're a policeman?"

"On leave, currently studying forensic science in the US."

He took a breath, then continued,

"My brother was murdered here during Holy Week."

"Ah, the young Nacional officer. I'm so sorry."

She stood.

"I'm sure Captain Ramirez will see you."

A few seconds later, Captain Ramirez strode out of his office, gripped Asuncion's hand.

"Captain Dagoberto Ramirez Palacios," he said. "An honor to meet the son of Colonel Ortega."

"Thank you, Captain. Pepe Ortega."

"My deepest condolences."

The Captain turned to the young woman.

"Elena, see to it we have some coffee and sweet breads."

In the Captain's office, Pepe declined an offered cigar. Ramirez selected one, settled back in his chair behind the big desk.

"A bad day," he said. "First, an American, a possible witness disappears, then your brother's death."

"Was there a connection?" Pepe said.

"A loose one. Spots of what could be the American's blood on the sleeve of your brother's jacket."

"You're not sure?"

"It was the same blood type we found in the missing American's room but we'd have to send it to the capital for a more complete analysis. We lack the resources here."

A knock at the door.

Elena came in carrying a tray with two small cups of dark Mexican coffee, a plate with two sweet bread rolls. She set them on the desk, then left.

Ramirez took a small bowl of dark, raw sugar from his desk drawer.

"Sugar?"

"I take it black."

Ramirez grumbled,

"No milk. Where's that woman's mind?"

Pepe sipped the strong coffee.

"This is fine," he said. "As for the forensic analysis, please send it on, Captain. My brother's associates will see to it."

Placing the cigar in a large glass ashtray, Ramirez pressed the tips of his fingers together.

"What bothers me is that this has none of the marks of a drug killing."

"Struck me the same way. Your thoughts?"

"The Gringo bled in the room– a small amount of blood. Our local physician thinks it could be from internal hemorrhaging– and your brother was struck in the throat with some object that crushed his windpipe."

He glanced over at Pepe.

"I hope this is not too hard for you."

"Please go on."

"His gun was holstered. He died where he fell. No other signs of violence, his wallet and ID untouched."

Ramirez leaned back.

"I was raised here, but I trained and worked in homicide for several years in Chihuahua. I've seen hundreds of killings, but I've never seen a drug deal end in a death this antiseptic."

"True, the absence of violence doesn't figure," Pepe said.

"You're a police investigator too?"

"Family tradition. After the Academy, I started in the Nacionales in my father's unit. Later, I worked with the US DEA, then studied advanced criminology in the US."

Folding his hands, Pepe went on,

"I got married last month. Now, I have an offer from the criminal investigation division of the LAPD to continue graduate school at the University."

"My congratulations," Ramirez said. "I wish you and your lovely bride every happiness."

"Captain," Pepe said. "Promise me that anything connected to this case, comes straight to me."

Ramirez went on,

"Please count on my complete support and full cooperation in all your efforts."

They rose together. Ramirez led the way to the door with his hand in the center of Pepe's back.

"You must allow me to take you to breakfast. Our local tamales are excellent, our cheeses made from mountain fed goats."

"I accept both the invitation and your promise of assistance."

Ramirez stopped in the doorway. Looking Pepe in the eye without smiling, he said,

"You have my word on it."

~*~*~

Intrigue
Hacienda el Aguila, Sonora, Mexico
Same day, 11:22 PM, Tuesday, March 31, 1970

Lucero kicked off his huaraches, stretched o u t listening to Nahuatl music droning in from the speakers surrounding the pool.

Doña Luz brought a tray with some hard cinnamon rolls then poured coffee in a large white cup, then set a glass of mescal on the table before leaving.

Drako came out, eased his big body into a deck chair, spoke in English,

"What's on your mind?"

"There was some trouble down in Santa Luisita a few days ago," Lucero said. "Some local coyotes smuggling workers were gonna move a large shipment of coke for us into the States when suddenly, the *Nacionales* show up."

"After the coyotes?"

"After the coke. A US DEA team was already in place. Lucky for us, someone recognized Armando Ortega's kid snooping around and they pulled out."

"So, what was the problem?"

"Fuchs's goon, that Cuban Jew, Volpez tried to force the coyotes to move the coke too soon. Some locals got involved, things got shot up– somebody offed Ortega's kid too."

"Killing Ortega's kid was stupid," Drako said.

"It wasn't us. We could send a letter of condolence to the Ortega family."

"In Serbia, we call that pissing on your enemy's doorstep."

A half-smile formed on Lucero's lips. He called to Doña Luz in Nahuatl,

"*Nantzun*, could you be so gracious as to bring our guest some of his favorite Serbian brandy?"

Doña Luz shot Drako a yellow-hazel eyed frown, then walked back to the house.

"I get the feeling she doesn't like me," Drako said.

"Aztec witch women never show their feelings, Ivo," Lucero said.

"Witch women?"

"There's really not a good word for it in Spanish or English."

"Gimme an idea."

"The *tepatiqui* is a woman who can cure you. The *axcualli* is one who can kill you."

"So, what's she?"

"Both."

"She's family?"

"She was my mother's closest friend."

Doña Luz appeared, sat a glass of slivovitz in front of Drako, then disappeared.

Lucero raised his glass of mescal. "Salud!"

Drako took a swig of slivovitz, then spoke,

"Back to Fuchs."

"There's more."

"Lay it out."

"The old bastard's been emptying accounts and moving lots of money from the Grand Cayman into Luxemburg."

"Don't our auditors catch this?"

"We get our dividends and shares," Lucero said. "But we never get to see the books. The numbers are all up front and what our accountants get matches the numbers."

"OK, Lucho," Drako said. "What're you hiding?"

Lucero extended his legs, wriggled his toes.

"My cousin had a maid whose kid was a whiz with numbers. I had him checked out and arranged for him to study accounting at the University at Guadalajara and then onto the National University of Mexico City. He did so well, when he finished I sent him to USC for an advanced degree in international banking. After that, I got him a job with the Banco Nacional, then marched him in front of some of Fuchs's pals. The old Zorro was so impressed with this kid, he hired him. He's the only person in the universe that Fuchs shares fiduciary information with."

Drako drew in a deep breath. "The old Zorro's never done that before," he said.

"But the fact is, amigo," Lucero said. "He's still a local boy and reports right back to me."

"How do we want to take care of this?"

"*How*'s not the issue, Ivo. It's *where* he's got the money."

"And?"

"Lucero brought his fingers together, chin resting on his thumbs, then sat that way.

"What're you thinking, Lucho?" Drako said.

"Did you see how the old Zorro made the joke about the name of the guy from Belarus?"

"Litzov?"

"It was a ploy."

"A ploy?"

"A signal, an overture, a sign of 'Let's make a deal."

"Interesting."

"Where did you find Litzov?" Lucero said.

"From a guy in the Moscow/Belgrade ring. They run all their money though him."

"What do you know about him?"

"He's a survivor. His family made it through the purges by running the international banking for Stalin's dog pack."

"Notice how he and Fuchs hit it off?"

"They're both Jews, they're both politicians," Drako said.

"Your Russian friends trust him?"

"Do Russians trust anybody?"

"If he's paid off the dogs, this makes him top dog."

"So, you think he'd climb in bed with Fuchs?"

"Fuchs lives only for the fast deal and deep sea fishing."

Drako stood, looked at Lucero then said, "Litzov holds his cards close to his tits but I'll check it out."

Lucero rose with a grin, patted the big Serb on his arm.

"Do that, amigo. You do that."

PART TWO

A book review
Tel Baruch, Negev Desert, Israel
3:52 PM, Friday, August 13, 1971

From the shade of the main tent, Ruth Hall watched the archaeological dig crew pile into the bus heading into town for a break from the broiling afternoon sun.

Snatching a can of beer from an ice-filled cold box, she located an aluminum camp chair, then pressed the cold can of Heineken's to her forehead. The battery-driven fan on the side table blew across her bare legs rattling papers and the topo-map covering the long table. She looked up when Harvey King stepped in the tent with mail.

"Ari brought us some mail," he said. "Too damn miserable to dig today."

Ruth took a long swig from the green Heineken's can.

"Supposed to be cooler tomorrow," she said.

Harvey tossed the pile of letters, magazines, large envelopes on the table.

Ruth picked up the wad, slipped off the rubber band binding it together, sorted through the pieces.

"Junk mail all the way out here," she muttered.

Harvey sat down in a chair at the end of the table, adjusted his glasses, took out the letter, then settled back to read.

Ruth looked over at him. "From Jeannie?"

Harvey grinned. "Yeah."

Ruth picked up one of the serial journals from the pile. Scanning the contents, a review caught her eye:

The Village Crier, v.62, number 2:4-6, April 23, 1971
"A new work, *The Secrets of Pedro Miguel: Reality and Substance in an Otomi Worldview [1971]*, opens a door that has been too long closed. The multiplex cosmos of a Native American people has suddenly been brought to the uninitiated. For the anthropologist striving to bridge the great cognitive gaps between a reality imposed on us by our Western civilization with its technologically dominated culture, and a worldview wrought by the

simpler, pragmatic existence of rural plain folk, this work is an eye-opener.

The author, Santos Villalobos, an anthropology graduate student, encountered Don Pedro Miguel Rojas, an Otomi Shaman who agreed to accept him as an apprentice. What follows is Villalobos's odyssey into other realms of awareness through alternate realities that lurk alongside, beneath and throughout the busybody everyday life of our society. Don Pedro Miguel challenges his young apprentice to release his grip on our world and enter the different shape-shifting cosmos that tunnels its way through, alongside and beneath that which we call reality. The passage on this voyage is often traumatic, fraught with peril but always enlightening. Emerging at the other end of this wormhole of consciousness, the sojourner finds himself having arrived, enthralled, a bit shaken but more aware of the several facets of his own being.

Two major issues arise in this work: First, we are given a peek into the world of a people living on the edge of our current civilized society with all of its material trappings, a world endangered by extinction and threatened by our Western Modern way of life. "This is an ancient world," Don Pedro Miguel tells Villalobos. "We were here before you but they (the ancients of this netherworld) were here before us." And, I would add, we are enriched by this view.

The other issue is the task of an anthropologist to bring this knowledge into the greater body of our science. The life histories imparted to Santos Villalobos by Don Pedro Miguel now form part of our archives and as such, will belong to the future for consideration long after you and I are gone. This record will live on and the secrets of Don Pedro Miguel Rojas now belong to the generations of social sciences to come.

The only other detraction I might tender is, alas, this kind of work will give license to those eager to abuse the quest for entrance into this alternative world that forms part of the Otomi cosmology. One hopes that this will not be the end result of this noble effort to explore that hitherto untrodden path to the outer reaches of reality.

P. Oliver Goldworthy, Professor of Anthropology, University of Los Angeles"

Ruth reread the review, going over it word by word.

Frowning, she dropped the magazine on her lap.

"I'll be damned," she said.

Harvey finished his letter.

"What's up?" he said.

"Something about this review is very unsettling," she said.

"What review?"

She handed him the publication.

Harvey read it then looked over at her.

"What bothers you?' he said.

"You remember my ex-boyfriend, Matt?"

"Crazy dude, right? Into psychological stuff with border Indians?"

"More like psychedelic stuff."

"What about him?"

"He was working with a group of Zaitequi in Sonora and was learning to be a shaman."

"Sounds like the guy who wrote this book did too."

"Damn funny coincidence, ain't it?"

"Yeah, I guess."

"Think I'm gonna get that book and read it when we get back to Haifa," Ruth said.

~*~*~

Another book review
Mira's Styling Salon, San Diego, CA
2:17 PM, Wednesday, November 22, 1972

Coming in early for a pre-Thanksgiving day appointment with her hair stylist, Ruth Hall sat in a vinyl and chrome chair. The chemical smell of cosmetic washes, tonics and liquids bit her nostrils. The chatter of voices permeated the interior of the shop. Ruth glanced over the other women, their bodies draped with plastic covers, their hair twisted in curlers.

Taking out a professional archeological review journal from her purse, she scanned the titles reviewed. One name grabbed her attention.

Santos Villalobos!

Kyklos Review, v.23, no. 3:16. September 12, 1972

The Road to Tlitzl,
by
Santos Villalobos
Los Angeles: Berkshire Press. (1972)
268 pp., $9.95

Reviewed by, Timothy O'Reilly, Professor of Psychology, Stanford University

For those readers who were not able to get enough to drink from Villalobos's previous work, *The Secrets of Don Pedro Miguel*, the drought is over. The work under review here is a revision of Villalobos's Ph.D. dissertation, *An Auto-Psychoanalytic Study of an Apprenticeship in Otomi Shamanism: The Secrets of Don Pedro Miguel,* USC, 1966. In this effort, Villalobos takes the reader through a maze of Freudian perspectives of the dream-state with its erotic symbols, sexual nuances and quests for ecstasy.

For Villalobos, the Freudian turmoil of the interaction of ego, id and superego, are merely a thin veneer of competing realities. He contends that the walls between the triumvirate of personality components are mere membranes through which the shaman is able to glide with the aid of hallucinogens, e.g., peyote, mushrooms, *Cannabis*, etc. Emerging on the other side, the shaman can grin at himself, as if, to paraphrase the Apostle, St. Paul, "through a glass darkly…"

Much of the text dwells less on the "trip" side of the experience and focuses on the structural analyses of what the vision affords in terms of explicative power. Of course, the explicative power in the model Villalobos develops is close to that of Freud, which seems to be acceptable to him and his colleagues at USC.

This work is well written but adds little that is not present in the previous works. The more psychedelic oriented will savor revisiting the same places Villalobos took them in his first adventure, while the more psychoanalytical oriented will appreciate his fitting the earlier work into a decidedly Freudian framework.

The rest of us will simply say, "more old wine in a shiny new bottle," with Freud's picture on the label, of course.

Stunned, Ruth bit her lip, sat back in the chair, arms folded, the magazine across her lap.

A voice intruded, startling her.

"Ruth, I'm ready for you."

Ruth gave a little convulsed twitch, stared up at her hair stylist, then looked back down at the magazine in her lap before she collected herself.

"Are you alright, Ruth?"

"Yeah. Sorry, Donna. My mind was just out to pasture."

Donna smiled. " Glad it's back. C'mon back and let's make you beautiful for turkey day."

~*~*~

More book reviews
Powell Library, University of California, Los Angeles
8:42 AM, Thursday, February 15, 1973

The desks and carrels along the walls of the archive section of Powell Library were devoid of people in the early morning. Ruth Hall found a table with a module for reading microfiche, settled in, inserted the film and scrolled down the long list of old records of land grants and entitlements dating back to the 1760s. She made notes of the sections she wanted, checked off squares on a data sheet, then removed the film plates from the monitor module.

Returning to the reference desk, she handed a stack of microfiche record envelopes back to the library clerk.

"What time does the photocopy center open?" Ruth said.

The clerk looked up at the clock.

"In about 10 minutes."

Ruth wandered over to the open stack of recent periodicals. Strolling down the stacks looking at the titles displayed, she stopped in front of one set of serials, stared at the faceplate of a periodical listing the names of anthropological books and articles under review, then took the issue from the stand to a table, sat down, read,

The Southern California Review of Books, XXXIII, number 1:22. January 9, 1973
Parallel Universes: More Secrets from Don Pedro Miguel.
by
Santos Villalobos, Ph.D.
Berkshire Press (Los Angeles), 1973

Play it again, Santos
Jerry Walters, MD, Ph.D., Psychiatry Dept. School Med., UC, San Francisco

When the first edition of *The Secrets of Pedro Miguel* hit the bookseller's racks 3 years ago, the story I heard was that, like Darwin's *Origin of Species*, the entire first printing sold out the first day. The age of psychedelia was upon us and everyone wanting a piece of the action in the Age of Aquarius now had something to get their hands on and stick in their heads. Rumor had it that there wasn't a Hippie pad in the Haight without at least three copies of Villalobos's book.

Berkshire Press had hedged their bets well by bringing the first edition out in an affordable paperback pocketbook— indeed, they only could have covered their bases better by printing it on Zig-Zag cigarette paper.

Now, a mere three years later, we see the appearance of a "new" Villalobos work on the same theme.

Well, Dooley Wilson in the classic film *Casablanca*, begins his refrain with "It's still the same old story..." which, at least in my mind, is relevant to this review: what we have here is more of the same.

In the first book, we were taken into the author's immersion into the spooky world of the Otomi *brujo* or witchman. We saw the kaleidoscopic scenery along the way, and even woke up like Gregor Mendel upon occasion. As one of my patients, a reader, told me, "it was cheaper than acid."

In the second book, a rehash of his forced attempt at a compromise between a psychedelic novel and a dissertation, we saw this vision dressed up in a psychoanalyst's suit with numbers, models and graphs. Now, what do we have?

Parallel Universes is a very disappointing read. One might consider it a psychedelic self-help manual, or a *"How to be a Shamanic Guru in Ten Easy Lessons?"* While Villalobos stops short of telling you where to obtain hallucinogenic drugs, he has no qualms in advocating their use– of course, with the proper supervision. As for new insights into the mind-musing of alternate realities, nothing new is offered.

So, play it again, Santos. You've got another best seller on the stands.

Ruth shattered the silence of the library with a loud cry, "Son of a bitch!"

~*~*~

Meetings
Santa Cruz Convention Center, Santa Cruz, CA
8:22 PM, Thursday, November 29, 1973

Carrying his bags into the lobby of the Santa Cruz convention center, Pepe Ortega stepped into buzz and hum of the vendors setting up tables for the annual convention of the National Anthropological Organization.

An old hand at conventions, Pepe knew a few hours later, these same vendors would admire their book display venues, then stroll out to go knock back a few shots with colleagues, friends, competitors talking about the trade.

Picking up his reservation materials, he stuffed them in his jacket pocket, then moved to the registration desk where a smiling efficient desk clerk assigned him a room.

"Would you like a bell captain to assist you with your luggage?" she said.

"I'll manage," Pepe said. "Thanks."

Walking to the elevator, Pepe heard his name.

"Pepe Ortega!"

A big man with a round face, a scraggly beard, a carnival prize fighter's nose rushed up, gave him an Alaskan brown bear-like hug.

"Ray," Pepe said. "Good to see you."

Ray released Pepe, spoke in Spanish.

"Good to see you too."

Ray's great grin faded, his lips molded into a sad smile, his voice soft.

"Lyla and I both cried when we heard about Ulrike," he said.

"Your letters helped me through a tough time," Pepe said.

"We couldn't get back for the funeral."

"Believe me, Ray, I don't know who was there."

Ray put his arm around Pepe's shoulder.

"Hey, *hermano.* You ain't alone."

Pepe gave a small laugh.

"How's Lyla?"

"Pregnant again."

"Again! I thought you two gave up being Mormons!"

"We did but we didn't give up balling each other."

His friend's homely face with wide set eyes reminded Pepe of a picture of Socrates he had seen in an old encyclopedia when he was a kid.

"Well, some things never change."

"Hey! What do you mean?" Ray said.

"Hay's the first stage of horseshit. Living in the apartment next to you two, we heard you making it every goddam night."

"Touché. How about we get some dinner?'

"I ate on the plane. I'm going to shower, crawl between the sheets and leave this planet until tomorrow morning."

"OK, but don't make any plans for tomorrow night. There's a restaurant in the old part of town that serves early California-style Mexican food and there are a dozen enchiladas with our names on them."

"Sounds good to me."

"See you then."

The big man turned, walked back into the busy lobby.

Pepe watched him go, emotion, pressure of tears building up behind his eyes. He picked up his bags, headed for the elevator.

~*~*~

A chance encounter
Harvest Room, Job listings, Convention center, Santa Cruz, CA
Next day, 5:22 PM, Friday

Pepe found the room with job postings where he was to meet Ray. Eyes on the listings posted on the board, he bumped into a shorter, chunky Mexican-American, wearing a tailored navy blue pin-stripe suit, dark cordovan Italian shoes. Throwing Pepe a short glance, the man apologized in Spanish.

Pepe laughed, then said, "My fault. Pepe Ortega."

The shorter man hesitated a second, then thrust his hand forward.

"Santos Villalobos."

Santos Villalobos. I should know that name.

"Enjoying the meetings, Santos?"

"Just checking out the job listings."

"Are you teaching somewhere now?"

"No. Just writing at the moment."

Bingo! That book. 'The Secrets of Don Pedro Miguel.'

Without letting on, Pepe nodded.

Ray came up, slapped Pepe on the back.

"Hey, you old bandit," Ray said, then turned, smiled at Santos.

"This is my friend Ray Errol. Ray, Santos Villalobos."

When Santos shook Ray's hand, a woman's voice chimed in next to them.

"Santos Villalobos, the famous author?"

Santos looked around, his brows pinched.

"I'm Santos Villalobos, yes."

An attractive blond stared at Santos through large, dark brown eyes, hand on hip, eyebrows arched, lips tight.

"Very interesting," she said. "Even more interesting, I bet, is where you got that fucking story."

She turned around, strode away.

Watching the swinging hips retreat. Pepe said to Santos,
"Friend of yours?"
"Never saw her before."
Ray then said to Santos,
"I'm very curious. I work in two Mexican villages near the Arizona border and I've never heard of an Otomi witchman or male shaman. Most of the Otomi I'm acquainted with have only female shaman."

Forcing a small smile, Santos glanced at his watch.
"I guess it is unusual. Well, gentlemen. I have to excuse myself. I'm late for an appointment."

After shaking hands, Santos paced off.

Ray scratched his head.
"Did I say something wrong?" he said.
"And who was that very attractive woman." Pepe said.
"An archaeologist and close friend of one of the archaeologists in our department. I'll ask Dana next time I see her."

Pepe laughed.
"If you remember, you mean," he said.
"You suggesting I forget?"
"Hah. You can't even remember the names of your kids."
"OK. Pick on me. But, let's go get something to eat. I'm as hungry as a desert coyote after all the rats have left town."
"Lead the way."

Following his friend through into the hotel lobby, Pepe spotted the blond woman. He was tempted to go over, strike up a conversation but Ray was already across the lobby, fixated on early California-style enchiladas.

As they left the center, Pepe glanced back at the attractive blond.

Maybe later.

PART THREE

Homecoming
Outside Tula de Allende, Hidalgo, Mexico
Three years later, Saturday, 11:55 AM, Monday, April 8, 1974

Sunlight poured out over the city of Tula de Allende in the state of Hidalgo some 100 km north of Mexico City. As the rain broke off, dark clouds broke into fragments lighting the surrounding hills and mountains in patches of green and gold.

Pepe looked over at the short, dark-skinned driver sitting next to him. Cipriano Flores had taught him to drive. Pepe smiled remembering how the little man had threaded the blue Mercedes through the congested traffic out of the capital.

The tarmac road leading into the town was clean. As the Mercedes passed, men doffed their hats, women and children waved. Chalupa was a small friendly town with was traditional architecture —white-washed adobe walls, red tile roofs, the legacy of an older Mexico.

Cipriano guided the big car toward a large house, pulled into its gated yard onto a curved pebble driveway, then stopped in front of a tiled landing. He jumped out, ran around, opened the door for Pepe.

"Welcome home, Don Asunción," he said.

Pepe looked over the house as Cipriano unloaded his bags. The door at the top of the semi-circular walkway swung open. A large woman with sparkling eyes, black and gray hair greeted him in Nahuatl,

"I see you, puppy."

Pepe laughed, embraced the woman as she kissed both of his cheeks.

"I see you too, Ixcheli," he said.

"Go in," she said. "Your Señora Madre awaits."

~*~*~

Same day, 10:28 PM, Monday.

On the veranda looking at the night sky, Pepe sipped a glass of mescal. Off in the distance, faint sounds of local music, smells from the smoke of cooking fires lingered in the night air.

Leaning back in the chair, the woven thatch against his back, he heard his mother wheezing as she came out on the veranda to take the chair next to him.

"We finally got those two monkeys down for the night." she said.

"I told them each two stories," Pepe said.

"Xochitl's on the phone with Rodrigo. He's coming up this weekend."

"The Deputy Chief Federal Prosecutor doesn't get much time off."

Doña Maria Guadalupe Cruz-Montez de Ortega folded her hands in her lap, then closed her eyes.

"It's a blessing your Papa died before Manolito," Doña Maria said. "It would have killed him outright– so proud was he of his sons."

"I'll never achieve what he did."

"Armando was Armando. Manolito was Manolito and you're you, each his own man. Now, just you carry the Ortega name."

Pepe swallowed the last bit of mescal, the liquor burned his throat. He set the glass on the table.

"What do you mean, just me. There's Xochitl, the kids, there's you..."

"I'll be dead before the next year ends."

Stunned, Pepe faced her– his hands on the armrests of the chair. "What?"

"This old body's worn out and the time comes soon to feed the worms, as your grandfather used to say."

"What are you talking about?"

"If I'd stayed in the city after your father died, I'd be dead by now. I'm sad to leave my Xochitl, my grandchildren and you. But, I have few regrets."

Pepe knelt beside her, took her hand in his.

"I'll take you to Los Angeles," he said. "We'll see the best doctors at the UCLA medical center. We'll..."

She raised her hand.

"I've talked to more Gringo doctors than you can imagine. Nothing can be done."

"Don't say that."

She pressed his head to her breast.

"We taught you never to fear the truth."

She stood raising him up with her, then pointed over the landscape in a sweeping motion.

"Our people have lived here since the times of the ancient Aztec gods. When the Spanish came, we fought them. Crushed under their heels, we fought on. We fought the French. We fought the Americans. Then, we fought our own corrupt government. Sometimes we won, sometimes we lost. But we kept the old ways. We mixed them with the new, knowing that if we didn't, we'd lose all of them."

She sat down.

"On the day your father and I married, I swore before my own mother and his that I would raise my sons and daughters in the old ways. That's why you, your brother and sister spoke our language before Spanish. That's why you boys spent your summers in the mountains with the herdsmen and Xochitl worked with the maids. That's why you and your brother, like your father, were beyond corruption. Because you are of the blood of Princes formed in our ancient ways."

"You never told me this before," Pepe said.

She gave a little laugh.

"I was never dying before," she said.

"I now ask you for something, for me."

"I will do anything you want– only let me take you to get some help."

She shook her head, raised her open hand.

"It's long past that. I ask– not just for myself but for your father and brother as well."

"What can I do for the dead?" he said.

"Bring their murderers to justice," she said. "If you can't make them stand in the courts of man to be judged, send them to God. He'll judge them."

"Murderers? Manolito was murdered but Papa died of a heart attack."

"It was the same as a bullet."

"What do you mean?"

"There's more than one way to kill someone," she said. "Armando worked for the last few years to arrest this one pack of pigs– day and night gathering evidence. Then, boom! A healthy man drops dead of a heart attack."

Her eyes narrowed. She looked him straight in the eye.

"I've never asked you for anything– but I'm asking you now— bring these dogs to justice. Let your father and brother's spirits rest in peace."

Pepe came up short as his mother spoke. He had never heard those words from her, never expected to hear them. He took a moment, let them sink in.

"This is my Roman Catholic mother?" he said. "Who goes to mass and prays the rosary twice daily? Now you ask me to follow the 'old ways of our Aztec ancestors' to be an instrument of revenge?"

"Not just revenge. These dogs didn't just piss on our flowers. They killed the innocent and ripped the fabric of family honor."

"There are laws, Mama. I'm a policeman. It's my duty to keep the laws."

Doña Maria let her eyes bore into her son. Pepe felt her wrath, her anger, her anguish when she spoke,

"There are laws– spider webs catch flies, but wasps fly through. If you let these beasts get away with killing your family, you soil the honor and truth they lived for."

Her gaze never wavered. When she touched his face with her cold fingers, Pepe knew what she was asking of him.

"I want your word, Asunción," she said.

Pepe hardened his face, glanced down at his hands. Even looking away, he felt his mother's fierce eyes burning into him.

"You have my word, *mi madre.*"

~*~*~

Later, same evening, Monday
Killers!

Doña Maria's words kept Pepe company as he entered his father's studio. On top of the chest of drawers under the old picture of both his grandfathers standing next to Pancho Villa and Emiliano Zapata, he found the US Army issue Colt .45, the same pistol his father had carried from the day he took his officer's oath at eighteen.

41

His father had taught Pepe and Manolito to shoot with the same Colt. When they in turn graduated from the National Police Academy, he had given each of his sons the same make of weapon.

Pepe sorted through pictures— friends, his father with Presidents of the Republic. Pictures of Doña Maria as a beautiful young woman, photos of him, his sister, his brother as children, his father and mother on their rare trips abroad.

Opening the top drawer to replace the pistol Pepe saw the notebook. Written in his father's hand, there were notes, sketches, names, dates, places, figures. He was about to close the notebook in the drawer with the Colt when the words, *La Trinidad*. 'The Trinity' caught his eye.

Trinity?

His father wasn't religious. A man among men, a Freemason to boot, he, like most Mexican men left the practice of religion to his wife.

Pepe read more.

References to the "Trinity" popped up page after page.

~*~*~

Sad departure
Hacienda Ortega, Chalupa, Hildago, Mexico
Four days later, 9:42 AM, Saturday, April 9, 1974

Coming back to his childhood home had been easy, leaving was not. At the door, Pepe he embraced his mother, hoping that it would not be the last time. He kissed his sister, her two children then promised to phone on their birthdays.

Walking to the car, Pepe took his brother-in-law, Rodrigo Rodriquez-Diaz by the arm, led him aside.

"Rodri, do you have any idea why my father would be writing about *La Trinidad*?"

"Don Armando?" Rodrigo said "The only time he ever went to mass was for a funeral."

"I came across some notes on an investigation he was tracking and the name 'Trinity' kept popping up."

Rodrigo's smile faded.

"*La Trinidad Profana* 'The Unholy Trinity,' " he said. "It's the biggest and most dangerous drug *familia* in Mexico. They're iron clad."

Pepe's eyes turned cold, his jaw muscles tightened.

"Let's take a walk, Rodri," he said.

Pepe led Rodrigo down the road, then spoke,

"Let's have it."

Rodrigo drew a deep breath.

"The Unholy Trinity was your Papa's last case," he said. "He was investigating two guys in Mexico City, Jacobo Fuchs and Enrique Alban. Alban's one of us, an Indio from the other side of the mountain. He spent some time in Cuba, got involved with the long-haul truckers' union then worked in the shadows for a long time until he got control of the biggest shipping company in Mexico."

"What about the other one?"

"Fuchs's into gambling, whores and everything illegal since the 40s. He paired up with Alban over 10 years ago. They've taken over the drug trade from the DF to Guadalajara to Monterrey."

"Not your typical Mexican Mafia."

"Fuchs, *el zorro viejo*, 'the old Fox,' runs the money. Alban— they call him "Lucero," because he loves flashy clothes, cars and women– is the enforcer."

"So what's all this 'Trinity' bullshit?"

"About a year before your father died, they hooked up with a crook from Yugoslavia, Ivo Drako. He's tied in with the Russian underworld and the three've gone international."

"So, Papa baptized them the 'Trinity.' "

"Yes, and was warned by the powers that be to back off."

"So, he went it alone?"

"No. He involved the Americans."

"How so?"

"Don Armando didn't tell me anything because he wanted to protect the family but Manolito dropped me a few hints."

"And that's all you know?"

"Manolito was the only one in the force your father could trust completely. Manolito brought in the Gringos."

"And then Manolito dies."

"These guys are beyond reach."

Pepe gripped Rodri's arm.

43

"No one's beyond reach, Rodri," he said.

"So your Papa used to say. But, '*Mano*, if anything happens to you or me, Xochitl and the kids are all out there by themselves. Don't try to go it alone."

"Rodri, can you get me more information on these bastards?"

"Well," Rodrigo said. "I may have a 'source.' "

"Who?"

"Truth is," Rodrigo said. "I don't know."

"You don't know?"

"A while back we were trying to bust a kidnaping ring, but the rats were always a step ahead of us. One day, I come in, find a note telling me to go to the lobby of the Prado and wait for a phone call at noon. So, I go. At noon, I get a call from a guy who tells me where they're keeping the hostages. When I ask for his name, he just says, 'A friend.' "

"Can you contact him?"

"How? I don't have idea one who he is or where's he's at. Maybe, just maybe I can get the word out but that's a big maybe."

"You know Mama is dying," Pepe said.

"Yeah. I've tried to keep it from Xochitl."

"You've got to help me in this 'Trinity' business, Rodri."

Rodrigo raised his eyes, looked over the mountains in thought.

"You sure, Pepe? You fuck with the bull, you get the horn."

Pepe looked at his watch.

"I better hit the road. Got a plane to catch."

~*~*~

Dan James
East Los Angeles State University, Los Angeles, CA
Two days later, 8:54 AM, Monday, April 22, 1974

Students hurrying, taking risks to get to class on time congested the normal heavy flow of traffic as rain poured onto the crowded streets close to the campus of East Los Angeles University.

Pepe drove along in silence until a yellow and black low-rider cut across two lanes, squeezed in front of him missing his front fender by inches.

Punching the horn, Pepe yelled, "Damned idiot!"

He drew a deep breath.

This isn't Mexico.

Pepe crawled along with the traffic into the campus parking lot. Pulling into a vacant spot, he spotted the low rider wheel into the zone marked FACULTY ONLY. Seeing the campus parking control's blue and white pick-up drive by, he signaled the attendant.

The attendant rolled down his window. "Yes sir?"

"Could you check that yellow and black car over there for a Faculty/Staff parking permit?" Pepe said.

The attendant made a cat seeing a mouse grin, swung the pick-up behind the low rider, turned on his overhead blinkers.

Coming into his office, Pepe shook off his raincoat, then looked through his father's notebook. Searching for patterns, he noticed the entries marked 'Trinity' alongside random appearing numbers in sequences of 22.

The phone rang. He snatched it to his ear. "Ortega."

"It's me, *hermano*," Rodrigo said. "I've got something."

"Talk to me."

"On Tuesday I got a note to be in the lobby of the Hilton at 1:00 PM. I go, am called to the phone and it's the same guy I told you about. He tells me to call Dan James if I'm interested in Fuchs and Lucero."

"Who is he?"

"DEA. Write this number down, then give him a call."

After Rodrigo hung up, Pepe punched in the number.

"DEA."

"Hello, this is Asuncion Ortega, in the department of Criminal Justice at East Los Angeles University. Is Agent Dan James available?"

"I'm Dan James, Dr. Ortega."

Pepe had not used his academic title.

"Are you familiar with a group of three in Mexico, Luis Alban, Ivo Drako and Jacobo Fuchs."

"The Unholy Trinity."

"You know that name?"

"This seems to be a family affair."

"What do you mean?"

"You're Armando Ortega's son. I knew your father. Your brother, Manuel was working with us. Like I said, it's a family affair."

"What can you tell me?"

"We've been working this case for a while but we're still in the dark about a lot of things."

"Maybe I can help."

"One cop to another—by the book, right?"

"Is there another way?"

"Okay. I'll be in touch."

~*~*~

Some news

Pepe's House, East Los Angeles
Two weeks later, 6:20 PM, Friday, May 17, 1974

Pepe pulled into the driveway just as the gardener slammed the tailgate of his pickup then headed down the street. Pepe liked Ernesto, he liked Ernesto's sons, he liked the job they did on the yard. Always edged, clean, lawn sheared close. Ernesto was from Michoacán. He had papers. An honest man in a corrupt world.

Entering his house, Pepe scooped up the pile of mail, tossed his briefcase in a chair, went to the liquor cabinet, poured a large splash of Jose Cuervo Especial tequila in a glass before collapsing in a soft chair with mail, drink in hand.

Scanning the bills, he tossed them to one side, flipped the junk mail into a nearby trash basket, then noticed the letter with a handwritten address, Mexican stamps.

Frente al Sr. Profesor Dr. Asuncion Ortega
2226 Sycamore Way
Los Angeles, California 90036
EEUU

Pepe opened the envelope with a small samurai sword letter opener, unfolded it, noting that the text was typed.

Esteemed, appreciated Professor, Don Asuncion Ortega,

Presente.

Please forgive the years of neglect that I have so thoughtlessly rendered since our last meeting shortly after the tragic death of your beloved brother, Manuel. I wish I could inform you with this writing that we have the cowardly dog that occasioned his demise in our custody at this time and are only awaiting the time to execute him. Unfortunately in the several years that have elapsed, we have made little or no progress.

Also, it was recently brought to my attention by a mutual friend, Carlos Madriaga with the National Police that you had lost your beloved Sra. wife to cancer, a number of years ago. I share your pain remembering your enthusiasm in informing me during our last encounter of your recent marriage and the joy it would bring in the face of the tragedy of losing your beloved young brother and your esteemed, respected equally beloved father.

I can, however, report that at the time of the former Lt. Manuel Ortega's death in the line of duty, our national authorities were closely investigating the possibility of our small community being the focus point in a large marijuana smuggling operation involving a Cuban, lately from Mexico City and involved with a crime syndicate there that your father had been investigating before his untimely death. In truth, I have no further substantive particulars on what might have occurred that night and offer this as a feeble excuse for not having put pen to paper of these long years.

However, I recently came across a file that served as a reminder of my neglect, and owing to the efforts of my beloved Catholic mother (I, myself, as you recall, am a member of the Freemasons, as are you and as were your beloved father and brother) I assuage my feelings of guilt by sharing its contents with you.

The mysterious departure of the North-American who left the bloody traces never resolved itself. We did manage to contact some people from the States from an address that had been abandoned in the wake of his departure.

The person whom we contacted was a Dr. Ruth Hall, who came to Mexico with the brother of the former occupant of the room, one Jacob Spyner, the name of the absent person being Matthew Spyner. Reviewing the file, I recall a most attractive young woman and a courteous, professional brother who was a member of his community's fire brigade. They collected the few personal items of the absent Sr. Matthew Spyner and departed. Hence, from our perspective in the department, we considered the matter closed.

However, recently, I came across a photo of the lovely young woman in a magazine article on Mexican archeology, an academic area in which I have more than a passing interest, given my own Indian roots on my mother's side. The photo was taken at an ancient site in Sonora and the text stated that the beautiful Dr. Hall, Archaeologist, an anthropological colleague of yours, it seems, is a professor at the Madison University nearby to you in San Diego, California.

My esteemed Professor, Don Asuncion, I tender this information in the hopes that a conversation with her about the bizarre circumstances of how her friend's blood got on your beloved brother, might yield something that could lead to something else.

I must say that my and my family's hearts reach out to you in your grief and hope the time of mourning will pass quickly with your complete recovery in spirit and health.

With no other particulars, I send you my most heartfelt affection and embrace you always.
Your faithful friend, servant and admirer,

Captain Dagoberto Jaime Ramirez y Guzman,
Chief of Police, Commanding the Police Department, Santa Luisita, Sonora, Republic of Mexico.

Pepe remembered Captain Ramirez. No better, no worse than anyone in law enforcement here, continuing in a struggle against bad wages, corruption, crime in his own back yard.

He looked at the name in Ramirez's letter again.

Ruth Hall,
Archaeologist.

Where have I heard that name before?
He decided to call her the next day, set the letter aside, took a swig of Tequila, turned to the small Spanish language newspaper he had picked up with the mail, shook it out.

The banner headlines caught his eye:

YOUTH LEAGUE RECEIVES GENEROUS DONATION FROM MEXICO

> Youth League and Community Center Director, Rodolfo Reyes G., announced today that the community center had become the recipients of an award of $750,000.00, from the Mexican Benevolent Agency, NUESTRA CAUSA. These monies will be used to completely refurbish the much needed game and meeting room at the center.

Pepe smiled. His friend, Rodolfo could find the dollars.

Glancing at the accompanying photo of Rodolfo standing next to a dapper shorter man, his eyes fixed on the shorter man's name, **Luis Alban M.**

Alban!
Pepe looked back at the face again.
So, that's what you look like, viper!
He read the article, most of it praising Reyes's skill and persistence in keeping the center funded, running. The last sentence in the caption of the photo print jumped out at him.

> "... Sr. Luis Alban will be present at the Community Center on Saturday, May 18, to present the check to Center Director Reyes."

Tightening his lips, Pepe set the paper down.
May the 18th..tomorrow's going to be a busy day!

~*~*~

SuperMex

East Los Angeles Youth Center, West Los Angeles, CA
Next day, 11:47 AM, Saturday, May 18, 1974

Rodolfo "SuperMex" Reyes knew how to handle a crowd. Just a half hour before, the former Los Angeles Dodger, the city's vice mayor, Francisco "Pancho" Contreras welcomed everyone to the new youth center. Now, Rodolfo stood with his benefactor, Don Luis Alban braced by his party of two lawyers with several bodyguards at the foot of the stage in the main hall.

After bouncing up the steps to centerstage Rodolfo seized the mike, then spoke,

"Ladies and Gentlemen, citizens and supporters of the neighborhood, please join me in welcoming our most distinguished Guest of Honor, Don Luis Alban, our primary benefactor and supporter coming here today from Mexico City."

Amid clapping and cheering, the small, dark dapper Lucero stepped forward accompanied by the two men in suits who made their way up to Rodolfo's embrace.

Rodolfo pointed to the three men who had joined him.

"Let me tell you. Our plans for this center were on the brink of failure. We were all going to mass twice a day to find the money to finish this project, when I get a call from Mr. John Rydell here."

Rodolfo pointed to a small light-skinned man standing next to Lucero.

"He told me the distinguished and honored Don Luis Alban, Mexican philanthropist and entrepreneur, had not forgotten his migrated friends and countrymen."

Rodolfo put his arm around Lucero.

"Don Luis called me," Rodolfo said. " 'Sr. Reyes,' he says, 'how much do you need to get this project off the ground?' "

Rodolfo tip-toed forward with his hand at his mouth as if hiding his speech from his guests.

"Now, when someone asks the old SuperMex 'how much?' I get kinda loco. So...," He crossed himself, winked at the audience,"...so I added a few more dollars to the kitty."

The audience roared in approval. Rodolfo held his hand up for silence.

"But," he said. "When I told Don Luis how much we needed, he said, 'That's not enough.'"

Rodolfo came back, put his arm around Lucero again.

"I thought I was hearing things. But, no. Don Luis says to me, 'I feel obliged to double what you are asking for.'"

"So," Rodolfo said. "I had no other choice but to accept. And here you are in this brand new facility for your and my children."

Rodolfo felt good listening to the crowd's cheers. Loving standing in the spotlight of approval, he spoke again,

"Don Luis, you're in your own home, can you say a few words?"

Lucero shook his hand, declined, smiling. Rodolfo turned to the short man next to him, then said,

"Mr. John Rydell. Give us a word."

Rydell accepted the mike, spoke in English,

"*Muchos gracias*, Rudy. I'm delighted to see the project come to fruition. I'd like to introduce my partner, Cassie Cortez, who first brought this project to my attention."

A good looking, well built Mexican American, Cortez waved at the crowd.

Rodolfo stepped forward to accept the mike.

"Ladies and Gentlemen, join me in persuading Don Luis to share a couple of words with us."

Rodolfo swept the protesting Lucero to the front of the stage, handed him the mike, then stepped back.

Lucero cleared his throat, then spoke in Spanish,

"It was a small gesture on our part to gain the pleasure of helping our former countrymen who have our beloved Mexico forever in their hearts. Speaking as a simple fellow Mexican, I'm happy and honored to be allowed to repay the joy and..."

A voice from in front of the stage interrupted the short speech.

"How about thanking them for using all the drugs you smuggle in and sell to their children and relatives for fat profits?"

Lucero glared at the man standing in front of the stage.

"Who are you?" he said.

"Just a grateful wretch who's glad to see you putting back some of the money you suck out of this community with your damned drug operations."

A big man pushed his way through the crowd toward the heckler who did not raise his voice or take his eyes from Lucero.

"Lucero Alban. You're a liar, a thief and a murderer. But we, the humble citizens of Los Angeles thank you for returning a tiny portion of our money which affords you your lavish lifestyle."

The big man grabbed for the heckler but was stopped by a blow to the throat. As the big man staggered back choking, the heckler faced Lucero, then spoke again,

"You should thank all the citizens and their children gathered here for buying your drugs, Lucero."

His dark face turned crimson. Lucero flung the microphone down, stalked off the stage.

Seeing four uniformed police pushing their way through the confusion, the big man scrambled to his feet, then shoved his way through the crowd after Lucero.

The Mexican-American police sergeant at the head of the others, pushed through to the heckler still standing in front of the stage.

"You OK, Dr. Ortega?" the sergeant said.

"Never better, Miguel," Pepe Ortega said. "Glad you could make it to the party."

~*~*~

Suspicions
Upper Marigold Drive, East Los Angeles, CA
Next day, 8:47 PM, Sunday, May 19, 1974

Santos Villalobos sopped up the last bit of sauce with the last piece of the last flour tortilla, plopped it in his mouth, then looked across the table at Lola.

"Those enchiladas were damn good," he said.

"That, you naughty boy, is my Tia Rosa's recipe. I always fry the tortillas and grill the onions in bacon grease, and use only real Mexican white cheese for the filling and sauce."

Santos drained the last swallow of a bottle of Tecate, wiped his mouth with the napkin, patted his belly.

"Next time you see Tia Rosa, tell her she has a big fan."

"She died about 5 years ago."

Lola carried the plates to the sink.

"Need some help?" Santos said.

"No, I'm just going to rinse them. Carmen comes in tomorrow."

Santos went into the front room, sorted through the mail on the coffee table, picking out a copy of the *Anthro Newsletter*, took it with him into the kitchen. After looking at it, he said,

"Sonfabitch!"

Lola grabbed a dishtowel, stepped to the table drying her hands. Santos was scowling, pressing his lips together when she came to his side.

"What's going on?" she said.

Santos threw down the newsletter, turned his head in a pout, his hand at his mouth. Lola sat down, picked up the Newsletter, then read aloud,

"The committee on Ethics and Academic Integrity has decided to hold a forum and inquest on the reported ethnographic work of...Santos Villalobos at the forthcoming meeting of the International Anthropological Association in Mexico City this December."

She looked over at this. "What does this mean, Santos?"

"It means they're going to do an axe-job on my ass."

Lola moved next to him, stroked the back of his neck.

"They can't do shit to you. Remember, Cassie said you were untouchable."

"I know that. But, now my name gets drug through the mud all because of that meddling bitch."

"What bitch?"

"Ruth Hall. I told you about this woman at the anthro meetings a few years back asking me if I was the 'famous writer?' "

"Yeah."

"Well, she was the girlfriend of the dip shit I took the manuscript from. Notice that Ed Singer's name is on that list. She and her asshole boyfriend were Singer's students."

"You mean she knew about the manuscript?"

"I'm sure she'd seen it. That why she confronted me in that smart ass way that night in Santa Cruz."

"But, Cassie said they don't have the original and can't prove anything."

"Legally, they can't do shit. But this pig bitch can crap up the scene so bad, I'll never show my face in public again."

"So what? We've got the money."

"These people want to crucify me for having a good idea and making it work."

Leaning against Santos, Lola nibbled his ear, she whispered,

"Let me make you feel better."

Lola took his hands, held them to her breast.

"Let me take care of this," she said.

~*~*~

Ignacio "Nacho" Santiago, wheeled the black Chevrolet van up to the gated property, roared in through the electronic opened gate, then parked in front of the multi-room 2 storey house inside the green enclosure.

His four German shepherds came running to the van. Stepping out, Nacho called the dogs to him by name, patted their heads, then checked the security cameras raking the grounds' perimeter.

Nacho entered the house through a hallway leading to the stairs bordered by a hardwood bannister. Black and white neo-realistic paintings of Mexican workers, revolutionaries in heroic poses hung on the walls in the front room.

Seeing the kitchen lights on at the end of the dining room, he came in, saw his sister Lola sitting alone with a phone directory in front of her.

"Hey. Lo," Nacho said. "Any of those enchiladas left?"

"In the oven."

"Tortillas?"

"In the fridge."

Nacho took a pan of enchiladas from the oven, set them on the table, went to the refrigerator for a package of flour tortillas, a Tecate beer.

"Brew?" he said to his sister.

"No."

Nacho heated up four tortillas on the range, wrapped them in a napkin, sat down at the table, popped the top of the Tecate, took a long swallow, tore a tortilla into pieces, attacked the enchiladas.

"Man, these are just like Tia Rosa's," he said.

Finished, Nacho picked up the pan, tossed it in the sink, opened the refrigerator for another beer, brought it back to the table.

"What's up?" he said.

"I need you to take care of something for me," she said.

"What?"

"There's this twat who knows about Santos's manuscript. I want her out of the picture."

"Say what?"

"You heard me."

"Man, I ain't offing no broads. You know that."

"Get Jorge to do it."

"That ain't gonna be easy. He's gone independent."

"I don't give a fuck," Lola said, raising her voice. "Santos will cover his costs."

Nacho dropped his eyes, made little circles with the beer bottle on the table.

"Nacho, if this bitch has something on Santos," Lola said, "it's all our asses."

Nacho puckered his lips, twisted the bottle in his hand.

"I don't like to bring Jorge in on family business."

"You ain't got to like it, Nacho. You just got to do it."

"Why?"

"Do you want to go back to hustling?"

"Fuck no."

"Then got off your ass and take care of this."

Lola passed him an address, a cut-out photo from a newsletter showing 3 women standing together.

"Take this," she said. "You'll need it."

She stored the phone book on top of the refrigerator, looked at her brother once more, then left the room.

Nacho sat rolling the empty Tecate bottle in his fingers. He scowled at the papers, the woman's photo circled in red pencil.

"Dr. Ruth Hall," he said.

He set the slip of paper with the name and address down, then leaned back in the chair.

"Shit. Damn. Fuck. Piss."

He got up, stuffed the papers into his jacket pocket, walked out to his van.

It started to rain.

~*~*~

The Rattler
Apartment complex, El Cajon, CA
Next morning, 2:31 AM, Monday, May 20, 1974

Rain thumped the top of the black Chevy van moving along the car crowded curbs of the street. The window wipers made loud thunks clearing the windshield. Scanning for a parking place, Nacho paid little attention to the noise. He swung the van into a narrow slot, killed the engine.

He checked his watch. 0332, set to military time. Nacho found it easier than remembering AM or PM.

He opened the door, squeezed out of the van, then bumped against the car parked next to him. A car alarm went off with lights flashing, shrills, sirens honks with an irritating bleeping sound.

Nacho slammed the van's door, wormed his way into the street looking around—no cops, no lights, no one calling out.

Then, his van's screeching alarm started.

Digging his keys out of his jacket pocket, Nacho inched back between the cars, opened the door, shut off the alarm. The car next to him stopped sounding as suddenly as it had started. When he got back to the sidewalk, he spotted Lola's note laying on the wet sidewalk.

"Damn," he said.

Nacho snatched up the wet paper, stuffed it into his jacket pocket, then ran for the cover of the apartment.

Like a big bear, he scrambled up the stairs to the landing, rushed along to the end. The apartment was dark but Nacho knew Jorge was awake because he had called him. He rapped on the door.

A voice from inside,

"Yeah?"

Nacho pulled the hood of his jacket up over his head.

"S'me, home," he said.

The door opened, Nacho slipped in. Standing behind the door, pistol in hand, Jorge closed the door, slipped the handgun into his pants top at the small of his back.

"Damn, man," he said to Nacho. "You're all fucking wet."

Nacho stripped off the soaked black cotton jacket, shook his long black hair, like a dog.

Jorge held his hands up, protecting himself from the spray of water.

"Hey. Cool it."

Nacho draped his wet coat over one of the two kitchen chairs.

"Sit down, homie," Jorge said. "I'll get you something dry to wear."

"Cool."

Nacho started to sit down by the lamp.

"Hold it, blood." Jorge said, pointing to the other chair. "That's where I'm sitting and I don't want your wet ass in my chair."

"Oh, yeah," Nacho said. "Cool."

Jorge stepped into the bedroom, came out with a set of sweats, socks.

"Get outta them wet clothes."

Nacho stripped to his shorts, draped his wet pants, shirt over the other kitchen chair.

Jorge sat down, picked up a bus transfer stub to mark the place in his book. Nacho looked over at him after Jorge settled into the chair.

"What ya reading?" Nacho said.

Jorge held up the cover.

"Catch 22, by Heller."

"I saw that movie."

"So did I. It was a piece of shit."

"Hey, I liked it."

"It was still a piece of shit."

"Book any good?"

Jorge picked it up, looked at it.

"It's OK. Best thing Heller ever did; never wrote anything worth a shit afterwards."

Jorge looked around at the stacks and piles of books around the room.

"You got more books, my man."

"Yeah."

"You read all these?"

Jorge looked around. "All except that pile by your chair. I just got those today."

Nacho frowned.

"Man, you got to get outta here– see some chicks, listen to some sounds. Why you stuck up here reading all the time?"

Jorge gave him a cold look, then smiled.

"Homie. You didn't drive all the way down here on a stormy night to give advice to the lovelorn. What's on your mind besides your ugly Mexican mug?"

Nacho rolled his eyes, looked around the room. "I need a favor, Man."

"What kind of favor?"

"Well, there's this chick that's causing problems for Santos and Lola asked me to come down here and have you take care of it?"

Jorge stared at him, his large yellow hazel eyes unblinking. 'You want me to kill her?"

Nacho kept avoiding looking at him.

"Yeah, something like that," he said.

Jorge didn't change expression.

"I don't do 'something like' killing someone. I either kill them or I don't. And, I don't do trimming– that's your specialty."

Nacho wriggled his toes, lowered his eyes to stare at them.

"Yeah, Man," he said. "Lola wants her offed."

Jorge drew a deep breath, sat back.

"Is this a contract?" he said.

Nacho looked up at him.

"Hey, home. We'll cover whatever you want. You know me, bro. You're family."

Jorge shrugged. "So, it's not a contract. You said you wanted a favor."

"Hey, Home. Either way. You want the bucks, Santos will cover it. You know that."

Jorge nodded. "Yeah."

Nacho looked over at him, arms open.

"Home. If this doesn't work for you, fuck it. I'll get someone else. Like I said, we're family, man. I ain't putting you out."

"Didn't say I wouldn't do it, homie."

"Only if you want to."

"Nach. I've never *wanted* to kill anybody in my life– except once."

Nacho laughed. "Lt. Cleo Gibson."

"I hated that Texas redneck motherfucker. If you hadn't pulled me off him, he'd be stinking up the worms now."

"And you'd still be seeing the view outside through iron squares in Leavenworth."

"Still did three years in the Marine stockade in Stanton."

"Yeah, but if you'd taken that pus-head out, you'd still be deep shit in the joint."

Jorge turned his head. "I'm hip."

"And who was there when you made the gate?"

"Your ugly Mex ass, homie."

"So, your choice, brother. I ain't pushing this one."

Jorge stared at him without words for nearly a minute. "Gimme the details."

"Hey, man. I really appreciate this. Let me know how much you want and I'll square it with Santos."

"This one's for old times, homie. I was glad to see your ugly face when I walked through that gate that day."

"OK. Here's the deets."

Nacho stood, reached for his pocket, realizing then that his pants and jacket were on the chair.

He dug out the papers stuffed in his jacket pocket. The wet magazine photo cut-out fell apart in his hands. The address slip was wet, smudged, barely legible.

"Shit," Nacho said.

"What's up?"

"The picture's crapped. Let's see... I got the address."

He handed Jorge the address slip.

Jorge looked at it. "I know this section of town. What's the mark's name?"

Nacho looked over. "It's written down there."

The name was wiped out into a blue Smudge. Nacho rubbed his head.

"Looks like Dr. something ending in '-all,' " Jorge said.

"Yeah, that's it," Nacho said.

"I'm supposed to go ask Dr. So-in so '-all' to step out and get her neck broke?"

"There's the description. Blond, short hair, about 5'2"..."

"Let me guess, 'eyes of blue.' "

"Yeah. I think so– how'd you know?"

"Lucky fucking guess."

"Hey, you got enough to go on, my man. How many 5'2" blond doctors gonna be living at that house?"

"You j u s t don't want to go back to your sister and tell her you screwed the mark's name and picture."

"Hey, man. You're a pro. You can do this one. I'll get back to you with some more details."

"When does this need to happen?"

"Are you tied up now?"

"Got a few things to clear up. I can get to it sometime next week."

"Cool. That'll give me some time to get some more info to you on this chick."

Jorge nodded.

Nacho stood up. "I'll be getting back to LA," he said.." Give you a call next week."

"OK."

Nacho gave Jorge an embrace, looked down at the sweats he was wearing, then said,

"Sorry, man. I'll change..."

"Let it slide," Jorge said. "I got more sweats. Stay warm going home."

Nacho took up his clothes, Jorge walked him to the door.

"It's quit raining," he said. "No sweat driving back to LA."

~*~*~

Jorge shut the door behind Nacho, dropped the slip of wet paper on the table, sat back down, picked up his book, read on.

Enter the fox

Officina Compania Pochteca, SA, Mexico City, DF, Mexico
Three days later, 11:17 AM, Thursday, May 23, 1974

Lucero stood when the door to his office opened. Fuchs came in leaning on a gold-headed cane, his bodyguard behind him carrying a brief case.

Coming out from behind his desk, Lucero shook Fuchs's hand, nodded to the bodyguard then led the old man to an overstuffed chair at a low table.

Sitting beside Fuchs, Lucero patted him on his knee.

"You look tired, Jacobo," he said,

"Too old to sleep anymore, Lucho."

Lucero looked up at the bodyguard standing behind Fuchs.

"Is he eating well, Tonio? Don't let him have too much ice cream."

Antonio Volpez forced a smile, answered in his musical Cuban dialect,

"He's well fed, Sr. Alban."

Lucero's secretary came in with coffee, a plate of pastries, set them before the men on the low table. After she closed the door behind her, Fuchs, taking a bite from a sweet roll, stirred three spoonsful of sugar in a small cup of coffee.

"Did you cement Mexican-American relations on your trip to Gringoland?" he said.

"Los Angeles is always interesting," Lucero said.

"Verbal attacks by some ex-Mexican turned Gringo are interesting?"

"It wasn't even worth thinking about."

Lucero stirred two teaspoons of sugar in his coffee, looked up to see Fuchs smiling at him.

"You knew old Armando Ortega's two kids who were both cops," the old man said.

"And one of them got in my face in Los Angeles."

"You're slipping, Lucho. When you were hungry, you'd have brought in someone to whack that snot-nosed son of a whore."

"It's not good policy to whack cops in La La Land, Jacobo."

"We popped this pup's pappy's ass and we can whack his too."

"That would create more problems than you can imagine."

"The competition will see your weakness. And they'll try to take you out."

Lucero launched himself from the chair, turned to face Fuchs. Volpez stepped to the old man's side.

"I was born piss poor," Lucero said. "My father was a farmer who had only his back and hands to sell. The land belonged to the local cacique..."

"You still have to resolve this situation," the old man barked.

Lucero strode to the wall to where an old machete hung from two hooks, snatched it down. Volpez stepped in front of Fuchs, his hand in his jacket.

Lucero held out the machete.

"With these," he said. "We took the corrupt bastards who were screwing us out in the fields and killed them."

Fuchs motioned Volpez to move back. Lucero replaced the machete back on the wall in its holder.

"Fat Tomás got me to start hauling dope," he said. "I took him out. I clawed my way up to where I am and I'll take out anyone who tries to take me down."

Fuchs pursed his lips, nodded, raised his hand.

"I've offended you, Luis," he said. "My apologies."

The old man stood, held out his arms, embraced Lucero.

"Forgive me, Jacobo, for losing my temper," Lucero said.

Fuchs made his way toward the door, looked back at Lucero then spoke,

"You're right. Let's concentrate on the business at hand. I'll be in touch."

After closing the door, Lucero stared at the machete hanging on the wall for a long time.

~*~*~

Foxes
Outside the Officina Compania Pochteca, SA
Same day, 11:26 AM, Thursday

On the way to the elevator, Fuchs shook his head.

"For a smart man, sometimes Luis acts like a complete *pendejo*."

"He's a viper, Jacobo," Volpez said.

"Vipers aren't dangerous as long as you handle them with a forked stick."

Volpez pushed the button for the elevator, then spoke,

"Lucero's an Indio. He'll come at you from behind."

"There's an old Yiddish saying," Fuchs said as they entered the elevator. "Trust a snake to be a snake. If you pick one up and get bit, don't complain."

"I heard my old grandmother say that when I was a kid back in Havana."

"I don't like Ortega's kid poking around," Fuchs said. "Get hold of Chibo and have him take that shit out."

"Here or in the States?" Volpez said.

"I understand the kid comes here from time to time," Fuchs said. "Take him out when he comes here."

"Consider it done, Jacobo." Volpez said.

Fox tails
Officina Compania Pochteca, SA, Mexico City, DF, Mexico
Same day, 1:20 PM, Thursday

The buzzer on Lucero's desk sounded.
Yes?" he said.
The voice of Carmela, his secretary came through.
"A call from a Sr. Melendez, Sr. Alban."
Lucero snatched up the phone, spoke in Nahuatl,
"Who am I?"
He heard the answer.
"You are you, as I am I."
The code was correct. Lucero went on in Spanish,
"What's up?"
"At the risk of sounding like a mystic, I've been seeing shadows in ledgers," the speaker said.
"Shadows?"
"We continually change sums of certain funds which we transfer in various accounts, shifting monies from one account to several and then into a separate fund to foil snoopers from tracing transactions."
"What's mysterious about this?"
"I've found that when the final liquidation is realized, not all the satellite accounts are accounted for in the sums of the central fund."
"What do you mean?"

"While all the satellite accounts are to be liquidated at the same time, some have been closed without a trace."

"Where to?"

"Good question."

"Can't you track these transactions?" Lucero said.

"Not when they're liquidated as cash closures. From there, they can vanish."

Lucero picked up a cigar.

"How much are we talking about?"

"Well, it could round out to over eight million a year."

Lucero froze, the unlit cigar stopped inches from his lips.

"Eight million a year?" he said.

"We move a lot of dollars. The cash we load into the Soviet banks is then recirculated into the Swiss and Luxemburg systems-- this can exceed 15 million a quarter."

"Where are these leaks going?"

"As you know, I pay the bills and I see every number the old Zorro calls from his personal and private phones."

"You're saying he's channeling these funds somewhere?"

"I came in late the other night and saw the lights on the phone console of one of the outer offices. Curious as to whom was working there that late, I saw that old gray head bobbing up, talking in Russian."

"Russian?"

"So, I did an audit of the international calls made from that office."

"And?"

"There were calls to a number in Minsk, in the USSR."

"Belarus, Probably talking to Litzov."

"As the clever cat doesn't always wait outside the same rat hole. I checked the phone logs of our other offices, and..."

"You found the same number popping up at different intervals made from different offices."

"You said the old bastard was clever and he'd never trust me completely."

"Very good. What's your next step?"

"This will be tough. They convert the cash into some same value commodity, such as gold or tobacco and then parlay that overseas through brokers to buy high demand items as capital assets."

"How will you pursue this?"

"The weak links are the brokers but I have connections exploring that end."

"Anything else?"

"Yes. A phone number for a bank in Tel Aviv kept popping up."

"Tel Aviv! The old goat's always going on how he hates Israel."

"I have a classmate from Guadalajara who works with the Federal Reserve in Washington, DC. I'll check with him."

"Don't try to contact the Jews as the word would get right back to the old Zorro."

"There's one thing that just crossed my mind."

"What?"

"A couple of years ago when the old Zorro got that cancer scare, he signed a power of attorney to me and gave me banking codes and passwords so I could transfer funds for him. This POA's still effective as he was under severe sedation at the time and must have forgotten about it. This means, of course, that if something were to happen to him and in absence of any will to the contrary, we would be able to liquidate any accounts of which he is a signer into our corporate holdings– as long as we know where the accounts are."

Lucero hung up the phone, looked at the cold cigar in his hand then threw it into the waste basket. He picked up the phone, punched in a number.

"Ivo," Lucero said. "Remember what I said about Litzov and the Old Zorro being in bed together?"

"Funny you should ask," Drako said. "Our Russian friends asked me the same thing. Seems their assets keep bobbing up and down and are always a little short when they reappear."

"Their own banker's screwing them?"

"Markovsky found out Litzov has a close friend who emigrated and now manages an overseas bank."

"Let me guess. This guy's bank is in Tel Aviv."

Drako clicked his tongue. "You know, Lucho, our partner, the Old Fox, is making some very sneaky and unfriendly decisions."

~*~*~

Voice from the past?
Pepe Ortega's Office, East LA University, Los Angeles, CA
A week later, 10:16 AM, Thursday, May 30, 1974

Striding into his office, Pepe threw himself into his chair, his mind a kaleidoscope on a runaway merry-go-round.

The letter from Captain Ramirez: Confronting Lucero. The name– Ruth Hall. Archaeologist–friend of the guy who disappeared.

Where've I heard that name before?

Grabbing his *Guide to Anthropological Departments*, he found her name.

Madison University. San Diego. Private, exclusive, well-endowed programs, attractive campus funded with a huge grant from the Early California Heritage Foundation.

She must be good to be there.

He punched the department number into his office phone.

A woman's voice answered,

"Anthropology."

"Hi, this is Dr. Ortega from East LA University. Is Dr. Hall available?"

"One second, I'll ring her office. Please hold."

Two buzzy rings later, an answer,

"Ruth."

"Dr. Hall, I'm Pepe Ortega, an anthropologist in the Criminal Justice Division at East LA University. Are you busy at the moment?"

A pause.

"No. Shoot."

"Captain Ramirez, in Santa Luisita, Mexico mentioned that you had cleared out some personal things of an American who disappeared from Santa Luisita about 10 years ago."

No immediate response– another long pause.

"Yes."

"As you may have heard, a police investigator was murdered that same night with traces of blood on his body that forensic analysis has linked to the man that fled the scene."

"I may've heard something, but I doubt if Matt had anything to do with it."

"I have a deep personal interest in this case. Would it be possible to meet with me to discuss this business?"

A hesitation. The answer was tense, words well chosen.

"As you know, Dr. Ortega. I wasn't there when it happened."

"Of course. Sometimes seeming innocent or irrelevant details can be very useful."

"Matt and I were involved for only a short while."

"I don't want to pry. I'm just following leads. I assure you it won't take too much of your time."

"Do you ever get down this way?"

"As a matter of fact, I'm going to be in San Diego on Wednesday giving an investigator's workshop."

"I've got a meeting downtown that evening... Tell you what. Why don't you come by my place. I should be free around 6:00 PM and we can talk then."

"That would be fantastic. How do I get to your place?"

She gave him the address, her home phone number, said goodbye.

Pepe sat there, for a moment, the phone still in his hand.

"I know I've heard that voice before…"

~*~*~

A short visit
Rosemont District, San Diego, CA
Two days later, 6:07 PM, Wednesday, June 5, 1974

Pepe found the old light green Victorian with wide front steps leading up to an arched covered landing at the door. Walking up to the house, he checked his pager.

No calls. He climbed the steps to the landing, rang the bell.

The light came on, the door opened with a chain lock, a blond woman with blue eyes peeked through the space in the door.

Pepe held out his business card.

"Good evening. I'm Pepe Ortega from East LA University. Dr. Ruth Hall asked me to come by."

The door closed, the reopened. A petit blond woman in a dark skirt and light pink blouse stuck her hand out. Her short hair was combed back, a tiny gold cross on a gold chain flashed at her throat.

"Hi, I'm Maggie Connall. Ruth said you'd be dropping by. She's not home yet but come in."

She led Pepe to a small breakfast table in the kitchen covered with a red and white checkered table cloth, four wicker bottomed chairs.

"We entertain all our important guests back in the kitchen. Coffee?"

"No thank you. I usually don't drink coffee in the evening."

"Caffeine intolerance?"

"No, the truth is, I can't stand American coffee, so I just use that as an excuse."

She poured herself a cup, motioned for him to sit down.

"Something stronger then?" She looked at his card again, "Dr. Ortega?"

"Pepe, please. I'm fine."

Maggie plopped into a chair across the table from him. "Ruth tells me you're a famous investigator from Mexico who works with the LAPD and teaches criminal justice."

"Former investigator, yes. Famous, no."

"How did you get from there into anthropology?"

"I got interested in the criminal culture. What do you do, Maggie?"

"Former psychiatrist. I run a program in addiction recovery for San Diego County."

"We're kind of colleagues, then."

"Yep. I come up against some pretty rough customers."

"Threats from your patients?" he said.

"No, threats from the assholes selling them the crap."

"That can be very dangerous."

"You learn to live with it."

The phone rang in the hallway, Maggie excused herself, went in, answered it.

"Pepe," she called in from the hall. "It's Ruth. Says she's tied up in this meeting, won't get home till late. Might be better to reschedule."

Pepe stood up.

"Tell her that's fine," he said. "I get down here from time to time."

Maggie spoke into the phone. "You heard that? OK. Bye."

Maggie came back into the kitchen.

"She sounded stressed," she said.

"Then it's better to catch her another time."

Maggie walked Pepe to the door, hands in the pockets of her skirt.

"Well, Pepe. It was nice meeting you."

She gave him a sidelong look, then said,

"Do you have a family?"

"No. I'm widowed."

"I'm sorry to hear that. Has it been long?"

"Nearly 5 years."

She looked up into his eyes. "I can see it still hurts," she said.

"You learn to cope."

"I hear you," she said.

At the door, he shook her hand, then looked into her eyes.

"Forgive me if I sound trite but you remind me of my wife."

"How so?"

"You're just you. No effort to be somebody else."

"Just pure shanty Irish. Poor as church mice. So's Ruth. She's the youngest of 4. Has three older brothers."

Pepe held out his hand.

"Well, it's been delightful," he said. "Are you two… a couple?"

"No. Just roommates," Maggie said.

"Okay," Pepe said, "I'll see you again."

"That would be nice," Maggie said.

~*~*~

Walking back to his car, Pepe took out the picture of his dead wife from his wallet. Little blond Maggie had reminded him of her.

His beeper interrupted. Looking at the number, he saw the red dot, an urgent call-back for Dan James.

"Damn!"

He drove to a gas station a few blocks away. After getting out, he stepped up to an open phone booth, digging in his pockets for change, he saw wires sticking out of the console.

Before he could step to the other phone, a young man in a car screeched into the station, jumped out, dashed over, snatched up the phone.

"Sorry, Man," the kid said. "I'll be quick but this is vital."

Pepe stepped back as the young intruder jammed in coins, pushed buttons, then gibbered into the speaker.

Strolling a few feet away, Pepe gazed over the urban scene avoiding the loud conversation.

He caught sight of a passenger that got off a city bus across the street– a big man in a gray suit over a dark brown shirt, buzzed hair, only a short black swatch on top of his head.

His large, light hazel yellow eyes reflected the shine of the street light like opal beads. His face evoked darkness.

Seeing the man scan his surroundings, Pepe looked away to avoid eye contact. The big man headed up the street in the direction Pepe had come from, his gait smooth, unlike the characteristic side to side swing of big men.

The voice behind him startled him back into his own head.

"Hey Man," the kid said. "It's all yours!"

Pepe called James who answered on the first ring.

"Agent James, this is Pepe Ortega. I got your page."

"I hear you confronted Alban at the new Hispanic Youth Center."

"I just thanked the little rat for returning some of the money he made from selling dope to our kids. It pissed him off. But his goons circled in, covered his retreat out the back door."

"You didn't mention anything, I hope."

"What's to mention? Lucero knows damn well you're after his ass."

"I just wanted to hear from the horse's mouth what went down, Dr. Ortega."

"Call me Pepe. Even my students don't call me 'Doctor.' "

"Great. Call me Dan."

"I don't blame Rudy Reyes for taking whatever support he can for his kid's center. If Lucero gives back some of the money he's stolen from the barrio, Rudy should take it."

"Agreed. Good night, Pepe. Talk to you soon."

"My pleasure, Dan."

Hanging up the phone, Pepe looked back across the street where he had seen the big man. He was gone.

~*~*~

Shocks and after-shocks
Rosemont District, San Diego, CA
Same day, 7:33 PM, Wednesday

Jorge Barrios walked up the porch stairs of the Victorian house, rang the doorbell feeling the calm that complete confidence affords. Inside, someone descended the stairs. The door opened a crack, a small blue-eyed blond peered at him from behind the chained night-latch.

"Yes?"

Jorge reached in his inside coat pocket, pulled out the black leatherette case, popped it open, showing his picture in a phony identification.

"Sorry, to bother you, Ma'am," he said. "I'm Agent Carlos Gonzalez, FBI."

"How can I help you?"

Replacing the ID, he took out the address Nacho had given him from his pocket, then made a frowning attempt to read it.

"I'm sorry– the name's been smeared. I'm looking for a Doctor, Doctor Small, Rawl,...."

"I'm Doctor Connall."

Jorge looked up at her from the paper, lips in a smile.

"Yes," he said. "That's it. May I come in?"

Maggie released the catch on the night latch.

~*~*~

Same day, 10:48 PM, Wednesday

Ruth felt a rush of relief when she spotted the familiar driveway of her house. The drug-out archaeological meeting had caused her to be caught in peak commute traffic, made worse by an accident.

After parking in the driveway, she climbed the back stairs, unlocked her way into the kitchen.

"Mag," she called out. "Finally back. I'm fixing drinks."

She threw her things on the table, took a bottle of bourbon down frown the kitchen shelf.

"Mag. It's just as easy to pour two as one. Speak up!"

Ruth peered out the back screen door. Maggie's car was parked in the garage.

She listened for the TV.

Nothing.

After pouring a splash of water in the bourbon, she stepped into the hallway. Then she caught sight of the still figure on the floor.

Ruth dropped the drink, ran to where Maggie sprawled in a twisted heap.

"Maggie!"

The body was cool. Ruth felt for the carotid artery.

Nothing.

Ruth looked into Maggie's eyes. The pupils were fully dilated.

"Oh God, Oh God."

She choked, reached for the phone.

"Oh answer, answer. Help me. My roommate. I just got home and found her. She's dead. No, I know. She's dead. Come help me! Please."

Ruth looked back at the twisted body.

"Just come, just come..."

~*~*~

Sitting in a chair in her front room, Ruth felt she was in a nightmare. Short recent scenes flashed by in her mind's eye.

The blare of the sirens.

Stumbling to the door when the policewoman came running up the steps.

The police officer looking over Maggie's body.

The fire department arriving.

A firemen helping her to a chair, then sitting with her.

The police officer asking questions.

A fireman appeared with a cup of coffee. Ruth took it from him.

Ruth overheard the officer-- her name was Mix-- call on her handheld radio.

"I need a forensic on site. Possible homicide."

Ruth chocked out, "Homicide?"

The officer pointed to the area around where Maggie's body was sprawled, said something about. "She has a bruise on the side of her throat... her body is a long way from the staircase,.. This positioning looks arranged to me..."

"But who'd want to hurt Maggie?" Ruth said. "Everybody loved her."

Everything was spinning. Ruth collapsed into the chair. Then, she became aware of a big man with a bulldog face kneeling next to her. Over 6', he wore neat, sharp-pressed gray slacks, a gray sport coat, light blue cotton shirt open at the throat, a new Panama straw hat on his large head.

"Bill Rowe, coroner investigator," he said in a deep voice. "What's your name, ma'am?"

"Ru...Ruth Hall."

"Hello, Ruth. Can you tell me what happened?"

"I came home, late. I called for Maggie, when she didn't answer, I came in here and found here on the floor."

Rowe looked around at the scene. "OK, did you touch anything before you called for help?"

"No. Just the phone."

Rowe patted her arm. "You did good. Hang in there."

Ruth saw him go over, look over the body.

Officer Mix pointed to a faint bruise mark on the throat. "That doesn't seem consistent with a fall," she said.

Rowe rotated the dead woman's head. "Neck's broken."

He stood. "Good job, Jude– proud of you. Let's take a look around."

A paramedic helped Ruth to the table in the kitchen. then refilled her coffee cup. Sitting down next to Ruth, Rowe looked over at the fireman.

"Pumper, that coffee doesn't just come in cups of one," he said.

Rowe looked at Ruth with deep blue sad eyes. "Feel like talking?"

"I'm OK."

He took a notepad and pen from his jacket pocket. "What was her name?"

"Maggie Connall."

Rowe nodded, wrote. "She isn't the one who's in charge of the County drug rehab program, was she?"

"Yes. She was."

"Damn. She was a fireball."

The questions came in short, simple phrases. Just as Rowe was finishing, another policewoman, an attractive 5'6" African-American came into the room.

"Bill Rowe," she said. "How in hell did you manage to beat me here?"

"Ruth," Rowe said. "This is Helen Davis, Forensic Investigative Unit. We're in good hands."

Davis came over and sat down by Ruth.

"Sweetheart," she said. "You've had one helluva night. Can I call someone? You shouldn't stay here by yourself."

Ruth gave her the name of a couple who lived nearby. Davis called, arranged for Ruth to come over. A women firefighter helped Ruth put some things together, then took her to her friend's home.

A calling card
Rosemont District, San Diego, CA
Same day, 11:28 PM, Wednesday

Rowe watched Ruth drive off, turned back into the room, patted Davis on the arm.

"Didn't know den mothering came with the job description," he said.

"Poor kid. That's a bitch of a thing to come home to."

Rowe went with Davis back into the living room.

"Judy's right," Davis said. "We got a killing on our hands."

"Glad to see we can agree on something, Helen."

Rowe liked how Davis marshaled her team into action. They photographed the area, dusted all over, found several fingerprints, bits, pieces of possible evidence which were collected, labeled, then filed away.

Looking over the door, Davis smelled something.

"This door was painted recently," she said.

Davis shined a light on the door. On the edge of the door she found another set of prints– fingertips. She called out to her colleague,

"Hey, Jerry. Be sure to get these."

Rowe came up with a business card in his hand.

"Found this in her pocket." he said.

Davis read it aloud,

"Asuncion 'Pepe' Ortega, MA, MS, Ph.D.,

Professor, Forensic and Investigative Science, Department of Criminal Justice, East Los Angeles University."

"I was at his talk earlier this evening," Rowe said.

"Heard of him," Davis said. "Criminal investigator from Mexico, does a lot of consulting on investigative matters with the Latino communities."

Davis looked over at the body being photographed on the floor.

"Wonder when she got the card?" she said.

Rowe wrinkled his bulldog face. "Don't know. But, I'll let you know when I find out."

~*~*~

Fox's den
Cafeteria El Águila, Mexico City, DF, Mexico
3:22 PM, Thursday, June 6, 1974

Fuchs sat down in a large curved booth in a nook in the back of the room of the old cafeteria. A waiter placed a cup of espresso in front of him while Antonio Volpez took the seat on his right, then relit his third cigarette from his second.

"Must you keep smoking?" the old man said.

Antonio stubbed the cigarette in an ashtray.

"I'm nervous and like the taste of Pall Malls."

"I have plans for you, you know," Fuchs said.

Antonio nodded, fought the urge for another cigarette.

"Luis came to me 15 years ago with a scheme," Fuchs said. "He was a truck-driver who'd murdered his way to the top of his union."

"So, you bankrolled him?"

"Yes," Fuchs went on. "Then, I heard about this big Serb who's got connections into the Russian and Asian opium markets."

"You brought Drako in too?"

"Of course. Do you think that poor idiot Indio who ran with the Castros..."

Antonio's eyes flashed. "Those sons of a whore."

Fuchs chuckled.

"You and your family lost your asses when they took over."

Antonio reached in his pocket, took out the red pack of Pall Malls, shook out a cigarette.

"We lost it all-- wound up in Miami with nothing. Lansky and those New York kikes kissed our asses when times were good then showed us the fat side of their asses when we needed help."

"American Jews have always been clannish. When they'd need something from Mexico, they'd wine and dine me, tell me how we're all circumcised and then screw me the first chance they'd get."

"Just like a bunch of Gringo kikes."

They both laughed.

Fuchs stopped laughing, looked over at Antonio. "We're both circumcised, Antonio. Do you trust me?"

"At least as much as you trust me, Jacobo."

They stared at each other for a second, then burst into laughter again. Fuchs went on,

"Luis's got the bug up his ass that he wants to be a gentleman."

"So I've heard," Antonio said.

"Before he met me, he'd ever eaten anything besides tortillas and beans. Now, it's French cuisine, California wines, Italian ice cream."

"I heard he's even going to church," Antonio said.

"Ten teams of priests in ten years hearing his confessions day and night couldn't give him enough absolution to squeeze his Indian ass into Catholic purgatory."

Antonio laughed, wiped his eyes, shook his head.

Fuchs took another slurp of coffee. "We don't even need Drako," he said.

"No? What about the heroin?"

"We have other sources."

"Ah, our circumcised brother, the Russian Banker."

"Litzov knows who has what."

"So, when do we move?"

"The accountant I stole from Luis hates his guts. Luis had Mauricio Placer kill his father and let him rape his sister. This kid's located all of Luis's assets."

"What about Drako?"

"Russians don't care who pays them off."

"So, what's the next step?"

"This business with Armando Ortega's kid: Luis's afraid the Gringos will implicate him."

"Won't they?"

"Of course, they'll know he did it– but. that's always been the case. One slip and it's all our asses., so what the fuck can they do?"

"Lean on him," Antonio said. "Stand on his ass every time he moves– those bastards don't forget."

Fuchs finished his coffee, sat back looking across at Antonio.

"That's why I want you to whack that Ortega kid next time he comes back to Mexico."

"You told me that earlier– I'm on it."

Fuchs stood, Antonio snapped his fingers for the bill, laid down a 500 peso note. When they were approaching the door, Fuchs leaned over to Antonio.

"You'll do a helluva lot better job running things than that uncircumcised Indio and that slew foot Slav," the old man said.

~*~*~

Later, same day, Thursday

Coming back into his office, Antonio told his secretary,

"Maria. Get me Chibo. Immediately."

Around two hours later, Antonio heard someone skip up the stairs, then open the door to his office.

A little hatchet-faced man with a deformed chest, a flat broken nose with small dark brown eyes set back under two prominent nodules on his forehead which with a straggly goatee gave his face a goat-like appearance stepped inside.

His nickname was Chibo, 'goat.' No one knew or cared what his real name was.

"You got here fast," Antonio said.

"Maria said it was urgent," Chibo said.

"Remember Armando Ortega?"

"That was one obituary I read with pleasure."

"I want you to take his oldest kid out."

"I'm interested."

Antonio handed him a folder with a picture of Pepe.

Chibo studied it, then said,

"Anything more you can tell me?"

"This guy was a cop with the Nacionales for a long time. Went to the States, stayed there. Teaches in an American school but comes back here to visit."

Chibo read the file, looked up at Antonio.

"He's from Hidalgo," he said. "And he's Rodrigo Gonzalez-Diaz's brother-in-law."

"That's right."

"Sweet as a pineapple ice! I'm tempted to do this one for free."

Antonio raised his eyebrows. "Oh?"

Chibo raised his finger. "Just tempted. A man's gotta make a living."

Antonio took out a pack of Pall Malls, offered one to Chibo.

Chibo whipped a lighter from his jacket pocket, lit Antonio's Pall Mall before his own, then settled back. "When does this have to happen?"

Antonio inhaled the smoke, blew it out in a ring.

"As soon as feasible," he said. "But, it's important that it gets done in country."

"Fine with me. Details?"

"Make it visible," he said. "And do it so we can lay it on Alban's ass."

"That makes it even easier."

Chibo put the straw hat back on his head, left without a word.

Unwelcome news
Pepe Ortega's Office, East LA University, Los Angeles, CA
1:17 PM, Thursday, June 13, 1974

The final presentation for Crim 109 had been hard. Professor Ortega had faced a long line of aspiring police investigators most of the morning.

Breathing a sigh of relief after the last student had left, Pepe was reaching for his coffee cup when the knock at the door stopped him.

"Come in," he said.

The door cracked open. A wrinkled clean shaven face with bulldog features peeking out from under a straw hat peered in then spoke,

"Dr. Ortega?"

"The same. Please come in."

Stepping into Pepe's office, he flashed a badge, an ID.

"Bill Rowe," he said. "Coroner's investigator for San Diego County."

"How can I help you, Inspector?"

Rowe withdrew a photo of a dead woman sprawled on a floor from a zippered binder, handed it to Pepe.

"My God!" Pepe said.

"You know her?" Rowe said.

"I talked to her just a couple of days ago."

"Her roommate came home around 10, found her lying in the hallway, her neck broken."

Rowe pulled a business card from his zippered binder, handed it to Pepe.

"I found your card in her pocket."

Rowe took a notebook, pen from the binder.

"Why were you there?"

"I'd come to talk to Dr. Hall. Maggie was there when I left."

"What was your interest in Dr. Hall?"

"It's a long story."

"I got nothin' but time," Rowe said.

Pepe explained about his brother's murder, the disappearance of Ruth Hall's ex-boyfriend as a runaway possible witness whose blood was on his brother's clothes.

"I'd just found a name for this guy," Pepe said. "I wanted to ask Dr. Hall about him."

"You think this ex-boyfriend killed your brother?"

"Can't say. My brother was working a drug case but I'd like to know more about the ex."

"Sounds reasonable," Rowe said. "What else did you learn from the murdered woman, Maggie that night?"

"She worked with a rehab program. She told me that she had gotten threats."

"From users?"

"From dealers."

"Did these threats seem to worry her?"

"Nah. She dismissed them."

"Did that strike you as strange?"

"In most cases, it would have. But, my impression was she wasn't much afraid of anything."

After glancing over his notes, Rowe looked back at Pepe.

"What do you think?"

"This killing doesn't make any sense. She did say she'd made enemies in the dealer's markets but why take her out."

Rowe flipped his notebook shut. "I think that about covers it, Dr. Ortega."

"We're colleagues. Call me Pepe."

"I'm Bill," Rowe said. "Can I call on you again if something else comes up?"

"By all means and please keep me in the know."

When Rowe stood up to leave, he glanced at the framed picture on Pepe's desk.

"You wife?" he said.

"My late wife. Maggie reminded me of her."

"They do look kind of alike," Rowe said. "What happened to your wife?"

Pepe picked up the picture and brushed it with his fingers before setting it back on the desk.

"Cancer," he said,

"Hell of way to go," Rowe said. "The big C gets a lot of us."

"How's Ruth Hall doing?"

"She's had a rough time but seems to be OK."

Rowe left, eased the door shut behind him.

Pepe looked up at the poster of Zapata with his sad eyes, then back the picture of his wife, recalling the image of the smiling little blond he'd left that night.

Not fair. She didn't deserve this

~*~*~

The Goat
Madera District, Mexico City, DF, Mexico
Three months later, 3:18 PM, Sunday, September 15, 1974

On the roof of an old apartment building, flanked by noisy traffic-filled streets, cluttered alleys, Chibo "the Goat" lounged under a canopied shade fixed to one side of an abandoned service shed. Plopped by a table in a large woven cane chair, feet up on a stool, Chibo looked through a newspaper.

On the table at his elbow, sprawled a near empty bottle of Cutty Sark scotch, a glass with ice cubes, an ashtray full of cigarette butts. The manila folder Antonio had given him lay next to an old television flashing images of a soccer match across its black and white screen. Chibo was ignoring the TV screen– his team was losing badly, when an article caught his eye.

'... Mexico City hosts annual meetings of the International Anthropological Association to be held in the Maria Teresa hotel this week. Delegates and members of this international scientific body will be attending conferences and meetings Thursday through Sunday of next week. Scientists dedicating their efforts to studying human beings will be coming from all over the world to be guests in our city ...'

Chibo snatched up the folder, thumbed through it, stopping at the line describing Asuncion Ortega's profession: *Professor of Forensic Investigative Anthropology.*

He jumped up, slipped his gnarled feet into a pair of worn huarache sandals, buttoned his shirt, clapped his hat on his head, took off for the stairwell to the street below.

Taking a bus to the the Maria Teresa hotel in the central part of Mexico City's Pink Zone, he found the concierge's station where a uniformed young man was sorting out papers and writing in a log book.

Chibo pulled out a press card identifying him as a reporter for LA VOZ PUBLICA, thrust it under the concierge's nose.

"La Voz Publica, Señor," Chibo said. "I understand you'll be hosting the International Conference of Anthropologists this coming December."

The concierge wrinkled his brow, scowled at the phony press card.

"Yes," he said. "What do you want?"

"I'm checking to see if you've received a reservation for a Professor Ortega from the US."

"That information is private, Señor. We don't give out our guest lists."

Chibo withdrew the press card.

"My apologies," he said. "I failed to show you my proper identification."

He thrust the press card forward again with two 100 Peso notes under it. The concierge looked around, took the press card, slipped the bills into his hand, then looked at his log book.

"His name's on the program roster but he's not staying here," the concierge said.

Chibo left, made the rounds of all the hotels in the immediate area until he arrived at a smaller hotel seven blocks away from the Maria Teresa. After passing some bills to the desk clerk at the Pensión Julio de Urquijo, he confirmed a reservation there for Dr. Asuncion Ortega.

Chibo caught the bus to another part of the city, got off outside a large shop with *Plomeria* 'plumbing parts' painted on the wall. Coming through the front door, four men playing cards, turned, looked up at him.

"Javier here?" Chibo said to them.

"In the back," one answered.

Chibo went in through a door behind a counter covered by a curtain into a room stacked full of plumbing parts. Two men stepped forward, hands inside their jackets. Recognizing Chibo in the dim light, they both relaxed.

Chibo called out, "Javier!"

An office door at the back of the room opened, a little man with a scarred face stepped out, grinned at Chibo.

"Chivito!" he said, then stepped forward, embraced Chibo.

"I need a tail pipe boomer," Chibo said.

"When?"

"No rush. A few weeks."

"How big?"

"Maybe 100 grams of military C."

"Expensive," Javier said. "It's hard to get C."

"Not for you."

"20,000 Pesos. Half up front, the rest when you pick it up."

Chibo blinked, swallowed hard.

"*Hermano*, that's impossible."

"Talk or walk, Chibo."

"Give me a little break on this, *viejo*. I'm working on a thin margin."

"You been working with those Jews too long," Javier said. "You're talking just like them."

"How about 10,000?"

"Seventeen."

"Javier, be reasonable."

"Fifteen."

"OK, OK. Twelve fifty and I'll pay it all up front."

"Fifteen, Chivito, means fifteen. You know you get quality from me and that adds up to fifteen in my book."

Javier burst into laughter along with the two men behind them when Chibo counted 15,000 Pesos into his hand.

~*~*~

Touching base
Professor Ortega's Office, East LA University, Los Angeles, CA 1:17 PM, Tuesday, September 17, 1974

Pepe picked up the phone, hesitated, punched in a number. It rang, twice, the voice that came on sounded tired, hoarse. "Hello."

"Hello, Ruth. This is Pepe Ortega. Sorry, I found out last June what happened to Maggie."

"Yeah. It was pretty bad."

"Forgive me for not calling right away but I knew you'd need some time and space to get this behind you."

"Yeah. I did."

"Inspector Rowe gave me some of the details. I'm so very sorry you had to endure all of that."

"So am I."

"Look, I don't want to keep you but I felt that I had to call and let you know that you're not alone in all this."

"That means a lot to me. I was late that night. Maybe if I'd been home on time instead of..."

"Ruth. Don't look back. The 'only if' game is fruitless."

"I suppose you're right."

"I am, trust me."

"OK. Say, by the way, are you going down to the international meetings in Mexico City in December?"

"Yes. I'm chairing a session down there."

"Let's get together down there and talk. Hopefully, the air will have cleared a bit by then."

"Sounds good to me. I'll be staying at a little hotel called the Pensión Julio de Urquijo on the Avenida Libertad."

"Sounds good. I think we're staying at the Maria Teresa but I'll give you a call."

"And, Ruth."

"Yes?"

"Hang in there."

"Thanks, I will."

After Pepe hung up the phone, he sat for a long time looking at the picture of his dead wife.

The Archeologist
Pensión Julio de Urquijo, Mexico City, DF, Mexico
11:10 PM, Thursday, December 5, 1974

The short flight to Mexico City had been easy, uneventful but the taxi ride from the airport to the central zone had been a nightmare of honking, dodging cars, trucks, bicycles. After checking into the Pensión Julio de Urquijo, Pepe made his way to the elevator past a group of Argentine tourists talking in loud voices.

After tossing his bags on the floor, he flopped down on the bed, forced himself to unwind, closed his eyes, then slept.

Pepe woke with a start.

His phone was ringing. Picking it up, he answered,

"Bueno?"

"Dr. Ortega?"

A woman's voice. Recognition set in.

Ruth Hall.

"This is Pepe," he said.

"Hello. This is Ruth Hall. I'm over at the Maria Teresa and was wondering if you'd like to come in a half hour or so for a drink?"

Pepe glanced at his watch. It was 2:10 PM.

"Sounds great," he said.

"I'll meet you by the concierge's desk on the first floor in the main lobby."

"How'll I know you?"

"I'll know you from that TV special you did on neighborhood Chicano gangs."

"Fine. See you then."

Pepe sat on the bed, phone in hand, a faceless but attractive blond woman swirling in his mind's eye.

~*~*~

The Maria Teresa, Mexico City's largest hotel, was only a short seven blocks walk. Pepe found his way to the concierge's station, then looked around.

"Dr. Ortega?"

Pepe turned to see a pretty woman with short blond hair, dark brown eyes, dressed in a red dress, dark hose, black high heels, carrying a bag that matched her shoes.

I knew it. I did see her before!

"Please call me Pepe," he said.

She extended her hand. "Ruth."

"Where would you like to go for a drink?"

"There's an annex with a bar right outside."

"Lead on."

He followed her out the door into a round open patio sprinkled with wrought-iron tables, chairs. A waitress appeared when they sat down, took orders for a tequila sunrise for Ruth, mescal for Pepe.

"I've been in a state of shock since Detective Rowe showed up at my door," Pepe said.

Ruth lowered tearing eyes, took a deep breath.

"I found her."

"Oh no!"

"The police said it was made to look like an accident."

"Any idea who'd wanted to hurt Maggie?"

"No. I'm still baffled."

They sat in silence for a while, both looking into the glasses in their hands.

"What was it you wanted to ask me about Matt?" Ruth said.

"He disappeared the evening my brother was murdered."

"Oh my god," Ruth said, touching his arm. "I had no idea it was your brother who was killed."

"Yes. They found your friend's blood on his clothing."

"Matt Spyner's the most unlikely person in the world to commit murder."

"My brother was investigating drug smuggling in Santa Luisita at the time."

"Even more incredible," Ruth said. "Matt used drugs but hated dealers."

"Where did he get his drugs?"

"Local sources, I'm sure. He'd worked with a Zaitequi shaman who used a variety of hallucinogens."

"So, where do you think he went?" Pepe said.

"This guy's unpredictable," Ruth said. "He could be in Timbuktu."

"Why do you think he bolted?"

"We've no idea," she said.

"We?"

"His brother, Jake and I went down there to collect his things. The police did mention a dead policeman and bloodstains but we were both at a loss to explain it."

"There's gotta be a connection," Pepe said.

"But, you do understand my reservations about Matt's involvement with drug dealers?"

"Certainly. You know this guy."

"Thanks for that," Ruth said. "I don't want to create any romantic misconceptions about my ex-boyfriend."

Pepe downed the last bit of mescal in his glass, then stared off across the patio for a while. He looked up to see Ruth looking at him, tears clouding her eyes.

"We've both been through the wringer," she said.

"It would certainly seem that way."

"Do you have plans for dinner tonight?" she said.

"What did you have in mind?"

"Would you like to join us at the Basque Club for dinner tonight? I'm going to be meeting up with the Singers, a Mexican public health official and Paco Arrechega."

"*The* Edgar Singer? Wouldn't I be intruding?"

"Not at all. Ed and Martha are real down to earth people. I'm sure they'd like to meet you."

"I'd be delighted to join you."

Ruth stood.

"Fine," she said. "I'll grab a taxi and pick you up at your hotel around 6."

~*~*~

Later that same evening, 6:22 PM, Friday

On the way to the Centro Español, home to the Club Vasco, Ruth said Pepe, "Have we met before?"

"We had an encounter once."

"How's that?"

"At the Anthro meetings in Santa Cruz some years back, I was with Ray Errol and Santos Villalobos..."

"Santos Villalobos! That sonfabitch."

"...when you sailed up and gave him a bit of your mind."

"You were there?"

"Not that you'd remember– you were too busy taking him to task."

"That asshole stole Matt Spyner's thesis."

"Your ex-boyfriend? The same guy in Santa Luisita who bolted?"

"Yes. His thesis was the basis of Villalobos's book."

"How can you be so sure?"

"I read Matt's thesis– it was all about becoming an apprentice shaman."

"Funny thing," Pepe said. "Ray Errol mentioned some strange business about Otomi male shaman at the time which prompted Villalobos to beat a fast retreat."

"Ray and I organized the inquiry on Villalobos," Ruth said.

"Inquiry?"

"Yes. An inquiry into the nature of the background of Villalobos's research will be made tomorrow night in open session."

"Who's involved?"

"A committee of selected scholars, including Ed Singer."

"Well, no one knows Southwest ethnography better."

"True," she said. "But I doubt if Ed says much."

"How so?"

"He's old school. He won't sully his hands beyond making a few perfunctory remarks on the substance or quality of the research."

"Why would he do otherwise?"

Ruth turned, looked Pepe in the eyes. "Because he is the only other person who read Matt Spyner's thesis. Villalobos called on Ed and he gave him Matt's name and location."

"When?"

"Just after Matt took off and before your brother was murdered."

"You're suggesting Santos Villalobos had something to do with all of this?"

"Suggesting, yes. Prove any of it? No."

"Ruth. Strong accusations require strong evidence."

"I know that. That's why Ray and I organized this panel to look at the ethnographic evidence."

Pepe didn't say another word until they reached El Club Vasco.

El Club Vasco
El Club Vasco, Centro Español, Mexico City, DF, Mexico
Same day, 9:10 PM, Thursday

Pepe followed Ruth out of the elevator, then paused to look over the polished brass plaque listing the Spanish ex-patriot clubs in *El Centro Español.*

Els Cercles Catalás,
As Socios Galegos,
Fijos de Asturia,
Asociación Madrileña.

The **Gure Herriberria Euskaldunetako**, *El Club Vasco* occupied an entire floor with an elaborate bar, restaurant and a Jai Alai frontón.

Walking into the large dining room, they were greeted by a dark skinned Mexican waiter in black tuxedo trousers, wearing a green vest under a bright red jacket.

"*Ongi Etorri, Jaunak.* Welcome to the Club Vasco," he said,

Taking in the dark skin, dark eyes, hook nose of the waiter, Pepe spoke to him in Nahuatl,

"For an Indio, you speak very good Basco."

The waiter replied in the same language.

"Thank you, my Don. But I'm afraid it's about all the Basque I know."

Ruth stood looking back and forth from Pepe to the waiter.

"Where'd you learned to speak Basque?" she said.

Both men laughed.

"Forgive our bad manners," Pepe said. "We were speaking Nahuatl."

Ruth rolled her eyes, then said to the waiter,

"We're with Dr. Solomón's party."

The waiter led them to an alcove at the back of the dining room, pushed aside a curtain. Three men stood when Ruth introduced Pepe.

"I've asked Dr. Ortega to join us."

Pepe shook hands with a man with thinning gray hair in his late 70s, tall, red-faced, gray moustache, dressed in a western style shirt, a bolo tie with an elaborate turquoise ring, dark brown western pants, pointed toe boots. His attractive wife, a few years younger than him wore similar western clothing, shook hands.

"Hello, I'm Ed Singer. My wife, Martha."

"An honor, Professor Singer," Pepe said. "I've read most of your work."

"It's Ed," the older man said. "And. I like your interesting work on forensic investigation."

"This is Hadim Solomón," Ruth went on. "Medical Director of the National Indigenous Health Program."

Pepe gripped his hand.

"You're famous– few get nominated for a Nobel prize."

"It's my pleasure to meet the son of the incorruptible Armando Ortega." Dr. Solomón said.

"Your father was Armando Ortega?" Singer said. "We met him once."

"Yes, I can see your father in you," Martha Singer said. "He was a remarkable man."

"Thank you," Pepe said. "He was."

Ruth presented Pepe to a stocky, 5'9" man, his grinning face showing short teeth with a wide frontal diastema, dressed in levis, a dark brown tweed jacket over a lighter brown turtle neck sweater covering a short, thick neck.

"This is our host, Francisco "Paco" Arrechega," Ruth said. "Medical anthropologist at the CDC, he worked with his fellow Basques in the Pyrenees and in California."

"As epidemiologist," Arrechega said. " I loved your paper on Latino inner-city drug culture."

Introductions over, they sat down to order.

"Paco, what do you recommend?" Martha said to Arrechega.

"Food here's like sex," he said. "Just varying degrees of good."

Martha and Ruth laughed, ignoring the discomfort of the men.

"We start with the pickled tongue," Arrechega went on. "Then we go on to the soup followed by the salad. Myself? I'm having calamari cooked in its own ink with saffron rice."

Arrechega ordered red wine. Corks popped, glasses filled, then raised,

"¡Salud!"

Pepe found the wine good, the food delicious, the conversation around the table lively. Arrechega made jokes in Spanish and English.

"Ruth," Martha said "We heard about your tragic experience with your roommate."

"Was it an accident?" Singer said.

"They're investigating it as a homicide," Ruth said.

"No!"

"I'm afraid so."

"Are there any suspects?" Arrechega said.

"Pepe said they might have some evidence but that's it."

"Who do you think might have done this?" Solomón said.

Ruth drew a deep breath.

"I honestly think–" she said. "Just think, mind you– that Santos Villalobos had something to do with this."

Singer looked down at the table, Martha stared, Solomón put his hand to his mouth– even Arrechega was quiet.

"What makes you think that, Ruth?" Martha said.

"That bastard stole Matt Spyner's thesis. Somehow– and I'm the first one to admit that I don't know how– he's involved."

Solomón looked over to Singer.

"Edward, aren't you on the panel inquiring into the authenticity of his work?"

Singer nodded without looking up.

"Ed," Arrechega said. "What's your read on this guy, Villalobos."

Singer gave a little embarrassed laugh.

"Honestly," he said. "I've never even read his book completely through."

"Hell," Arrechega said. "I wasn't able to stay awake to get past the first chapter."

Frowning at his hands, Singer spoke,

"Since I'm on the panel, the least said, the least mended."

"Did you ever meet Villalobos, Edward?" Solomón said.

"Once," Singer said. "He asked me to recommend some possible field sites. I did. He left and that was that."

He looked over at his wife. "It's been a grand evening but I feel all talked out. Shall we go back to the hotel?'

Martha patted his hand.

Looking over at Ruth, Pepe saw her glare at Singer who didn't return her look.

Everyone reached for their pocket books.

"Where's the bill?" Martha said.

"It's on the house," Arrechega said.

Everyone protested. Arrechega just shook his head.

Stepping out to the elevator, Pepe heard a noisy group come walking up the stairs. Four beefy red-faced men came up arguing in loud Basque voices. Arrechega said something to them. They burst into laughter, came over shook his hand, chattering to him in Basque.

After Arrechega made introductions all around, the Basques invited everyone for drinks. Arrechega waved his hand at his dinner companions.

"I'll make the self-sacrifice of drinking with these wild guys," he said. "See you at the meetings tomorrow."

"You hope," Pepe said.

~*~*~

In the taxi ride back, Pepe noticed Ruth staring out the window. Then she spoke, her voice soft,

"This is a beautiful city at night."

"It is."

She looked over at him.

92

"I'm glad you came."

"So am I."

When the cab pulled up in front of his hotel, Pepe paid the driver, leaned toward Ruth, kissed her on the lips, then stood on the curb waving as the cab pulled away.

~*~*~

Inquest
Grand Ballroom, Maria Teresa Hotel, Mexico City, DF, Mexico
7:10 PM, Saturday, December 7, 1974

Pepe sat between Ruth and Ray Errol, the organizers of the conference in the huge ballroom surrounded by gilded walls with Aztec warriors locked in warring bas-relief with Spanish conquistadors. A huge fresco of a circular Aztec calendar dominated the wall behind the stage.

The five panelists emerged onto the stage from the wings to a round of applause. P. Oliver Goldworthy, current president of the International Anthropological Association, stepped up to the lighted podium to announce the purpose of the forum as an inquest to consider the validity of the ethnographic content of the book, *The Secrets of Don Pedro Miguel* by Santos Villalobos.

Goldworthy went on to say,

"An invitation to appear and speak on the issue at hand was extended to Dr. Villalobos, but, his lawyer declined on his behalf, stating 'The work stands on its own.' "

Following Goldworthy, Professor Edward Singer addressed the ethnographic aspects of the work in question.

"I have serious questions about the ethnographic authenticity as a serious study of the Otomi people," he said.

Professor Immanuel Barber, Santo Villalobos's dissertation advisor at USC, came on board with a scathing comment.

"I required the original research to be presented less of a personal narrative as is seen in his first book and more ethnographic. And he published his dissertation as his second book. Frankly, I'm greatly disappointed by Santos's refusal to address the questions of fraud and manipulation of data before a body of his peers."

The next commentator, Professor Swami Prajñaparmitra–
formerly Heinz Rippenkauf– discussed the religious and symbolic
aspects of the work, noting in a heavy Austrian accent that the entire
series by Villalobos was simply "bad mysticism."

The last speaker Robert Groswalt, Professor, Jungian
Psychiatry, University of Lucerne School of Medicine, stated,

"The entire psycho-scenario of Villalobos's drug-induced
perception of an alternative reality is consistent with other
chemically induced warped perceptions. However, I'm curious as to
what the furor is about, since the books read well as entertainment."

When the speakers had finished, Goldworthy gave a summation
of the inquest, recalling his initial review of the book, then declared
his second thoughts about his initial review,

"We anthropologists proceed on an act of faith– that is 'I'll
believe your ethnography if you believe mine.' "

Goldworthy finished up the session by announcing Professor
Ray Errol, University of San Antonio, along with Professor Ruth
Hall of Madison University would review the ethnographic and field
work supporting the research, then report on their findings in the
Association's journal.

~*~*~

Frustration
Grand Ballroom, Maria Teresa Hotel, Mexico City, DF, Mexico
Same day, 9:16 PM, Saturday

When the session concluded. Pepe saw Ruth jump out of her
seat, then stand over Ray Errol.

"I'm pissed," she said. "All blather. That sonfabitch Villalobos
stole another man's work, called it research, made a fortune off it
and they accepted it."

"But Ruth," Errol said. "Wasn't that what they were telling us?"

"No, goddam it," Ruth said. "That was just a slap on the hand."

Errol shrugged his big shoulders.

"Let's see if we can show the holes in his data reveal that his
field work wasn't done with the Otomi," he said.

Errol stood up, hugged an irate Ruth, grabbed Pepe's hand.

"Gotta run," he said. "I'll catch up to you two later."

Ruth turned back to Pepe, her hands still on her hips.

"You must think I'm a first class bitch," she said.

"I understand frustration," Pepe said.

Crossing her arms over her chest, Ruth glared at the departing panelists.

"Bastards," she said. "They just covered their own asses."

"Let's go somewhere and unwind," Pepe said. "I know a little place not far from here where we can get a quiet drink."

"I feel like getting drunk and running screaming down the street."

"Let's hope it won't come to that," Pepe said.

Pepe led her outside, found a cab, then told the driver the name of a bar.

After they arrived, Ruth plopped down at a table, then gave the waitress an order for a "triple margarita."

"Thirsty?" Pepe said.

Ruth wrinkled her eyebrows, looked at her fingernails.

"Oh well," she said. "Tomorrow's another day."

"I think that Scarlet O'Hara may have already used a line like that," Pepe said.

"I guess I was going off the deep end."

"Let's put Santos Villalobos out of our heads for now," Pepe said. "Tell me about Ruth Hall."

"What's to tell? I was raised in the South Central Valley of California. My dad worked for the Southern Pacific Railroad. I have three older brothers. One's a lawyer. One's a teacher and one's a pilot in the Navy."

"How'd you become an archeologist?"

"As a kid, my dad and I used to go looking for arrowheads and I loved reading about Indians. As an undergrad, started out as a geology major, took an anthro course, went on a summer school dig as a shovel bum and got hooked. Been playing in the dirt ever since."

"How did you wind up at Arizona?"

"I heard Ed Singer speak about border tribes and decided that's what I wanted to study."

The drinks arrived. Ruth hoisted the large frosted, salt-rimmed stemmed glass of margarita, clinked Pepe's glass of mescal.

"*Salud!*" she said.

She took a big swig of the drink, licked the salt residue from her lips, looked over at Pepe.

"Tell me about yourself, Dr. Ortega," Ruth said. "What're you investigating at the present?"

"Not investigating, investing," Pepe replied.

"Was that kiss last night part of your investment?" Ruth said.

"I'm not sorry about that if you're asking."

Then, without a pause, Ruth picked the previous topic back up, saying she dug in the dirt, wrote papers, but got pissed when thieves steal, then pass off other's work as their own.

"How involved were you with this Matt guy?" Pepe said.

"I've not been too lucky with men. Matt was a lost soul– a dreamer. Basically a gentle, hardworking guy who could fix anything mechanical. In another lifetime, he'd have been a monk."

"Were you in love with him?"

"Are you investigating or investing?"

"I'm a cop. I like to know everything about my informants."

"I felt sorry for him."

"That's poison for a relationship.

"Amen," Ruth said. "We'd long broken up before he took off for Mexico."

"Did the affair just wear itself out?"

"You do like to know everything, don't you?"

"I can take notes in my little policeman's notebook if that will make you open up."

Ruth sipped her margarita then licked her lips.

"Matt wrote this wild psychedelic diatribe," she said. "Then he gave it to Ed Singer as an MA thesis. Ed looked it over, kindly handed it back and suggested he do it over– from the beginning."

"That must have stunned him."

"It crushed him. He personalized the rejection and took off. Truth is, he wasn't all that stable. Another round?"

She signaled the waitress.

"I'll pass," Pepe said. "Going back tomorrow."

The waitress brought the margarita. Ruth raised it to Pepe, downed a big swallow, set the glass down, leaned back in her chair looking over at the man sitting across from her.

"Why do you think someone killed Maggie?" she said.

"It could have been drug-related," Pepe said.

"Well, it sucks."

"Yes. It certainly does."

She eyed him over the rim of the margarita glass and then, a slight smile played across her lips.

"Y'know, I think we should spend the night together." she said.

"Now who's doing the investing?" Pepe said.

"You're a genuine stud," Ruth said. "A rare quality among the men I've met."

"It's a bad cop takes advantage of his consultant."

"I'm not drunk or frivolous," Ruth said. "If I didn't want to be with you, I wouldn't be here."

After dropping a wad of pesos on the table, she leaned over, kissed him on the lips, took his hand, then led him to the door.

Breakfast

Ruth's room, Maria Teresa Hotel, Mexico City, DF, Mexico
Next day, 7:20 AM, Sunday, December 8, 1974

A beam of light leaking through the split in the drawn curtain spiked Pepe's eyes. Awake, he turned to Ruth who clung to his back. She murmured, eyes still closed, wiggled, snuggled nearer to him, curling up against his chest.

"Buenos dias, Dr. Ortega," she whispered.

He put his arm around her, pulled her close, appreciating her softness, her warmth.

"You think we can spend the day this way?" he said.

"Damn. I guess you're right."

He held her, letting his hands trail over her skin. She said *"umm"* a lot before kissing him with a mouth that still sang of margarita.

"You're still here and there's no note saying you'll call." she said.

"No note?"

"We're still friends, aren't we?" Ruth said.

"A bit more than that," he said. "Let's talk about it over huevos rancheros and a glass of OJ," Pepe said. "Let me run back to my hotel. I have to pack and then you come meet me there."

"Eggs with chorizo beats a note," Ruth said

She pulled him to her, rolled on top of him, kissed him again.

"There's no need to hurry," she said.

~*~*~

Later, same day, Sunday

The lobby of the Pensión Julio de Urquijo was total chaos. Outside, footmen waved for taxis. Tourists packed the sidewalks in disorderly lines. People jumped out to grab available taxis. Others complained, argued who was first in line.

In the lobby, Pepe waited for Ruth, reading *El Diario*.

"Hola, Dr. Ortega."

Ruth was now all archaeologist: levis, a khaki work shirt, plain toed brown Redwing work boots. Her hair was pulled back into a bushy puppy's tail under her cap.

Pepe folded the newspaper while sizing her up from boots to cap. She didn't fidget under his gaze but stood there taking it as a compliment, knowing she had a hold on him.

"Feel like breakfast?" Pepe said, coming to his feet.

"After last night, a girl's gotta eat."

Escorting her to the adjacent dining room, Pepe seated her at a table, then sat next to her.

Ruth scanned the menu. When the waitress came up, she said,

"I'll have fresh squeezed orange juice, *tamal* with scrambled eggs, rice, beans and three corn tortillas. Bring me a *café con leche* afterwards."

Pepe smiled at the waitress.

"A girl's gotta eat," he said. "Double that. It was a long night."

Ruth sat back, looked at him.

"Where do we go from here?" she said.

"Wherever it goes, I want to be there. You're a fascinating woman."

"Sorry, I went on and on last night about that asshole Villalobos."

"You're a scientist. Where's the proof?"

"Fuck science, Pepe. My gut of guts tells me this shitbird is in this up to his eyeballs."

"I'm a cop. Hunches whisper, but evidence sings. What you've got now is hearsay and circumstance. Show me something solid."

"A friend of yours bakes a cookie," Ruth said. "You wake up, find it's gone, learn your friend has split—maybe even killed. Then you see a fat rat with cookie crumbs in his whiskers. You do the math."

"That's still pretty subjective."

The waitress brought orange juice. Ruth grabbed the glass drained half of it in one swallow.

"You're right. Speculation and guesstulation. Unsupported. Only hints and traces of any solid empirical evidence, but that voice inside my head keeps screaming his name."

"Guesstulation?" Pepe said. "I love it when you talk dirty."

The waitress served up breakfast. Ruth's appetite at the table was equal to her appetite in bed.

"I like a woman that likes her food," Pepe said.

Ruth shrugged her shoulders, tore off a piece of tortilla, scooped up beans and rice, stuffed it into her mouth.

"Musta been a Mexican in a former life," she said. "I love Mexican food– I eat it at least twice a week."

After breakfast, they took coffee out on the veranda at a table under the shade of some trees.

"Every time I come to Mexico," Ruth said, "I hate to go back home."

"It's the same for me too," Pepe said.

"You still have family here?"

"I'm from Hidalgo, just north of the capital, Tula de Allende."

"Besides your brother, do you have other bloodlings?"

"Bloodlings? You have a unique way with words."

"Do you? Anybody to make you watch your step with wild women?"

"My sister, Xochitl. She's a lawyer here in the Federal District."

"Does she have a family?"

"Two wild Indians– her husband's the Chief Prosecutor in the Ministry of Justice. He's a hometown boy. We went through college and the National Police Academy together. I landed in investigations but Rodrigo left the force after a couple of years and went to law school."

"That's amazing."

"After he landed his first job, he proposed to my sister. She accepted only on the condition that he would support her way through law school too."

"Sounds like my kinda woman." Ruth said.

When they finished their coffee, Ruth looked at her watch.

"I gotta get my buns in motion," she said. "Finish packing, talk to some friends and check out. I'll get back tonight. This coming week is going to be crazy for me."

"I'm going back today as well," Pepe said.

"Call me. You have my number."

"I won't leave a note," Pepe said.

Ruth held her hands out. Pepe stood. She kissed him. He flushed with the heat of her body. He didn't want it to end.

"More than friends?" she whispered. She left him standing.

Pepe felt emptiness sweep over him. He'd call her all right.

A near miss
Pensión Julio de Urquijo, Mexico City
Same day, 1:10 PM, Sunday

Coming down the steps his bags in each hand, Pepe nodded to the curb attendant who flagged a cab. When the attendant reached for the back door, a dirty pock-faced man in ragged filthy clothing, a broken brim hat pulled low over his face, pushed past Pepe, then sprayed window-wash on the taxi's windshield.

The cab driver yelled, "Get the hell outta here."

The dirty man grinned at Pepe.

"For a peso, I'll clean all his windows."

"Why not?" Pepe said, then handed the dirty man a 10 peso note.

When the curb attendant opened the cab door, put the bags in the back, the little man scurried around the car spraying, wiping windows. When he stepped to the rear of the car, he dropped his spray bottle, bent down to retrieve it. Glancing around, he pulled a metal cylinder from inside his jacket sleeve, stuffed it into the exhaust pipe, then disappeared into the crowd.

When the hotel attendant opened the front door, Pepe started to get inside. Then his billfold fell from his jacket pocket onto the ground.

Stepping back, Pepe bent over to pick up his wallet.

The cab exploded in a burst of flame, metal and smoke. The rear of the chassis leaped from the ground, the doors blew out, tires popped, the hood flew off, windows burst, hurling shards like bullets over the surrounding area.

A shockwave of dust, debris swept over the immediate area, blowing Pepe from his bent over position into a gaggle of people standing on the curb in front of the hotel.

Then, everything turned blank.

~*~*~

Pepe came to with a start.

He was in a bed.

Putting his hand to his face, it felt burned, tender, his joints ached.

Then, he remembered.

It came in bits, pieces, fragments.

An explosion.

The odor of cordite.

A taxi.

A dirty window washer.

Some funny business at the rear of the cab.

"You're awake?"

Pepe startled at the voice.

He looked up. A male nurse stood next to his bed.

"You were lucky," the man said.

"Yes," Pepe squeaked.

"The police said someone was after you. Why?"

"I work with the US DEA and National Narcotics Control to pin down drug dealers."

"You're still alive," the nurse said.

"Let me outta here," Pepe said.

"No, Sr. Ortega," the nurse said. "You stay here for tonight."

"Can you get the police in here?" Pepe said. "I need everything I can get on these drug dealers?"

"You'd not find out anything you don't already know," the nurse said. "Just rest for now."

Pepe groaned.

"I need some help," he said.

The nurse reached into his pocket, pulled out a brown half-pint bottle.

"This is good mescal," he said. "Now get to sleep and they'll get your ass outta the country tomorrow morning."

The nurse left the room.

Pepe drank the mescal, then spent the night in a deep sleep.

PART FOUR

Phone message received
Rosemont District, San Diego, California
Next day, 9:14 PM, Monday, December 9, 1974

Ruth toted her heavy suitcase into the hall, dumped it on the floor at the entrance to the living room, scooped up the pile of mail on her rug below the mail drop in the front door, then plopped down in the front room into an overstuffed chair, her stretched out on the coffee table.

"What a pile of crap," she muttered.

Sorting through the mail, she tossed advertisements, fliers, circulars into a pile on the coffee table in front of her, then setting one or two bills aside, her gaze shifted to the large suitcase visible in the hall.

Gotta take less stuff next time, she thought, knowing she had made that vow many times before.

Ruth pushed herself into the hall, grabbed the handle of the suit case, then bumped it upstairs to her bedroom.

Opening the door, she pushed the bag into her room, then dropped it on the floor. Satisfied that nothing was out of place, she gave the side of the bag a soft kick, then went back down stairs.

In the kitchen, she made coffee spiked with a double shot of brandy. Cup in hand, she checked the messages on her answering machine.

First two nothing, then she froze, the coffee cup suspended at her lips hearing a voice she had not heard for years.

"Hi, Ruthie. This is Matt, I know, out of the blue, I mean, you could be married with a bunch of kids running around, but I kinda doubt it."

"Anyway, I been in Chile and Bolivia for the best part of the last four years."

He was nervous, kept clearing his throat. Typical Matt. Speaking volumes while stating nothing. But then came the shocker,

"I was ripped off, Ruth. This guy came down to Santa Luisita to see me. Said Ed sent him. We got to talking, he listened to my ideas. I told him how Ed had shit on my thesis and we got to drinking, doing a couple of numbers and next thing, we're back in my hotel

room and he says I ought a sell my work as fiction. Said it'd be a great seller."

He cleared his throat again.

"Well, I got pissed– guess I was pretty spun and told him that I'd fucking burn it before I'd whore away my life's work. All I remember telling him was this was my work, my experience. Tried to explain how what I did was real anthropology. But, then I musta fallen or something."

Another pause-- a long silent gap.

"When I came to, my face was covered with blood, there was blood on the floor and the chair– looked like I'd been in a fight. My head hurt, my eyes burned..., and the guy was gone."

Ruth was right. She had been right all along and here he was telling her what had happened. She thought about Pepe Ortega and his dead brother as she rewound the tape to catch it again:

"Then I met this anthropologist in Chile studying local fishermen. We got to talking and I told him about my field work. When he heard it, he said, that sounded like the Secrets of Don Pedro Miguel."

His voice became higher, more strident.

"When I told that name didn't mean shit to me he goes on to tell me that some guy named Santos Villalobos wrote this book about learning to be a brujo from this Otomi shaman named Don Pedro Miguel. Ruth. Santos Villalobos was the sonfabitch who I was drinking with that night in Santa Luisitia. That motherfucker stole my thesis and published it— not as a piece of fiction but as his own fucking work. Look, I gotta run. I'll call you back in a few days."

He didn't leave an address or a call back number.

Ruth felt a twinge of guilt. She thought of Pepe, his honesty, his caballero manners, even his vulnerability so different from Matt. He'd only been a small part of her life and now like an unguided missile he was back.

But he had been ripped off. Santos Villalobos had screwed him, had made a fortune off his work.

That pissed Ruth off.

So, what was she going to tell Matt if he did call back?

~*~*~

Family in grief
Mexico City International Airport
Same day, 8:43 AM, Monday

Chaos reigned over the traffic at Mexico's City's International Airport. Pepe stared out the window of the yellow Mercedes seeing nothing.

A policeman sent by an old friend had taken him to the airport where he got the phone call from his sister that his mother had died. Now, Xochitl was driving him to her home.

"We knew it would happen," Xochitl said, weeping. "We just didn't expect it so soon."

"It's always a shock," Pepe said.

"She never let on. She never complained, she..."

Xochitl's tears came again. A near miss. She changed lanes at the last possible moment after giving the blinker two flashes. More brakes squealed, horns blared, fists, hands were shaken, shouts from rolled down windows rang out— all ignored by the weeping woman steering the yellow Mercedes.

"Would you like me to drive?" Pepe said.

Ignoring him, Xochitl went on, "Ixcheli came in with Mama's morning coffee and found her. She'd died in the night."

"*Menos mal*," Pepe said. "It could've been worse."

"How much can we take, Pepe?"

"Grief and death don't care whom or when they visit."

She looked over at her brother, her face a mask of grief, weeping. They said nothing more on the way home.

~*~*~

After arriving at Xochitl's house, the children greeted their uncle with subdued enthusiasm. Pepe's luggage was taken to the guest room.

Old Ricardo, the house attendant, greeted Pepe in Nahuatl,

"Don Asuncion. Our hearts break at the passing of your blessed Sra. Madre, our beloved Doña Maria Guadalupe."

Pepe patted his arm. "Thank you, Ricardo."

They went out onto the patio where a maid brought coffee, pastries. Xochitl dropped into the chair, her face in her hands, wept. Clara and Juanito came over to their mother. She clutched them to her, crying.

Pepe rose when Rodrigo came out onto the patio. They embraced each other.

"She was like a mother to me after my own beloved mother died, *Viejo*," Rodrigo said.

"I know, Rodri. We all loved her."

Rodrigo motioned for Pepe to follow him.

"I heard about the taxi blow-up," Rodrigo said. "What happened?"

"A street vendor pestered me beside the cab. Then it blew up before I got in."

The servant, Ricardo brought Pepe a glass of mescal on a tray. Taking the drink into the next room, Pepe picked up the phone, dialed Ruth.

She answered on the first ring, her voice strident, tentative.

"Hello."

"Ruth. You sound tense."

"I got home today to find a call from Matt Spyner on my recorder."

"Really?'

"I tried to call you. I'm just coming to grips with this whole Villalobos business. I've met a man I like a lot and I don't want Matt and his warehouse of problems in my life."

"I'm still in Mexico."

"Oh?"

"A bit of trouble..."

"What?"

"Yesterday, someone tried to kill me when I was leaving for the airport."

"Kill you! How?"

"Long story– they blew up the taxi I was taking."

"Are you all right?"

"Fine. But when I got to the airport this morning, I found out my mother had died."

"O my god. You poor man."

"I'm at my sister's now. We'll be making funeral arrangements.

"Pepe. Can I help? I'm willing to come..."

"It's too dangerous. I know how to protect myself."

"I'm so sorry."

"Thanks, but tell more about this call."

"Matt said he'd gone to South America for a few years, then only recently found out about what Villalobos had done. Now, he's after him."

"From what I've read and heard, Villalobos has pretty much gone underground."

"That won't stop Matt."

"If he calls back, get in touch with me immediately. I'll be back in a week."

"I'm so sorry to drop this on you. You're already having a rough time of it."

After he hung up, Pepe looked up at his reflection in the glass of a framed bull fight poster featuring the famous matador, El Gallo.

The English words of St. Paul ran through his mind, *... **and through a glass darkly...***

Pepe couldn't remember the rest.

~*~*~

Repercussions

Volpez's office, Cordoba District, Mexico City
Same day, 1:47 PM, Monday

Jacobo Fuchs stormed into Volpez's office, rapped his cane on the floor, his faded gray eyes sparking the reflected light from Antonio's desk lamp.

"I thought this job was to be done quickly, efficiently and visibly," he said.

"I don't know what you're talking about, Jacobo," Volpez said.

"That stupid monkey, Chibo, blew the wrong car, killed the driver and cut up a bunch of people. Now, the cops are all over the place and Ortega's kid's still walking the streets."

"I hadn't heard."

"Damn your not having heard! I tell you to do something, you tell me it's done. Then, I turn on the television and there's Ortega's spawn still alive."

"I swear I didn't know," Volpez said.

"Your damned ignorance makes little excuse for failure."

"Let me find out what went wrong."

"We know what went wrong. The job was botched."

The phone buzzed.

"Alo?" Volpez looked over at Fuchs, mouthed "Chibo," then said, "Send him in."

The door opened, Chibo slipped in hands raised, palms extended.

"Let me explain before you get pissed on. I set it up just right. I got the right amount of military C for the tailpipe, I slipped it in, knowing it would go off as soon as the car accelerated, I made sure the target was Ortega's kid."

Fuchs's gray eyebrows met in a V over his sharp hooked nose.

"So what went wrong?" the old man said.

"Ortega didn't get his ass in the car."

Fuchs pursed his lips into a tight knot.

Chibo went on, "I did everything I could right. Unless I popped Ortega on the spot with hundreds of witnesses, there was nothing else I could do."

Chibo held up his hands again for attention.

"And, I've not been sitting on my ass," he said. "I just learned Ortega's mother died."

"The old bitch died!" Fuchs said. "At least that's some good news."

Chibo heaved a sigh of relief.

"So, what do you propose now, Jacobo," Volpez said.

"Get some boys together," Fuchs said. "Go up to Tula and take out the whole damned family at the funeral."

"I can do that," Chibo said.

"And, make it look like Alban set it up," Fuchs said.

"I can do that too."

"Make damn sure you pop Ortega's brother-in-law too." Volpez said.

Chibo grinned. "I'll personally shoot that trouble-making son of a whore in the head."

Chibo went to the door, then stopped.

"What about the kids?" he said

"Nits grow into lice," Fuchs said,

Chibo swallowed hard, nodded, walked out the door.

~*~*~

Back in town
Los Angeles, California
same day, 8:10 AM, Monday

The once gray paint of the four door 62 Chevy now faded to a color between dirty fog or neglected laundry, showed patches, peeled spots, splotched by dents, nicks. Its chrome bumper, flecked with rust pustules, scratches, skewed out on the passenger's side, then twisted down on the driver's.

But its big V8 engine purred like a fat, cream-fed tomcat.

Behind the steering wheel, Matt Spyner's attention stayed fixed on a van with a Pacific Bell logo, making sure the driver did not notice him.

A bit after noon, he saw the van pull into the parking lot of the Alpine Hut Doggy Diner, then watched the driver get out of the van, go into the restaurant.

After parking the Chevy around the corner, Matt slipped up to the van, inserted a curved flat metal rod down the window slot, tripped the locking lever, climbed in. Seizing the wiring from under the dashboard, he selected two wires, pierced them with alligator clamps, brushed them together, started the van, then drove out of the lot onto the street.

He drove along the back streets to the Santa Ana freeway, cruised into a run-down neighborhood of West Los Angeles, pulled into the driveway of a small house with a detached garage. After parking the van in the garage, he got out, walked to the corner, caught a bus downtown.

After transferring buses twice, he came back to the Chevy, then drove to a Working Man's clothing store specializing in uniforms where he bought a telephone serviceman's khaki pants, short sleeve shirt.

He drove back to the little house, went inside, picked up the thick LA phone book, found a number.

"Berkshire Press," A woman answered. "How may I direct your call?"

"Dr. Harlan Higgs. Professor of anthropology, Valparaiso, Chile, I need to contact one of your editors."

"Do you know the name of the editor?"

"I've lost the name but this is the one who reviewed the *Secrets of Don Pedro Miguel.*"

"I'm afraid Ms. Dunham is not available at the moment. May I take your name and have her secretary return your call?'

"Please don't bother. I know how busy your editors can be. I'll drop her a line later."

"Thank you for calling Berkshire Press, Dr. Higgs.

~*~*~

Next day, 10:45 AM, Tuesday,. December 10, 1974

Matt stepped out of the elevator, the tool bag clinking around his waist, came over to the blond receptionist guarding the interior offices of the Berkshire press.

"Phone company," he said. "Got a call to check one of your phones."

The blond waved him toward the door, continued her honeyed conversation into her phone.

Matt made his way back to a circle of glassed-in offices, stuck his head in one.

"Ms. Dunham's office?" he said.

A woman looked up from her desk, shook her head, pointed across the way.

After mumbling, "Thanks," he ambled over to the office, stuck his head in again.

"Ms. Dunham?"

A red-headed woman in her forties, scowled up at him. "Yes?"

He pulled out a paper, made a show of looking at it. "Office sent me here to check out problems with your phone."

"Don't recall having any problems," Ms. Dunham said.

Matt wrinkled his face. "Take just a moment to check out your phone. I'd hate to have to come back."

"Be my guest," Ms. Dunham said, then went back to her work.

Matt disconnected the hand set, plugged the contact into his utility monitoring unit, dialed in a call-back code, recording the number in the utility unit's memory.

He took out the speaker unit, attached it to a power-driven monitor, charged it, watching the needle record the frequency range. When he reinserted the speaker assembly, he slipped a small disk into the handle-well before snapping it back in place.

"There was a loose contact," Matt said. "I replaced it and it seems to be working just fine now. If you have any problems, just give us a call."

Ms. Dunham gave him a fleeting glance. "I'll do that. Thanks."

Matt left.

~*~*~

That evening, Matt called Ms. Dunham's office number. When the phone rang, he punched in a code. The recording device sounded out the outgoing, received numbers. Matt recorded, decoded and wrote them down. Consulting the reverse directory he had taken from the van, he found that none of the numbers suggested anything to do with Santos Villalobos.

He erased the numbers, reset the recording device.

~*~*~

Mobilization
Barrio Dominguez, Mexico City
Same day, 6:05 PM, Tuesday

Chibo jumped off the bus at the busy corner, shouldered his way into the bar, CANTINA MARTINEZ. Ignoring the noise, the milling crowd, he pushed his way back to a curtain covered doorway. Brushing it aside, he met two men standing at the door.

One of them grabbed the little man. "Hey, where do you think you're going?" he said.

Chibo whipped out a P38 pistol, shoved the barrel in the man's nose, pulled back the hammer.

"Hands off me, fathead or I'll put a lead booger up your nose."

The man let him go, stepped back. Chibo pushed his way inside where a dark, heavy-set man sat playing cards with five others. Looking up at the intruder, the man said,

"Chibo. What're you doing busting in here with heat in your hand?"

"We gotta talk, Jose," Chibo said.

"So, talk."

"Just us."

Jose threw his cards on the table, jerked a thumb toward the door. "Outside," he said.

The five left without words.

Jose whipped out a silver cigarette case, took one out, tapped it on the case, put it in his mouth, accepted the light from Chibo's lighter, then offered him one.

"What's so damn important you come here flashing a piece, breaking up my card game?" he said,

"I need some guys and cars for a big hit," Chibo said.

Jose drew deep on the cigarette, blew out the smoke.

"Who?" he said.

"You remember Armando Ortega?"

"*El Jefe*? Hell, yes. I got drunk with joy the day that bastard died."

"We're going to take out his family."

"Here in Mexico City?"

Chibo drew in on his cigarette. "No. Up in Hidalgo. I got word his old bitch wife died and their kids will be gathering for the funeral. I need enough muscle to take them all out."

"Who's paying for this?"

"The old Zorro."

Jose smiled. "I smell money."

"We do it right, there'll be a bonus," Chibo said.

Jose took a stub of a pencil from his pocket.

"Let's see," he said. "There'll be the family, some local officials and the rest will be Indios..."

"As soon as we open up on the family," Chibo said, "The rest'll run like chickens."

Jose wrote down some names.

"OK. We'll take the car. I'll drive, German and Cristobal in the back. The pick-up with Jorge and Luis and the three Sandoval brothers in the back."

Chibo shook his head. "Sounds light. What if there are cops?"

Jose returned to the notepad. "OK. I'll bring the van with Roberto and Chato, Pancho Cruz and Libio in the back with Ruben and Faustino in the jumper seats."

Chibo pulled his straggled goatee. "Man, we can't have no fuck-ups."

Jose leaned back, raised the cigarette in the V of his fingers. "These guys are all pros– none of them will choke."

"Any of them know Hidalgo?"

"I doubt it. These guys are from the city. Pancho Cruz is from up north somewhere but not Hidalgo."

"We gotta move right away," Chibo said. "How long will it take to get these guys together?"

"I can have everything ready to go by day after tomorrow morning, latest."

Chibo sucked smoke in, stubbed the cigarette out on the table top.

"We do good on this one, Jose," he said, "it's easy street from now on."

Liar, Liar. Pants on Fire
Downtown Los Angeles
Next day, 11:05 AM, Wednesday, January 11, 1974

Matt dialed Ms. Dunham's office from a pay phone.

"This is Margery."

"Miss Dunham, I'm Harlan Higgs, professor of anthropology at Valparaiso University in Chile. I have a manuscript my friend, Santos Villalobos suggested I send you to look at."

There was a brief silence.

"I doubt that," Ms. Dunham said.

"What do you mean?"

"Listen. I don't know how you got my number but there's no way Santos Villalobos recommended me."

"Are you calling me a liar?"

"Only because I'm a lady and won't call you anything worse."

"But, I assure you, this is true. You can verify this with him."

"We have no contact with him. Everything is done through his attorney."

"Who is?"

She laughed.

"Well, if you're such good pals with him, you should know. Goodbye, asshole. Don't call back."

The phone clicked off.

Matt smiled.

~*~*~

That evening, Matt retrieved the data from the earlier calls.

After noting the number dialed following his call from the pay phone, he went back to the reverse directory, found the number.

"Casimiro Cortez, attorney at law," he read aloud.

~*~*~

Requisat in Pace
Chalupa, State of Hidalgo, Mexico
8:47 AM, Thursday, December 12, 1974

Pepe stared at the black polished wood open casket holding the thin body of Maria Guadalupe Cruz-Montez de Ortega, her head resting on a lace-covered cushion, her face screened with a knitted silk black veil draped over the open lid of the casket, her hands clutching her rosary, crossed at her chest.

He remembered the drive into town, the local people lining the way to the house. The men stood in silence bareheaded, hats in hands. The women covered their heads, children held green branches. No one waved or cried.

Ixcheli came up to his mother's casket. The big woman smiled, embraced Pepe, kissed him on both cheeks, spoke in Nahuatl,

"I rose before the sun, went into the hills, spilled corn, fruit and the blood of a slaughtered goat. I cried her name to the four winds. I sang her song to the rising sun. Our ancestors await her."

She brushed at Pepe's tears, then spoke to him again,

"Ease your sadness. Know that the Señora takes her place beside those who gave her life. Your father, your brother– all who loved her and who've gone before greet her. She suffers none of our pain. She loves us no less than when she was among us."

Pepe looked away, tried to smile. Ixcheli looked long, deep into his eyes, a tiny frown showing at her eyes.

"Something troubles you beyond this?"

"It's nothing."

"Nothing means nothing. I see worry beyond pain."

"You worry too much. I'll be fine."

The frown spread over her wide face. "Puppy. I was there when you were born. I washed you and placed you in your mother's arms. I watched you grow. Don't tell me otherwise."

Pepe looked over at his mother's body, the candles flickering.

"Someone tried to kill me," he said.

Ixcheli did not react.

"Who?" she said.

"Some bad people."

"Over your father and brother's business?"

"You could say that."

Ixcheli pursed her lips, then looked back at him. "This is time for you to spend with her and hers. Put all else from your mind."

"I'll give it my best effort," Pepe said.

Patting his face, she pushed him to go sit by his sister and family.

More guests were arriving to pay their respects. Ixcheli snapped her fingers. One of the boys attending a food table, came over to her. She spoke in Nahuatl. "Go get Cipriano. Now."

When Cipriano came into the kitchen, the women preparing food gave him only a glance. The little man took off his hat, sat down at the table. Without a word, one of the women set a cup of coffee in front of him. Pouring in milk, adding sugar, he stirred, then spooned it into his mouth in silence. The women's low chatter went quiet when Ixcheli came in, sat down across from Cipriano. He looked up at her when she spoke.

"Bad men mean to harm Don Asuncion," she said. "They will come here."

Cipriano lowered his gaze to his coffee, stirred, scowled.

Ixcheli did not take her eyes from him. "I want you to get the men and watch out."

Cipriano nodded. Ixcheli got up, left the room.

The women took up their gossip in low voices. Cipriano sat frowning, drinking his coffee like soup.

On the trail
Los Angeles, California
Same day, 8:14 AM, Thursday

Dressed as a phone serviceman, Matt found the phone line gang box for the law office. After checking the lines, he found the eight numbers that formed the bloc he wanted. He called one.

It rang once.

"This is Cindy."

"Sorry, Cindy. I was trying to call Mr. Cortez."

"He's in court today but I can connect you with his voice recorder."

"That'll be just fine."

Two clicks later, a secretary's voice came on. "To leave a message for Mr. Rydell, press 12; for Mr. Le, press 13, for Mr. Cortez, press 14..."

Matt pressed 14, noted the number that came up on the monitor, disconnected before the voice recorder was activated. He connected a number recording device to each of the office phones before replacing all of the wires back into the gang box.

He left the building, drove home in the stolen van, parked it in the garage.

~*~*~

The next day at a pay phone, Matt dialed Cortez's office.

The phone buzzed.

"Cassie Cortez."

"Mr. Cortez, I'm Dr. Harlan Higgs from the university of Valparaiso, Chile. I wish to speak to your client, Santos Villalobos."

"Who told you Santos Villalobos is my client?"

"His publisher indicated to me that you were handling his affairs."

"You didn't get my name from the publisher. So, how did you get my number?"

"You're listed in the phone under attorneys."

"This is bullshit. I have no idea what you're talking about."

"Oh, Mr. Cortez. Please understand that I'm completely legitimate. You can check with Santos to verify my credentials."

"Listen, Higgs, Piggs or whatever name you're using, I got nothing more to say to you."

Matt grinned at the click on the other end.

~*~*~

That evening, he retrieved several numbers from Cortez's line, checked them against the reverse directory. The unlisted name for the third call caught his eye.

SDPM Enterprises.

"Ess dee pee em. Secrets of Don Pedro Miguel," he said aloud.

Bingo!

~*~*~

Next day, 6:16 AM, Friday, December 13, 1974

Matt parked the phone van in the same spot from where he had stolen it outside the Alpine Doggie Hut Diner. After donning latex gloves, he had wiped the insides clean, replaced the equipment. Now, he removed the hot wire link on the ignition wiring, tucked it back under the instrument cowling, locked the door, walked two blocks away, caught a bus back to West LA.

After changing his clothes to a dark green shirt, pants, matching cap, he drove to Cortez's law office. Finding the maintenance closet on the floor below the office, Matt opened the door with a penknife, removed a rolling trash barrel, took the elevator up to the next floor. Then he dialed Cortez's number from a public phone booth in the foyer of the building.

"Cassie Cortez."

"Listen very carefully, counselor. This is the guy who Santos Villalobos ripped off. You tell that slimy little sonfabitch that I've got his balls in a vise."

Matt hung up before Cortez could answer.

He stepped over to the wheeled trash barrel, pushed it to the elevator, went up to the floor of the law offices. Taking out a cleaning rag, he wiped down the walls outside the office. A few minutes later he noticed a dark skinned man in his 30s hurry out of the office toward the elevator.

Matt tossed the cleaning rag in the trash barrel, dashed over to the stairwell, raced up to the parking structure on the roof then crouched behind a parked car with a view of the exit to the elevator.

He saw Cortez unlock a blue Mercedes, then drive out in a rush. Matt wrote down the car's license plate, then left the building.

Getting in his car, Matt drove for several blocks until he spotted a police car pull into a hamburger joint. He parked, watched the two officers go into the restaurant. Noticing they were sitting just out of sight of the cruiser, Matt used a slim-jim tool to open the car door. Stretching down on the seat, he clicked on the radio speaker.

"Adam 27, base," he said.

"This is base, Adam 27."

"Need an address to go with a set of vanity plates, CASSIE, Blue '75 Mercedes."

"Ten four, Adam 27. Wait one."

Matt kept his eye on the door of the restaurant.

"Car is registered to Casimiro Cortez, address, 1039 Glorietta drive, Venice Beach."

"Ten four, Base. Thanks much."

"Base clear."

He slipped out of the cruiser, making sure he locked it before walking back to the Chevy.

Matt found the address, a condo in Venice beach. He drove past it several times, then found a nearby pizza parlor, bought a medium-sized pizza, stationed himself in full view of the condo. He put on the earphones to his Sony Walkman, ate the pizza, settled back, watched. It was about 6:30 when the Blue Mercedes pulled up into the driveway, waited for the garage door to open, then drove in. Matt ate the last of the cold pizza, waited.

Around 7:45, the garage door opened, the Mercedes backed out, took off down the street.

Matt started the Chevy, followed it, keeping a good distance behind. He followed the blue car out onto the crowded freeway, moved along with the slow traffic toward West Los Angeles, where it pulled off.

Still keeping his distance, Matt followed the car out into a driveway into a large residence surrounded by a high iron grate fence. Matt stopped around the corner, watched as the Mercedes honked. Through the rolled down window, he could hear dogs barking. A few seconds later, the gate swung open, the Mercedes roared inside, as the gate closed behind it.

Writing down the address Matt waited a few minutes, then drove to a nearby gas station, went to the phone booth, dialed the number in his notebook. It rang twice before a woman's voice answered.

"Hello."

"I want to speak to Santos."

A pause. "You got the wrong number."

"Bullshit. Tell that asshole this is Matt Spyner."

Another pause, the sound of the receiver being covered with a hand, then a soft male voice. "Who's this?"

"Your worst nightmare, Greaseball."

"What do you want?"

"I've got your balls in a mop squeeze, Santos, and both hands on the handle. You and I are going to have a quiet discussion about the importance of being honest."

"When and where?"

"I'll be in touch, asshole. I know where you're at. Don't try to take off because I'll find you, motherfucker."

Matt hung up, drew a deep breath, pulled over to the pump, went inside, paid for the gas, bought a newspaper. As the gas tank filled, Matt looked through the *Help Wanted* section of the paper for available jobs for journeyman mechanics.

~*~*~

Intrusion
Outside of Tula de Allende, State of Hidalgo, Mexico
Same day, 10:17 AM, Friday, December 13, 1974

Leaning on the open window of the dusty black sedan's front seat, Chibo sneered as they passed rural farmers walking along the road

We ride while the country bumpkins walk.

Behind the sedan trailed a faded blue van followed by a dirty white pick-up with 3 men in back. Inside the sedan at Chibo's feet, weapons lay on the floor covered with blankets.

"Where's this pisspot town, Chalupa?" Chibo said.

Jose, the heavy-set man behind the wheel, said, "It's about 15 or so kilometers west of Tula, up in the mountains."

Chibo picked at his spraddled teeth a tooth pick.

"So, how we gonna find the house?" he said.

"Any local will point it out for you for a few pesos," Jose said.

"So, we'll ask nice and polite," Chibo said. "Just don't forget, we don't leave no witnesses."

Jose shivered.

"You getting squeamish?" Chibo said.

"I don't like busting in on a funeral," Jose said. "It's bad luck."

"What's a fucking funeral got to do with it?"

"Flaco, you're messing with the dead. That means Indian Spirits. These guys are Aztecs."

"Jose. We're going up there to kill a bunch of people and you're worried about someone already dead?"

"It just ain't right." Jose said, his mouth tight.

Jose turned onto a side road up into the surrounding mountains.

"You sure we're on the right road?" Chibo said

Jose shook his head. "No. The damn map wasn't clear."

Coming around a curve, Chibo pointed out an old man watching a herd of goats.

"Ask that old bastard," Chibo said.

Jose pulled up alongside the old man, rolled down his window. The old man came over, doffed his ragged sombrero, clutched it to his chest, murmured a greeting.

"Hey, *viejo*," Jose said. "Is this the road to Chalupa?"

"*Si, Señor.*"

Chibo leaned towards him, said, "How far?"

"About 12 kilometers, Señor."

Jose nodded thanks, pulled back on the road, the other vehicles following.

The old man watched them go, then ran to a pile of weeds, brush, green leaves heaped up around a dead bush. Lighting the pile with a match, he fanned the flames with his hat until it blazed. The dry brush crackled, sparked. The burnt green leaves sent sparks into the air borne by thick smoke from the dried wood's fired oils.

When the quick burning brush became a smoldering, smoky pyre, the old man whipped off his faded serape, flung it over the smoking pile, then popped it off, causing the smoke to billow into a gray puff ball, spinning into the air.

After repeating this act twice more, he kicked dirt on the dying embers then walked back to round up his goats.

~*~*~

Driving into the town of Chalupa, Chibo looked around at deserted streets, closed houses, shuttered shops, no traffic.

"Looks like nobody's home," Chibo said.

"Probably all at the funeral," Jose said.

Chibo pointed to a gas station with an open, empty service bay adjoining a small windowed office. A flatbed truck with a canvas tarp thrown over the bed stood parked in front of the station near the edge of the road.

"There's a guy in that gas station over there," Chibo said.

Chibo reached under the blanket, pulled out his old German P38, slid the receiver back, until he heard the round click into the chamber.

"What're you doing?" Jose said.

"Soon as we find out where the house is, I'll pop him."

Jose drew a deep breath. "Man, I don't like this."

"You don't have to like it," Chibo said. "Until we get the ski masks on, our faces are hanging out. We ain't leaving no one behind who can pick us out."

Jose signaled to those behind him, then pulled into the little gas station. The other vehicles followed, lining up behind him.

Jose honked.

From inside the station, a small, dark man peered out at him. "We're closed today, Señor," he said.

Chibo leaned across Jose. "Can you tell us how to get to Casa Ortega?" he said.

"Of course, Señor," the man said.

Stepping out, the small, dark man swung up a double barreled shot gun, blasted Jose through the open window. The force of blast blew the side of Jose's head off.

A second blast struck Chibo in the face, throwing him back against the open window on the passenger side. His straw hat punctured with shot pellets flew out through the open window.

Four men poured out from the open service bay of the station, guns in hand, blasting away at the three vehicles. Throwing back a tarp covering on the flatbed truck, four men rose up, guns in hand, then shot straight into the three vehicles.

When the driver of the pick-up tried to jam it in reverse, four more men ran around from behind the gas station firing their guns into the cab. The pick-up lurched, stalled, died– the driver slumped over the steering wheel.

The three men in the back of the pick-up grabbed for their weapons covered by blankets. The rapid fire from the flatbed riddled all three before they laid hands on them. One man in the van managed to lift an automatic pistol before his head was shredded by a shotgun blast from a man crouched inside the service bay.

The man in the passenger seat of the pick-up opened the door. A bullet from the flat bed struck him below his chin. He tumbled forward to the ground, clutching at his throat. A rain of bullets struck his body, causing him to convulse, twitch before he rolled still.

A man from the service bay shot the driver of the van through his eye. He jerked, fell across the seat, slumped to the side. The man seated next to him, raised his hands in surrender but another man from the service bay put a bullet in his forehead through the windshield.

The four men in the two sets of back seats of the van scrambled for the guns at their feet. One raised up to see a man outside his window point a shotgun in his face, then fire. The shot, the glass turned his face into a mass of blood, bone, tattered flesh.

The man sitting next to him, lurched to the floor using his partner's body as a shield. Half a dozen bullets tore through the thin metal paneling from the other side, striking his body as he dropped his unfired weapon.

The two men in the rear seat managed to get to their weapons. One turned to return fire out the side window. As he pulled the trigger, a shot from the rear of the station crashed through the rear window, striking him in the temple. The man's eyes rolled as he jerked from the impact, yanked his machine pistol back, discharging it into the face of his partner at his elbow.

The small, dark man who had killed Jose and Chibo, popped open the old side-by double-barrel 10 gauge shotgun, popped in two rounds, swung the barrel smashing the rear window of the sedan, blew the face off the man in the back seat behind the driver. The man seated behind Chibo, threw down his pistol, raised his hands.

"I'm unarmed!" he screamed.

The small, dark man pointed the shotgun, blew the top of his head off, spraying brains on the rear of the roof of the back seat.

Then, the small, dark man raised his hand, yelled, "*¡Alto!*"

The others stopped firing. The smell of cordite stung the noses of the living.

Reloading, the small, dark man walked from the car to the van to the pick-up, looking at the carnage, then looked around at the dozen men holding guns.

"We'd better clean up," he said. "We gotta be at the funeral in an hour."

"*Muy bien*, Cipriano," one of the men said.

Inside the Ortega house, Father Delgado, a big bear of a man was leading the rosary when the reports of gunfire echoed through. He raised his deep bass voice.

"Hail Mary, Full of grace.

The Lord is with you.

'Blessed are you among women

and blessed is the fruit of your womb, Jesus."

The mourners intoned in response,

"Holy Mary, Mother of God.

Pray for us sinners now and at the hour of our death. Amen."

The bereaved moved their fingers to the next bead on the decades of their rosaries.

Father Delgado repeated the refrain.

No one looked up in the direction of the noise of the gunfire.

New plans
Officina Compania Pochteca, Mexico City
11:14 AM, Monday, December 16, 1974

The knock at the office door, prompted a quick removal, stowing of Lucero's horn-rimmed spectacles. "Come in," he said.

Daniel Soto, his attorney, made a rapid entrance, swung the door shut behind him. Dressed in his usual dark blue, three button, pin stripe suit with a vest, he paced over, plopped his 5' 4" body down in a chair in front of Lucero.

"*Compadre*, you got to let me in on what's going on," he said. "Don't make me have to find out things like this from the law enforcement."

"Daniel," Lucero said. "I've no idea what you're talking about."

"You can sit there and tell me you didn't have a bunch of local monkeys o up there to take out the Ortega family during the widow's funeral?"

"What?"

"Three carloads of gun-bunnies rolled up to Chalupa, stopped at a gas pump and got their asses shot off by the local Indios."

Lucero stared at Soto.

"Don't joke with me, Daniel," he said. "I'm in no mood for this."

"Jokes, Luis?" the lawyer said. "This morning, my offices were swarming with reporters, the secretaries swamped with calls from the warehouses where cops are crawling all over them. Then, I get a call from our mutual friend and admirer, Dr. Rodrigo Gonzalez-Diaz who wants to talk to me about an attempt on his and his family's life."

"On my mother's soul, I swear I know nothing of this," Lucero said.

"Well, the chickens have come to roost in your barn, beloved friend."

Lucero rose, walked over, stared out the window.

"The old Zorro," he muttered.

"Fuchs?"

"He set this up."

"Now, beloved friend," Soto said, "it's my turn to ask 'are you joking?' "

"That old bastard's grooming Antonio to take over the unions and transportation, he's cutting a deal with the Russians for the product. He figures now we're just in the way."

"What're you going to do?"

Lucero snatched up the phone, dialed a number.

It rang twice. "Bueno."

Lucero spoke in Nahuatl,

"Who am I?"

"You are you. I am I."

"What do you know about this business in Chalupa?"

"This had to be Antonio's brain child, but you know the whole adventure turned to shit."

"I heard."

"Old Zorro's not too happy with Antonio right now but they'll mend their fences. They need each other."

"If I whack Antonio," Lucero said, "the old bastard will have every little independent drug dealer in Mexico gunning for us."

"Not if the old guy disappeared."

"What about all the banking and finances?"

"I'm close to having that all nailed down."

"That's the first good news today."

"Then, let me give you some more. In a few days after the new year, the old guy's going with Antonio on a fishing trip for a week off the coast of the States."

"But, he never leaves Mexico..."

"Technically, he does. He slips out to go deep sea fishing three or four times a year in the waters off the States."

"How'd you find out about this trip?"

"The guy who used to take him out died and the old Zorro asked me to set him up with a boat."

"When?"

"In a couple of weeks."

Lucero winked at Soto, touched his cheek below his eye for emphasis. "Lemme call you back tomorrow with the name of a reliable fishing boat."

After hanging up, Lucero looked over at Soto.

"As the English say," Lucero said, " 'Lunch has arrived.' "

Lucero dialed again. "Lemme call my lawyer in the US."

Hearing the voice answer, he said, "James. I need a big favor."

"What can I do for my favorite client?"

"I need a mechanic who can handle a fishing boat."

"Hmm. When?"

"Yesterday."

"That soon. Let me talk to Cassie Cortez. He has good connections."

"The guy has to speak Spanish."

"Not a problem in Southern California. Let me call you right back."

"Do that."

Lucero leaned over to Soto.

"The old bastard's going a fishing trip off the States," Lucero said.

"So I heard."

"I'm gonna turn Zorro and his pack of Cuban Jews into fish bait."

The phone rang.

"Bueno."

"Cassie's got a Mexican-American contactor who's not only super-good but who's worked as a commercial fisherman," Rydell said. "I know this guy– smart, careful and quiet."

"What's his name?"

"I'm not sure. They just call him the 'Rattler.' "

"Like in rattlesnake?"

"The same."

"Set it up. Get back to me with any problems."

Lucero hung up. The door popped open, Drako strode in.

"You heard about Hidalgo?" he said.

"Sit down, Ivo," Lucero said. "We're gonna turn our moment of surprise and anguish into joy and profit."

Lucero recounted the entire morning's conversations with Soto nodding confirmation and agreement at the important points. Lucero concluded.

"I won't undertake this without your agreement, Ivo. If you are unhappy with any of this, we can make other plans."

Drako took out his gold cigarette case, picked one of his gold-ringed Turkish tobacco cigarettes.

"I like it," he said. "All of it."

~*~*~

Some business
Jorge's Apartment, El Cajon, CA
9:15 PM, Wednesday, December 18, 1974

Jorge Barrios sat in the threadbare overstuffed chair, the glare of the lamp falling across the worn, dog-eared, spine broken paperback book titled *The Red and The Black.*

He reached for a cup on the nearby lamp-table. The coffee in the cup had gone cold over an hour ago but he took a shallow swallow, set the cup back down on the table, read on.

The phone's ring screeched like a shout in the quiet room. Jorge turned a page, then picked up the receiver without taking his eyes from the book.

"Yeah," he said.

The voice spoke in barrio Spanish. "Jorge, my man. Howzit hanging, brother?"

"Same old. What's up, Cassie?"

"Are you open for a job?"

Jorge looked up from the book. "Who for?"

"Y'know my partner, Jim Rydell?"

Jorge searched his brain for an image, a face, an impression. A face formed in his mind's eye.

"I'm listening," he said.

"We need someone to provide personal security for a guy."

"Don't do security. Just the opposite. I whack people."

"That's the kind of security they want. This involves a fishing trip. I told Rydell you'd worked as a commercial fisherman."

"What kind of fishing trip?"

"The man'll have all the details, Bro," Cortez said. "I'll arrange for your payment transfers."

"What's the money?"

"Whatever you think's right, my brother."

"Works for me."

"When can you come up here?"

"Tomorrow."

"Excellent Tamales."

"OK."

The last phrase was in English. "You da man, Jorge."

Jorge hung up the phone, took a sip of the cold coffee, went back to reading his book.

~*~*~

More business
Bus Terminal, Downtown, Los Angeles, CA
9:47 AM, Thursday, December 19, 1974

Jorge stepped into the bus terminal carrying a canvas book bag with the cartoon image of Garfield, the cat. After finding a row of pay phones, he searched his pockets for change, then dialed.

A voice answered, "Rydell."

"This is Smith."

"Yes, Mr. Smith. Do you know where our office is?"

"I prefer neutral turf."

"Understand completely. There's a bar, Barny's Barn off the corner of Sepulveda and Grant. Meet you there in half an hour."

Jorge returned the phone to its cradle, went over to look at local bus schedules.

~*~*~

Jorge walked into Barney's Barn. Four unsmiling men at one end of the bar turned, sized him up and down when he took a stool at the bar.

A burley black bartender came over. "What can I get you?"

"A coke."

The bartender took a glass, poured in a handful of crushed ice, filled it with a hand-held vacuum tube, gave it a stir with a twisted metal swizzle stick with a red ball on the end, dropped a maraschino cherry in it, stuck in a red plastic spangled straw, set it in front of Jorge.

"That'll be $4.00," he said.

Jorge laid four one dollar bills on the counter.

The bartender took the cash, rang the cash register, went back to talking to the men at the end of the bar in a low voice. The door swung open, a short man in a dark blue suit walked in, a red rose pinned to his lapel.

Upon seeing him, the bartender said, "Morning, Mr. Rydell."

"Morning, Walt."

"The usual, sir?"

"That'll be fine."

Jorge turned to look at Rydell who strode over, extended his hand.

"Mr. Smith." he said.

Jorge's limp hand met Rydell's firm grip.

Rydell pointed to some empty booths in the back. "Let's sit back there."

Jorge followed him to the back booth. When they sat, Walt, the bartender set a tall frosted glass in front of Rydell.

When the bartender left, Rydell said, "So, you're the famous Rattler."

Jorge ignored him. "What's up?"

Rydell lowered his voice, leaned over the table.

"Here's the deal," he said. "There are some people coming to town who want to go on a fishing trip. One of this party is a partner who's giving my client a lot of trouble."

Jorge made a noisy slurp of his coke.

"Cassie said you've worked as a fisherman and know boats," Rydell said.

"Yeah."

"I'd like for you to arrange to take this party out for a cruise."

"How many?"

"There'll be the old man, his personal bodyguard and two or three more goons."

"And, you want them whacked."

Rydell turned his face back toward the bar. "I didn't hear that."

Jorge grunted.

Rydell looked back at him. "If you need some extra muscle, I have the budget."

"Might not."

Rydell sipped his drink. "How much for this job?"

"250 K. Give me 20 K for the set-up and the rest when the job's done."

Rydell flinched. "Two fifty large? That's big bucks for a job."

"It's a big job."

"There can be no margin for error," Rydell said.

"This is Mexican mafia," Jorge said. "There won't be any comebacks."

Rydell looked around again. "No one said anything about the Mexican mafia."

Jorge drained his drink, rattled the ice, sucked at the straw again.

"No details," he said. "The less I know, the better."

"Let me be perfectly clear," Rydell said. "My clients want complete satisfaction, no mess..."

Jorge interrupted him. "Or, both our asses get whacked."

Rydell just stared at Jorge who crunched ice from his glass.

"When?" Jorge said.

"Is 2 weeks enough time?"

"Yeah. I think so."

"You think so?"

Jorge put down his glass, spoke in a quiet voice,

"I've agreed and I'll deliver. But, I ain't heard you agree."

"You guarantee this'll get done?"

"I'm staking my ass on it."

"My balls are hanging out on this one," Rydell said. "But, Cassie swears by you."

He reached into his coat pocket, took out a thick envelope, handed it to Jorge.

"Here's 10K. I'll have the rest of the front money transferred to you tonight."

"Cassie knows where to send it."

Rydell got up, looked back at Jorge. "These guys are damn dangerous..."

Jorge stood, looked down at the lawyer, spoke in the same low voice,

"You think I'm a cretin who's not aware of the risks?"

Rydell stammered, "I didn't mean to sound patronizing. I apologize..."

When Jorge picked up his Garfield canvas bag, a worn paperback copy of Plato's *Republic*, spilled out the table. Rydell blinked at it for a second before Jorge scooped it back into the bag, then walked out the door, ignoring the stares of the other men at the bar.

~*~*~

In the moonlight

Al's Auto Repair Palace, West Covina, CA
6:10 PM, Friday, January 3, 1975

After getting off work, Matt Spyner threw some of his personal tools onto the floor of the passenger side of his Chevy, then drove to a nearby gas station. He dialed Santos's number at a pay phone then recognized the soft male voice.

"Hello."

"Let's talk," Matt said. "Tonight."

"Where?"

"The Shrine Auditorium out by the USC campus. North corner at 11:00. If I even suspect someone else's there, I won't show."

"I understand."

Matt hung up, got in the Chevy, drove through the Watts area of Los Angeles, parked across the street from the Shrine Auditorium where he had a full view of the corner.

~*~*~

From the front window of the car, Matt watched the corner through through a falling mist. Around 10:30, he saw a van pull up past the darkened auditorium. Santos got out of the car, leaned back inside to say something to the driver.

Just as the van pulled around the corner, Matt screeched up alongside Santos.

"Get in!" Matt hollered.

Startled, Santos pulled his hands out of his pockets, got in the car. Matt wheeled the Chevy in a wide U turn then roared off down the street.

"Take it easy, man," Santos said. "You'll get stopped."

"I'll worry about that."

Racing up the freeway heading north, Matt took the first off-ramp, rolled over the overpass, returned to the freeway driving south.

Matt drove into rural Orange county onto a side road leading into a crop field. Turning off the paved road, he drove along a dirt frontage road, then parked in the dark alongside an irrigation canal bordering the planted field behind a wind break of eucalyptus trees.

They both sat there for a few minutes as the engine cooled down listening to the sound of the irrigation water running along the ditches.

"You ripped me off, Man." Matt said.

"You had something and had no idea what it was worth," Santos said. "You spun out on mescal, weed and mushrooms, went goofy and passed out. So, I took it."

"You don't even fucking deny you ripped me off."

"I crafted your halfassed work into a piece of art," Santos said. "It's made me wealthy enough that I'll never have to sit in some academic hole where the big birds on top shit on the little ones below. I can go where I please, do what I want and not have to worry about it."

"It took me two years to find that old Zaitequi shaman," Matt said. "I bribed him, did his shit work, even blew him to get him to teach me what he knew."

"You're not the only one who's had to whore to get what they want."

Matt pounded the steering wheel, then exploded,

"I've always been the failure, the flake, the loser. But, my thesis was original!"

"Tried to tell you that in Santa Luisita. The manuscript was a brilliant piece of psychedelia."

"Psychedelia! That was research–I told what it was like to experience all this."

"Well, I saw how it could work," Santos said. "And, it did-- more than if it had been stuck in some academic journal where disinterested people like Ed Singer would just criticize it."

"It was still my work."

"I don't deny that. But what came out of it was greater than anything you could ever have done by yourself."

"What're you saying?"

"The thesis was your work. But, the *Secrets of Don Pedro Miguel* is _our_ work."

Matt's mouth twisted into a snarl. "What the fuck do you mean 'our' work?"

"Don't flatter yourself thinking all this success has just been your doing."

"Asshole!"

"Yeah. But, an asshole who's willing to see you'll never have to work ever again in your life."

Matt struck the seat between them. "It's not about money, shiteater."

"Oh?" Santos said. "What's it about then?"

"You stole my work," Matt screamed. "You made it into something it's not and now have the balls to offer me a payoff? I want my respectability back."

Santos went quiet. "What do you mean?" he said.

"I want you to own up that you swiped my thesis."

"I haven't denied that."

"No!" Matt roared. "I mean go public, asshole. Put in the fucking papers. Let people know what happened."

Santos took a long breath.

"That would create more problems than you can imagine in your worst nightmares," he said.

"Then you leave me no choice. I'll take it to the newspapers."

"You're cutting off your nose to spite your face."

"And your fucking thieving nose and balls too, shithead."

"Don't you see what's at stake here? We're talking several million. You can live like a king. I'm not greedy."

"You're from another planet, Santos."

Santos's words came faster, his voice higher, "You can't prove anything. I destroyed the original manuscript."

Matt sneered. "I have another copy."

Santos's eyes were wide open now. "I don't fucking believe you."

"I made a copy and gave it Ruth to keep for me in case I ever lost the original."

"You're lying."

"You willing to take that chance?"

"OK, OK," Santos choked. "How much do you want?"

"You just don't get it, do you? I'm going to nail your balls to the wall."

Santos's foot bumped a large socket wrench on the floor. Snatching it up, he swung, struck Matt in the temple.

Matt cried out, raised his hands.

Santos struck him in the head, in the face, in the back of his head, on the top of his head, again, again, again.

~*~*~

Panting, exerted, Santos stared at the bloody mess that was Matt's head. He looked down at the wrench in his hand, then again over at the body slumped against the window on the driver's side of the Chevy. Dropping the wrench on the front seat, he backed out of the car, then fell to his knees, supporting himself on his fists.

After a short while, he got up, took a handkerchief from his pocket, wiped down the door handle. Going inside, still covering his fingers with a handkerchief, he took Matt's wallet, went through his pockets before he rummaged through the glove compartment looking for anything that would identify the owner. Then taking the keys, Santos went back, unlocked the trunk.

Inside, he found an open two-quart coffee can with some nuts and bolts, a Phillips screw driver, some rags. Pouring the nuts and bolts out into the trunk well, he scooped up the can, the screw driver, the rags.

Going to the passenger side, he picked up the bloody socket wrench from the front seat, went to the rear of the car, got down on his knees, pounded the screw driver into the gas tank with the socket wrench, then filled the can with gasoline.

Plugging the hole in the gas tank with the screwdriver, Santos came back, splashed gasoline over the front seat seat of the Chevy.

Santos refilled the can again and again, each time splashing the gas over the car's interior. He wiped down the passenger side of the car with a rag soaked in gasoline, then pushed in the cigarette lighter in the dash.

When the cigarette lighter popped out, he pressed the glowing end to the gas-soaked rag. When it burst into flame, he tossed it into the front seat, stepped back from the whoosh of igniting gas.

He picked up a broken branch from a eucalyptus tree, brushed away his tracks until he reached the paved road where he walked four miles or so until he came to a convenience store with an icon for a public phone.

~*~*~

"Is this ' Ruth?' "
Rosemont District, San Diego
7:15 AM, Monday, January 6, 1975

The wooden steps on the porch of the old Victorian creaked to the thump of Ruth's running shoes as she ran up to the landing on top then unlocked the door. Coming in out of a light early morning rain, she grabbed a towel off a nearby chair, wiped her face, plopped down in the chair. Leaning over, loosening her shoe laces, the blinking red light on her answering machine caught her eye. She pushed the playback button.

"Hello, this is the Orange County Sheriff's office. We are calling for Ruth. Could you please call us back at 714-366-2525. Ask for Detective Shermer, extension 27."

Ruth dialed the number, keyed in the extension. The phone rang twice.

"Detective Al Shermer, how can I help you?"

"This is Dr. Ruth Hall returning your call."

"Is this Ruth? Sorry for the morning call, but I may have some bad news."

Ruth swallowed hard. "I'm listening."

"One of our patrol units was called to a farm site in rural Orange County about 3 this morning to investigate a reported car fire. Turns out, there was a man in the car that had been apparently beaten to death and partially burned."

Ruth gasped, "O God. Who was it?"

"There was no identification on the body. But, we did find a scrap of paper under the seat with your first name and phone number on it."

"My name and number?"

"We ran the plates on the car and they were stolen. We ran the Vehicle Identification number and found out that the car had been junked in Arizona a year or so ago. So, your number's the only solid lead we have."

"I've no idea who this person could be. I'm an archeologist. I do contract work for the State and teach at Madison University here in San Diego. I cross paths with lots of people."

The Detective sighed into the phone. "I was afraid of that. Professor Ruth..."

"Hall."

"Sorry, Professor Hall, could we ask you to come up and possibly identify this body. I realize that's asking a lot because it's far away and this won't be a pleasant experience."

Ruth swallowed. "I suppose so. I have an afternoon class today but I could drive up there some time in the early morning."

"Thanks. We really appreciate it and I know how trying this is."

Grabbing a pencil, Ruth said, "Give me the directions to get there."

~*~*~

Red Sails in the Sunset
Sunset Marina, San Diego, CA
Next day, 3:15 AM, Tuesday, January 7, 1975

Jorge Reyes dressed in gray trousers, ball cap, shirt with **YARD MAINTENANCE** stenciled on the back, tugging a wheeled trash barrel behind him, noticed the night watchman sound asleep in the lit, glass cubicle outside the Marina. The marina facility peeked through the dark of the early morning, spotlighted by a single flood light over the gate.

Jorge inserted two curved picks them into the gate lock, twisted, jimmied open the door.

The incoming tide's choppy waves through the Marina caused the tethered boats to bob, dance, bump against the sides of their slips. Jorge walked down the slip until he came to a 65 foot fishing yacht tied at the end of the center slip. He lifted the heavy trash barrel onto the deck, then, climbed aboard.

Switching on a flashlight, he stalked around the bow, then the canopy covered rear platform deck. Going below, he inspected the engine, checked through the interior of the below deck cabins, then the stowage compartments. Scouting out the control cabin, he turned the radio equipment on and off. He retrieved a tool box from his trash barrel, took out a pulley mounted in a square block, inserted a head with two protruding notched keys into the ignition lock, twisted the ratcheted fitting until the two picks expanded tight against either side of the lock cylinder, then jacked the cylinder out of its mounting by tightening the pulley.

Cutting the ignition wires from the lock cylinder, Jorge disconnected the battery, stripped the insulation of the starter wires, twisted them, screwed them down onto a new key cylinder he took from his pocket. He reconnected the battery cables, then jumped over the gunwale down onto the dock, slipped the lines from the bollards, threw them on board, pulled up the fenders, scrambled back to the wheel-cabin, started the engine, backed the yacht out of the slip into the waterway, throttled her forward into the morning tide.

He took the craft several miles south of the Naval facility at Coronado to an inlet where an old rickety pier thrust into the bay. Just as the sky was turning pink with the threat of dawn, Jorge pulled the yacht alongside the pier, jumped off, secured one of the lines to an old worn cleat, then lashed another over a protruding end of piling.

Jumping back aboard, he rigged a maintenance platform over the yacht's stern, took a hammer and chisel from his tool kit, climbed on the platform, removed the brass letters spelling the name GORGEOUS, SAN DIEGO on the stern plate, then replaced them with similar brass letters spelling GUADALUPE, SAN PEDRO. He took the platform to the bow, suspended it over the starboard side, took a stencil frame with a square cutout, sprayed over the hull registry with white paint, then repeated this on the port side. While the paint was drying, he taped off the trim over the after canopy, spray painted the red striping to black. He replaced the dull brass porthole covers with shiny brass, took down the red, white blue San Diego Yacht Club pennant, hoisted a gold, white one in its place. He picked the locks on the long deck storage cabinets, removed the fishing tackle, checked out the lines, reels, poles, hooks.

Taking out two large live bait containers from the trash barrel, he secured them along the side of the stern chairs, then set up the fishing poles in the stands along the canopy. He rolled the trash barrel over to the galley, removed other boxes containing groceries, deli meats, beer, wines, tequila, juices, soft drinks, stowed these into the refrigerator, cabinets, side containers. He returned to the side, climbed onto the platform, taped on transparent registry number stickers to both side of the prow, then taking a set of clothes out of the trash barrel, he dressed in light khaki pants, a long sleeve tee shirt, a worn yachtsman cap with captain's braids.

Mounting a square box along the side of the wheel cowling, he placed a Beretta Px4 Strom 9mm along with two extended filled magazine clips, then closed it with a key. After stowing the tool box, trash barrel in a corner of the forward cabin Jorge started the engine, backed the yacht off the pier, headed off out to sea. Keeping an eye out for Coast Guard patrol boats, he steered south towards Mexico.

~*~*~

Tough times
County Morgue, Santa Ana, CA
Same day, 9:52 AM, Tuesday

Coming into the old hospital in a dress, high heels, Ruth asked a young female deputy behind a reception window for the directions to the morgue.

Looking Ruth up and down, the deputy said, "Do you have an appointment?'

"I need an appointment to go the morgue?"

"We require all visitors to the morgue to register prior to visiting."

"I'm Ruth Hall. One of your detectives asked me to drive up here from San Diego."

"Which detective?"

Ruth rummaged in her purse. "Hold on. I've got his name here. Shermer. Detective Al Shermer."

The deputy straightened up. "Inspector Shermer is our chief homicide investigator. You probably have been already scheduled." She scanned her list. "OK. I see your name. Just a moment and I'll call him."

She mumbled into a handheld radio that squawked an incomprehensible reply.

"He'll be right up, Ma'am," she said.

A minute or so later, a door banged, a short, wiry man in a rumbled gray pin-stripped suit, with short black graying hair that looked like it was made of unruly steel wool, popped out of a door. "Professor Hall," he said. "Thank you so much for coming."

Ruth followed him through the door, down a long corridor to a room with a large viewing window covered by a curtain.

"This isn't pretty," Shermer said. "If you need anything, I'm right here."

Ruth nodded, bit her lip. The curtain parted.

The body on the gurney was covered to the chest with a sheet, the face was burned black on one side. The other side of the head showed abrasions, rips in the scalp, the white of skull bone peeked through a laceration over the temple. Ruth looked, shook her head. Then, she peered closer at the face.

"Could you turn him so I can see the side of his face without the burn?"

Shermer rapped on the window, made a circular motion with his fingers. Inside, the morgue attendant nodded, swung the gurney around. The body shifted from the motion, the attendant straightened it, setting the head on the support.

Ruth gasped, her hand went to her mouth.

"O God, it's Matt!"

Shermer stepped up, caught her arm, led her to a chair.

"Do you recognize him?" he said.

Ruth nodded, hand at her mouth, tears coming to her eyes.

Shermer grabbed a packet of tissues from a table near the window, put it in Ruth's hand, pulled another chair next to her.

"Take your time," he said.

Ruth gave a convulsive whimper, choked back the tears.

"His name was Matt Spyner," she said. "We used to date. He was... a friend."

Looking at her with tired, sad eyes, Shermer said in a soft voice, "Were you lovers?"

"For a while. But, that was a long time ago."

"How long ago?"

"Over 10 years ago. We were both graduate students at the University."

"When was the last time you saw him?"

"Nearly 10 years ago... No. It was in '64 when he went back to Mexico."

"He was from Mexico?"

"No. He was an anthropologist, working in Mexico."

"What was he doing?"

"Studying to be a shaman."

Shermer blinked.

"Studying to be a shaman?" he said.

"It's not as crazy as it sounds. He'd found this old Zaitequi shaman who agreed to take him on as an apprentice. He spent over a year with this guy."

"Let me get this straight. He studied to be a shaman for a year."

"That's right."

"And, as I recall, a shaman is a kind of Indian medicine man or witch doctor."

"That's right."

Shermer took a long deep breath. "OK. Go on."

"Well, Matt wrote all this stuff up into a master's thesis."

"About being a sorcerer's apprentice."

"That's about it."

"So what happened then?"

"He came back to the University and showed it to our major professor, Edward Singer."

"Who's he?"

"He's one of the foremost authorities on Southwestern Native American cultures."

"So, what did he say about this thesis on learning how to become a shaman."

"Being a gentlemen, he said it wasn't a valid anthropological study."

Shermer breathed something amounting to a sigh of relief.

"Did you see this thesis?" he said.

"I read it."

"What did you think?"

Ruth paused, wiped her eyes.

"I agreed with Ed Singer," she said. "I told Matt I thought it was a piece of crap."

Ruth started to cry.

"He didn't say a word," she said. "He picked up the thesis, walked out the door and went back to Mexico."

"Did you hear from him after that?"

"Some time after Easter, we got a message from the Mexican police that he had disappeared and there was blood all over the place he'd been staying. We went down to gather his things."

"We?"

"Matt's brother and I. Jake's a fireman, an arson investigator in Anaheim."

"What did you find down there?"

"Precious little. But, we did find a big pile of ashes that could have been the remains of Matt's thesis that the Mexican police had swept in a box."

"He burned his thesis?"

"I thought so at the time. So did Jake. We thought he'd just gone into one of his famous manic moods, got drunk, stoned or both, burned the damned thing and took off."

"Where to?"

"No idea. Matt was never very stable."

"You said that you thought at the time, he burned his thesis," Shermer said. "But, now you don't?"

"Here's where it gets weird. I got a message earlier this month while I was at an international conference in Mexico from someone who said he was Matt. He said that he'd been in South America for these last ten years."

"So, he took off to South America from Mexico after this thesis burning incident."

"It gets better, Detective Shermer."

"Go on."

"Well, after Matt disappeared, this guy named Santos Villalobos writes this book, *The Secrets of Pedro Miguel.*"

"I think I heard of it."

Ruth's eyes went hard. "It's a blatant revision of Matt Spyner's thesis."

"What?"

"This book is damn near word for word in substance what Matt wrote in his thesis."

"You're saying this Villalobos guy stole the story?"

"When I saw the book, I knew he'd stolen the story. It was Matt's work."

"No possibility of a coincidence?"

"Too many identical details– it was a rip off."

"Can you prove that?'

"Not in any way you could take to court."

"Are you suggesting this Villalobos guy might have had something to do with Matt Spyner's death?"

"I am."

"What makes you think that?"

"The message I got said Matt had only recently learned about the book's existence. He said he was going to get hold of Santos and confront him with the evidence."

"Did he?"

"I wasn't totally convinced the voice was Matt. So, I thought I'd just wait and see what happened next. That was the last I heard from him."

"Did you save the tape."

"I'm afraid I erased it and recorded over it."

"Don't discard it," Shermer said. "Our forensic people can work wonders with tapes."

He put his hand on her arm. "I'm truly sorry, Dr. Hall. This has been very traumatic for you. Can you give me the name of Matt Spyner's next of kin?"

"I have Jake's number somewhere at home. I'll call him and have him get directly in touch with you."

"If you like, we can call him."

"No. Jake's an old friend, a very sweet guy. He used to get very frustrated with his brother but he loved him dearly. I'll call him."

"That will be fine." Shermer said

"What happens next? "Ruth said.

"We'll get in touch with this Santos Villalobos and talk to him. But, realistically, there's little to try and build a case on. My guess is that Villalobos will have his lawyer at hand, an alibi tight as a rat's ass and there will be damn little we'll be able to pursue anything from beyond that.'

Shermer looked over to see Ruth on the verge of tears again.

"Do you need for me to have someone see you get home OK?" the detective said.

"I'll be fine."

Ruth left the morgue, drove home without crying.

~*~*~

A friendly Cuban welcome to Mexico
Boca Zorillo, south of Tijuana
Same day, 4:05 PM

Jorge pulled into the dock at a small private marina. Two uniformed inspectors came aboard as soon as he docked.

"Your papers and registry, Señor," the senior officer said.

Jorge handed them some forged papers with two one hundred dollar bills inserted into the fold. The inspectors glanced at the papers, pocketed the bills, stepped off the craft passing a big man in a tailored blue suit standing on the slip. After the inspectors walked away, the big man looked up at Jorge.

"You Lopez?" he said.

Jorge nodded.

Flicking the ash from his cigarette, the man scowled at Jorge. "Man, you took your damn time getting here."

Noting the man's Cuban accent, Jorge looked at his watch. "My orders were to be here around 4:00 PM. It's only 4:20."

The big man frowned. "Like I said, you took your goddam time. Four o'clock means four o'clock, not 20 minutes later."

"Sorry."

"Here's the deal, asshole," the man said. "I'll be here, right here in this fucking spot tomorrow morning at six in the morning. If your ass isn't here, I'll feed you to the sharks."

"Not a problem. I'm going to pick up a few supplies and will stay docked right here."

Antonio Volpez shot him a scowl. "See to it. I meant what I said."

He turned, walked off down the dock.

Jorge climbed onto the dock, hailed a guard. "Where can I get some fishing supplies and the boat fueled?"

The young man with a rifle slung over his shoulder pointed toward the end of the dock.

"There's a store over there You can get what you want from there."

"Thanks." Jorge turned to walk away, then stopped. "You saw the guy who I'm taking out tomorrow, no?"

The young guard nodded.

"Then, I don't need to point out to you that it is in both of our best interests that no one goes on board my boat while I'm over at that store, right?"

The young guard's eye brows knit in a worry knot.

"I understand completely, Señor," the guard said.

Jorge slipped a hundred dollar bill in the guard's shirt pocket, then walked to the store at the end of the pier, bought some items, arranged for the boat to be fueled. When he returned to the yacht, the young guard nodded assurance.

After checking around the yacht until he was satisfied nothing had been disturbed, Jorge went down into the bunk room, lay down, read a translation of Merleau Ponty's *Signs* until nearly midnight.

Follow Ups
Upper Marigold Drive, East Los Angeles, CA
Same day, 8:47 PM, Tuesday

Rainfall like soft water flowing from a showerhead with millions of holes lulled Lola as she sat at the kitchen table, staring out the window at the drops becoming little drizzles across the surface of the glass.

The coffee cup, the cigarette in the ashtray before her were cold, forgotten. When Santos walked in, she glanced at him, turned her eyes back to the falling rain outside.

"I thought you'd quit smoking." he said, his voice soft.

She kept looking out the window.

"I did," she said. "Same time as you. Remember?"

"So, what's that dead dill doing in the ashtray."

"It's not every day someone you love goes out and kills somebody."

"I wish it hadn't happened."

"This ain't some cop in some out of the way place in Mexico. This is right here in California. This is gonna come back to you."

"I took his wallet. It had all his ID. There's no way they can trace it back to me."

"That's what you said last time."

"And, it didn't happen."

"No?" she said. "What the fuck do you call this weirdo showing up, calling your publisher, then Cassie and finally you? How many others did this nutcase call?"

"This guy was a loner. I doubt he had any friends."

"Oh yeah? He had a girl friend."

Santos gave her a hard look. "Speaking of which, we could have a long discussion on fucked-up killings."

"OK, OK," Lola said. "We nailed the wrong bitch. Nacho screwed it up, gave Jorge the..."

Santos raised his voice. "That was your call, Lola."

"I only wanted to protect you."

"Fact: no one's ever come forward since we published *Secrets*."

"But, that guy told you his girlfriend had a copy of the manuscript."

"I don't take that very seriously."

"That's a damn weak hook to hang your hat on."

"They had damn near ten years to kick up a fuss."

"So why did this guy suddenly pop up out of the blue?"

"My guess is he only recently found out about the books."

The phone's ring made them both jump. Lola looked at Santos, then picked it up.

"Hello."

The voice was male. "Good evening. This is detective Al Shermer, Orange County Sheriff's Department. May I speak to Santos Villalobos?"

Lola covered the mouthpiece. "It's the Orange County Sheriff's Department."

Santos flinched, reached for the phone.

"This is Santos Villalobos."

"Good evening, sir. Sorry to disturb you but we found a body with evidence of foul play yesterday."

"What would that have to do with me?"

"During the identification phase, your name came up as a possible connection to the deceased and we're just following up on that."

"Who was this person?"

"We've tentatively identified the deceased as Matt Spyner, a former anthropology student at New Mexico University."

"I'm an anthropologist. But, the name doesn't ring a bell."

"You don't recall having met him?"

"I'm afraid I don't."

"Have you been in Orange County recently?"

"No, it's been years since I was in Orange county but I'm happy to cooperate with you in any way I can."

"We certainly appreciate that Mr. Villalobos. Is it possible for us to get together and talk?"

"Not to sound defensive, but would you be able to meet with me tomorrow at my lawyer's offices?"

"Do you feel the need to have your attorney present, Mr. Villalobos?"

"As you may be aware, Detective, having written a couple of books, I'm very sensitive to negative publicity."

"I understand. When would it be convenient?"

"How about tomorrow afternoon, say around 3:00?"

"That would be ideal."

Santos told him the address, how to get to the office, hung up.

Lola stared at him wide-eyed. "This is bad shit."

"Only a ripple on the surface of the pond."

"A minute ago you said they'd never connect you to this guy. Now, you got a cop on your ass asking questions."

"If they had anything solid, they'd be here with a warrant in hand. Call Cassie and set up this meeting for tomorrow afternoon. I'm going to get back to work on my book."

~*~*~

Sailing along
Calistina Marina, south of Tijuana, Mexico
Next day, 5:08 AM, Wednesday, January 8, 1974

Jorge jerked awake, scrambled out of the bunk, peed in the head, made a pot of coffee, checked everything once more. A bit before 6:00 he saw Antonio followed by two men pushing an older man in a wheel chair come down the dock up to the rail.

"You ready to go?" Antonio said to Jorge.

Jorge nodded.

Turning to the men standing by the older man, the Cuban said, "Go check it out."

The two men climbed aboard. One of them pushed Jorge to the side of the cabin, frisked, patted him down, front and back. The other went through the boat probing, poking, turning things over. About a half hour later, the two helped Jacobo Fuchs board the boat.

Fuchs took a look around the yacht, then eased himself into the seat of a deck chair under the canopy. Antonio made one last sweep of the yacht, then came up, put his face in Jorge's.

"You know, if anything goes wrong, I'll have your entire family killed."

Jorge nodded again.

Fuchs pounded the deck with the end of his cane. "Enough threats, Antonio," he said. "Let's go catch some fish."

"Cast off," Jorge yelled at the slip attendants.

He fired up the engine, pointed the yacht's bow into the blue waters of the Pacific.

~*~*~

Once underway, Jorge set the helm on autopilot, hurried back to get a pole baited.

The two men helped Fuchs into the stern chair. Jorge stepped to the stern, adjusted the weights at the end of the line, bent the pole back, heaved a long cast out into the wake of the boat, placed the end into a cup at the base of the chair, then passed the pole to Fuchs.

The old man grinned, grabbed the pole with both hands. "Ah, yes. Thanks."

Jorge turned to one of the men standing at Fuchs's side. "When he needs the bait reset, call me," he said. "I'll be forward."

The man nodded, turned his attention back to Fuchs who was reeling out the line, giving it periodic yanks. Jorge made his way forward to the galley, took out two long loaves of French bread, sliced them down the middle, spread mayonnaise on the sides, brown mustard on the others, laid out slices of ham, salami, provolone cheese, sliced onion, chopped lettuce, hot peppers, put the two halves of the loaf together, sliced these into eight equal sections. He arranged the sandwiches on a rolling table he took out of the galley cabinet, set out the pot of coffee, drinks in a cooler filled with ice, rolled the table back to the stern chair, locked the wheels in place close to the old man working the fishing pole.

Antonio stepped up, picked up one of the sandwiches, handed it to Jorge. "You eat the first one," he said.

Jorge bit off a large bite. "Thanks."

He walked back to the helm, sandwich in hand, selected a coca cola, took the boat off autopilot.

Antonio came to his elbow. "Where'd you learn to speak Spanish?" he said.

"Thought we were speaking Spanish," Jorge said.

"Well, I know I was," Antonio said. "I just wasn't sure what you speaking."

The two men lounging around the old man wrestling with the fishing pole in the stern chair laughed.

Jorge shrugged his shoulders, kept his eyes in front of him.

Antonio took a red pack of Pall Malls from his pocket, shook out a cigarette, lit it.

"Where'd you get this boat?"

"Bought it from a guy in Pedro."

"No, wise guy. I mean where'd you get the money to buy it?"

"Stole it."

The men laughed.

Antonio frowned. "So, you're a comedian. A funny guy. Full of jokes."

"Just answered your question," Jorge said.

Antonio blew smoke in Jorge's face. "I don't like funny guys."

"No one said you have to like me, Sr. Antonio." Jorge said.

Antonio frowned, then burst into laughter. "Hey, this guy's good."

The two men stared back at Jorge without smiles.

Jorge looked around.

"Do you guys want some music?"

Antonio stepped away, leaned back on the front passenger seat. "We're Cubans. We don't want any of that shit you Chicanos listen to."

Jorge switched on the shortwave, searched until he found a Cuban station, turned on the speakers, so the sound went throughout the yacht.

"At least you got enough sense to find some decent music," Antonio said.

Jorge kept his eyes on the ocean in front of him, scanning for US coast guard or Mexican maritime patrol boats. "Thanks," he murmured.

Antonio sneered. "It wasn't a compliment."

Jorge did not respond, his hand tapped the metal box next to the helm in time to the Afro-Cuban music coming over the speakers.

Antonio gave a shiver, crossed his arms, moved around. Jorge looked at Antonio, lighting his second cigarette from his first.

"Doe this fucking scow have a heater?"

"It does but by the time it would warm up this area, we'd have to turn it off because it would be too hot."

"Turn on the fucking heater."

"You got it."

Jorge flipped on the heater switch. Warm blew out of the vent.

Antonio looked over at him. "See, it's getting warmer already."

"Glad to accommodate," Jorge said.

Antonio frowned again, lit a fresh cigarette, muttered, "Asshole."

Fuchs gave a cry from the stern chair. "Got one! Feels big."

Jorge set the autopilot, moved back to the boat, picked up a snare hook. The two body guards stepped in front of the old man, their guns in their hands, pointed at Jorge.

"Put those goddam guns away," Fuchs yelled at them. "If I lose this fish, I'll use both of you for shark bait."

The men put the guns away under their jackets, stepped back. Jorge came to Fuchs's side, pulled the line taut, then reeled in the slack.

"Just keep doing what you're doing," Jorge said. "You're bringing him in good. A little more now."

Leaning out over the stern, Jorge hooked the big albacore in the gill slit, hauled it aboard.

When the big fish started to thrash, Jorge brought the round side of the hook down, striking the albacore behind the head.

The fish gave two convulsive jerks, lay trembling as Jorge freed the hook.

Fuchs rose out of the stern chair. "Look at that! Now, that's a fish."

Their faces encased in smiles, the two guards patted him on the back.

"Very good, Mr. Fuchs."

"That is some fish."

Fuchs looked down at the fish, then grinned at Jorge. "Bait me up. Let's get another."

Jorge baited the second pole, cast the line, passed the pole to Fuchs who yanked the line, pumped the handle as before.

"Now, let's see how many fish I can get into this boat," he said.

Office call
Law Offices: Rydell, Le, Cortez & Yoshizumi, Los Angeles, CA
Same day, 2:31 PM, Wednesday

Santos and Lola arrived at Cortez's office a half hour before the scheduled interview. Cortez escorted them into his office, shut the door.

"OK," he said. "I want both of you nice and relaxed. Answer each question curtly. Don't elaborate. Don't give any more information than is absolutely necessary. If you have any doubts, look over at me and I'll pick up it up from there."

"Cassie, how did they get on this so soon?" Lola said. "They must have something."

"They ain't got shit," Cortez said. "This is a fishing expedition."

"Yeah, but what if they do?" she said.

"If and 5 bucks gets you lunch at Mickey D's," Cortez said.

Cortez turned to Santos.

"I called in the guy who does our background work," he said. "He checked the office phones and found a device in the wiring that records numbers. He went over to the gal at Berkshire Press's office, checked her phone, found another recording device in her phone. Apparently, these can be activated from another phone. This was how this asshole found our numbers."

"He was a busy boy," Santos said.

"A smart rat always finds a little hole to squeeze through," Cortez said. "So, we gotta be careful with these cops. The Orange County Sheriff's Department aren't a bunch of country hicks. They handle the urban criminal investigations around Santa Ana."

Cortez's phone buzzed. His secretary announced the arrival of two detectives.

"They're here early," the lawyer said.

He opened the door, admitted Shermer and a tall African-American plainclothesman.

"Cassie Cortez, gentlemen. My clients, Dr. Santos Villalobos, his associate, Ms. Dolores Santiago."

"I'm chief investigator, Lt. Al Shermer. My partner Sgt. Paul Reeves."

Cortez seated the two men across from Santos, Lola, then moved around behind his desk.

"I apologize for having you guys come all the way up here, but all legal activities are required by our corporate charter to have an attorney present."

"Not a problem, counselor," Shermer said. "We just want to ask Mr. Villalobos some questions."

Cortez corrected him. "Dr. Villalobos."

"Sorry. No offense intended."

"None taken." Santos said.

Shermer cleared his throat. "Dr. Villalobos. Do you know a Ruth Hall?"

Santos shot Cortez a glance. Cortez intervened. "Who's she?"

"She's a professor and archeologist who initially identified the deceased. His brother's since confirmed the identification."

"We met once," Santos said.

"At that time did she accuse you of stealing her boyfriend's thesis?"

Santos laughed.

"It was several years ago. I didn't know who she was at the time. But, no, aside from a sarcastic comment, I don't remember any accusations."

Cortez shot Santos a dirty look.

Shermer wrote this down. "I see. Do you recall the remark?"

"Not verbatim. It was something like, 'So you're the famous writer.' "

Cortez flinched.

"How did you respond?" Shermer said.

"I confessed to be Santos Villalobos."

"Did you know Matt Spyner?"

"I've no idea who he is."

Shermer turned his gray eyes on Santos.

"He's the supposed author of a thesis based on his anthropological study about learning to be a shaman from a Zaitegui witch doctor," the detective said,

Cortez started to speak, but Santos raised his hand.

"Since I've written *The Secrets of Don Pedro Miguel,* we've received dozens of reports and accusations from various individuals claiming to have gone through the same experiences that I did in preparing the research upon which my book is based."

"And all of these claims have proven baseless," Cortez broke in. "When we've asked to see the original data or the manuscripts, they've all failed to stand up to close scrutiny by reputable investigators."

"I can well imagine," Shermer said. "However, we did follow up on Dr. Hall's report of the deceased having completed such a work by calling Professor Edward Singer at New Mexico University."

Cortez didn't bat an eye. "And?"

Shermer raised his eyes, looked at Cortez, then at Santos. "He confirmed that Mr. Spyner had indeed written a thesis along the lines of your client's work."

Cassie leaned back in his chair, brought his two hands together. "Could he say for certain if it was the same?"

Without taking his eyes from Santos, Shermer went on,

"Professor Singer couldn't say because he said he hadn't read your client's book."

"Did this Professor Singer have a copy of this said thesis?" Cortez said.

Shermer kept looking at Santos,

"No. He didn't," he said

"Well," Cortez said. "There you have it."

Shermer looked over at him, then back to Santos.

"On the other hand," he said. "Dr. Hall had read the thesis in question and your book, and is quite certain the thesis is essentially the same as your client's book."

Cortez's smile was gone. "Does she have a copy of this alleged thesis?"

Without flinching, blinking or taking his eyes from Santos, Shermer said, "I don't know. She didn't say."

Cortez leaned forward, folded his hands, placing them on the desk.

"So, where is this famous thesis, Detective?"

Shermer's response came as if from a statue. "Seems no one knows– could be lost."

"Well, Cortez said. "Until we do have it in hand, these comparisons remain just so much speculation."

"No argument counselor," Shermer said.

"Well, gentlemen," Cortez said, looking at the two policemen. "Anything else you'd like to ask my client?"

Reeves leaned forward. "Dr. Villalobos, where were you a week ago on the night of January the 3rd?"

"I was at a board meeting with the members of my working group," Santos said,

"Who were these members?"

"My attorney here, Ms. Santiago, her brother, Ignacio and two other officers, Mr. Gabriel Sanchez and Enrique Alire, our accountant."

Reeves wrote down the names. "How late did the meeting last?"

"Quite late. We didn't get finished until well after midnight."

"Are your meetings usually so late?"

"My attorney, here, was busy with another client and detained."

"What did you do when the meeting concluded, Dr. Villalobos?" Reeves said.

Lola reached over, patted Santos's hand.

"I can answer that," she said. "We went to bed."

Reeves nodded at Shermer. Then, both detectives stood. Shermer put his note book back in his pocket.

"Dr. Villalobos, Ms. Santiago, Counselor," he said. "We'll call you if any further developments arise."

Cortez stood. "Thank you for coming by, gentlemen. I hope your case is resolved quickly."

The two men left the office. Lola let out a deep breath.

"Well, that went well," she said.

Cortez stared at the door. "Not that well."

"What do you mean?"

"Did you notice they made no effort to shake hands while they were here?" Cortez said.

~*~*~

In the elevator, Shermer looked over to his partner. "What do you think, Paul?"

Reeves let out a little burst of air through his lips.

"Ruth Hall's right. He did it."

Shermer shook his head. "Ain't shit we can do about it, though."

"He's covered his ass pretty well."

"Were there any prints on that branch he used to sweep his tracks away on the dirt road."

"We went over everything, the can, inside and out of the car. Whatever prints may have been there were burned off when he threw the gas in there. Nothing."

"So, we might as well close the lid on this one."

Reeves looked over at his partner, as the elevator door opened. "We ain't got shit. Just gut feelings."

"Damn shame," Shermer said.

~*~*~

Down and dirty
Off the coast of California, near Coronado, CA
Same day, 12:45 PM, Wednesday

Antonio's voice rang out over the sound of the backwash of the propellers at the stern. "Can you get your fat Chicano ass up here and turn off this fucking heater?"

Leaving Fuchs pulling the line, Jorge made his way to the helm, switched off the heater fan, took the craft off auto pilot, then steered closer to the shore.

Antonio had taken the cabin chair to the right of the helm. "What the fuck are you doing?" he said.

"Moving to a better fishing spot."

"Well, land us in Gringoland and your ass'll look like a hairnet."

Jorge turned parallel to the shore line, scanned the surrounding area. Antonio scowled over at him again.

"What're you looking for, asshole?" he said.

"Coast Guard."

"If we get stopped, it's your ass, dreamboat."

"I'm aware of that."

"Keep it in mind."

Jorge looked back at Fuchs, pulling and reeling. After setting the boat on autopilot, he went back, spoke to the old man. "There are swordfish in these waters and I want you to troll a bit."

Jorge pointed to a spot off a point of the coastline.

"The navy sunk an old ship out there. I'm going to make a couple of runs over it. Don't tire yourself out because if we get a hit, you're going to need all the strength you got to get it in."

Fuchs's eyes lit up, his head nodding up and down.

Jorge put his hand on the old man's shoulder. "Unless you want me to land it," he said.

"No. This is what I came for."

Jorge smiled for the first time, patted the old man's shoulder, went back to the helm.

Taking the craft off autopilot again, Jorge gunned the throttle, brought the boat about, turning her into the wind. Firing up the sonar sounder, the fathometer, he headed for a spit of land extending out into the sea.

Antonio sat with his feet on the runner of the cabin chair, smoking a fresh cigarette.

"Do you know what the fuck you're doing?" he said.

Jorge ignored him, looked back at Fuchs playing the line from left to right.

"The old guy's pretty good," Jorge said.

Antonio shrugged. "He loves this shit. Can't wait to get out here."

Jorge smiled.

Nice to have off my ass for a second, shithead.

On the second run, Jorge felt the craft give a slight tremble, looked back. Fuchs now had the line in both hands, pulling it in, reeling in the slack as fast as possible. Jorge set the throttles at medium speed, turned on the autopilot, then went back to the stern chair. Fuchs was pulling the pole back to his chest, reeling as fast as his hand could move, repeating the action.

Jorge stepped up beside him, buckled the shoulder belts across the old man's chest, centered the rubber butt of the pole into the holder cup at the base of the stern chair.

"Let the pole pull you to your feet," Jorge said. "Brace yourself against the foot rests, then lean back and let your body weight pull the pole. Don't overwork your arms trying to pull against the fish."

Fuchs nodded, did as he was told. The taut line pulled him to his feet. He gripped the pole, leaned back pulling the pole with the weight of his thin body.

Jorge stepped forward, passed a leather belt loop behind the old man's back, closed the two rings at either end with a double snap, then clipped the other to the pole.

"This will give you some more leverage," he said. "And, if you lose the pole, we won't lose the fish."

Fuchs kept pulling, leaning back, reeling the slack out of each pull. Antonio and the two body guards stood there, hands at their sides, mouths open watching the old man fighting the fish with the pole.

Jorge picked up the landing hook.

"It's a sword fish. Bring him in like you're doing."

Fuchs kept up his constant yanking, jerking, reeling, his face red, the veins standing out on his neck and head. His long billed hat had fallen to the deck, the large blue veins could be seen though his spotted white skin. He kept pulling.

Jorge slipped on a leather glove, gripped the line, reached over, hooked the sword fish in the gill slit, let go of the line, grabbed the swordfish's pointed nose, hauled it on board, landing in a heap.

The two body guards stepped back from the thrashing fish, as Jorge reached down, gripped the gaff where it fit into the handle, jerked it free of the gill slit, swung it, bringing the heavy curved hook behind the sword fish's head. The big fish gave a couple of whips with its body, quivered, lay quiet, flopping its long tail.

Jorge got his feet under him, slipped on the deck, went over, unbuckled Fuchs from the stern chair harness and pole belt. The old man got up, looked at the swordfish.

"I've never caught one. I've had them on line before but couldn't land them. I finally did it."

The guards clapped their hands, cheered. "Bravo, Sr. Fuchs. A courageous job."

"You did it, Sr. Fuchs."

Antonio was standing at the edge of the deck canopy watching the men admire the fish, his nose rolled up in boredom.

Jorge slipped forward, unlocked the metal box next to the helm molding, took out the automatic, jacked a round into the chamber, stepped behind Antonio, struck him behind the head.

As Antonio sprawled forward on the deck, Jorge shot each bodyguard in the head before they could reach their handguns. Fuchs turned, staggered backwards, slumped into the stern chair.

"So, this was a set up," he said.

"I'm afraid so, Sr. Fuchs," Jorge said.

Fuchs stared at him, his eyes adjusting to the shock. "Alban set this up?"

"I don't ask who signs the check."

Fuchs looked at Jorge, gave a faint smile. "You're good. Damn good. In fact, you're the best I've ever seen. I'll double whatever you're getting to come over to me and take out those other two bastards."

"I believe you, Mr. Fuchs. But, I can't do that."

"You know they'll take you out. They don't like loose ends."

"Guess I'll cross that bridge when I come to it."

Fuchs looked over at the fish, then back at Jorge. "You could have taken us anytime."

"More or less."

"So why'd you wait?"

"I wanted to see you catch that fish."

"You knew I could do it?" Fuchs said.

"I did."

Fuchs looked down at the two fish. "Well, I thought I'd be eating you tonight but looks like your relatives will be eating me."

He gazed at Jorge, eyebrows knit.

"You and I could make an awful lot of money together," he said. "You're throwing it all away for an early grave, you know."

"It's a risk of this business, Mr. Fuchs."

The old man looked out over the sea.

"Every race ends," he said. "The winners stand in the sun for a minute, the losers go their way. In the end, we're all in the same place.'

He looked back at Jorge. "Can I ask a favor?"

"What?"

"After you shoot me, will you put my fish over the side with me."

"Yes."

"Do it."

Jorge fired one shot into Jacobo Fuchs's heart.

Then Jorge heard Antonio groan.

Jorge went back to a drawer, took out a roll of duct tape, broke off a long swatch with his teeth, seized Antonio's hands behind his back, jerked him to his feet.

Antonio groaned, shook his head, looked down at his clothes.

"You ruined my suit, motherfucker. This is a $10,000 suit. You got it all fucked up."

"Sorry."

Antonio gawked at the bodies of the two body guards on the deck, Fuchs in the stern chair, then stared over at Jorge.

"You did this?"

"It wasn't the fish."

"You're dead," Antonio said. "Your fucking family's dead. You're going to be flushed down a shithole."

"Not today, Antonio."

Jorge shoved Antonio to the stern of the yacht. Antonio twisted his neck to look at him.

"I ain't going to beg for my life, you piece of shit."

"You got a bad mouth, Antonio," Jorge said. "Someday it's gonna get you in a lot of trouble."

"Piss in your teeth, you fucking Chicano."

Antonio ducked his head, rammed like a bull at Jorge, lunging forward like a fullback with his hands lashed behind him. Jorge shifted his weight to one side. Antonio fell forward onto the slippery deck.

Jorge reached down jerked him to his feet, then noticed the red pack of Pall Malls on the deck. He reached down, put them into Antonio's inside jacket pocket, shoved him back to the stern of the boat.

"You'll want these. Where you're going, you'll have no trouble getting a light."

Antonio spat blood, snot in Jorge's face.

"Fuck you, bastard," he said.

Jorge shot him in the side of his head; Antonio's body pitched over the stern into the yacht's wake.

A flash of light caught Jorge's attention. There was a US Coast Guard patrol boat about three miles off the stern. Jorge rolled the bodies of the body guards overboard.

Turning to Fuchs's body still sprawled in the chair, eyes open, Jorge closed the eyes, picked up the body of the old man, let it slip into the wake, then slid the two fish over the side as well.

Making his way to the helm, he spun the wheel turning the prow of the yacht toward the shore, shoved the throttles to full, felt the yacht's bow lift when the powerful Grey-Marine engine bit the water whipping the twin screws into a frenzy.

Jorge looked back. The patrol boat was changing course, swinging his direction.

He knew he could outrun the patrol boat but not a round from the 8mm canon mounted on its forward prow. The patrol craft had to get within three hundred yards of him, try to hail him to stop before it would open fire.

He knew this stretch of beach from his old drug running days with Nacho. Around the spit of land thrust into the sea, there was a little cove. Jorge forced everything else from his mind, concentrated on getting to that spot.

~*~*~

A chase
Off the coast of California, near Coronado, CA
Same day, 1:25 PM, Wednesday

165

It had been a boring morning starboard lookout watch aboard the USCG Patrol craft GA1109. Seaman Henry Walkins gave the yacht a mile or so away a passing glance, took another sip of his coffee. Wishing he had some music, he looked over at the green coastline, thinking about the whores in Tijuana when his attention was pricked by a faint sound– a snick.

Walkins wrinkled his nose.

What would make a snick?

He looked around, shipmates on the main cabin watch were laughing, talking about some party they had attended.

A snick?

Walkins remembered. Sound waves travel far across water. Lifting his 8 X 35 watch binoculars to his eyes, he returned his gaze toward the shore.

Nothing.

He scanned back along the sea way. The yacht was churning its way toward the shore.

Man, that dude's trying to make that boat fly.

Walkins turned to the pilot house. "Skipper!"

Chief Warrant Officer, Samson "Skip" O'Dell turned his head to the starboard side deck.

"What's up, Wilkins?"

"Walkins, Sir."

"OK, Wiggens."

"There's a pleasure craft hauling ass toward shore about two miles off the starboard beam."

"I see him. Guess he's in a hurry to get home."

"Well, he wasn't doing that before I heard the snick."

"The snick?" O'Dell said.

"Yessir. I heard a snick."

"Walker, what'n the hell do you mean by a 'snick?' "

"Walkins, sir. You know a snick, like in a gun shot."

O'Dell snatched up his binoculars, fixed on the speeding yacht. "He's hauling ass for sure. Walkman, check him on the 32 power scope."

"Walkins, aye, aye, sir."

The seaman tracked the retreating yacht through the fixed 32 power binocular spotting scope. "I got a visual, sir."

"Pennant?"

"Yessir. Looks red and white."

"See any identifying marks?"

"Yessir. US flag at the after mast, Name, Guadalupe, San Pedro."

"That doesn't wash," O'Dell said. "Let's take a look at him. Could be a druggie."

Turning to Reilly, the quartermaster, he ordered,

"All ahead full. Come right. Get on that guy's ass."

"Do we go to GQ, Skipper?" the quartermaster said.

"Not yet," O'Dell said.

He turned back to the quartermaster.

"Is there any place he can land along here?"

Reilly looked at the chart. "Not really, sir. The closest docking facility is at the Naval base."

"We got his ass now," O'Dell said.

The patrol boat followed the fast moving yacht keeping it in view until it turned behind the little peninsula.

From the starboard flying bridge, O'Dell scanned the shore line with his binoculars. "Where'n the hell did that big bitch yacht go?"

"This stretch of land runs along here for about 5 miles," the quartermaster said. "It's dotted with little coves and inlets. We'll just have to drag along here until we can see something."

O'Dell ordered the patrol boat in close to the shore along the spit of land.

Walkins spotted the cove. "I see it, sir."

"Where?"

"About 600 yards off our starboard beam."

O'Dell, Reilly scanned the area.

"Got it. Good job, Walking."

O'Dell spoke to the cabin crew,

"Don't want to take the ship in there. Full stop!"

As the patrol craft's engines chugged down, O'Dell cried out to his deck crew.

"Simmons, take a boarding party in there to that yacht. Reilly, alert the San Diego Sheriff's office."

"Aye-aye, sir."

O'Dell watched the five armed men in the landing party steer a motor whale boat into the cove. Five minutes, the intercom buzzed.

"Charlie 1, this is unit 1."

"Go ahead, 1."

"Skipper, we've boarded the craft. It's been abandoned."

"No one on board?"

"Not a soul, Skipper but there's blood all over the aft deck and stern."

"Doesn't sound good."

"Hold on, Skipper. Henderson just found some shell casings."

"Roger. Secure everything down, keep a tight ass until the Sheriff's guys get there. Reilly, call ahead and tell them they'll need a forensic team there as well."

"Roger, Skipper."

"And, Simmons."

"Yes, Skipper?"

"Tell the guys to keep their paws off any booze or goodies aboard. I'll have their asses if someone screws this up."

"Roger, Skipper."

~*~*~

More plans
Upper Marigold Drive, East Los Angeles, CA
Sam day, 11:47 PM, Wednesday, January 9, 1975

After Santos had gone to bed, Lola sat at the kitchen table with her brother, Nacho.

"We may have dodged a bullet," she said.

"Yeah?"

"Cassie made mincemeat out of those two cops yesterday. They left with their tails between their legs."

"Cool."

"But there're still some loose ends dangling out there."

"What?"

"Did you hear they did an axe job on Santos at that convention in Mexico City last month?"

"Sort of."

"Well, there's this guy who's been stirring up a mess and we can't afford another crap-stained sheet on the line."

"Thought you said we were cool on this one," Nacho said.

"For the moment. But, we need this guy off Santos's case."

"So, what do you want?"

"I want you to go out and take care of it."

"Where's the guy?"

"The University of El Paso."

"Man, that's in Texas."

"And don't fuck it up like you and Jorge did on that other one."

"Hey, man. That wasn't my fault."

"Bullshit. You gave Jorge the wrong goddam name. If this'd been done right, we wouldn't be in the shit we're in now."

"How close you want this guy trimmed?" Nacho said.

"Take him out," Lola said without emotion.

Some feedback
Convention Center, Holiday Inn, Irvine, CA
Next day, 11:22 AM, Thursday, January 9, 1975

After giving a paper at a morning session of the annual Southwestern Anthropological Convention, Ruth came up to her hotel room to freshen up. The little blinking red light on the phone caught Ruth's eye when she came into her hotel room but she went straight to the bathroom.

Her colleague archeologist from Nevada State College in Yerington, Janet Johnson came in a minute later, saw the light, called for the message.

"It's for you, Ruth," she called out,

Ruth washed her hands at the sink before sitting down on the edge of the bed to take the phone message, a call-back request from the Orange County Sheriff's Investigative Office. She called the number.

"This is Al Shermer."

"Ruth Hall, returning your call."

Detective Shermer related having met with Santos, his lawyer, told how he brushed off the accusations, constructed himself an ironclad alibi, saying he'd never met Matthew Spyner.

"He said he never met Matt?" Ruth said.

"I'll quote: 'I've no idea who he is.' "

"That's bullshit."

"My impression too, Dr. Hall, but I can't take impressions to the DA."

"Did you talk to Jake?"

"He came in the same evening as you and confirmed the deceased was his brother."

"Was it hard for him?"

"It's never easy, but he's a real pro– an arson investigator who gave us some interesting information."

"Anything that helps?"

"Everything helps. He pointed out that the body had only been splashed with gasoline and not doused, something our guys had passed over."

"What's that prove?"

"That whoever did this was an amateur and in a hurry."

"So, you can't take any of this to the DA?"

"My DA would reserve a soft room for me if I did."

"What about the obvious theft of a piece of work that made Santos a fat cat? Surely, this is a valid motive?"

"Where's the original work? All we have are your and Professor Singer's impressions. His lawyer would slice and dice that in a heartbeat."

"You talked to Ed Singer?"

"He said that the work that Spyner submitted to him seemed very similar but that he had not read Villalobos's book."

"Horseshit."

"What that says to me is 'I don't want to get involved.' "

"That's Ed Singer."

"Did Spyner ever have another copy of his work? Who writes a thesis with just one original?"

"Apparently, Matt did. When Jake and I went through his stuff in Mexico, we couldn't find anything besides a pile of ashes that the police had swept up into a shoe-box."

"Dr. Hall. I had my doubts. Shaman, anthropologists, lost manuscripts. But, after meeting Villalobos, my feelings about this case are much closer to yours."

Ruth hung up, sat back on the bed. "Shit," she said.

Janet looked over at her. "What's up?"

Ruth stared at the ceiling, spoke through tight lips. "That tick turd, Santos Villalobos is literally getting away with murder."

"That sucks," Janet said.

Ruth flopped back on the bed, her eyes toward the wall. She sat up, grabbed her purse, took out a notebook, picked up the phone, dialed. Janet looked over at her.

"What're you doing now?"

Ruth cocked the phone to her ear between her shoulder, looked back at Janet. "I'm getting a date with a good-looking Mexican."

"Does he have a friend?" Janet said.

Ruth rolled her eyes. A voice at the other end came on after the third ring.

"Hello, this is Pepe?"

"Hi, Pepe. This is Ruth."

"Hello, *querida*. How are you?"

"To tell you the blunt truth, I'm bummed out and need to have dinner with a good-looking Mexican."

"Well, I'm a Mexican who's willing to have dinner with you. You'll have to decide on the good-looking part."

"Sounds good to me. I'm here in Irvine for a convention, so where can we meet?"

"Irvine. OK. Do you like Thai food?"

"Love it."

"There's a restaurant called the Tiger Fish about three blocks off the UC campus on Valencia, near Jamboree Road. What if I meet you there in an hour?"

"See you then."

As Ruth hung up, Janet spoke out. "Hey, you forgot to ask him about a friend."

Ruth shook her head. "No, and if I had of, your husband would never speak to me again."

Janet stuck her nose back in her reading.

~*~*~

The Tigerfish
Tiger Fish Thai Food Palace, Irvine, CA
Same day, 6:24 PM, Thursday

Ruth entered the small restaurant with a large hand-painted tiger fish in the front window. A smiling Thai hostess in a traditional shimmering gold dress greeted her, showed her to a table in the rear of the dining room.

Ruth was looking at the menu when Pepe came over, kissed her on the cheek, sat down facing her.

"I see you found the place," he said.

"Yes. No problem."

"The food here's great. A friend of mine on faculty at UC took me here and I've been coming back every chance I get."

They ordered Thai noodles, skewered grilled chicken with peanut sauce, Thai beer.

Ruth took a long drink of her beer. "Thanks for rescuing me."

"Actually, it's the other way around. I just finished a novel and was about to condemn myself to an evening of TV."

"I haven't had a chance to tell you but I had to identify Matt Spyner's body."

Pepe's eyes opened wider, his face startled. "No!"

"His body was found in a car in Orange County. He'd been beaten to death with a wrench and his body burned in the car."

"Do they know who did it?"

"Think about it. Matt disappears off the face of the earth..."

"The night my brother was killed."

"There's the missing thesis, this pile of ashes and then, boom. A few years later, *The Secrets of Don Pedro Miguel* hits the stands. Time passes. I get on the trail of this business. We go to the convention in Mexico. Suddenly, out of nowhere, when I get back from Mexico, there's this message from Matt."

"Go on."

"Then, a couple of days ago, I get this call from the Orange County Sheriff's department to come up and identify a body. It was Matt."

"So, you think it was Santos?"

"Yes. Matt said he was going to confront him over the theft of his thesis."

"That's pretty thin evidence, Ruth."

"I know that but every bone in my body tells me this sonfabitch did it."

"Did you share this with the police?"

"Yes. I told all this to detective Al Shermer in the Sheriff's office."

"I know Al Shermer– top notch investigator. What did he say?"

"He talked to Santos Villalobos with his attorney by his side and wasn't able to come up with anything substantial."

"What about evidence from the forensic investigations at the crime scene?"

"Nothing. No fingerprints, no footprints, nothing left behind, nothing, *nada*."

"That more or less leaves it as a dead end."

"Shermer did say that he felt Santos was hiding something."

"And, that there was nothing they could do but keep looking, try to find something to build a case and keep you informed."

"Shermer told me that Jake, Matt's brother, who's an arson investigator, pointed out that the burning was a half-assed job."

"What do you mean, 'half-assed?' "

"It wasn't professional. The killer had splashed some gas inside, lit the thing and ran off."

"That certainly doesn't sound professional."

"My point exactly."

"But just to play the devil's advocate, it doesn't mean it wasn't a set-up either."

"What do you mean?"

"I mean some of these guys are very clever and will do anything to throw an investigation off the track."

"You think this could have been done by professional killers?"

"When we drove home to Chalupa to bury my mother, they sent a bunch of wise-guys up there to wipe out my whole family."

Ruth's mouth dropped open, she sat there stunned.

"Were any of you hurt?"

"No. Mercifully, our local constabulary neutralized them before any harm was done."

Ruth put her hand to her forehead, stared at a spot on the table.

"It's like we're in a war zone. First, your brother, then, Maggie, Matt, and now you."

She raised her head. "Maybe I'm next."

"You're out of the loop," Pepe said. "Even if Santos is somehow involved in this, he wouldn't dare to lay a finger on you. It would come right back on his head."

Ruth sat back, her face in a sad frown. Looking up at the man across from her.

"You think that's what Shermer thinks too?" she said.

"I don't know what Al thinks but I do know if he had a shred of credible evidence, Santos and his lawyer would be down in Orange County having a long chat with him."

Ruth sat silent for a long time.

"Al Shermer's a top cop," Pepe said. "I'll stay in touch with him all the way on this."

"OK. I'm going to be out at my field site for most of the rest of the month."

"I'll still keep you in the loop."

"Well, here comes the food and I'm starved. Let's order another beer to go with it."

Pepe smiled, lifted his glass. "An excellent suggestion, Dr. Hall."

PART FIVE

Strange catch

Off the California Coast, Near the Mexican Border
5:01 AM, Friday, January 10, 1975

The trawler plowed through the wind-whipped sea into rolling waves with streaks of foams, her red and green running lights gleaming in the dim predawn light.

On deck, the 5 man crew in foul weather gear rushed to clear the net lines for the first trawling run. They moved nets, lines, floats and other gear in practiced routine, shouting at each other over the noise of pounding waves.

The Captain stepped out of the pilot house, called down, "Ready Manuel? First run."

A burly man in rubber boots with a foul weather jacket grinned up at his older brother. "Hell yes, we're ready."

The Captain yelled, "Off your Portagee asses. Let's net some fish and make some money."

Yelping back friendly obscenities in Portuguese, the men scurried to their tasks. The trawler turned into the undulating waves, nets peeling off the stern into the water, the men feeding them slack, freeing them from tangles. The trawler chugged on into the wind, the rising swells pulling the nets taut.

At Manuel's signal, the lines tightened, the nets hauled in, then the catch of. fish dumped. The after landing deck shimmered with wriggling fish bodies.

Eduino, a younger man spotted something among the teeming mass of fish.

"Hey, Manny," he said. "What in the hell is that?"

Making his way through the slippery, flopping fish, the big man looked down at the remains of a human body tangled among the squirming fish.

He crossed himself, muttered, *"Mai de Deus!"*

"Joao!" Manuel yelled up to the pilot house. "Call the Coast Guard. We've just pulled in a floater!"

~*~*~

Same day, a little before noon.

The Coast Guard arrived to remove the body the crew had packed in ice, then placed in a waxed cardboard fish container. The Coast Guard work party replaced the body into a polyethylene body bag, then stowed it aboard the patrol boat

One of the Coast Guard seamen puked over the side of the patrol craft next to the trawler after handling the cadaver.

~*~*~

The remains were landed at the Coast Guard Receiving Station in San Diego, then transferred to the morgue at the San Diego County medical facility. There, the body was logged in, scheduled for a postmortem examination the following Monday.

~*~*~

Post Mortem
San Diego County Morgue,
Next day, 8:04 AM, Monday, January 13, 1975

County Medical Examiner, Viet Nguyen, MD, came in to the post mortem examining room carrying a cup of coffee and a sweet roll. After changing into his surgical greens, he donned a fresh autopsy apron, took his breakfast with him into the examining room. He looked over the kit of instruments laid out on a stainless steel tray-table beside the dissecting table, then walked over to the body bag, set his coffee and roll down on one side of the tray-table, adjusted the mike so it would carry his voice to the recorder fixed to his belt, took his first bite of the roll, washed it down with a swig of coffee.

Turning to a heavy Mexican-American man in white pants and shirt with his nose rolled up, he said, "What do we got, Danny?"

"Dunno, Doc, but my money says you'd better finish scarfing that roll before we open that bag."

"Lay him out," Dr. Nguyen said.

Daniel "Danny" Quintero, the morgue orderly, unzipped the body bag. The pathologist looked over the visible remains while Danny cleared the body through the opening of the bag.

"I've seen worse," Dr. Nguyen said. "The fish left most of his head, so we'll get a good dental to make an ID. Also, there's a lot of his clothing left."

"Nothing the Salvation Army will want," Danny said.

Dr. Nguyen munched on the roll. "The way his right arm's twisted back, looks like it was seized behind him."

Danny moved toward the door. "OK, Doc. Just let me know when you're ready to pop that chest so I can find something to do in the next room."

"Danny," Dr. Nguyen said. "Where's your sense of duty?"

"Over in the next building checking out the asses of those good looking nurses."

After Dr. Nguyen finished his roll, drained his coffee, he put on latex gloves and a surgical mask. Then, he examined the remains, speaking into the mike in a dispassionate monotone,

"Subject is male, age undeterminable at this point. The skin and muscle tissue on the face are largely gone; teeth are visible and appear to be intact; the right malar bone is exposed, abraded and broken, the left is missing; the frontal edge of the skull is likewise abraded, the exterior of the nose is gone, the... Just a moment: An unusual abrasion in the side of the left parietal bone... looks like a bullet hole."

He stopped, pulled down his mask, called out. "Danny!"

The door at the end of the hall opened and Danny stuck his head in, "You called?"

"Yeah. Get on the horn to the coroner's office. We got us a homicide."

~*~*~

Same day, 4:21 PM, Monday,

Sporting a light yellow and black checked sports jacket, no tie, over a lemon colored shirt tucked in cream colored slacks, William A. Rowe, Chief Coroner's Investigator for San Diego County, strolled into the morgue. A *Racing Form* peeked out from his jacket pocket, the sport section of the *San Diego Times* stayed tucked under his arm.

"The mysterious and sinister Dr. Fu Man Nguyen," he said. "What's up, doc?"

Dr. Nguyen motioned him over, pointed to the examining table.

"This guy wasn't in the water more than a day or so. The tissues have not gone into severe decomp and the parts of the corpse that have been attacked were those exposed."

Rowe walked around looking at the body. "Where's the other half of his left leg?"

"Probably in the gut of some big shark, judging from the way that the tibia and fibula have been sawed and the patterns of the rips below the knee."

"Pleasant thought."

"He was dead before he hit the water. Shot in the side of the head and dumped in the drink."

Dr. Nguyen pointed to an array of small items and a pile of tattered clothing. "I had a hard time keeping this ring out of Danny's pocket."

Dr. Nguyen tossed the ring to Rowe.

Catching it like an infielder, Rowe turned it in his fingers. "Very expensive. We should be able to get a trace on this."

"OK Bill," Dr. Nguyen said. "I got a stack of paper work. If you need any more from me, you know where to find me."

Rowe bent over the pile of tattered clothing.

Danny spoke from near his elbow. "Do you want me to bag up that stuff for you?"

Rowe dropped the ring into his pocket.

"No, Danny. I'll have a forensic team here in a little while to pick up everything. But, you can do us a big favor."

"What's that, Boss?"

"Make damn sure no one touches anything because it will be your ass if they do."

~*~*~

Forensics calling
San Diego County Forensic Lab,
2 days later, 3:22 PM, Wednesday, January, 15, 1975

The forensic lab was cramped, crowded with lab materials, examining stands, beakers and other items. In a corner of the cluttered room, Dennis Holly, the Coroner's Office's forensic technician spun his desk chair around, scooted to a nearby IBM typewriter, pecked out an entry, then rolled back to double-check the results. Satisfied, he grabbed a nearby phone, punched in the numbers.

"Bill? Denny. Can you come down here? Got something to show you."

Ten minutes later, Rowe walked into the lab without knocking.

"Anything good, Denny?" he said.

"I just finished the clothing," Holley said. "It's made from imported Scottish wool and high quality Japanese silk lining. The label was still preserved on the inside of the jacket."

"Yeah?"

"I've traced the label to one of the most exclusive tailors in Mexico City."

"So, we're talking big bucks."

"There's more– this is cool, incredibly cool. Inside the jacket pocket was a pack of smokes, Pall Malls. The pack had deteriorated from the sea water but I turned up a print off the cellophane wrapper."

"You're shitting me."

"I shit you not. What must have happened is the oil from the print was stained by the red dye from the pack and fixed to the cellophane. Lying squashed against the silk lining of the pocket, the sea water didn't dissolve it. There's enough left of the print that we can run it and I've already got it in the works. Let's see what the Feebees can do with it."

~*~*~

Back on the third floor of the Coroner's Office desks sat in islands faced each other with worn chairs drifting alongside. In a glass nook in the far corner of the room, Bill Rowe leaned back, feet in the seat of a chair beside his desk, staring once again at the folder in his hand.

When the phone on his desk rang. He growled, "Rowe," then recognized Helen Davis's voice.

"Remember those two prints we found in the case of the doctor with the broken neck?"

"Yeah?"

"We were looking over an abandoned yacht..."

"An abandoned yacht?"

"Yep. Someone boosted this yacht and then abandoned it in the ducklands south of Coronado. The Coast Guard found blood stains on the deck, then we got involved and found blood samples from four different individuals and full sets of prints of five people."

"Wow."

"But here's the best part. One of the prints matches the one we lifted from that Doctor's house."

"Fax that information over here to Denny Holly."

"It's done, baby. Call you back when I got more."

Rowe returned the phone to its cradle, then jumped when it rang.

"Yeah?"

Holly's voice chirruped,

"Bill. Come down here. Got something."

"On my way."

~*~*~

Rowe came crashing into the forensics lab.

"Whatcha got?" he said.

Denny cleared his throat, "Pull up a chair because this is good stuff."

Rubbing his hand over his thinning blond hair, he made a dramatic gesture like a conductor calling the orchestra to order.

"First, the suit. Got in touch with the tailors, Hafez Brothers of Mexico City. They code their labels so that when they make accessories, they have the customer's details. The guy's name is Antonio Volpez."

"Volpez. Doesn't mean anything to me."

"Ran the ring though my jeweler contact. It's distinctive, made in Turkey for a jewel seller who is in, are you ready for this?"

"Mexico City."

"Miami."

"Miami? Like Florida?"

"Damn sure ain't Miami, Ohio."

"Why would a Mexican hood buy a ring in Miami?" Rowe said.

Denny's light blue eyes sparkled like a hungry cat holding a fat bird.

"When I got the name, I contacted Mexico forensics who told me this guy Volpez is an enforcer for a Mexican drug Mafioso named Jacobo Fuchs."

"Fuchs. Sounds German."

"Or Jewish. Remember? A lot of the old Jewish Mafia, like Meyer Lansky and Bugsy Siegel had extensive connections in both Cuba and Mexico."

"Bingo! Miami. Cubans. Betcha this guy was a Cuban."

"We're good," Holly said. "Damn good."

"Got anything on that phantom print you lifted from the cigarette pack?' Rowe said.

"You bet. It matches the one that Helen sent me."

"No shit?"

"No shit."

"Any word yet on whose it is?"

"Nothing yet. But, the day is still young."

Rowe patted Holly on the shoulder.

"I owe you big time for this one, my man. Get me the reports at your earliest."

Denny grinned like a fox.

"Merry Christmas," he said. "Got the papers right here for you."

Rowe walked out of the lab, leafing through the stack of papers.

~*~*~

Dinner for two
Coroner's Office
Later that evening, 9:22 PM

Alone, Rowe wrote names on a blackboard, drew lines connecting them, then scrawled questions about each name.

Twiddling a pencil in his fingers, he heard the office door creak open.

Helen Davis made a grand entrance in a clinging red dress, matching shoes and handbag. A string of large white pearls circled her throat in contrast with her dark skin above an ample bosom. "Keeping some long hours, aincha Sweetie?" she said slipping into the chair beside Rowe's desk.

Rowe leaned back, enjoying the faint scent of her perfume.

"All in a day's work, Helen."

"So howcum you ain't home with your family?"

"Family? Twice divorced. Waiting to find a woman who'll put up with my work hours and playing the ponies."

"Well, since you so sweet, I decided to bring you a little something."

When he read the papers, he jumped to his feet, then cried out, "Sacred feces!"

"Yep," Helen said. "We've got a name and face to go with the prints we lifted."

"Here he is. Jorge Barrios. He's got a rap sheet."

He looked over at Helen.

"You made this guy, Antonio Volpez's prints too?" he said.

"His prints turned up on the yacht too. The Feds have a long rap sheet on him: Cuban, came to Miami after Castro, went very dirty then skipped to Mexico when the local vice moved in on him."

He looked over at her.

"This coulda waited until morning," Rowe said.

"So, get off your wild Irish ass and figure out where to feed a hungry girl from the 'hood," she said.

"You like fish?"

"Love 'em."

Rowe picked up his hat, put it on, took her arm.

"Come along, my dear. I know just the place."

~*~*~

Snake killer
Coast of Oaxaca, 25 km south of Acapulco
11:32 AM, Thursday, January 16, 1975

The moisture on the big white house's red tiled roof perched on the rugged cliffs over the sea, sparkled in the morning light. Overlooking the drop to the sea, a blue tile veranda extended from the house to the edge of the cliffs. Men in dark suits and sunglasses carrying automatic weapons strolled the perimeter of the veranda.

Lucero sat at a table, the plate of tamales, rice and beans, a glass of pineapple juice unattended in front of him. His attention fixed on papers in his hands. He looked up when a maid in a red skirt, white blouse came to the table.

"Sr. Drako's arrived, Sr. Alban," she said.

"Show him in."

"Would you wish for something else for breakfast?"

"Take it away."

Lucero focused again on the papers until Drako strolled out on the veranda.

Lucero waved to a chair.

"I've been going over the accounts since the old Zorro disappeared," he said.

"And?"

"Fuchs was screwing us blind, siphoning off huge sums and sticking them in a bunch of off-shore banks."

"How do we stand now?"

"We got enough cash on hand to settle the big shipment of heroin the Russians are bringing into Monterrey. By then, Montoya will have tracked down these rat-holes that the Zorro set up."

Drako turned his head, looked out over the surf. "He found out that rattlesnakes eat rats."

"Yes, I have to admit," Lucero said. "That one went off very smoothly."

"I was skeptical," Drako said. "I couldn't see how one man could take out the Zorro and his shields without a war."

Lucero gave a little laugh. "Oh, ye of little faith."

Drako took out his silver cigarette case, selected a gold-ringed Turkish cigarette, lit it with his silver lighter.

"So, what do we do about the snake?" he said.

Returning his gaze to the accounting papers, Lucero murmured, "Rattlers are very dangerous. We Mexicans kill them."

"Definitely a loose end that could snap back at us."

Lucero nodded, then called out,

"Adelita!"

The maid came out again. "Sr. Alban?"

"Have Mauricio come."

When she left, Drako wrinkled his face.

"You're thinking of sending Mauricio to whack the rattler?"

"It will take some real talent to put this guy down. Here's Mauricio."

In his perpetual dark blue suit, white shirt, black narrow tie, the big man moved across the veranda with an athlete's grace. Unlike his fellows, Mauricio seldom wore sunglasses.

"You called for me, Señor Alban?" he said.

"I want you to take a trip to California and arrange an accident for a Mr. Barrios," Lucero said

"The one they call the Rattler?"

"The same."

"When do you want this taken care of, Sr. Alban?"

"Leave tonight, Take your time setting it up."

"Be careful," Drako said. "This guy's damn dangerous."

Mauricio smiled.

"So am I, Mr. Drako," he said.

~*~*~

More news
San Diego County Coroner's Office
Same day, 3:16 PM, Thursday

Bill Rowe's desk phone startled his attention away from his *Racing Form* where an interesting horse was scheduled to run that weekend at Hialeah Park.

"Rowe."

"Bill, Denny. This guy Volpez worked for this Fuchs guy, right?"

"Yeah."

"My Mexican connection tells me Fuchs is missing and for all intents and purposes may have skipped the country."

Rowe dropped the racing form, sat up straight in his chair.

"Damn!" he said. "This Barrios guy offed Fuchs and Volpez."

"Huh? What makes you think that?"

"Barrios was on that yacht along with Volpez and Fuchs. I'm getting back to Helen on this right now."

Rowe punched the numbers for CSI.

"Helen. Can you get in touch with anybody and find out if any of those prints might belong to a guy named Jacobo Fuchs. What? You did? They do. No shit!"

Around the room, people stared at Rowe, jumping up and down.

"Get right back to you," Rowe said. "Gotta call someone."

~*~*~

Shared information
DEA's California task force, Los Angeles, CA
Same day, 3:22 PM, Thursday

Assistant Director Dan James tapped his pencil on a yellow pad in front of him during the meeting of the War on Mexican Drug Trafficking Task Force. Having slept little the night before, he forced his attention to the speaker's droning presentation.

Carla, his section's secretary entered, handed him a note.

"Thanks," he mumbled, ignoring a disapproving look from his department head.

After reading the note, he spoke out,

"Excuse me, Dick. I've just received something that we all ought to hear."

The department head, Gene Fredson frowned at him.

"What's so important that it can't wait until after the briefing?"

James ran to the door.

"Carla," he shouted. "Can you reconnect me with that last call? Great. When it comes in, pass it through to the speaker phone in the conference room. Thank you."

Returning to the table. James said, "Sorry. You all need to hear this for yourselves."

Fredson frowned, thumped his fingers on the table.

The phone rang.

"I've put you on conference mode, Bill," James said. "You can share your information with all of the task force."

"Gentlemen, a few days ago some local fishermen retrieved a half-eaten corpse from off the coast of California and turned it over to us," Rowe said. "After a standard forensic, we've determined it's the body of one Antonio Volpez."

"Did he say 'Volpez?'" Fredson said.

"That's right, Volpez," Rowe went on. "Our investigation also turned up a stolen yacht with blood stains and prints. We've identified those of Volpez, Fuchs and a couple of his goons with matches from the Mexican National Police."

"Fuchs? Dead?" Fredson gasped.

Rowe continued. "We've cross-typed Volpez and are working on the rest but we found something else that spins this entire pile of evidence."

"What's that?" James said.

"A loose print on the personal effects of Volpez survived being in the water and matches one from the yacht, a local enforcer named Jorge Barrios. We've also established he's involved in other drug-linked killings."

"OK, but what makes you think Fuchs is dead?" Fredson thundered.

"His chief bodyguard's damn sure dead," Rowe said. "His blood's on the yacht and we got the tracks of a professional who's likely whacked him as well."

"That's hardly conclusive," Fredson said.

"I'll leave that one in your backyard, sir," Rowe said. "Just sharing what we've found."

"This has been great, Bill," James said. "Thank you so much for getting the word to us."

"My pleasure. Bye."

Fredson wrinkled his face. "What do you think, Dan?"

"I think Fuchs is out of the picture. Which means Alban and Drako now control the wherewithal and finances. The banking and money laundering operation were the old guy's life insurance. They must have done an end run and got control over the bank accounts."

"And, you think this info from this coroner guy is solid?"

"As solid as it gets, sir."

"Alright, gentlemen," Fredson said. "Run with it."

He left the room.

Dan James went to the head of the table, tore off the page on the flip chart, wrote names in squares on the paper.

~*~*~

Death of a conspiracy
Pepe Ortega's house, East Los Angeles
Same day, 8:16 PM, Thursday, January 16, 1975

The strains of Pepe Romero's rendition of Rodrigo's *Aranjuez* filled the darkened room. A swatch of light lit Pepe's book where he sat in the overstuffed chair, feet on the suttee.

The phone's jarring ring, shattered the guitar music.

"This is Pepe."

"Pepe, Bill Rowe. Sorry to intrude on your evening..."

Rowe related all the recent events, the discovery of Antonio's body, uncovering the fingerprints.

"You think this same person is involved in Maggie Connall's death?" Pepe said.

"The fact this guy's fingerprints keep popping up sure suggests some kind of drug killing," Rowe said. "Barrio's a pro but sometimes even the pros get careless."

"How can I help?"

"You said you might have some ideas about connections to a Mexican drug cartel. So, could we get together with friends of mine from the San Diego PD and the DEA to kick around some possibilities?"

"I'd be pleased to meet with you."

"How about we come up to meet with you? You're mid-point between all of us."

"Sounds good. When?"

"Day after tomorrow OK?"

"Yes. Come up for lunch. I know a Mexican restaurant where we can meet."

"Just as long as the food is good."

"This is the Topaztlan on Broad street and 23rd. The owner's brother is the chef. They're from my home state in Mexico."

"Fantastic. We'll see you there at noon, day after tomorrow."

Pepe hung up, sat for a while, chin in his hand.

Well, there goes Ruth's Santos Villalobos conspiracy.

~*~*~

Some Mexican food
Topaztlan Restaurant, East Los Angeles
11:17 AM, Sunday, January 19, 1975

Topaztlan restaurant stood like a Mexican beacon at the corner of Broad Street and 23rd. White table clothed booths and tables were topped with woven thatch place mats, spotted with place settings wrapped in white napkins.

Spicy dish smells scented the air. The soft melody of the old Mexican love song, *Usted*, hung in the air.

Walking into the main dining room Pepe embraced a man in dark slacks, a white guayabera shirt.

"Your health, Don Paquin," Pepe said. "You received my request for a meeting place?"

"To be sure," the owner said. "Come this way."

He led Pepe to a room at the rear set off of the main dining room with a white and red flowered curtain. "You'll be comfortable here and not disturbed."

Five minutes later, Don Paquin ushered in Bill Rowe in his ever-present straw hat, accompanied by an attractive African-American woman in a dark blue dress.

Rowe introduced Pepe to Helen Davis when the curtain parted again. Don Paquin showed in a tall African-American man in a dark blue suit, a red and yellow striped tie over his white shirt.

"Hi, Dan," Rowe said.

After introductions, they all sat down.

"I feel like I already know all of you," James said.

Pepe raised his hand.

"First, we eat. You guys are on my turf now and have to respect the rules. Mexicans never talk on an empty stomach."

Having not taken her eye off Dan James, Helen Davis said,

"Sounds fine. How about ordering for me?"

"How spicy do you like your food?" Pepe said.

"Sugar, this sister's from the ghetto. They don't make it too hot."

"I can't eat onions," Rowe said. "A rare allergy. Outside of that, there's no problem."

"I'll put my appetite in your hands. Pepe, "James said.

"Only, you have to let us handle the tab," Rowe said. "Today's meal's brought to you by the taxpayers of San Diego County."

"Well then," Pepe said. "We'll have the best."

The food pleased everybody. Helen Davis saved half of hers for later.

The dishes were cleared. Dan James spoke first,

"We've confirmed that Jacobo Fuchs has fallen out of sight after going on a fishing trip."

Rowe handed them each a folder.

"These are the records and photos we've put together. We're getting warrants to pick up Barrios."

"Do we have a fix on him?" Helen said.

"He does have a current California driver's license and an address," Rowe said.

Pepe stared at Jorge Barrios's photo.

"I've seen this guy somewhere before," he said.

"Friends, contacts, ideas?" Rowe said "Anything can help..."

Pepe closed the folder. "It'll come to me."

Glancing at his watch, Dan James said, "Gotta get back. I'll be in touch as soon as anything crosses my desk."

He smiled over at Helen, his voice soft when he spoke, "It was nice making your acquaintance, Helen."

"Same here."

Rowe stood. "Dan. Always a pleasure."

Pepe wrung James's hand. "Nice to meet at last."

James hurried out the curtain.

Rowe looked over at Helen. "You'd met him before?"

"Just talked on the phone," she said. "Why?"

Rowe rolled his eyes at Pepe. "I just got the impression you two were old friends."

Helen's eye brows shot up, her hand went to her hip.

"What do you mean?" she said.

"He did seem quite taken with you," Pepe said.

Rowe nodded. "Struck me that way too."

Helen snorted, picked up her bag. "A woman meets an attractive man and everybody goes ga-ga over the event."

Rowe wrinkled his nose. "Didn't have that effect on me. Did you react that way, Pepe."

"Not really."

Helen threw up her hands. "Men. You'd agree with each other on anything."

~*~*~

Back in his home, Pepe sat the folder on his desk, looked once more at its contents, staring again at Jorge Barrios's picture.

I know you, cabrón. But, from where?

The phone rang. "Hello this is Pepe."

The voice was stressed, tearful.

"Pepe, this is Lyla. Someone assaulted Ray last night. He's in the hospital."

"No! What happened?"

"Some man attacked him in the parking lot when he was getting in his car. Campus security found him unconscious."

"How bad is it?"

"He's conscious now and has been asking for you. Can you come?"

"Of course, Lyla. I'll book a flight and be there tomorrow. I'll call and let you know when, OK?"

"Thank you, Pepe. You're a friend."

"No, Lyla. Were family."

He reached for a rolodex of phone numbers, found the one he wanted, dialed.

"Hello, Heidi. Pepe Ortega. How soon can you book me a flight for El Paso, Texas tonight? Excellent. I'll come right over and pick up the tickets. Yes, I'll need a car there but I'll be coming home the same day. Thank you."

He dialed another number.

"Gary? Pepe. Can you cancel my classes until the weekend. I have a family emergency and will be gone a couple of days. Thanks, *hermano*. I owe you."

After hanging up the phone, he sat for a long staring at the photo in the folder in front of him.

~*~*~

Rough stuff
Mercy Hospital, El Paso, Texas
Next day, 10:47 AM, Monday, January 20, 1975

Pepe followed Lyla Errol through the door to the Hospital's ICU, a large room filled with light green curtains, setting each unit off from the others. Inside one of these sections, Pepe saw Ray Errol lying on a raised bed. A tube descended from his nose, IV tubes sprang from his arm. His eyes and cheeks were a map of spotted stitched abrasions. An open face cranial cast circled his head. The white of one of his eyes showed blood red bruising against the purple, red blotches on his face.

He looked up when they came in.

Pepelote," he whispered. "Man, I knew you'd be hitting on my woman as soon as I got tossed in the slammer."

Lyla kissed him, gave a sweeping slap at his arm. "Behave. I don't want to have to kick your butt in front of company."

"Better do as she says, *hermano*," Pepe said. "She's tough."

Lyla fussed over him like a mother hen, pulling his sheet straight, arranging his pillows. "How're you doing today, Sweetie?"

"Ready for round two with that big Mex," Ray wheezed.

Lyla shook her head. "Men."

She turned to Pepe.

"I'll leave you two alone. Don't overtire him. He's got no sense."

"We know that," Pepe said.

When she stepped out, Pepe pulled his chair next to the bed.

"Can you talk?" he said.

"I'll give you all I got."

"I'll ask. Give me short answers."

"Hey, you're the cop."

"Tell me about the guy who grabbed you."

"Big bastard. Definitely, Chicano."

"How do you know?"

"The clothes, the hair, the shades, the face and the voice."

"He spoke?"

"Yeah, said, 'You going' down, motherfucker.' "

"Voice?"

"Deep, male, Barrio lilt."

"What happened then?"

"He rapped me, a bunch of times, something hard, like a pipe."

"What happened next?"

"I popped him in the side of his head with my briefcase."

"Remember anything else?"

"Naw, I passed out. Woke up here."

"You musta hurt him," Pepe said. "Lyla said campus security saw the guy. I'll talk to them but I think you saved your life when you hit him."

"Hope his fucking head hurts as much as mine."

"He didn't go for your wallet?"

"Naw. He wasn't after money?"

"What do you mean?"

"This has to do with that Santos Villalobos inquiry."

"Huh?"

"Couple of weeks back I get a call from this LA lawyer. Warns me any character attacks on Villalobos would be considered libel."

"What lawyer?"

"Name was Cortez."

"What did you say to him?"

"Told him my work was strictly ethnographic. I didn't give a shit about his client."

Pepe sat in thought before he spoke.

"Did you ever hear of anything about a Mexican drug cartel called the 'Unholy Trinity.' "

"Naw, Pepe," Ray said. "We used to blow a little weed when we were younger, but now Lyla won't let anything stronger than aspirin around with the kids and all."

"Not what I mean. Did you ever come across any connection to the Mexican Mafia?"

"Never heard of them."

"So, how do you tie this to Santos Villalobos?"

"When you step outside into dogshit, you know a dog's been in your yard."

"I'm gonna get Lyla back in here and do some poking around. Sorry you're caught up in some bad shit here."

"So am I."

"I'll see you, *hermano*."

Ray caught Pepe's hand.

"Pepe."

"Yes?"

"Nail that sonfabitch for me."

"Count on it."

~*~*~

The campus police office at the State University of El Paso occupied a basement section of the tall administrative building. Pepe went down the stairs, showed his identification to the clerk at the black vinyl counter, then she ushered him into the watch captain's office.

Captain Immanuel Gutierrez, a big man, clean shaven with a buzz cut and two cauliflower ears, shook Pepe's hand.

"I can't tell you how distressed we are at this," he said. "Dr. Errol's a big favorite around here."

"I was wondering if you might have anything to add," Pepe said.

Gutierrez picked up a folder. "The patrol attendant saw the attack, called it in and immediately went to the aid of Dr. Errol."

"Did he get a look at the attacker."

"Yes, she did. I'll have her come in."

"Was there a forensics done on the attack site?" Pepe said.

The Captain shook his buzz cut head, "Just a routine investigation. Here's Martha."

A large framed woman, over six foot tall with broad shoulders stepped in the door. Her long braided dark hair rolled tight in a bun at the back of her head, her dark eyes and skin revealed her Native American background. Gripping Pepe's hand, she looked straight into his eyes, her face devoid of expression.

"Martha Hewana, sir," she said.

"Thank you, Martha."

She notched her dark eyebrows in a slight knit.

"For what?"

"Saving my friend's life for one, your quick thinking for another. Did you get a look at the assailant?"

"Damn sure did. If I'da been carrying, I'da shot the sonfabitch."

"Any details?"

"Nothing more than is in my report. I was making my rounds that night and saw what looked like a scuffle next to a car in the faculty lot. Then I saw this big guy clubbing Dr. Errol with something. I called for back-up as I went after the guy. About the time I got outta my pickup, Dr. Errol smacked his attacker in the side of the head with his metal briefcase."

"What happened next?"

"The guy stumbled back holding his head. Then he spotted me and bolted off over the lawn toward the street. I saw Dr. Errol lying there and went to him. By the time the patrolmen got there, the dirty shit had got away."

"Can you describe him?"

"Big man. Likely Latino. Wore shades, a light jacket, gray over black pants. Hair was black, long, combed back. Looked like he was wearing tennis shoes."

"And they didn't do a forensics?"

"There wasn't a lot there, "Gutierrez said. "All the blood was Dr. Errol's.

"Our main concern was to get him to the hospital," Martha said.

"Did you find the weapon?"

"No." The big woman shook her head. "The attacker musta wagged it off."

"Thanks for your help," Pepe said. "I'll keep you informed if I find out anything."

Martha stood, shook Pepe's hand.

"Ray Errol's a pal," she said. "If I coulda got my hands on that slimy sonfabitch, I'da pounded his head to shit."

Pepe looked into her dark, unsmiling eyes.

"I believe you," he said.

~.*~.*~

Protect the meal ticket
Upper Marigold Drive, East Los Angeles, CA
Same day, 10:47 AM, Monday

Under a covered deck in back of the house, Santos looked up at Nacho sitting next to Lola.

"So," Santos said. "You beat this guy up and took off."

"Kinda like that," Nacho said.

Lola yelled at her brother, "Goddamit, you bungholed it again. Now, everything's worse."

Shifting his cracked sunglasses, Nacho rubbed the bruised side of his face.

"Sorry, man," he said.

"¡Pendejo!" Lola yelled again.

"Cops showed up," Nacho said. "Had to split."

"Too late now for instant replays," Santos said.

"Yeah, man," Nacho said, looking down at his shoes. "Shit got complicated fast."

"I know about that," Santos said.

"Things are going so well," Lola said. "All that shit from the Anthro Association has both your other books flying off the shelves."

"So, what's the problem? "Santos said.

"The problems are a lot of loose ends." Lola said.

"How so?" Santos said.

"You said Spyner told you there was only one copy, and no one'd seen it but his professor," Lola said.

"And his girlfriend."

"How do we know he wasn't just bullshiting you."

"How do I know he wasn't just bullshiting me the other night?"

"We don't!" Lola screamed. "Do you want to stake everything we've got on a pile of loose ends?"

She turned back to Nacho.

"Homeboy here fucked up by not taking that guy out."

"Hey, man," Nacho said. "Don't lay all that shit off on me."

"You're screwing up didn't help either, turdhead," Lola snapped back.

Santos rose, walked towards the door with his hands in his pockets.

"Ray Errol doesn't know anything," he said. "The only loose end is Ruth Hall."

"The girl friend?" Lola said.

Santos stopped at the door, stared at the ground for a time, then looked back up at them.

"I'm gonna let Cassie handle the funds and we'll split to Brazil."

Lola startled. "Brazil?"

"Brazil," Santos said. "No extradition, more bang for your buck. With our income, we can live like royals."

"Hey man," Nacho said. "I don't speak Brazilian."

"Portuguese, you ignorant shit." Lola said.

"Don't speak no Portuguese either."

"It's close enough to Spanish that in a year, you'll be speaking it just fine." Santos said.

"OK, we split," Lola said. "But we need to cover our asses damn good before we get the hell out."

"I got a headache," Santos said. "I'm going to take a nap."

Santos went inside, shut the heavy door behind him.

~*~*~

Without looking at her brother, Lola spoke, "We gotta take that broad out."

"What broad?"

"Ruth Hall. The one that's bugging Santos."

"Oh, that broad."

"We'll get outta here but with no loose strings."

Lola went to the door, peeked through it, then came back to her brother.

"We keep Santos out of this," she said.

"Cool."

"We still got that shack outside of El Centro?"

"Yeah."

"What kinda shape's it in?"

"Everything's cool. We got the electricity on and even a phone."

"If we snatch that bitch, haul her over there, we can get to the bottom of this manuscript bullshit," Lola's said.

"Dunno about all this 'manuscript bullshit,' but we can do it."

Lola looked back at the door where Santos had gone inside.

"In the meantime," she said, "we'll get Santos to hang out in Cassie's cabin up at Rice Canyon. Nobody knows about this but us."

"But Lo, he's still gonna have to talk to that broad about the manuscript. I dunno shit about it. Neither do you."

Pursing her lips, Lola didn't make a sound for a minute.

"OK," she said. "We snatch her, take her out to the shack and then get Santos to meet us there. Once we get the shit straight with this twat, then he'll get his ass back to Rice Canyon."

"Cool," Nacho said. "If there's any clean up, he's off the set."

Lola went to her purse on the table, took out a pencil and writing pad.

"OK," she said. "Here's the way I see this thing going down…"

Nacho leaned over, giving her his complete attention.

~*~*~

A name recalled
Frontier Air, flight 2220 en route to Los Angeles
Same day, 10:44 PM, Monday

In the darkened airplane on the flight home, Pepe tried to sleep. Failing that, he tried the crossword puzzle in the airline magazine. After a few minutes, he stuffed the magazine into the seat pocket in front of him, leaned back, closed his eyes.

He jerked awake. Flight attendants were checking seat belts, tray tables and seat positions for landing. Looking around to gathered his things, Pepe stopped, froze.

He remembered someone.

"Rudy Reyes, the SuperMex," he muttered.

Another job offer
Jorge's Apartment, El Cajon, CA
Same day, 7:15 PM, Monday

Jorge Barrios sat in the chair under the light of the lamp. Eliot Fisk playing Francisco Tarrega's *Adelita* competed with salsa and Mariachi bleeding in from the outside. The book, Bertrand Russell's *Unpopular Essays,* held his attention until the phone rang.

He waited until Fisk completed *Adelita* before picking up the receiver.

"Yeah?"

"Mr. Barrios. John Rydell. Would it be possible for you to come by tomorrow? We have a job for you."

"Can't. Day after tomorrow, 1:30."

"Excellent. See you here then."

Jorge hung up, returned to reading his book, listening to Fisk's guitar playing.

~*~*~

Missed appointment
Anthropology office, Madison University, East San Diego, CA
Next day, 3:47 PM, Tuesday, January 21, 1975

The white stucco buildings with red tile roofs of Madison University of San Diego lay among the hills above the city. In a patio surrounded by curved column-supported archways, Lola Santiago in a black dress, hair pinned at the back paced her way into the anthropology department.

A secretary near the entrance looked up at her.

"May I help you?" she said.

Lola flashed a press card.

"Carmen Lopez with the *El Cajon Tribune*. I'm supposed to interview Dr. Hall."

"I'm afraid she's not on campus this semester."

"Oh no! We'd scheduled this interview for this morning."

Looking over at the Admin Assistant, the secretary said, "Jerri, do you know where Ruth is?"

"Out at her field site," Jerri said.

"Even better," Lola said. "I can get some photos. Where is this place?"

"Haven't the foggiest" Jerri said without looking up.

A student assistant in levis and a dungaree shirt inserting mail in the faculty mailboxes, looked over at Lola.

"I know how to get there," she said.

Pulling out a pen and pad, Lola jotted down the directions, then rushed out the door saying, "Thanks," over her shoulder.

~*~*~

Jake Spyner
East Los Angeles State University, Los Angeles, CA
Nest day, 10:22 AM, Wednesday, January 22, 1975

Unlocking his office, Pepe came in, set his briefcase on the floor, plopped into his chair. Leaning back in the subdued light, he reflected on his recent trip to see his friend. A knock at the door brought him back to attention.

"Come in," he said.

A big man stuck his head inside the door. "Professor Ortega?" "Please come in."

Standing 6'2", over 220 lbs., he wore levis, a long sleeved shirt, brown western boots. Pepe noted a wide, triangular burn scar on his left cheek.

"I'm Jake," the man said. "Matthew Spyner's brother."

Pepe rose, shook his hand.

"My condolences on your loss," he said. "Believe me, I understand."

"I heard you lost a brother too."

Pepe flinched, motioned to a chair.

"How did you know?"

"I was in Santa Luisita and had a long conversation with Captain Ramirez."

"Oh?"

Jake took a note book along with a small tape recorder out of the case in his hand.

"Have you talked to Ruth Hall?" he said.

"Not in the last few days."

"Did she tell you about her suspicions?"

"Many times," Pepe said.

"I think Santos Villalobos's involved too," Jake said.

Pepe drew a long, slow deep breath.

"A week ago," he said, "I'd not have believed you."

"A week ago I'd not have believed me either," Jake said, "But, that was before I went to Mexico."

"Talk to me," Pepe said.

Jake opened his note book.

"Years ago I got a call from Ruth– she and Matt were close at one time."

"She told me."

Jake stopped, his eyes misting, then went on,

"Matt was always on the edge– our family was delighted when he went off to New Mexico to study anthropology. When he got involved with Ruth, we were ecstatic."

"I see."

"Matt was bright but hard to get along with– his relationship with Ruth went on and off. Then one day, Ruth gives me a call that he'd showed up at her door with a thesis about learning how to be a *brujo*."

"You speak Spanish, Jake."

"Raised on the Tex-Mex border– spoke Spanish since we were kids."

"So, what happened next?"

"Ruth said that Matt had a falling out with his professor and took off to Mexico. A few months after that, we got the word that he'd disappeared. So, Ruth and I went to Mexico, talked to Captain Ramirez, then picked up some of Matt's personal things, including a box of ashes that we thought was his burnt thesis."

"I was in Santa Luisita after my brother was killed," Pepe said. "Captain Ramirez mentioned blood on the floor and furniture."

"The blood matched Matt's, but as there was no evidence of foul play, I came home and threw all this stuff in my shed."

"What happened then?"

"As an arson investigator, I've an intuition about unstable people. I didn't buy that Matt was dead. I loved my brother but knew chasing after him would've been a waste of time."

"So, you never heard from him again?"

Jake choked, then went on,

"Ruth called earlier and told me that she'd heard from someone claiming to be Matt. Told her he'd been in Chile. Then, I got the call from the cops."

"I'm so sorry."

Jake wiped his eyes.

"Taking care of the funeral arrangements, Ruth told me about all this Santos Villalobos business."

"So, you didn't know about the stolen thesis or the book?"

Jake turned his eyes away.

"I never read crap like that," he said. "I'm too busy cleaning up the messes these assholes leave behind."

"After you talked to Ruth, what did you do?"

"I had one of our lab techs in arson forensics look at the ashes. He told me the fiber residues that hadn't completely burned weren't notebook paper-- they were burnt book and newspaper pages."

"So, the burning was just a ruse."

"My guess is that this Santos swiped his thesis then burned a pile of papers to make it look like the thesis was burned."

"Where's any solid evidence to get Santos into the picture?" Pepe said.

Jake picked up the tape recorder.

"I talked to the hotel clerk," he said. "Nothing. But the old cleaning lady had a memory like an elephant. Listen to this."

He set the recorder down, pushed *play*. The questions and answers were in Spanish,

Jake: Maria, can you recall that day you discovered the bloody room?

Maria: Yes sir. I had to work. it was the first day of Holy Week and I wanted to be in the procession with my relatives, but what can a poor person do but work. So, in spite of the fact that I wanted to be at the church, I came in to work early that morning.

Jake: What did you find?

Maria: When I knocked on the door, I saw it was open. When I went in– O my God, what a mess! Tables, chairs, plates were thrown all over. Then I saw that blood on the floor and chair. I was sure someone was killed. So, I went to the manager.

Jake: Did you know the man who lived in the room?

Maria: I'd seen him many times. He was very strange. Always looked hungry, scared like a coyote. Always wore the same clothes. He spoke Spanish very well, like you.

Jake: When was the last time you saw him?

Maria: The night before. I work sometimes in Ovelardo's cantina and he was there that night drinking and talking to the other American.

Jake: (pause) What other American?

Maria: I don't know. I'd never seen him before.

Jake: What did this American look like?

Maria: He looked like a Mexican.

Jake: What do you mean?

Maria: Well, Americans look different. The guy who lived in the apartment, he was a Gringo. You know, light skinned, blue eyes, typical Gringo-- like you. But this other guy looked more like a Mexican.

Jake: How do you know he was an American?

Maria: His clothes were American, he talked Spanish like an American Mexican– besides, the way he cut his hair, his mannerisms were American.

Jake: Did you get a good look at him.

Maria: Oh, yes. I was cleaning tables. I saw him up close.

Jake: Did you catch any of their conversation?

Maria: I don't remember anything they said.

Jake: Can you describe this Mexican-looking American?

Maria: He was shorter than the Gringo, maybe one and a quarter meters, chubby, long black hair combed straight, big dark eyes, a fleshy, bulbous nose and acne scars on his cheeks.

Jake turned off the tape recorder.

"I'd brought a magazine photo of Santos Villalobos. I showed it to her and she was pretty sure it was the same man."

"So, we can put him there at the time which means he had an opportunity to steal the thesis."

"I'm convinced." Jake said. "That's why I took along that picture of Santos in case someone might remember."

"You know we're a long way from making a case that any DA would take seriously. I'm ashamed to say that Ruth had told me that Santos was involved in all of this, but I was so focused on this drug cartel that I didn't buy it."

"Drug cartel?" Jake said. "Matt wouldn't have had anything to do with that. He was a user, but a real puritan about drug dealers."

"I never associated your brother with them. It goes back to my father's investigations."

"Ruth told you that Santos was involved somehow?"

"Not with these drug guys. She said Santos was involved in Matt's disappearance."

Jake put his hand to his head. "This is confusing."

Pepe brightened, raised his finger for emphasis.

"It is but it's starting to clear up for me," he said. "Lemme make a phone call."

~*~*~

Job details

Law Offices: Rydell, Le, Cortez &Yoshizumi, Los Angeles, CA
Same day, 1:35 PM, Wednesday

Jorge came into the office, molded sunglasses hiding his hazel eyes. The young African American receptionist with green and black nails, smiled at him.

"May I help you?" she said.

"I'm here to see Rydell."

"Do you have an appointment?"

"Yeah."

"Your name, sir?'

"Smith. Joe Smith."

She checked her appointment calendar, punched a number.

"Mr. Rydell. Mr. Smith is here for his 1:30."

She looked up at Jorge, a smile painted on her face. "Someone'll be right out."

One of the four doors circling the reception area opened. An older gray-haired woman in a polka-dot print dress came out, extended her hand to Jorge, said, "Hello, I'm Angela, Mr. Rydell's personal secretary. Come this way, please."

Jorge followed her through the door into a large office. Angela opened the door, ushered Jorge in.

John Rydell came around from behind the desk. "Hey, amigo."

Standing 5'4", dressed in a tailored dark blue suit, a bright red tie over a light blue shirt, Rydell's shined cordovan oxfords sparkled in the overhead light as he embraced the larger, unresponsive Jorge.

"Coffee?"

"I'm fine."

Rydell indicated a chair for Jorge, then plopped in his own, leaning back with his foot on the edge of his desk.

"Our clients were so impressed with how you took care of things we have some more work for you."

"Talk to me."

Rydell handed Jorge a slip of paper.

"The guy who lives there's causing a lot of trouble for our friends. We'd like you to insure that he won't be a bother anymore."

"50 large."

Rydell picked up an envelope, handed it to Jorge.

"Expenses, plus. This guy works nights at card clubs. He'll be showing there about 4:00 AM. We'll settle later."

Jorge looked at his watch. "Tonight, then?"

"Excellent," Rydell said.

Jorge stood. Rydell came around from behind the big desk and led Jorge to the door.

Rydell said, "Cassie's got your numbers, right?"

Jorge looked at Rydell like he was a numbskull, then left without a goodbye.

~*~*~

Rydell closed the door, brushed his hand over his coiffured hair. He snatched up the phone, dialed a number. It rang. A click at the pick-up, then Lucero's voice,

"Bueno."

"It's me," Rydell said. "He bit."

"Problems?"

"None at all."

"Did he say anything?"

"Not a word... he's a cold fish."

"Too bad to lose this guy," Lucero said. "He could have done OK in our organization."

"Wanna bring him in?"

"He's a loner, too smart. And now, he knows too much."

"Well, it's in hand, Luis."

"Excellent. Get back to me when Mauricio gets things done."

~*~*~

Jorge paid cash to rent a car, drove straight to nearby Norwalk, found the address, an old building off a side street.

Parking the car, he walked past the tenement without giving it a glance. Around the block, he found the alleyway that ran behind the building then jogged down to the rear of the tenement.

It was an old fashioned building with an iron grated fire escape. Climbing up on a dumpster, Jorge seized the lower rung of the sliding ladder, shuffled up the ladder to the third floor, then peered through the window. The hallway inside was empty.

The old fashioned lock on the window presented no problem, he pushed the thin jimmy tool through the jamb crack, sliding back the seal. Opening the window, he made his way down the hall to the target's apartment.

The doors were old with no over-seals. Jorge worked the latch back over the strike plate with a credit card, entered a dark deserted room, looked around. No signs of anyone living there met his gaze.

Thought so. Dust on the fixtures. Cobwebs in the corners.

Jorge left just like he came in.

~*~*~

At the dig site
Los Medanos State Park, San Diego County, CA
Same day, 3:24 PM, Wednesday

Twenty miles south of Coronado below the US Naval Station lies Los Medanos State Park, a series of shrub covered canyons rolled along the coast. One of these ravines, closed to the public, opens to the rocky shore where tide pools with sandy areas sprawl among the dark gray rocks.

An old rocky pathway twists up a steep hill from the shore to a grassy meadow, surrounded by trees and bushes. A rushing creek cuts through the area descending into the sea parallel to the path.

At the end of the meadow connecting to the path, dressed in military camouflage fatigues, her hair pulled back under a cap, Lola watched twelve workers pockmarking the ground with excavation trenches from the bushes adjoining the clearing. Nacho crouched beside her, his dark hair tucked under a black hair net.

Her attention fixed on a campsite pitched at the other end of the grassy flat, three hundred yards away from the digging area, along the creek. The flap of one tent was pulled back.

Inside, Lola saw Ruth Hall dressed in shorts at a table cataloging artifacts.

"In the tent– that's her," Lola whispered.

Nacho squinted in the direction she was pointing.

"Man, there's a lot of people hanging around," he said. "How're we going to grab her?"

Motioning for Nacho to follow Lola pulled back, moving through the bushes like a cat, her brother stumbling after.

Twice she gave him angry gestures to be quiet. Coming to a clearing where a stand of trees blocked the view from the campsite, she pointed to a trio of Porta Potti chemical toilets.

"They set these crappers out here for privacy," she said.

"You mean, grab her here?" Nacho said.

"Yes. Now, get your ass in those bushes over there."

Connections
East Los Angeles Youth Center, West Los Angeles, CA
Same day, 4:22 AM, Wednesday

Pepe led Jake through the door to the secretary in front of the Director's office.

"Good morning, Esperanza," he said. "Rudy in?"

Esperanza flashed him a smile. "Always in for you, Dr. Ortega."

When she went into her director's office, Pepe whispered to Jake,

"I want you in on this."

Rodolfo Reyes, a bear storming out of his cave, popped open the office door, embraced Pepe.

"Beloved, honored and respected professor, Dr. Pepe Ortega."

After giving Pepe a rib-cracking squeeze.

Indicating his companion, Pepe said, "Jake Spyner, arson investigator, meet SuperMex Rodolfo Reyes– community coordinator for the Barrio Youth Program of the Urban league."

"Hello Rudy," Jake said.

"Welcome to the den of the SuperMex," Rudy said. "Esperanza, bring us some coffee."

Ushering the two men into his spacious office, Rudy plopped down in an armchair in front of a couch. Esperanza sat a tray with a coffee server, three cups along with a plate of cookies on the the flat table.

Rudy poured coffee into the cups.

"Esteemed and distinguished Professor Ortega," he said. "How can the old SuperMex be of service to his beloved friend and brother?"

"We can speak Spanish," Jake said.

"Rudy," Pepe said. "Let me apologize for that confrontation business with Alban."

"No apology necessary, brother. It was great publicity. Now we get his money without his snooping to see how we spend it."

"So, how'd you connect with such a deep pocket in the first place?" Pepe said.

"His lawyer called me."

"Here in LA?"

"John Rydell. Handles a number of Mexican Mafia clients' interests here in the States. Alban's the biggest."

"You knew him before?"

"A year or so ago, I did lunch with Rydell's partner, Cassie. Mentioned we could use some help getting kids off the street. As he's from the Barrio, said he'd look into it. A few months ago, got a call from Rydell's secretary and got the bucks."

"Cassie?"

"Casimiro Cortez. Rydell's junior partner."

"Is he connected to the Mexican Mobs too?"

"Naw. He's got a fat cat client that keeps him in a Mercedes."

"Hollywood?"

"A writer. Shacked up with Cassie's cousin, Lola Santiago."

"The political shaker and mover?"

"The same."

"Who's the writer?"

"One of your boys, the anthropologist alternative reality guru, Santos Villalobos."

Pepe stared at Jake for a few seconds, then retrieved a folder from his briefcase.

"Rudy," Pepe said. "Ever hear of a guy named Jorge Barrios?"

"*El cascabel*?" Rodolfo said. "Hell yes."

"The Rattler?"

"His nickname. He's from the San Diego barrio and was in the marines with Nacho Santiago."

"Who's he?"

"Lola's brother."

"How do you know about him?" Pepe said.

"When he was a kid Nacho ran with the local LA gangs. At age 18, the court told him to choose: military or jail. He hooked up with Barrios in there. Barrios did hard time for nearly killing an officer."

"That's pretty intense," Jake said.

"Nacho got out, got back into the local drug scene. When Barrios made the gate, they teamed up. Barrios got the name *Rattler* because he's quiet and damn deadly. Killed a bunch of guys. Word on the street's he's gone freelance since Nacho went to work for his sister's boyfriend."

"What does Nacho do for Villalobos?"

"Who knows? Chief gopher, enforcer– all of that."

"Rudy, do you think there's any connection between this Rattler and Alban's outfit?"

"Wouldn't surprise me."

~*~*~

Back in his office, Pepe said to Jake,

"There's the connection."

"I don't quite see it all," Jake said.

Pepe wrote names on the pad.

"Here's Alban and Drako," he said. "They want their partner Fuchs dead. Alban has his lawyer get the "Rattler" to grease Fuchs and his gang. Then, Fuchs's main wise guy floats up, we get lucky, link him to the Rattler. Now we've connected the Rattler back to Santos through his girlfriend's gangbanger brother."

"OK. I see it now."

"The Rattler's the key," Pepe said. "He murdered Ruth's roommate but left a print. Everyone thought it was a drug killing because Maggie was an anti-drug activist."

"Ruth mentioned that," Jake said.

Pepe got up, looked out the window.

"Only, I don't think it was that at all," he said.

"Oh?"

"I think Maggie was killed by mistake or was in the wrong place at the wrong time. And, I think this Nacho guy had the Rattler kill her."

"Wow. That's a stretch."

"Not a bit," Pepe said. "The Rattler has his feet in both camps. He's in with Santos and with the Mob."

~*~*~

The snatch
Los Medanos State Park, San Diego County, CA
Same day, 6:41 PM, Wednesday, January 22, 1975

The sun had already set when Ruth Hall threw a sweat shirt over her shoulders, walked back around the trees to the Porta Potti. She was inside for a few minutes.

When Ruth stepped outside the door, Nacho snatched her back, clamped a gauze pad soaked in chloroform over her mouth and nose. Lola slapped the tape over the gauze, fixing it over her mouth and nose. Ruth struggled, kicked, made some muffled sounds, then went limp in Nacho's arms.

~*~*~

Lola grabbed Ruth's ankles, wrapped them in duct tape, bound her wrists behind her. Nacho slung the moaning Ruth over his shoulder, then they moved out through the thicket of bushes.

Nacho stumbled, wheezed, shifted Ruth's body several times en route to his van parked inside the park less than a mile from the digging site.

After checking for passerbys, Lola pulled the van around, jumped out, helped Nacho load Ruth into the back, then hopped in beside her. Nacho closed the double doors, climbed in, then drove away.

Lola wrapped Ruth with more duct tape, then crawled up into the passenger seat. She took off her cap, then glanced back at Ruth rolling in the back.

"How long do you think it'll take to get to El Centro?" she said.

"As long as it takes," Nacho said, "'cause I'm driving the speed limit all the way."

~*~*~

Ricochets
On the street, Norwalk, CA
Next morning, 3:08 AM, Thursday, January 23, 1975

Jorge parked the old Chevy van across the street from the tenement, placed a clothed manikin with a ball cap and shades into the driver's seat, slipped out of the side door, then crouched in a nearby darkened doorway.

At 3:15, he saw a black van screech around the corner, pull up alongside the old Chevy. Three machine pistols thrust out from the open side panel stitched the manikin in the Chevy's driver's seat with bursts of sound-suppressed gunfire.

Jorge sprang out, rolled two grenades under the van, stepped to the left rear, shot the driver in the head, then rolled to one side when the grenades exploded.

The van lurched, buckled, then rocked onto its left side.

Jorge ripped open the rear door, pumped four shots into the men inside, then jerked open the front passenger door, hauled the man in the front seat onto the pavement.

He thrust the hot barrel of the automatic into the man's face.

"Who set me up?" Jorge said.

The man's face was bleeding, his right hand hung useless, punctured from the blast and shrapnel of the grenades. Focusing his eyes, he glared at Jorge.

"Fuck you," he said.

"Ain't got time for this shit. Who set me up?"

He spit blood into Jorge's face, then choked out,

"Eat shit, *cabrón.*"

"Wrong answer."

Jorge squeezed two rounds in his face

Hearing sirens, seeing lights coming on, Jorge stepped over the body, then ran to the other car he had parked a block away.

After getting on the freeway, Jorge drove to his apartment in El Cajon. Slipping upstairs with no more noise than a big tomcat, he went to his bedroom, threw some clothes along with some bank papers with a forged passport in a canvas suitcase.

Coming out of the room, he snatched a shopping bag of paperback books, took them with the suitcase to his car with even less noise than before.

Jorge drove north on the freeway to the outskirts of Long Beach to a run-down motel, then rang the bell outside the office for the night clerk.

An Indian woman came padding out.

"You want room?" she said.

"Yes." Jorge said.

"How many?"

"Just me."

"You want girl?"

"No. Just a room."

"How many hour?"

"Just one day."

"All day?"

"Yeah. No disturbances."

"OK. $65.00. Sign here."

"Are the sheets clean?"

"Oh yes. Clean every day."

Jorge scrawled 'Joe Smith' on the registration card, handed the woman a hundred dollar bill.

The woman gave him a key fastened to a heavy sprocket, then held the bill up to the light. Satisfied the currency was not counterfeit.

"No change right now," she said.

"Keep it," Jorge said.

"*Shukria*," the woman said. "Most generous."

Jorge found the bedraggled room, made sure the sheets were clean, then kicked off his shoes. Setting his pistol on the night stand by the bed, he turned on the bed lamp, took a paperback book from the brown paper grocery bag, flopped down on the bed, then turned to the first page to read.

~*~*~

Captive audience
65 km south of El Centro, CA
Same day, 1:43 AM, Thursday

Sprawled on the carpet floor of the van, Ruth tried to open her eyes.

Images floated in her head.

Stepping out of the Porta Potty.

Grabbed from behind.

A woman, tape in her hand.

Kicking, lifted from behind.

Her mouth taped shut.

An astringent chemical smell– drowsy, so drowsy.

Sleep, dreams, bumped along, thrown over a donkey's back, hands in shackles, her older brothers laughing at her, tied up again.

Can't call out!

Lying on the floor of their old tree house.

Her brothers saying they were selling her to the Gypsies.

Dark men and women, leering, dark smiles, dark eyes, white shining teeth, red scarves on men's heads, women in flouncy dresses wearing round gold earrings, men with scarred faces– can't open her eyes.

Tethered.

Hanging in space, dangling like a chicken about to be butchered, hands sewn together, feet in chains.

Gypsy wagons, the rattle of pots and pans, the smell of a campfire, pangs of hunger...

The bump brought her back.

Her head hurt.

She was lying on the floor, couldn't see.

Tape over her eyes. Her mouth was taped too. Hands, feet bound, taped.

She felt the carpet on the floor of the van with her fingertips. Sounds came to her, out of the darkness.

Voices.

She listened.

"It was smart to travel parallel to Interstate 8."

A woman's voice.

"Yeah. Didn't want no cops stopping me."

A man this time.

"Lucky you still have that place outside of El Centro."

Her voice shrill, accented.

"Yeah. We never got rid of it."

Man's voice seemed familiar– maybe not.

"When's he coming?"

When's who coming?

"He'll be there later this morning."

The man again.

"I'm getting hungry."

"Me too. Let's have some coffee."

Rummaging sounds, clanks, rattles. Pouring. Smell of coffee.

My bladder's full.

Slurping sounds.

"How's she doing?"

The man again.

Another rustle, a clink. Someone turned in the seat, seat belt hitting something.

"Still lying there."

Her again.

"Think she's awake?"

"We'll check her when you pull off the road up ahead."

Her accent: Chicana, Mexican American. The man too. Who are they?

Ruth breathed through her nose, nostrils wide. Her duct-taped eyes couldn't open. She felt the tape loosen, tear at her eyebrows.

Fight panic, fear, force yourself, relax.

She had to pee.

Can't see– but, I can still hear, smell, feel– the pain in my bladder.

She'd not hallucinated it. She had been seized, kidnaped, taken prisoner. She had to maintain reason. That was her only hope. See it through.

Don't lose it. That's what they want: me to panic, to lose it, to turn to shit. It's me against them.

Ruth pushed against her bonds.

They took me for a reason. They had no right to. No fucking right!

She had to pee.

She remembered peeing her pants as a kid. She had held it and held it. When the pain came, she had let it go. The other kids had laughed...

The van stopped. Ruth braced herself.

Doors opened, then the side panel slid back. Rough hands grabbed her pulled her out the door, then shoved her to her feet. The tape was ripped off of her mouth.

The woman spoke, "Don't do anything stupid, it's your ass if you do. Do you want something to drink?"

Ruth spat back. "No, bitch. I have to pee."

A few seconds of silence.

"Well, bitch," the woman said. "I guess you'll just have to fucking wait."

The tape was slapped back over her mouth. She was pushed back into the van.

Ruth pushed against her bonds, listened carefully to each sound, smelled everything, touched the carpet with her fingers, tried to open her eyes.

Keep busy.

Every little bit of sensory input told her a bit more about her environment. She summed up what she knew:

She was in a van.

Two people– both Latinos; the bitch mentioned El Centro. That's east– towards Arizona.

The stop.

I smelled the desert. Early morning but already heating up.

Ruth repeated these bits of information to herself over and over for the next hour.

Then, a slowdown. A turn. A bumpy road. Ruth smelled dust. In her mind's eyes, dust clouds arose from behind the nondescript van.

She welcomed the pain of her bladder.

She listened. They had not spoken to each other since the stop.

The van bumped more now. The road was rougher. It went that way for nearly another hour.

The man spoke, "Here we are."

The van turned, lurched to a stop. Again, the sound of doors opening, then, the rough drag to outside.

She felt herself grabbed, then thrown over a shoulder. A big man.

Damn, that hurts.

Tempted to pee on him, she heard them enter a building. The woman spoke,

"We'd better let her piss. Don't want her stinking up the place."

Ruth heard a door open. She felt her feet hit the floor. Her shorts were unbuttoned, pants pulled down, then, she was pushed onto a cold toilet seat.

The woman spoke again,

"Piss, shit or whatever you want now, bitch. Don't count on our being so sweet the next time."

Ruth did not hesitate. She evacuated.

"Done?" *The woman again.*

Ruth nodded.

Jerked to her feet, she felt her shorts pulled up. Hoisted to the man's shoulder, taken a few steps away, she heard a door open.

She was tossed on a bed. It felt, smelled dusty but more comfortable than the floor of the van. A hard pillow supported her head. She relaxed her eyelids behind the tape, released a long breath. She slept.

~*~*~

Distressing report
Pepe's Office, East LA State University, Los Angeles, CA
Same day, 9:26 AM, Thursday

After two quick knocks on his office door, Pepe looked up to see Jake Spyner barge in.

"Ruth disappeared from her worksite last night," he said.

"What?"

"A friend, a State Park ranger called me this morning. Ruth's crew reported her missing last night just before suppertime."

"Where could she have gone?"

"They did an intensive search last night and it's continuing today. Her vehicle's still at the site and none of her things are missing. They found her sweatshirt near a portable toilet."

"This sounds bad. Who's on scene?"

"The sheriff's department's out there today."

"They don't have the resources to deal with this. That means it'll be nearly two days before the FBI gets into this."

"Shall we go out there?"

Pepe sighed, shook his head.

"I'm afraid we'd only be in the way."

"Where does that leave us with Ruth?" Jake said.

"Can't say. But let's get some help with this."

Pepe went to his rolodex, dialed a number.

"Officer Rowe, please. This is Dr. Ortega at the University of. East Los Angeles. Could you have him call me back. This is urgent. Thank you."

Back to the rolodex, Pepe dialed again.

"Helen Davis, please. Hmm..., may I leave a message. Please call Pepe Ortega ASAP. Urgent. Thanks."

He looked at Jake, said, "One more."

Pepe dialed Dan James.

"Damn, a recording!" he said.

"Dan. Pepe Ortega. Get back to me immediately. Something urgent's come up."

Jake stared at Pepe. "Are we dead in the water?"

Pepe sat in thought a moment, raised his eyes. "We use this situation."

After grabbing the rolodex again, Pepe dialed, then held the phone so Jake could hear.

The voice answered, "Ed Singer."

"Professor Singer. This is Pepe Ortega. We met at the International Anthropological meetings last December."

"Ah, yes. The forensic specialist. Please call me Edward. That was a most pleasant dinner."

"It was indeed. But, Ruth Hall's disappeared and may have been kidnaped."

"Oh no!"

"I'm afraid so. I must ask you something personal that may be related to her disappearance."

"By all means."

"You mentioned that Santos Villalobos had called on you asking for field sites prior to the disappearance of Matthew Spyner."

"Yes."

"You'd seen Matthew Spyner's thesis. Was it the same as *The Secrets of Don Pedro Miguel?*"

Singer gave a long sigh. "Not having been able to bring myself to read the book very closely, I can't say for certain but from everything I've heard, and know, yes. I'd say the entire Villalobos book appears to have been plagiarized."

"But you gave no indication of that at the time."

"It was a nasty business. I wanted nothing to do with it. Any accusations I would've made couldn't have been substantiated. I'd only seen the thesis proposal once and told Matthew that in its present form, it wasn't adequate anthropological research."

"What was his reaction?"

"Very disappointed. He took the manuscript back and said he'd be in touch. That was the last time I saw him."

"Were there any copies of the thesis made?"

"Not to my knowledge."

"Edward, is there any doubt in your mind that Santos Villalobos somehow obtained Matthew Spyner's master's thesis and published it as *The Secrets of Pedro Miguel*?"

A long pause, followed by a sigh. "None whatsoever."

"Thank you. I'll keep you informed as things develop in our search for Ruth."

"Please do. She's a sweet girl and we'd be heartbroken if anything has happened to her."

Pepe hung up, looked over at Jake. "All we can do now is wait to hear from our police friends."

The phone rang.

"This is Pepe."

"Bill Rowe. You called?"

"Yes. Ruth Hall may have been kidnapped last night."

"Oh, shit! The disappearance at the State Park."

"I may have a lead."

"Bill. This is complex. When can we get together and talk?"

"Can you come down? I'm kinda tied up right now."

Pepe looked over at Jake. "You doing anything today?"

"Just hanging out with you."

"Bill. We can leave here now and meet you somewhere in about 2 hours. Can you get hold of Dan James."

Bill laughed. "No, but our friend Helen can."

"Oh?"

"Little romance blooming there. I'll call Helen on her pager. I think she's with him now."

"That's convenient."

"You guys meet us in Oceanside. There's a bar and grill called Curley's outside of Camp Pendleton and we'll meet there 3 hours from now."

"OK, amigo. We're on our way."

~*~*~

A nice quiet chat
Lola's cabin, outside of El Centro, CA
Same day, 1:28 PM, Thursday

Ruth lurched awake at some new sounds. Aside from an earlier bathroom break, she had heard nothing from her two captors. They brought her a sandwich around noon, untaped her hands, freed her mouth, then replaced it when she'd finished. She'd fallen asleep.

Noises. Voices bled through the door.

There was a new one.

She listened, froze. She knew that voice.

Santos Villalobos.

About twenty minutes later, she heard the door open.

She felt rough hands pull to her feet, strip tape from her boots, then push her through the door. Stumbling to her knees, they jerked her to her feet, then shoved her into a chair.

She winced when the tape was pulled from her mouth.

Santos's voice was soft, coaxing.

"Dr. Hall. I regret the brusque invitation to have a quiet chat."

"I don't know who these other two assholes are, Santos," Ruth said. "But I damn sure know you."

Ruth heard Santos chuckle.

"Take the tape off her eyes," he said.

Ruth felt the tape rip from her face, pull her eyebrows. She blinked in the bright light. Santos sat in front of her. A scowling Latin woman, her long hair pulled back stood to his right while on his left. stood a big man with cracked sunglasses, his face scratched, bruised.

"We met before," Santos said.

Ruth literally spit her words.

"I saw you once, buttface. That was enough."

The woman stepped forward, slapped Ruth in the face, snarled,

"Watch your mouth, bitch."

"Lola," Santos said. "No rough stuff."

"Piss on you, Santos," Ruth said.

"We just need to have a heart to heart and you can go home," Santos said.

"Then make an appointment with me during my office hours, turd," Ruth said.

"Why do we have to do it this way?" Santos said.

"You're a murdering kidnaping sonfabitch, Santos."

Lola smacked Ruth again, knocking her out of the chair.

The big man jerked her up, plopped her back in the chair.

"My friends did use some unorthodox means of inviting you here, but we're not holding you for ransom," Santos said.

Choking back anger, frustration, Ruth said,

"Don't give me that shit. I know you killed Matt Spyner."

Lola jumped for Ruth, but Santos restrained her.

"Prove it, bitch!" she screamed.

"I can't. But I know it."

"Matt's death was a tragic accident," Santos said. "But, that's not what we're here to discuss."

"So, let me go," Ruth said.

"We talk. You can go. My word."

"Your word doesn't mean shit," Ruth said. "You kidnaped me— that's a major felony. How're you gonna let me go when you know I'd have the FBI on your ass like stink on shit."

"You'll have a very hard time proving it without witnesses," Santos said.

Ruth pursed her bruised lips. "Jesus, you must think I'm stupid."

The women leapt forward, fist doubled.

"Lola. Please!" Santos's voice was sharp.

Lola flopped down in a nearby chair, folded her arms, scowling at Ruth.

"Nacho, sit down too," Santos said. "This is getting out of hand."

Ruth, her face smarting, glared at Santos. "Nothing to say."

"You and Matt Spyner were lovers," Santos said.

Ruth glared at him, tight-lipped.

"When did you become disappointed in him?"

"Go to hell," Ruth said.

Lola came in swinging, knocked Ruth off the chair, drove her boot into Ruth's ribs, raised her foot to give her another kick when Nacho pulled her back.

Santos stood.

"This is no good. Nacho, put Dr. Hall back in the room until she's a little more reasonable and Lola's calmed down."

Nacho pushed his sister into a chair, then picked up the tape, plastered it over Ruth's mouth, swung her to his shoulder, carried her to the bed in her room, retaped her feet, then closed the door.

Ruth heard Lola let go a stream of Spanish,

"Let me handle her. Give me ten minutes and I'll have her squawking like a papagallo."

"Slapping her around won't work," Santos said.

"Man," Lola said. "All we need to know is where she's got that other manuscript..."

"Shut up!" Santos snapped. "She probably understands Spanish."

"Cool it, Lo," Nacho said. "Let's go outside."

"Good idea," Santos said.

Hearing the door bang, Ruth lay back on the bed.

Other manuscript? What other...?

It hit her.

This tidbit can save my ass.

~*~*~

Heads together
Main section of downtown, Oceanside, CA
Same day, 6:22 PM, Thursday

Pepe led Jake into the bar flashing an old fashioned neon tube sign, *Curley's Bar and Grill* .Inside, Ritchie Valens's nasal voice intoned *Donna* from an old juke box. Marines of varying ages talked in loud voices amid the acrid smell of stale beer, cigarette smoke. The bar's walls sported mementos, memorabilia, exploits of USMC battles from around the world.

Spotting Bill Rowe with Helen Davis in a corner booth at the end of the bar, Pepe walked over, introduced them to Jake.

"You guys must have walked here," Helen said.

"LA traffic," Pepe said, then glanced around. "Dan couldn't make it?"

Helen lowered her eyes. "He's tied up with a big break in his Mexican drug case."

"I ordered hamburgers," Bill said. "Everything here tastes the same here anyway."

"Sounds good to me," Jake said. "Haven't eaten since this morning."

A waitress appeared loaded with plates of hamburgers, French fries and beer, set them in front of everyone, then went to the next table.

Turning to Pepe, Bill said, "What do we have?"

Pepe laid out the papers showing the links to the Trinity and Santos through Jorge.

Jake told his discoveries in Mexico.

"So," Rowe said. "You think this Santos guy killed Jake's brother after swiping his manuscript?"

"Yes-- several years later," Pepe said. "In between, he wrote this book based on the manuscript."

"I read that book," Davis said between bites. "It was just about getting zonked on drugs and seeing weird shit."

"How does all this tie into our Mexican mafia murder?" Rowe said.

Davis interrupted, "Or the murder of Maggie Connall?"

Pepe said, "My read is that Barrios, whose nickname, by the way, is *cascabel* 'Rattler,' killed them both."

"You mean 'Rattler' like the pit viper kind?" Rowe said.

"Detectives in our office have been after an unidentified hitman," Davis said. "Their only lead is he's called 'Rattlesnake.' "

Pepe nodded. "Sounds like the same guy."

"If he whacked both Maggie and Volpez, he was doing it for the mob," Rowe said. "Where does this Santos guy fit into this picture?"

"Santos's girl friend has a brother, Nacho," Pepe said. "He and the Rattler were in the marines together."

"That's a damn thin connection to the mob, Pepe," Rowe said.

"No argument," Pepe said. "But, something about this Santos business eats at my guts."

"Santos was in San Luisita when Pepe's brother was killed." Jake said.

"There are lots of loose ends we can't tie up now," Rowe said. "First thing. We gotta get the Rattler out of the henhouse."

"We may have a lead," Davis said. "A snitch told a detective this "Rattlesnake" guy likes bookstores."

"What's a snitch know about bookstores?" Rowe said.

"I'm just telling you what I heard."

"Balls in our court," Rowe said. "Pepe, Jake. You guys, keep on this Santos guy and we'll collar the Rattler."

"You're overlooking something," Pepe said.

"What?"

"Santos is likely behind Ruth Hall's disappearance."

"What?" Davis said. "That archeology teacher who disappeared out at the State Park was Ruth?"

"She's the only one of two people who knew about the manuscript," Pepe said.

"My team went out there and didn't find anything conclusive suggesting foul play or a kidnaping. Nothing– nada."

"That could mean they just covered their tracks well," Jake said.

"They'd have to have been very good," Davis said.

"Or very lucky," Jake said.

"We're spinning our wheels," Rowe said. "Let's call it a night and get back to work."

Davis shook Pepe and Jake's hands.

"I'll get this info to the suits," she said. "This may open the door to nailing this asshole."

Pepe grinned at her. "Say hi to Don."

Davis gave a little cough.

"Almost forgot," she said. "He said he'll be in touch with you real soon. Had something to tell you."

"What?"

"Didn't tell me."

Pepe and Jake left.

~*~*~

The drive back from Oceanside unfolded in a depressed silence. Pepe looked over at Jake Spyner sitting with his chin on his fist, staring out of the window.

Good guy. Unassuming, competent and hurting.

"Any family besides Matt?" Pepe said.

"Married once."

"Oh?"

"She left me for an investment banker. Nice gal but wanted a lot more than an under-achieving fireman could give her."

"Sorry to hear that."

"Been a number of girl friends since. How about you?"

"Married once. She died."

"Wow, that was tough."

"Yeah."

Jake looked at Pepe.

"From what Ruth tells me, she likes you a lot."

"I like her too."

"She deserves someone like you."

"I'm very worried about her."

"Me too, but you know, somehow I think she's OK. We just need to find her."

Pepe reflected on this thought for the next several miles until they arrived at the University.

Pulling up to Jake's car, Pepe said,

"Let's hope for some breaks."

"We'll keep pushing this until we make our own breaks," Jake said.

~*~*~

Life insurance
Lola's Cabin outside of El Centro, CA
Same day, 9:55 PM, Thursday

Outside the cabin, Lola watched her brother stretch his arms.

"January," Nacho said. "And it's gonna be hot again tomorrow."

"It's the desert, stupid," Lola said.

"Thank you, sister. Driving all night made me forget."

"Cool it," Santos said. "No need to add to this crap-pot situation."

"OK, OK," Lola said. "It's just that twat thinks she's better than us."

"Forget it," Santos said. "I was making some progress when you screwed it up."

"You call getting cussed out 'progress?'"

"Notice how she didn't try to bargain, not even a hint of another manuscript," Santos said.

"You want to bank your ass and our future on that?" Lola said. "If some pile of shit turns up while we're off in Brazil, they could have your assets tied up for years."

Strolling a few paces away, Santos stared off down the dusty road.

"Cassie can only do so much," Lola said. "If another manuscript surfaces, it could mean shit up to our eyeballs."

"I know that," Santos said.

Coming up to Santos, Lola put her hand on his shoulder, her voice purred, "She recognized you. She knows you won't let anything happen to her."

"So, what are you suggesting?"

"Go up to the cabin and wait for us."

Santos looked her in the eyes. "So you can torture her?"

"Once you're gone, she'll fold."

Nacho frowned. "Man, I ain't beating up no chicks."

"I said, I'll handle it," Lola said. "You just do what I say."

"She's not dumb," Santos said. "The 'good cop, bad cop' routine won't work with her."

"I know what I'm doing," Lola said.

"Don't let on about the manuscript," Santos said. "If she does know something, she'll clam up."

Lola kissed him on the mouth.

Nacho took a pistol from his waistband, thrust it in Santos's hand.

"Here's a piece," Nacho said.

"What's that for?"

"You never know, homie."

Santos got in the car, laid the gun beside him on the seat, rolled down the window.

"Be careful," he said to Lola.

Lola leaned through the car window, kissed him again.

"We will."

~*~*~

Ruth heard the car drive away from inside the bedroom.

Santos's taking off. It's going to get tougher.

Steps outside, crunching on the sand.

The front door banged shut.

More steps. Her door opened. Nacho pulled her to her feet, stripped tape from her ankles, then led her inside to a chair.

Taking the tape from her mouth, Lola said, "You can yell but no one's gonna hear you."

Ruth glared.

Lola sat in front of her.

"We just need to know more about this Spyner guy."

"Why'd you kill him?"

"I didn't kill him."

"The fuck you didn't."

Lola breathed deeply, then let it out.

"Watch the mouth," she said. "And I won't slap you around, OK?"

Ruth nodded.

"Cool. So, how long were you two a thing?"

Ruth swallowed, then said,

"Cut the bullshit. This is about that Xerox of Matt's thesis."

Lola glanced at Nacho, then back at Ruth.

"Oh?" Lola said.

"You think I didn't know this was all about that fucking manuscript Santos turned into a goldmine after Matt took off?"

Lola looked at her brother.

"Make us some coffee."

The big man went to the kitchen, filled a kettle with water, rattled cups, opened a coffee can.

Lola looked at her fingernails.

"Go on," she said.

"Matt gave me a copy for safekeeping. I've made arrangements that if anything happens to me, it goes to the police."

Ruth saw Nacho stare back at her from the kitchen area.

"That's too neat," Lola said, her face in a smirk.

"There's a book written with his stolen thesis that's printing money," Ruth said. "My friend gets brutally murdered and I got the only copy that can prove it's all bullshit. You damn right it's 'too neat.'"

"Why didn't you just out it before now?" Lola said.

"Because it's my life insurance."

Lola's smirk eroded. She knit her eyebrows at Ruth.

"Nacho," Lola said. "Where'n the hell's that damn coffee?"

~*~*~

Mexico Calling
Pepe's house, East Los Angeles, CA
2:08 AM, Friday, January 24, 1975

The phone shattered the silence in the bedroom where Pepe lay in the quiet lull of deep sleep. He shook his head, looked around. The numbers 2:08 on the digital clock face pierced the bedroom's darkness.

The phone rang again. He answered,

"Pepe."

"*Hermano*, I have news."

Recognizing his brother-in-law's voice, Pepe sat up straight.

"Xotchitl? The kids? They OK?"

"They're fine– I'm on Alban's ass."

Pepe slid his feet to the floor. "What do you mean?"

"I'm getting arrest warrants for him and Ivo Drako today and will have them in jail tomorrow."

"What happened?"

"A few days ago, I got a call."

"A call?"

"I recognized the voice. Same guy as before. He gives me the address of a warehouse in Guadalajara and then tells me to dig in a precise location in the sand along a road in Sonora outside of Immures."

"You followed up on this?"

"That day we impounded 275 kilos of cocaine and around a thousand kilos of marijuana from the Guadalajara place and dug up two bodies in the desert."

"Who were they?"

"Carlos Lopez Carrillo and Alberto Mondragon– two missing judges who resisted taking bribes from Alban."

"No kidding!"

"I took this to my boss and he took it to the President today."

"And?"

"It's election year. The President told Sanchez to put Alban's ass away. I'll have warrants today as soon as Superior Court Judge Joaquin Cabrillo signs them in the morning."

"Someone in Alban's organization gave you the tip?"

"Has to be. Your Papa tried to get someone inside for years. Never happened."

"And this guy just calls up out of the blue?"

"As we say back home, Pepe, don't look a free chicken in the ass."

"I'll pass this on to my friends over at DEA."

"Good. Go back to sleep. I've been up all night and have a full day in front of me."

Pepe found a number, left a call-back page for Dan James, then lay back on the bed, closed his eyes.

The blast of the ring startled him awake.

"Pepe."

"Dan. You paged me, urgent."

"I just got a call. The Mexican court's issuing arrest warrants for Alban and Drako."

"Who told you?"

"My brother-in-law's the Assistant Prosecutor to the Mexican Minister of Justice."

"Then there's some real shit going down. Can you meet with us this morning?"

"What time?"

"Ten O'clock. I'll buy the coffee and donuts."

"I'll be there. How're things going with you and Helen, by the way."

James chuckled. "I'll ask her."

Pepe heard a woman's voice say "asshole," followed by a thump.

"Ouch. That hurt, woman."

"See you at 10, Dan," Pepe said.

~*~*~

Early wake-up call
Casimiro Cortez's Condo, Venice Beach, CA
Same day, 5:48 AM, Friday

Making no noise, Jorge glided into the beach cottage's bedroom reeking with the odor of cannabis. He spotted the naked couple asleep between burgundy sheet, exhausted from recent sexual pleasures. The man's light brown skin contrasted with the black skin of the woman in the dim glare of a night light from an open bathroom door.

Jorge grabbed the man, clapped his hand over his mouth. The man kicked when Jorge jerked him upright.

The woman woke up. "What the fuck?" she said.

Shoving the man against the wall, Jorge jammed his foot on his neck, grabbed the woman's head, jerked, twisted, snapping her spinal cord.

She convulsed once, fell back dead across the bed.

Jorge pulled up the man, drug him over the edge of the bed, then thrust a pistol into his scrotum.

"You got two seconds to tell me who set me up," Jorge said.

Casimiro Cortez's eyes adjusted to the dark.

"Jorge?" he choked. "What the fuck you doing, man?"

Jorge's finger tightened on the trigger. "One second, Cassie."

"Wait, Man. Take that gun outta my balls. What's going down?"

"You know what's going down. You set me up."

"Hey man. I swear. I don't know what you're talking about."

"Answers, Man. I want answers– not bullshit."

"Home– it's me, Cassie. Man, I'd never set you up."

Jorge whipped up the gun, stuck it next to Cortez's nose.

"Your partner, Rydell set me up."

"*Hermano*– we're from the same family."

"You're in the same fucking office– you called me to pop that old Jew."

"I did, man. But, I didn't know nothing about this, I fucking swear."

Jorge shoved the barrel of the pistol against Cortez's nostril.

"Lie to me, motherfucker and I'll feed you parts of your own body."

"It's gotta be Alban and the Mexican Mafia. Rydell didn't say shit to me. I can prove it."

"How?"

"Man, I just got back from Brazil today. I've been gone damn near a week clearing things so Santos can get his ass outta the country."

Jorge lowered the gun.

"Whadda mean get Santos's ass out of the country?"

"You know Santos stole some guy's manuscript."

"Yeah. The one he used to write those shitless books all the heads love."

"Well, the guy showed up and tried to shake him down. So Santos caved in his crust. Now, he wants to take the money and run. They can't extradite him from Brazil."

"What about Lola?"

"She's going too. I can get you out with them."

"Where's Nacho?"

"He and Lola grabbed some twat that has something on Santos. They're out in the old Santiago coyote hole near El Centro."

"I know where that is."

"OK. I'll call them and let them know you're coming. Once you get to Brazil and go underground, Alban will never find you."

"They'll be after my ass from now on."

"Let me handle this. Everything's negotiable. That fucking little short-dick prick Rydell didn't tell me shit."

Jorge backed off.

Cortez took the phone near his bed, dialed.

"Lola?" he said. "Yeah, I know it's late. OK, OK, lemme get a word in. Look. Jorge's here. The mob tried to kill him tonight. I'm sending him out there. Hold on."

He handed the phone to Jorge.

"Yeah, Lo," Jorge said.

"What happened homie?" Lola said.

"Rydell set up some homeland boogers to grease me."

"OK. Get your ass down here. Cassie will set things up for you so you can get outta the country with us."

"Cool. See you in a few hours."

Jorge looked at Cassie.

"Wanna say any more to Lo?"

Cortez shook his head, then looked at the body of the woman sprawled across the bed.

"Why'd you whack her?" Cortez said.

Jorge shrugged.

"I was planning to off you too," he said. "She a friend?

"Naw, just a hooker."

"Sorry. Want me to clean up?"

Cortez nodded.

Jorge picked up the limp body of the dead woman.

"Were you really gonna shoot my balls off?" Cortez said.

"No," Jorge said. "I was gonna buckwheat you."

"Buckwheat?"

"Yeah. Shoot you in the guts through your balls."

~*~*~

Noticias no muy Buenas
Coast of Oaxaca, 25 km south of Acapulco
Same day, 7:08 AM, Friday

Sitting in the patio in the streaked early morning light, the bright red, blue and green cover of the magazine in Lucero's hand, *Deportes Mexicanos,* contrasted with his bleached white cotton peasant farmer clothes. He was turning a page when the tap-tap of rapid footsteps on the patio caught his attention.

He looked up into a worried frown on the face of his attorney, Daniel Soto.

"Daniel," Luis said. "What brings you here?"

"Bad news," the lawyer said. "Gonzalez-Diaz has gotten Superior Court Judge, Joaquin Cabrillo to issue arrest warrants for you and Ivo. I flew here from the Capital to tell you in person."

Lucero stood. The magazine dropped to his feet.

"The President will never let this happen," he said.

"This is an election year. Politicos throw their mothers and children to the wolves for a vote."

"I'll throw those motherfuckers to the wolves."

"I want you and Ivo out of sight until I can get this worked out."

"I'll have his whole family whacked."

"Later. Right now you and Ivo get your asses out of town."

Soto plopped down in a chair beside Lucero, catching his breath.

"We've kept you well insulated," he said. "So how in hell did Rodriquez Diaz come up with enough evidence to go to the President."

Lucero's eyes narrowed.

"There's a rat in our house?" he said.

"Old Zorro had lots of moles. You go somewhere people know about, there'll be guys on your back like horny roosters on hens."

"OK. We go underground."

"I gotta get right back to the Capital, "Soto said. "The pilot's got the plane's engine running on the strip right now."

He embraced Lucero.

"Don't delay, Luis," he said, then scampered off over the blue tiles on small feet in shiny shoes.

Lucero called his maid.

"Call Sr. Drako," he said. "Tell him it's urgent."

Two minutes later, a frowning Drako strode out in a terrycloth robe.

"What's going on?" he said.

"Rodriquez Diaz is getting warrants for our arrest," Lucero said. "We gotta go underground."

"We've just landed a huge shipment of heroin. The competition will steal us blind and we'll lose our asses."

"Daniel can smooth things out in time but we've to get out of sight now."

Drako plopped down in a chair, whipped out his silver case, lit a gold-ringed cigarette.

"What if Daniel's just overreacting?" he said.

"Let's check it out."

Lucero snatched up the phone, dialed a number.

A voice answered at the first ring.

"Yes?"

Lucero spoke in Nahuatl.

"Are you the one?"

The reply in the same language,

"This is the one who listens."

"Daniel Soto just told me Rodriquez Diaz's getting warrants for my and Ivo's arrest."

"Impossible!"

"Seriously. Daniel said we got to go underground for a while."

"Let me call you right back."

Lucero hung up.

"Why did this have to happen now?" Drako said.

"This will all blow over."

"All our asses and chips are on the table now, Luis."

The phone rang. Lucero snatched it off the cradle.

"Bueno."

The question in Nahuatl, "Who am I?"

"The one who speaks."

"Dr. Soto's correct. This could be only so much political window dressing. But you should play it on the safe side."

"What do you propose?"

"We have a place in the Guatemala highlands no one knows about. You and Sr. Drako can stay there until Dr. Soto gets things settled here."

"What about business?"

"You can still keep a close eye on what is happening here. I'll keep you in the know on the details on the money side."

"Sounds reasonable."

"You know our private airstrip outside of Acapulco. I'll have a pilot take you both to Guatemala tomorrow evening."

Lucero's smile broadened, he hung up. "We're going to take a little trip, Ivo."

"Where? Brazil?"

"First we go like Gringo tourists outside of Acapulco. Then, on down to Guatemala."

"Guatemala? Why?"

Lucero took a cigar from a box on the table, sliced off the end with a silver cutter, picked up a box of long cigar matches, then looked over at the big Serb.

"Think of it as a much needed little vacation, Ivo." he said.

Bookstore connection
Buyer-Seller Used books, El Cajon, CA
Same day, 10:08 AM, Friday

Helen Davis had photos of the Rattler distributed to the entire department. Patrolmen, plainclothesmen, detectives flashed his picture around used bookstores.

A policeman in El Cajon showed the photo to the owner of a used bookstore on his beat. The woman at the counter looked at the photo in her hand.

"I know this man," she said. "Comes in from time to time. Very quiet. Likes the classics. Always pays cash."

She looked in a card file by the cash register.

"We have a frequent reader's club," she said. "If someone's looking for a title and we don't have it, we call around to other bookstores and send them a card when one comes in– here's his address. Joe Smith, 2227 Ballard Way, apartment 27, El Cajon. No phone number."

The policeman thanked the woman, took the card, called San Diego Central.

~*~*~

Run for the hills
Airstrip at Rio Riego, 25 km outside of Acapulco, Mexico
Same evening, 11:48 AM, Friday

From the back seat of the black Mercedes limousine, Lucero watched the black Chevy van lead the way down the grass covered road. Behind him, another black van hugged the rear bumper of the Mercedes.

The little parade of vehicles bounced over a grated cattle guard between a fence spanning a pair of twin peaks, then stopped before a high cyclone wire fence with a steel bar gate.

A sentry in khaki stepped out from a small grove of palm trees, his automatic weapon pointed at the car. The window of the lead van buzzed down. The guard raised the muzzle of his weapon. The steel gate swung open, the sentry stood watching the cars go in, then turned back into a shaded grove of palms.

Lucero leaned back in the leather seat of the limousine, a glass of mescal in the cup holder at his elbow.

"We're almost there, Sr. Alban," the driver said.

"Thank you, Juan." Lucero said.

They pulled into a fenced-in air field. A landing strip stretched out near an open door hanger with a white pole topped with a wind-sock. A two storey wooden frame house sprawled behind the hanger. Lucero's driver pulled up to the parking area in front.

The two vans parked near the hanger. Men got out, guns in hand, positioning themselves face-out in a circle around the two limousines along the perimeter of the house.

A guard seated next to the driver, got out, walked around the protected area. At his signal, four men ran up the steps into the house. The guard waited a minute or so until the four men came out, each one nodding affirmative.

The guard opened the door. "It's all clear, Sr. Alban."

Lucero looked back as Drako got out of the limousine behind him.

Lucero looked over a long, roofed veranda that ran along the entrance to the house. Coming inside, he saw a table near the door laid out with coffee, pastries and a phone. He sat in one of two wicker chairs with cushions nearest the phone, motioned Drako into the other.

"All the comforts of home, Ivo," Lucero said.

Drako frowned behind his dark glasses. "I'm still concerned about who set us up."

"I got some people working on it."

"Could be anyone– even one of these hired guns."

Lucero shook his head.

"These men are all hand-picked from my home town."

"How could Rodriquez-Diaz have found out all that information? Someone very close to us keyed him in."

Lucero poured a cup of coffee, selected a pastry.

"What about the product?" Drako said.

"I brought it with us. I didn't want to take any chances on someone tipping the Nacionales to where we have 12 million dollars of heroin."

"So, what do we do with it now?"

"We can't risk going off to Guatemala and having it ripped off right under our noses. We're taking it with us."

"To Guatemala?" Drako said.

"We can ship it out of there easier than from here. Besides, most of our customers want to handle the shipments themselves."

"Look, carrying that heroin with us is dangerous."

"Leaving it here is more dangerous– it's got to come with us."

"This worries me."

Lucero ate the pastry, washed it down with coffee.

"Try some of these *pan dulces*," he said. "They're made in Acapulco. The baker graduated from a French baking academy."

"You're being very cavalier about this setback," Drako said. We've got a rat in the pantry."

"Whoever did this will trip over his tail. I've got people I trust on this."

"So, what do we do now?"

"Our pilot will be here tomorrow evening. Until then, we relax."

"Relax?"

"Yes. No one knows about this place but us."

"How in the hell can I relax when the guy in the next room might have a gun for me?"

Lucero poured some more coffee, spooned sugar, then stirred it.

"Ivo. There's a good football game on this afternoon. We've a stock of your favorite French sex films and the boys can bring us in some girls from Acapulco."

Ivo ran his hand over his hair, scowled at Lucero.

"Great. So then we can get our heads blown off by hooker assassins."

Lucero chuckled then took a slurp of his coffee.

~*~*~

Too late again
2227 Ballard Way, El Cajon, CA
Same day, 2:10 PM, Friday

Six black and white police cars, two vans screeched into the apartment complex. Two SWAT teams outfitted in tactical battle gear deployed in a run around the apartment building.

Children stopped playing their noisy games. Women quit their gossiping. Men gathered to watch from across the street.

The Tactical Unit troopers hurried residents out of their apartments. Uniformed patrol officers cordoned off spectators, bystanders. The SWAT teams approached the end apartment on full alert, weapons drawn.

A squad leader went to the door of apartment 27, rapped on it, then retreated.

"Police!" he called out. "Open up!"

No response.

He signaled. Two more Tactical Officers in body armor ran up with a steel battering ram, smashed the door in with one swing. Men poured into the apartment, weapons at the ready.

Inside, they found books laying in piles. The record player was still. The sink board was clean. The apartment was empty.

The Tactical Squad leader called his shoulder mouthpiece, "All clear."

Helen Davis's forensic team came in, went through every corner of the apartment. While they were taking everything apart, Helen stepped out on the walkway, used her radio.

"Coroner's office? This is CSI unit three. Inspector Rowe in? Bill? The rattler bolted. Yeah. His clothes are gone. I'd say he's been gone no longer than a day or so. We're talking to the neighbors now. Why not give that lawyer Pepe mentioned a call and see what you can stir up. Unit three clear."

~*~*~

Bill Rowe thumped the radio speaker into the receiver on the console, said, "Shit!" then stomped out of the radio room.

Back in his office, he picked out a Los Angeles phone book. Finding the number he wanted, he punched it in.

"Law offices of Rydell, Le, Cortez and Yoshizumi."

"This is inspector William Rowe, San Diego Coroner's office. Is Counselor Cortez in."

"Please hold and I'll check."

Two clicks later.

"Cassie Cortez. How can I help you, inspector."

"Counselor, are you acquainted with Jorge Barrios?"

A long breathy pause.

"That's privileged information, Inspector."

"We're trying to locate him as a material witness in a homicide."

"I regret I cannot be of assistance."

"Counselor. This is a homicide. Do I hafta get a subpoena?"

"Tell you what, Inspector, you get one and I'll be happy to tell you the same fucking thing. So, till then, screw off."

The click resounded in Rowe's ear.

"Shit," Rowe said again.

He picked up the phone once more.

The voice at the other end clicked on.

"Hello, this is Pepe."

"Bill Rowe, Pepe. They missed the Rattler."

A short silence.

"Pepe, are you still there?"

"Let me look into something, Bill," Pepe said.

"Whatcha got in mind?"

"I'm meeting Dan and the DEA guys later today."

"They won't do anything."

"Then, we'll have to try something else."

"I don't have to tell you about not doing anything illegal."

"We're still brother officers, Bill." Pepe said.

Eyebrows pulled tight, Bill hung up, shaking his head.

Big hearted bureaucracy
Federal Annex, Los Angeles, CA
Same day, 10:01 AM, Friday

Pepe showed his ID to a guard at the turnstile. After studying the ID and Pepe's face, the guard checked his name on a roster, then said, "Sign here."

The guard handed Pepe a numbered clip-on badge inscribed **GUEST**.

Pepe rode the elevator to the 12th floor, then walked to an office behind frosted glass doors. Coming in the large room, a secretary behind a front counter looked up at him.

"Yes?"

"Dr. Ortega, here to see Agent Dan James."

"He's expecting you, please go on back."

Walking to the back of the office down an aisle cutting through the prairie dog burrows of cubicles, Pepe saw Dan James through the glass wall sitting at a long table with several other men and women.

James greeted him at the door, shook his hand.

"Pepe," he said. "Come in. Meet the gang."

James put his arm around Pepe's shoulder.

"This is one of the crown jewels of our investigation team. Dr. Pepe Ortega, Professor of Criminology and Anthropology at East LA University.

A young dark complexioned man with big eyes stepped forward, hand extended.

"You might also mention, his family is legendary in Mexican law enforcement," he said.

He took Pepe's hand, then said in Spanish,

"Jaime Morales. I was in the academy with Manolito."

The handshake became an embrace.

"I've got to leave immediately," Morales said. "But when I heard you were going to be here, I had to come."

Pepe, coughed, his voice cracked.

"Forgive us," he said. "We Mexicans are an emotional bunch."

Everyone there laughed.

James spoke again,

"Jaime, born in Mexico is a US citizen by choice. He's FBI and has been working with us on drug money laundering."

When Jaime left. James ushered Pepe into a chair, strode to a flip chart, then said, "Let's get to work."

"We've got a drug cartel that's been operating in the open for several years. They bloomed from an underground network of small time suppliers and buyers to one of the largest importers and exporters of opium, heroin and cocaine in the Western hemisphere."

At the head of the table, Supervisor Fredson waved his hand.

"Dan," he said. "We know all this. Get to the point."

James returned to the chart.

"Thanks to Dr. Ortega, we've seen a shake-up in the triad with the removal of Fuchs, confirmed by his disappearance and the surfacing of the body of his enforcer, Volpez."

Fredson interrupted again. "Dan. This is history."

"Well, Pepe called me this morning and gave me advance word that warrants have been issued for the arrest of Alban and Drako."

Startled, Fredson looked around the table. "Now, this is news!"

"Moreover, I've just learned from a CIA source that a large shipment of heroin arrived in Mexico from Russia. If we move now together with the Mexican authorities, we can catch them with the goods."

Fredson spoke out again, "Now, that's what I like to hear."

Pepe raised his hand.

"Gentlemen," he said. "I need your help in something that touches on this situation."

Fredson frowned. "What's that, Dr. Ortega?"

"The man who killed Fuchs and Volpez was a local hitman called the Rattler. He murdered a psychiatrist in San Diego, an antidrug activist, named Margaret Connall."

Fredson interrupted, "What's that got to do with this case?"

"Drako and Alban contracted Barrios to kill Fuchs and Volpez."

"And?"

"He murdered Dr. Connall as a favor for his friends who have kidnaped an archeologist named Ruth Hall."

"That's way outside of our jurisdiction," Fredson said. "You should go to the FBI."

"The San Diego police have filed a missing person's report and have already contacted the FBI," Pepe said.

"And?"

"Since there were no witnesses, no evidence of foul play and no ransom demands, the FBI can do nothing beyond look at this as a missing person case which they defer back to the local police who initiated the request for their assistance."

"Well, there you have it," Fredson said, rolling his eyes.

"Has the San Diego PD picked up this Rattler guy?" James asked.

"I'm afraid he's bolted."

"Well, there's nothing we can do," Fredson said. "And, as you can see, our plates are already full."

Pepe looked into Fredson's eyes.

"So, you're telling me that even though I know this murderer killed the partners of your targets, you're washing your hands of further involvement?"

"This office can do nothing more in that regard," Fredson said.

Pepe stood, gathered up his papers.

"Then, I can contribute nothing more here. Gentlemen, thank you for your time."

Fredson's lips formed a tight smile. "Thank you for coming in, Dr. Ortega."

James walked Pepe to the door.

"I'm sorry, Pepe," James said. "You know I'll try to help in every way I can."

"I understand, Dan. Good luck."

"Stay in touch," James said. "We're on the brink of something big."

Back in the elevator, Pepe stared down at his boots until the door opened.

Then, he decided.

Inside the building he found a payphone, then made a call,

"Jake? Pepe. We need to talk. Now."

~*~*~

A literary chat
Lola's Cabin outside of El Centro, CA
Same day, 9:55 PM, Friday

Ruth heard a new voice. It was soft, low.

Now what? Who's this?

Ruth remembered the phone ringing early in the morning. Lola talked so fast, Ruth couldn't make out what she was saying.

It made sense now. She was inviting a friend.

Who in the hell is he?

She heard the conversation through the thin wall.

"You bring any food, homie?" Lola said.

"You didn't ask me," soft voice said.

"I gotta make a call, Lo," Nacho said. "We can pick some stuff in town."

"Go ahead, call," Lola said. "We got a phone."

"Gotta use a pay phone," Nacho said.

"Why?"

"He's gotta make a call that can't be traced," the soft voice said. "If they've bugged the number, the fuzz can trace it back here."

"Why didn'cha say something before?" Lola said.

"Didn't think we'd be here so long."

"You and Nach go to town," soft voice said. "He makes his call, you get some grub and I stay here."

"What about the mouth in the room next door?" Lola said.

"Jorge can watch her," Nacho said.

Jorge. A name for the voice.

"You cool with that?" Lola said.

"No worries."

"She ain't had nothing to eat since last night," Lola said. "Can you fix her something?"

"I'll take care of it."

"Awright. It's just she's got a bad mouth..."

"C'mon, Lo," Nacho said. "Quicker we go, quicker we get back."

Ruth heard Lola grumble some more, then the door bang shut.

Who is this guy? He seemed anxious for them to leave...

Ruth heard footsteps to the door, then it squeaked open.

A big man with a pockmarked face stood in the doorway. He stared at her with big, bright yellow hazel, eyes, then took out a knife, snapped open the blade.

She tensed.

"No one's gonna hurt you," he said. "That tape's chaffing your wrists."

In one swift motion, he sliced through the duct tape binding her wrists, then cut her ankles free. Snapping the knife shut, he slipped it into his pocket then helped her sit up.

His touch was gentle-- even stripping the tape from her had a soft demeanor. He helped her to her feet, then guided her into the kitchen to a chair.

"Sit down here for a minute," he said.

Stepping over to a canvas bag near the table, Jorge took out a green can labeled, *BAG BALM*, then brought it to the table.

"Rub some of that on your wrists while I rustle us something up to eat."

Ruth rubbed the pungent, oily cream on her reddened wrists.

"I found some eggs, a can of chili beans and some corn tortillas," he said.

Ruth choked back tears.

Is this a good-guy/bad-guy routine?

Jorge sat a paper napkin with a knife and fork in front of her.

"There's coffee. Don't see any milk but there's sugar."

"Black's fine," Ruth murmured.

Jorge poured her coffee in a chipped white cup, then rinsed out a small Mason jar, poured himself some.

"This was cleaner than the cups," he said. "How do you like your eggs?"

"Scrambled," Ruth managed to say.

"Cool. So do I."

Jorge found some butter, spread it on the skillet, then heated up the stove. Breaking 6 eggs into a bowl, he whipped them up with a fork, poured them into the hot skillet. Then, he opened the can of chili beans with his knife. Stirring the eggs once more with the fork, he shook the beans out on top then stirred the mixture as it heated.

"Don't see no salt or pepper but the beans will cover it," he said.

Separating the food into two plates, he set one in front of Ruth, turned to warm the tortillas.

Ruth stared at the case knife beside her plate, then at the back of the man firing the tortillas on the stove. She didn't move.

Jorge set a plate of warmed tortillas on the table, then said,

"Let's eat."

Not having eaten since the night before, Ruth scooped beans and scrambled egg up with the tortilla, plopped them in her mouth. Jorge looked over at her.

"You part Mexican?" he said.

"No. Just love Mexican food."

"Huh."

Ruth looked down at the knife by her plate.

"Weren't you worried about turning your back to me with a knife on the table."

"No," Jorge said without looking up from his plate.

When she had finished, Ruth wiped her mouth with the paper napkin.

"You hooked up with Santos too?" she said.

"Nacho's friend," Jorge said.

Ruth didn't say anymore as Jorge took the dishes to the sink, rinsed then stacked them.

"More coffee?" he said.

"No. Makes me pee."

Jorge sat down near her, picked up a book, started to read.

Ruth looked over the book.

"You're reading *Ulysses*?" she said.

"Yeah. Read it couple a times."

"Why?"

"Liked it. Don't usually read a book more'n once."

"You liked it?"

"Joyce's cool. He kinda turns Homer's Odyssey topsy turvey."

"Really."

"Leopold Bloom's counterpart to Odysseus but Molly's hardly Penelope and Stephan Dedalus's kind of a weird combo of Telemachus and some of the gods."

"You've read the Odyssey too?'

"Lotsa times," Jorge said. "Some things you just gotta keep reading over and over."

Ruth blinked, rubbed her wrists.

Jorge returned to his reading.

PART SIX

Surprise, Surprise, Surprise
Parking Structure above Law Offices, Los Angeles, CA
Same day, 11:48 PM, Friday night

The ceiling lights in the parking structure cast long shadows over the few cars parked along the long wall. The muted light blended colors into mottled dark shades of gray, brown and black.

Pepe and Jake crouched in the shadows next to a navy blue Mercedes.

The light over the elevator door blinked. A bell chimed. The door slid back with a subdued clink. Casimiro "Cassie" Cortez stepped out, loosened at the neck, suit jacket open, briefcase dangling in his hand.

Walking over to the navy blue Mercedes, he reached in his pockets for his key.

Pepe and Jake come at him from both ends of the Mercedes, pinned both his arms behind his back. Pepe had the fiber-lined strapping tape strip in his hand, popped it over Cortez's mouth. Cortez tried to yell, kick with his feet.

Pepe grabbed his ankles, wound the tape around them. Jake slung Cortez onto his belly on the hood of the car. Pepe peeled off another stretch then wound the roll around Cortez's wrists and hands.

Cortez struggled to get to his tethered feet.

Pushing Cortez into Jake's open arms, Pepe retrieved the Mercedes key from his pocket, opened the back door. Jake, heaved Cortez inside onto the floor between the back and front seats, then grabbed his brief case, threw it in on top of him.

Pepe took the driver's side, Jake in the front passenger seat. Pepe started the car, drove out toward the exit.

Stopping at a key pad, Jake punched in numbers. The arm raised, Pepe drove out into the traffic.

"Nice thing about being a fireman," Jake said. "You have access to emergency entrance codes to gated parking lots."

~*~*~

Comrade Banker

Central Minsk, Autonomous Republic of Belarus, USSR
10:12 AM, Saturday, January 25, 1975

It always snows in Minsk during the winter. Sharp winds whipped snow-flurries over the sidewalks, streets, roadways. It was almost noon, traffic was light. The black Zil crept along the street with lights on, wipers slapping, two faces peering through the frosted windows. Sergei Ivanovich Kasherov pulled his overcoat over his shoulders, looked over at his KGB, colleague Mikhail Svyatislavovich Sharpinsky huddled over the steering wheel.

"Do you think that maybe one day," Kasherov said, "they'll give us a car with a heater that works?"

"Why do that, Comrade? We have our love for the party to keep us warm."

"I'd settle for a big roaring fire, near a comfortable chair, my feet up and a glass of French cognac in my hand."

"So," Sharpinsky said, "you're not above capitalist indulgences."

"Misha, I'd send my mother to Siberia for a bottle of French cognac."

"Spoken like a true party member."

Kasherov pointed out the window. "Here's the bank."

They parked the car in front of the bank, hurried inside through the falling snow. Kasherov flashed his KGB ID to the woman at the front desk before she said a word.

"Where is Director Litzov's office?" he said.

The woman looked at the two big men through round horn-rimmed glasses, pointed to a large office sealed off by frosted, opaque windows, another secretary stationed in front.

They marched there without thanking her. The IDs came out again. The secretary hit a buzzer that opened the door to the inner office. Coming in, they found Litzov talking on the phone. He frowned.

"Yes?" he said.

Kasherov stepped to Litzov's desk thrusting out his ID.

"Comrade Director Isak Davidovitch Litzov, I am Captain Sergei Ivanovich, Kasherov, KGB and this is Sergeant Mikhail Svyatislavovich Sharpinsky."

Litzov excused himself, hung up the phone, scowled at Kasherov.

"So?" he growled.

"I must ask you to come with us, Comrade," Kasherov said. "We have a few questions to ask you down at headquarters about your banking operations."

"Then, I must suggest, Comrade," Litzov said, "that you make an appointment with my secretary and I'll be delighted to discuss it at a more convenient time."

Kasherov smiled a tired smile.

"You'll come with us now, Comrade Litzov."

Litzov leaned across the desk, his face a mask of contempt.

"Listen, ratshit," he said. "One call to your boss, Comrade General Leonid Petrovich Gruznitsky and you'll be pushing paper in Siberia."

Kasherov indicated the telephone. "Call."

Still glaring at them, Litzov snatched up the phone. "Galena. Put me through to Moscow, Comrade General Gruznitsky, director KGB."

Litzov put his hand over the speaker, sneered at the two men.

"I hope you two turds enjoy your new assignment in Novaya Zemlya," he said.

Scowling at the two men watching him, he returned to the call.

"Hello, this is Director Litzov, People's International Bank in Minsk. I would speak with General Gruznitsky."

Litzov's eyes bulged. "What?" he choked, then stammered, "When? Who's in charge? Oh."

Litzov stared up at Kasherov, the phone still in his hand.

"Alas, Comrade director," Kasherov said. "General Gruznitsky has met with a terrible accident. We're here at the orders of our new Commandant, General Slushikov."

Litzov stared, unbelieving first at Kasherov, then at Sharpinsky. Then, the banker sank down in his chair, murmured, "A moment. A moment, Comrades."

Kasherov shrugged. "A moment, then."

The KGB man stepped back. Litzov reached under his desk, snatched up a small nickel plated automatic, pointed it at the two KGB officers.

"Back!" he snarled.

Kasherov and Sharpinsky stepped back, hands raised.

"This solves nothing, Isak Davidovich," Kasherov said. "Put down the gun."

Litzov thrust the gun, first at one, then the other.

"Back!" he snapped. "Hands raised."

When the two moved toward the rear of the office, Litzov thrust the pistol into his mouth, pulled the trigger. At the muffled, hollow bang of the report, the back of Litzov's head popped off. He fell forward across the desk, blood running down the desk, leaving the back of his expensive suit spattered with blood, the gore from brains.

Karsherov and Sharpinsky slowly lowered their hands. Sharpinsky stepped over, pried the gun from Litzov's fingers, put it into his pocket.

"Shit!" he said. "He caught us like a pair of amateurs."

Karsherov flopped down into a chair. "This complicates things."

A crowd gathered outside the door. Karsherov looked around, heaved himself to his feet, opened the door.

"Touch nothing," he said. "An investigation team will be here in minutes. Who's in charge of foreign accounts?"

Karsherov saw a man raise his hand. "Round up whatever records you can find and make yourself available for questions."

Sharpinsky sidled up to his colleague. "Maybe the team can turn up something."

Karsherov looked at him.

"And, maybe they can't."

Sharpinsky stared at the dead man's body stretched across the desk.

"You know, Sergei Ivanovich," he said. "That Jew sonfabitch could've been right. We just might be protecting the fatherland in Novaya Zemlya."

Karsherov stared at his colleague, but did not laugh.

A rattily friend
North of El Centro, Colorado Desert, SE California,
Same day, 6:05 AM, Saturday

Pepe looked back at Cortez kicking, trying to hit the seats with his knees and heels.

"Save your energy, amigo," he said. "It's gonna be a long ride."

After a while Pepe noted Cortez had tired, was laying still, then pulled off at an all-night gas station. He stayed in the car while Jake went to the enclosed cashier's window, paid for gas.

When Cortez kicked, banged the door, tried to yell through the tape. Pepe turned the radio on. Inside the enclosed window, the cashier did not even glance in their direction when Jake returned, filled the tank.

They drove back down the road, then Pepe turned off at Jake's directions onto an unmarked road leading into out the desert. After several miles, he turned off onto another unmarked road, driving along for about a half hour until they came to a rocky outcropping, splotched with bushes, scrawny mesquite trees.

Pepe stopped at Jake's command.

Jake got out, opened the door, jerked Cortez out, then leaned him back against the car as Pepe come to his side.

Cortez glared, tried to talk. Then Pepe ripped the tape from his mouth.

"Ow, that hurt, motherfucker," Cortez said.

"Sorry," Pepe said.

Cortez looked from Pepe to Jake. "Who the fuck are you two?"

"Not important," Pepe said. "Where's Ruth Hall?"

"Who?"

"Don't get cute," Jake said.

"I dunno what you're talking about."

"Bullshit," Jake said.

Cortez leaned back against the car, balancing himself on his bound feet. "You two crapheads are in some serious shit."

"No kidding," Jake said.

"Kidnaping is a capital offense in California," Cortez said. "Both your asses will be in for life."

"Assuming you'll be around," Jake said.

Cortez looked around. "I gotta piss."

"Tough," Jake said.

"Tell us where Ruth is and we'll cut you loose," Pepe said.

"Fuck you."

"OK," Pepe said. "Piss on yourself."

Cortez squirmed. "C'mon, man. I gotta go bad."

Jake said to Pepe, "Think Ruth got to take a whiz after his pals grabbed her?"

"I doubt it," Pepe said.

"All right, fuckers," Cortez screamed. "I can take anything you give me."

"That makes it easy for everybody," Pepe said.

Jake grabbed Cortez by his tie.

"Where's Ruth?"

"I don't fucking know."

When Jake drew back his fist, Pepe raised his hand.

"That won't do any good," he said.

Jake dropped his hand, took a few steps away, looking around the landscape.

"You talk to this shit," he said. "I'm gonna take a little walk."

He strode over to the rocky outcropping, climbing over the dried crusted rocks, sparse bushes.

Pepe turned back to Cortez. "Where're your cousins?'

"Fuck you."

"They grabbed Ruth to cover Santos's ass?"

"I dunno what you're talking about."

"That guy is Matt Spyner's brother."

"Who the fuck's that?"

"The brother of the man Santos robbed and killed."

Cortez twisted his head to look back where Jake had gone.

"The only thing keeping him from twisting your head off is me," Pepe said.

"Let him twist," Cortez said. "Fuck with me and you still got nothing."

"We got nothing now, Cassie. And, nothing to lose."

Cortez shot him a frown.

Maybe we can work out a deal," he said.

"What do you have in mind?"

"Lemme go and I'll do what I can to spring the gal."

Pepe turned, bent over, looked into the side mirror of the car.

"Excuse me," he said. "I just wanted to see for myself if I really do look that stupid."

Pepe stuck his face in Cortez's.

"Let you go, *chavalito*? Well, then we're busted and Ruth's still in shit."

"Back off, man," Cortez said. "You can't bully me."

Pepe saw Jake coming back with something wrapped around his arm.

Jake came straight up to Cortez.

"I'd like you to meet a friend," Jake said.

He thrust a four foot rattlesnake coiled around his arm into Cortez's face, its shovel shaped head wedged between his fingers.

"Not just your ordinary buzztail– this is a Mojave Green," Jake said. "It's the only pit viper in the world with neurotoxic venom and he's not in a very good mood because I've disturbed his winter nap."

Cortez's pants darkened with urine. He leaned back making choking, gasping sounds.

Jake squeezed the snake behind its head between his thumb and forefinger. The snake opened its mouth, fangs protruding. Jake held it next to Cortez's face.

"This guy's bite's like a cobra's," Jake said. "You'll be dead in about an hour and a half, two hours. During that time, your tongue'll swell, you'll try to breath. But you won't. The venom will shut down the nerves that work your respiratory system. You'll be fully conscious and in great pain as you suffocate, slowly."

"Take that fucking snake away," Cortez screamed. "Take it away!"

Jake unwound the tail from around his arm. "Pepe, pull his pants open," he said.

"What...?" Cortez gasped. "What're you doing, man. Stop it. Stop! Oh, God. Stop!"

Pepe loosened Cassie's belt as Jake slid the thrashing tail of the snake down into the front of his pants.

"I can only hold this snake for about another minute, fuckhead," Jake said. "It's loaded with venom. It'll bite you a dozen times once I let go."

"Don't do that, man. Don't do that. Oh, shit. Don't..."

"My fingers are starting to cramp."

"Where's Ruth?" Pepe growled.

"Nacho and Lola got her in a shack over near El Centro."

"Where near El Centro?" Pepe said.

"Their family has an old coyote shack outside of town."

"We need a map." Pepe said.

"There's one in my brief case."

Pepe opened the door, took out the briefcase.

"Locked," he said. "What's the combo?

Cortez rolled his eyes, the snake's body was thrashing in his pants. Jake held the snake's open mouth closer to Cortez's face.

"Eight, five, four, eight," he screamed.

Pepe snapped it open, rummaged through papers, pulled up a county map, looked it over.

"Got it," he said.

"We're not done, " Pepe said. "Who all is there?"

"Just Santos, Nacho, Lola and Jorge."

Pepe looked over at Jake.

"Hey, man I played it straight," Cortez said.

He was in tears.

"Don't let that snake go on me– I told you what you want."

Jake pulled the snake out, walked to the bushes, released it.

The snake twisted off into the brush like a dart.

Cortez's eyes were wide, his cheeks pale, his face in a sweat.

"Ain't you gonna kill that goddam thing?"

"No reason to." Jake said.

Pepe looked at his watch.

"Let's go," he said. "If we lean on it, we can be there in a few hours."

Cortez lurched forward. "Hey, what about me? You can't leave me here."

"Oh, I almost forgot," Pepe said.

He grabbed Cortez, turned him around, cut a nick into the tape holding his hands.

"What're you doing?" Cortez screamed over his shoulder. "That ain't fucking off."

Pepe folded his pocket knife, slipped it back into his pocket.

"No, amigo," he said. "Not cut through– but, it's got a nick. You can worry around and get it off your hands by tonight."

"Hey, you're not going to leave me here."

"Afraid so," Jake said. "We gotta go get Ruth away from your pals."

"Hey, man. I told you what you want. Don't leave me out here."

"Tell you what," Jake said. "I'll just trade you a canteen of water for your shoes."

Reaching over, he slipped off Cortez's shoes, threw one in the bushes, broke the heel off the other, threw into the rocks.

"Be careful when you retrieve those shoes," Jake said. "Mojave Greens have a nasty disposition this time of year."

Pepe sat a polyethylene canteen on the ground next to Cortez.

"See you later, counselor," Pepe said.

Cortez was still screaming at them when Jake and Pepe drove away.

~*~*~

Preflight jitters
Airstrip at Rio Riego, 25 km outside of Acapulco, Mexico
Same day, 4:48 PM, Saturday

Lucero awoke from his nap with a start, sat on the edge of the bed, looked out the window.

The setting sun threw shadows from the nearby hills over the landing strip. Looking around for his shoes, he stood, stretched, slipped them on, then left the room.

Downstairs he found Drako pacing.

"You should have taken a siesta, Ivo," Lucero said. "I feel like a new man."

"Some new developments on the financial front," Drako said. "I just talked to Moscow."

"What about our Russian friends?"

"Litzov's dead."

"How?"

"Change in Moscow. They left the back door open. The KGB got in."

"What happened?"

"Litzov blew his brains out rather than be taken."

"So, who's running their money?"

"You're gonna like this. Your boy, Montoya."

Lucero gasped, then said, "When?"

"This kid's good, Luis. He dug into the old Zorro's connections and hooked up with his rogue banker in Israel."

255

"No!"

"The Russians have passed their money problems off to him."

"He never mentioned it to me." Lucero said.

"You trained him good. He keeps his eyes and ears open but his mouth shut."

"When did all this happen?"

"Today. Montoya arranged all the money transfers for the heroin purchase."

Lucero's face paled. He grabbed the phone. It rang.

"Bueno."

"The wind sings," Montoya said in Nahuatl.

"The mountains listen," Lucero said. "We're here at Rio Reigo."

"Did you hear the Old Zorro's pal, Litzov, was set up by the Russians to take a fall? He killed himself in front of the KGB."

"Ivo just told me."

"The Russians asked me to take over running their accounts. One of Litzov's stooges contacted me. He can do the same transfers in and out of the Soviet Union as Litzov was doing through this guy in Israel."

"Oh?"

"They just made this offer earlier today. I tried to call to clear it with you, but they said you were out. I passed this on to Sr. Drako. But, it's your final decision. What do you think?"

Lucero heaved a sigh, smiled, looked over at Drako, winked and said, "As the Gringos say, 'go for it.' "

"This will work well for all of us."

Luis hung up, breathed a sigh of relief.

"When's the pilot supposed to get here?" Drako said.

"Have you forgotten that I know how to fly? We can take off anytime we want."

Drako flinched. "I'll wait."

"No problem, Amigo."

Drako looked away. "Whatever happened to the guy, the Rattler?"

Lucero frowned, poured himself a glass of water, then walked over to the window, looking out into the yard. Turning back to Ivo, he wiped his mouth.

"Rydell called me earlier today," Lucero said. "He said the guy got wind of the trap, took out Mauricio and bolted to ground."

"He took out Mauricio? Impossible!"

"I'm afraid that's what happened."

"There's gotta be a tie in to all this shit going on here."

"Naw. The Rattler and Rydell are completely out of the picture. Rydell's a twit and screwed things setting this guy up."

"What're you going to do about that?"

Lucero looked over at the hanger. "Mauricio was like family– from my home town. I'll hang Rydell's ass out to dry when we get back."

"And, this Rattler guy, is he a loose cannon?"

"He's what the Gringos call a 'local yokel–' just a hired gun who's a long way from here and has no direct links to us."

Drako looked around. "When are we taking off?"

"The pilot will be here around sunset," Lucero said. "We'll take off at dusk, fly out over the sea and on down to Guatemala. We'll be in there sometime this evening."

"So, what do we do till then?"

Lucero stood, stretched. "Don't know about you, Ivo. But I'm going to have a bite to eat."

~*~*~

Un par de pendejos
75 miles outside of El Centro, CA
Same day, 5:44 PM, Saturday

Pepe fed directions from Cortez's map to Jake who drove, sweeping the landscape, scanning through the rear view mirrors for Highway Patrolmen. Sparse traffic presented little obstacle as the navy blue Mercedes hit over 90 mph on the straight stretches of road.

"What do you call a smoke-eater and an ex-cop professor out to take on a rip-off author, two professional killers, a mad Mexican woman and God knows who else with no plan of attack?" Jake said.

"*Un par de pendejos*,' 'Pepe said. "A pair of dummies' comes to mind."

"Back home we say 'more balls than brains.' "

"We say that in Mexico too."

Pepe went on, "A primatologist colleague of mine who studies baboons told me that when a female monkey comes into estrus ..."

"Into what?"

"Estrus. Heat. Sexual receptivity."

"Ah, horny in the animal sense."

"... the dominant males keep the subdominant males away."

"Makes sense."

"But, turns out there are smaller males who get a big fuss started with the nearby sub-dominant males, so that when the bigger guy comes over to investigate, the little guy sneaks over, mounts the ovulating female and pow, pow, starts humping like crazy."

"Just like us."

"Then, he takes off like hell."

"Interesting. What do they call these guys?"

"SLFs."

"SLFs?"

"Sneaky little fuckers."

Jake shrugged his shoulders, said, "We know there'll be this guy Santos, Nacho, the Rattler and the girl friend– frankly, she's the one who scares me the most."

"How so?"

"Barrio Chicanas are ranker than cornered cougars."

It was early afternoon when they pulled off toward where the map showed the house. Driving through the rolling, sandy hills, Pepe pointed to a stand of Joshua trees.

"Pull over there," he said.

Jake rolled the car to a dusty stop in the sparse shade of the desert trees. Pepe spread the map on the car's dashboard, then pointed to a sharp curve in the road that forked behind low-lying hills.

"From what it shows here," Pepe said, "the house is about a mile or two down that road."

"Can't drive in," Jake said. "They'd see the dust and hear us coming long before we'd get there."

"They'd know the car. But then what? We can't jump out, assault guns blazing."

"Yeah. No assault guns."

Pepe poked Jake's shoulder with his outstretched fingers.

"You mean you didn't bring the assault guns?"

"Coulda brought a fire hose."

Pepe checked his belt holster. "I have my piece."

Jake looked at the Colt 45, M1911, Army issue.

"Looks like an antique left over from the 1899 Philippine insurrection."

"Probably is," Pepe said. "Also got my ankle piece."

Pepe striped a holstered Sig-Sauer P229 from his ankle, then handed it to Jake.

Jake drew the pistol, jacked a round into the chamber, then slipped the small, compact weapon into his pocket.

"Let's hope we can get the jump on them," he said.

"Our advantage is surprise and cunning."

"Just our being here screws the cunning part," Jake said.

"It'll be dark soon," Pepe said. "Did you remember the flashlights?"

"Firemen don't go anywhere without flashlights. I brought us each two."

Jake took two heavy cast aluminum flashlights out of his bag, handed one to Pepe, then slipped a smaller one into Pepe's pocket.

"Never know when you'll need to use both hands," Jake said. "You can hold this little MiniMag in your teeth."

After parking the Mercedes behind a hillock, Pepe set off with Jake alongside the road. After walking about three miles, Jake spotted the house around a foothill. They scrambled up to the top of the foothill, laid on their bellies overlooking the house about 200 yards below them.

Pepe stuck his hand out to Jake.

"Hand me the binoculars," he said.

"What binoculars?"

"Forgot them with the assault rifles, huh," Pepe said. "Amigo, next time I pack for the trip."

Jake surveyed the house. "Two cars. One's a van."

"Down!" Pepe said. "Someone's coming out."

Two big men in loose-fitting shirts, slacks sauntered out of the cabin beyond the parked cars. The first man wore sun-glasses, his long black hair swept straight back. The other's hair was cut to the scalp around the edges, buzz cut on top.

Pepe heard only murmurs of their conversation on the breeze as they unzipped their pants, backs toward the house, then urinated.

"At least they're gentlemen," Jake whispered.

"I've seen the buzz-cut before," Pepe said.

"Where?"

"I saw him get off the night Ruth's roommate was murdered."

"Must be the Rattler."

"That other big bastard is Nacho."

The snick of a door-bang spanked their ears. A woman strode out. The men below buttoned pants.

"And Baby makes three," Jake said.

~*~*~

Off we go…
Airstrip at Rio Riego, 25 km outside of Acapulco, Mexico
Same day, 5:22 PM, Saturday

Lucero saw the guards outside raise their weapons. A red Porsche open convertible wheeled into the space beside the limousine.

"What do we have here?" Lucero said.

Ivo stood at Lucero's side.

"The pilot finally got here," Drako said.

Lucero saw a tall Mexican wearing a light blue shirt with black shoulder boards showing four white stripes, uncoil his legs from the roadster, then step out of the car with his hands raised.

"Gentlemen," he said. "Don't shoot or your boss will have a long walk to Guatemala."

Reaching back into the Porsche, The pilot pulled out a flat-toped brief case, popped a pilot's peaked cap on his head.

One of the guards stepped forward, looked inside the briefcase, patted the pilot down front, back, then stepped back.

"Follow me, *Capitán*," he said.

Lucero and Drako stepped out to meet him on the veranda. Lucero frowned.

"Where's Javier?" he said.

The pilot brushed his chin with the tips of his fingers.

"I've no idea, Señor Alban. Cardo Montoya told me to come here and fly you to Guatemala."

"Who're you?" Lucero said.

"Hector Delgado," he said, handing Lucero his wallet case.

"Come inside," Lucero said.

Without taking his eyes from him, Lucero went over, picked up the phone, punched in numbers, waited for the voice to click on.

"Bueno."

The question in Nahuatl. "Who am I?"

"You are you. I am me."

"Who's this pilot?"

"Hector Delgado. He knows where to take you very discretely."

"You're sure there's no problem?"

"I trust Hector with my life..."

"Where'd he learn to fly?"

"Mexican Air Force. He's very good"

"Anything else?"

"All arrangements have been made for you to be met upon arrival."

"Very well."

"Happy landings," Montoya said.

At a Georgian hot springs
Djugashvili Hot Springs, Tbilisi, Republic of Georgia, USSR
2:32 AM, Sunday morning, January 30, 1975

When the four big men in ski masks trotted into the steaming spa with guns in their hands, the naked men and women sprawled around the sides of the indoor pool, ran for cover.

The armed men fanned out, pointing the muzzles of their guns at a door of a room at the back of the spa.

One of them yelled,

"Niolai Sergeyevitch!"

The voice that boomed from inside was angry, impatient.

"Who wants to know?"

"We have a message from Viktor Gladkov, Comrade."

"What?"

Some rustling sounds emerged from inside. The door opened, Markovsky, naked with a towel around his middle, poked his head out. Seeing the guns, he jumped back, slamming the door.

The guns erupted, shredding the door, filling the air with splinters of wood, paint, smells of cordite. The men emptied their automatic weapons, snapped taped banana-curved magazine clips into the chambers, then emptied these into the doorway.

The man who spoke, stepped up, smashed open the remains of the tattered door with a kick revealing a bed splattered with blood. Markovsky's body lay back, splayed over the bloody sheets. A teenage girl's trembling body slumped against the blood-spattered, hole-filled wall.

Blood oozing from his mouth, Markovsky moved his lips, blinked his eyes.

The man whipped out a pistol holster, fired three rounds into Markovsky's forehead, than stalked out of the spa with the others behind him.

Unpleasant alternatives
Lola's cabin outside of El Centro, CA
Same day, 6:04 PM, Saturday

Lola's voice rang carried over the sandy slopes.

"Just like a pair of dogs, gotta come out here and piss. Why didn't you piss on the tires?"

Nacho ignored the remark.

"What's up?" he said.

"She ain't got any manuscript," Lola said. "She's bluffing."

"You sure?" Nacho said.

"Sure as I'm gonna be."

Nacho turned, looked out over the landscape, muttered something too low to be heard.

Lola raised her voice,

"There's nothing to her story- no manuscript to send to the cops or any shit like that."

"What's your call?" Jorge's said.

Nacho walked away a few steps.

"I ain't offing no girls," he said.

"I didn't say you had to off her," Lola said.

"We talk to Santos first," Nacho said.

"This bitch's standing in the way of our getting outta here," Lola said. "If she gets loose and blabs, it could be our asses."

"They can extradite you from Brazil for kidnaping," Jorge said.

"So, what you saying, homie?" Nacho said.

"Man, like your sister says," Jorge said. "Got an obstacle–remove it."

Nacho looked over at Jorge. "Can you do it, Man?"

Jorge shrugged. "No problem."

Nacho just stared at the horizon. Lola came over, patted him on the back.

"We'll call Santos later."

Nacho lowered his head for a while, then turned.

"I'm getting hungry," he said.

"Didn't you bring anything besides tortillas and beans?" Jorge said.

"We got some more canned chili con carne," Lola said.

Jorge shrugged. "Same shit."

The three turned, walked together back to the house.

~*~*~

... Into the wild, blue yonder

Airstrip at Rio Riego, 25 km outside of Acapulco, Mexico
Same day, 6:14 PM, Saturday

Lucero watched the pilot lugging his flight case, slip between two armed guards into the hanger. The guards scowled but then stepped aside when Lucero and Drako approached.

The silver gray Lear jet crouched like a huge hawk on the hanger floor. The 4 man maintenance crew greeted the pilot as he scrambled up the accommodation ladder to the cabin. A few seconds later, Lucero saw him emerge with a clip board, then walk around doing the aircraft's ground check.

After the guards stowed their bags aboard, the pilot strolled over to Lucero and Drako.

"Gentlemen," he said. "Ground check completed. Let's be off."

"I'm a pilot too, Captain," Lucero said. "If you need a rest, I can spell you."

The pilot flashed Lucero a wide smile.

"Thank you, Sr. Alban," he said. "Always comforting to know I have a copilot."

Lucero climbed aboard into the passenger's cabin, took the seat across from Drako.

Juan, the only guard accompanying them sat facing Lucero and Drako in the seat behind the flight cabin.

Lucero looked out the porthole at the maintenance crew starting the engines, then heard the pilot rev them up when they kicked over.

After he taxied the aircraft to the end of the runway, the pilot braked, ran the engines up to full throttle. The Lear jet trembled like a sky creature lusting to become airborne.

Lucero felt the brakes release, the aircraft gather speed, then lift off at the end of the runway.

Lucero looked over at Drako, the knuckles of his hands pale from gripping the arms of the leather passenger chair.

"Relax, Ivo," Lucero said. "We'll be there soon."

Drako glared back at him.

The pilot's voice came over the cabin speaker.

"Welcome aboard, Gentlemen. It'll be about a three hour flight. I'll be taking a longer route, because some of my former colleagues in the Mexican Air Force might be looking for us along the Western coastline. So, we'll be taking the scenic route, coming into Guatemala from the Caribbean just south of Belize."

"See, Ivo," Lucero said. "Nothing to worry about."

"Nothing to worry about!" Ivo said. "Some rat lurking to turn us, 12 million dollars of raw heroin in the luggage compartment, every cop and hood out there looking for us..."

When the plane leveled off, Lucero loosened his seat belt, lit a small cigar.

"Juan," he said to the bodyguard. "Could you be so kind as to get your old *patrón* a glass of mescal."

Juan unbuckled the seat belt, made his way to the bar section to the aft of the cabin.

"Something for you, Ivo?" Lucero said.

"No," Drako said.

"Juan," Lucero said. "Get him a vodka."

Ivo glared at Lucero. "I'm not a Russian."

Lucero looked over at Juan.

"Of course," Lucero said. "Bring him a slivovitz."

~*~*~

Insertion
Lola's cabin outside of El Centro, CA
Same day, 7:54 PM, Saturday

Pepe said to Jake, "It's as dark as it's gonna get."
"What's the first step?"
Pepe pointed to the cabin.
"See that window at the back?" he said. "Ruth might be in there."
"Right behind you," Jake said.
They jogged down to the back side of the house in the darkened shadows. The old fashioned two panel window was open at the top, a frame screen covered the outside. Looking into the darkened room Pepe saw Ruth lying on her side facing the door, her hands and feet taped.
He shined the flashlight on her face.
She jerked around, caught her breath.
Holding his finger to his lips, Pepe cut the screen with his pocketknife. After taking it off, he opened the window, crawled into the room.
Coming to the bed, he slit the tape holding her hands, then cut her boots free.
The bedroom door opened. Jorge stepped in with a plate of beans.
"What the fuck...!" he yelled.

~*~*~

Moscow nights
Krasnaya Zvezda District, Moscow, USSR
Earlier, 4:44 PM, Sunday

Vladimir Pavlovich Potapov waved to the armed guard at the iron gate as he left his house. In the front seat, his body guard surveyed the passing traffic with a pistol in his lap while the driver turned the Mercedes onto the street leading out into the main avenue.

Coming into downtown, Potapov took out a silver cigarette case, selected a hand-rolled Turkish tobacco cigarette with a gold band at the filter, tapped it on the case before putting it into his mouth. He reached into the pocket of his overcoat for his lighter, as the driver slowed down for a slow-moving truck on the traffic choked street.

A tarp covering the back of the truck in front flew open. Two men kneeling on one knee raised rocket propelled grenades to their shoulders, then fired into the front window of the Mercedes in a single burst of flame. At the same time, another man fired an RPG into the Mercedes's back window from behind a parked car on the side of the street.

The big black car bucked up at the simultaneous dual explosion, then rolled to its side after the third burst, becoming a blazing ball of torn metal, burning flesh.

The man on the street tossed the empty firing frame of the RPG, ran out from behind the car, climbed onto the back of the truck with help from the two men in the back.

The tarp over the back of the bed truck flapped down, the truck screeched away from the stopped traffic blocked by the burning wreck on the busy avenue.

~*~*~

Confrontation
Lola's cabin outside of El Centro, CA
Same day, 8:04 PM, Saturday

Pepe dropped the knife, pulled his pistol from his holster.

Jorge slammed the plate against his hand knocking the gun to the floor, grabbed Pepe off the bed, then sprang on his back. Pepe shoved his feet against the edge of the bed, driving his body back into Jorge. Both men rolled to their backs on the floor, Jorge groping for Pepe's throat.

Pepe threw his head back smacking Jorge in his face, then heard a thunk when Jorge's head struck the floor. Stunned, the big man loosened his grip.

Pepe rolled off to one side.

Jorge recovered, rolled to his left, pulling a pistol from his belt.

Jake's flying body smashed down on Jorge, crushing him to the floor, pressing the pistol against his chest.

In reflex to the impact, Jorge jerked the trigger. The gun discharged into his chest.

He shuddered, groaned, then relaxed.

Nacho burst through the bedroom door gun in hand, popped two shots.

Jake rolled off Jorge's body, crossing his arms over his chest. Pepe leapt up onto Nacho, knocking the pistol out of his hand. Nacho fell back, clawing at his attacker's face.

Snatching the small flashlight from his pocket. Pepe shoved it into Nacho's throat, feeling the soft crack of the hyoid bone crushing his windpipe.

Nacho gasped for air, gurgled. Gripping his throat with both hands, he staggered back, then fell to the floor on his knees. He clutched at his throat, tried to rise. He stumbled forward, kicked his legs, convulsed for a few seconds then pitched forward on his face.

Lola lunged through the doorway, slashing at Pepe with a butcher knife, screaming.

"You killed my brother!"

Pepe rolled away from the attack.

Lola, her face a Greek masque of rage. fell on him, raising the knife. Throwing his arm up to fend off the blow, Pepe heard a smack, then saw Lola's eyes roll. The knife dropped from her hand, she flopped to the floor.

Ruth stood there, Jake's heavy flashlight in her hands.

Happy landings
Aboard the Lear Jet, over Mexico
Same day, 9:04 PM, Saturday

The flight went on. Lucero smoked little cigars, read his magazine. Ivo fidgeted with his fingers, smoked cigarettes, looked around him. Juan sat watching them, hands in his lap, a half-smile on his lips.

A shift in the attitude of the aircraft made Lucero look up.

"We're turning again," he said.

Laying down his magazine, Lucero unbuckled, made his way to the flight cabin, opened the door, stuck his head in.

"How're we doing?" he said to the pilot.

"Be there in about 25 minutes," the pilot said.

Lucero glanced at the compass.

"North?" he said.

"Yes," the pilot said. "We picked up a military contact south of Yucatan. He got on my tail and I kept going south. Lost him about ten minutes ago over Nicaragua."

"You sure you lost him?"

"For sure. We're only slightly behind schedule."

Lucero closed the door, went back to his seat.

"We dodged another bullet," he said to Drako.

"What?"

"We were being trailed by a military aircraft but we gave him the slip over Nicaragua."

"Military aircraft?"

"Yeah. They sneak up on and track private flights looking for drug runners. The Gringo Air Force will challenge suspicious flights and shoot them down but the Mexican Air Force just tracks them."

"That doesn't sound good."

"This kid, Delgado, knows what he's doing."

"If he doesn't, we're screwed."

The plane banked again.

"See, Ivo. What did I tell you? We're coming in now."

Ivo caught his breath, released it in a loud wheeze.

"I'll be glad when this day is over," he said.

The night outside was cloudy. Wisps of clouds brushed by the porthole windows. The cabin vibrated with the sound of the flaps, the landing gear locking in place. The landing strip lights rolled by the portholes as the aircraft banked into its final approach.

Their ears popped as they dropped down, straightened for the final approach over the airstrip.

The plane leveled off, bleeding off speed, jarred, thumped down on the tarmac.

There was a halting motion as the jet engines reversed thrust, followed by a braking motion then a turn.

They taxied for a few hundred yards, then stopped. The engines shut down.

Lucero looked around.

"That was a short taxi," he said.

Juan unbuckled his seat belt, started to rise.

The pilot stepped through the cabin door, shoved Juan to the floor, stuck a foot on his back, pointed a pistol at Lucero and Drako.

"Gentlemen," he said. "For your health and safety, don't move."

Rattling sounds from outside rumbled through the aircraft, the door popped open, the accommodation ladder unfolded out onto the tarmac.

Dan James hopped up into the aircraft followed by four DEA agents, guns in hand.

"Welcome to the United States, *Señores.*" he said.

Lucero glared at the pilot. "Delgado. You're dead."

"Forgive a little white lie, Sr. Alban," the pilot said. "The name's Jaime Morales, FBI."

"You turncoat bastard. I'll see you and your family dead."

Sitting in a state of shock, Drako made no resistance as he was jerked to his feet, then handcuffed.

An agent cuffed the prone Juan, disarmed him, pulled him to his feet.

Dan James seized Lucero, pulled him to his feet.

"Take your fucking nigger hands off me," Lucero said.

James twisted Lucero's wrists, snapped a ring on one, then clicked the mate on the other.

"Talk like that can get you in serious trouble, Sr. Alban," James said.

James jerked Lucero up, shoved him toward the door.

"You're dead, *cabrón!*" Lucero screamed at Morales.

"I don't think so, Lucero," Morales said.

He turned to James, said, " Dan, you'll be delighted to see what I brought you back in the luggage compartment."

Lucero was still screaming as the DEA agents loaded him, Drako and Juan into the waiting van.

~*~*~

Aftershocks
Lola's cabin outside of El Centro, CA
Same day, 8:14 PM, Saturday

Pepe looked over at Jake.

"You OK?" he said.

"Shit no, I ain't OK," Jake said. "That sonfabitch shot me."

"Where are you hit?" Ruth said.

"Upper arm. Went clean through and missed the bone. He was a lousy shot. The first one missed me."

Ruth and Pepe helped Jake to the bed. Ruth tore off the pillow case, ripped it into strips.

Jake pressed them against his shoulder.

"This will staunch the bleeding," he said.

Looking around the room, Pepe shook his head.

"Helluva mess," he said.

Ruth stripped the rest of the tape from her hands.

"Damn near peed on myself when you shined that light on me," she said.

"We got lucky," Pepe murmured.

Jake winced. "They all dead?"

Pepe looked over the three bodies on the floor.

"Both of the guys bought it," he said. "Home girl's still groaning."

Jake grunted.

"Don't trust her," he said. "Those barrio bitches lie."

"Jake," Ruth said. "That was a sexist thing to say."

Jake looked over at Pepe, said. "Once a feminist, always a feminist."

Pepe knelt beside the groaning Lola.

"Ruth, do you know if there's any more of that tape?"

Ruth stepped over Jorge's bloody body into the outer room, came back with a roll of duct tape.

Pepe retrieved his knife, cut a stretch of tape then taped Lola's hands behind her back.

"I'll resist temptation and not kick her in the ribs," Ruth said.

"What happened to you?" Jake said.

"It was fast," Ruth said. "I went to the toilet at the site, stepped out and bam! That Nacho guy grabbed me and she slapped tape over my mouth, drugged me and next thing I knew, we were on our way here."

"Where's Santos?" Pepe said.

"He was here and then took off– they've been keeping him out of it as much as they could."

"Protect the goose that lays the golden egg," Jake said.

Ruth looked down at the body of Jorge.

"He was the most gentle one of the bunch."

Pepe and Jake looked at each other. Both men blinked.

"He was a reader," Ruth said. "Only person I've ever talked to that understood Joyce's *Ulysses*."

Lola groaned again, sat up, looked around, gurgled a loud cry, then screamed,

"They're dead. They're dead. Oh, you dirty bastards."

Pepe helped her to her feet, led her into the other room. Lola wept in a hoarse voice.

"You ruined everything," she said. "You shitty assholes."

Pepe sat down in front of her, looked into her eyes, said, "Where's Santos?"

Lola moaned, "They're dead, they're dead."

Pepe looked again into her tear streaked face.

"Lola, Where's Santos?"

She focused on the face in front of her. Her face twisted into a snarl.

"Who the fuck are you?" she said.

"Not important," Pepe said. "Where's Santos?"

"Why the fuck do you want to know?"

"Where's Santos?"

"Fuck you."

Jake came in, holding the bandage against his shoulder.

"Weren't there two maps in Cassie's briefcase?" he said to Pepe.

"Cassie!" Lola screamed. "Not him too! You dirty sons of bitches, filthy motherfuckers."

Pepe nodded to Jake.

"I'll go get it," he said. "Stay here and watch her– Ruth can drive me down in one of their cars."

Ruth found a set of keys on the table.

"I think these are for the van," she said. "Let's go."

Pepe and Ruth went out the door as Jake sat down in front of Lola.

Lola wept.

~*~*~

Confirmation
CS&FI Office, SDPD Building, San Diego, CA
Same day, 8:45 PM, Saturday

Bill Rowe came into the busy office. Helen Davis came running over, gave him a rib-cracking hug.

"They did it," she said.

"Thanks for the columnar readjustments," Bill said. "You saved me chiropractor treatments for next year.

"They brought down the Mexican drug cartel!"

Rowe blinked. "No shit?"

"No shit."

He looked around, saw an empty chair, eased his big frame down into it.

Helen plopped on a nearby desk, one shapely leg dangling over the edge.

"I just got the call from Dan. They lured the two major bigwigs back on US soil and caught them with a shit-pot full of smack and money."

"How in the hell did they do that?"

"Turns out that a Mexican-American feebee who was raised in Mexico as a kid ..."

"Jaime Morales," Bill said. "I met him. Educated and trained in Mexico, he flew jets in the US Air Force."

"Apparently, he had a cousin whom a druggie bigwig had running the books for the outfit."

"The cousin ran the books?"

"He kept Morales in the know and tipped off the Mexican authorities which got the druggies to bolt."

Bill took off his expensive panama, turned it in his fingers, then said,

"Any word on Ruth Hall?"

"Nothing I've heard."

"How about Pepe? I've been trying to call him since yesterday."

"I tried to call him too and so did Dan."

"He's just dropped off the radar," Rowe said.

~*~*~

More revelations
Lola's cabin outside of El Centro, CA
Same day, 8:54 PM, Saturday

Pepe followed Ruth outside. After unlocking the passenger's door for Pepe, she climbed in, pulled the car onto the road.

"How'd you find me?" she said.

"We persuaded Cassie Cortez to share your location." Pepe said.

"Who's he?"

"He's Lola's cousin and Santos's lawyer."

When they came to the parked Mercedes, Pepe jumped out.

"I'll follow you back to the shack," he said.

After the short drive back, Pepe and Ruth came into the cabin together.

Jake still sat on the chair in front of the sullen, weeping Lola. She looked up when they came in.

"That's Cassie's brief case," she said. "You dirty thieving bastards."

Pepe sat it on the table, opened it.

"There is another map," he said, "– to Rice canyon."

"Dirty bastards," Lola screamed. "*¡Pinche chingados!*"

"That's confirmation he's there," Pepe said.

"You killed my brother, you bastard," Lola growled.

"Sorry," Pepe said. "He was trying to kill me."

"*¡Hijo de puta!*"

"I'll call Bill Rowe in San Diego," Pepe said. "He's the only one who knows the full range of what's going on."

Lola yelled again, "Bastards, *¡Pinche cabrones!*"

"We came to get someone you kidnaped, not to hurt anybody," Jake said.

"I ain't got nothing to say," Lola snarled.

Jake s face lost expression.

"Santos killed my brother," he said.

Lola turned her tearing eyes away from his face.

"Somewhere I've got Bill Rowe's number," Pepe said.

"I can get it through the public safety information network," Jake said. "We can have them pick up Santos as well."

Lola gave a cry. "Why?" she said, "Why drag him into this?"

"Because he stole Matt Spyner's manuscript," Ruth said. "Then killed to protect his theft."

"He didn't mean to," Lola said.

"Bullshit!" Ruth said. "You got the guts to sit there and tell me he didn't mean to kill Matt Spyner?"

"No, he didn't. The other one either."

Pepe, Jake and Ruth stopped, then Pepe looked back at Lola.

"What other one?" he said.

"That cop in Mexico– it was an accident. Santos didn't mean to hurt him."

Pepe stared at her, the phone still in his hand.

"Santos killed my brother?" he said in a loud whisper.

"I don't know shit about your brother," Lola said. "It was a cop that stopped him in Mexico."

Pepe slammed the phone down, eyes blazing.

"That was my brother!"

Lola trembled under his gaze. "Well, he didn't mean to."

Pepe collapsed into a chair, put his hand to his forehead.

"It wasn't the mob," he said. "It was Santos. He killed Manolito over that shitting manuscript."

"But, it was an accident," Lola whined.

Pepe stared at her. "This had nothing to do with the drug racket– it was the manuscript."

"Then who killed Maggie?" Ruth said,

"The Rattler," Pepe said. "I saw him get off the bus that night. I had no idea he was on his way to kill her. I didn't hear about her death until a week later."

"I thought the Rattler was a hitman for the mob," Jake said.

Lola looked down at that table, her eyes misting again.

"Nacho got Jorge to do it. But, Nacho screwed up.

When he gave him the name and address, Jorge got one doctor confused with the other. It was a mistake."

"So, he meant to kill me," Ruth said. "They killed Maggie over this fucking manuscript too."

Lola looked away saying nothing.

Pepe rose, paced for a minute hands on hips, then snatched up the map to Rice Canyon.

"I'm going after Santos," he said.

"No, Pepe," Ruth said. "Let the cops handle this."

Jake stood. "I'll go with you."

Pepe shook his head.

"No– I've got to do this. Ruth, get hold of Dan Rowe and explain. Jake's in no shape to do anything but stay here with you."

Pepe picked up the map, snatched up the keys to the Mercedes.

"I don't like this, Pepe," Jake said. "At least take your gun."

Pepe strode toward the door, then turned, looked back at them. "I don't need a gun," he said.

Lola raised her head. "Please don't hurt him."

Pepe stared at her for a few seconds, then said, "I'll be in touch."

He left out the door.

~*~*~

Checking in
Bill Rowe's apartment, San Diego, CA
3:04 AM, Sunday morning, January 26, 1975

The phone's ring pierced Bill Rowe's ears like an electric needle. His hand shot out from under the covers, groped for the receiver, found it, then drug it back under the down quilt covering his bed.

"Goddam it, I'm off today."

"Officer Rowe? This is Ruth Hall."

Rowe sat up, blinked, searched the night table for his glasses.

"Ruth? Where are you?"

"It's a long story. But, I'll make it quick. I was grabbed a few days ago and Pepe and Jake Spyner..."

"Who?"

"Let me finish. Jake's the brother of my former boyfriend."

"Former boyfriend...? All right, I got it. Met him and Pepe in Oceanside..."

"They found me– don't ask how. Santos Villalobos's girlfriend and her brother kidnapped me."

275

"Holy shit."

"Yeah. Then, this guy called the Rattler..."

"The Rattler!"

"...they were holding me here..."

"Where's 'here?' "

"Well, I'm not quite sure but Pepe and Jake..."

"He's the ex-boyfriend, right?"

"No. His brother– anyway, they rescued me from those guys holding me prisoner."

"Wow. How'd you get my number?"

"Jake's an arson investigator and has been calling all night getting friends up all over the state running down your number."

"Where are you now?"

"I'll let you talk to Jake."

Rowe heard a man's voice come on.

"Detective Rowe. Jake Spyner, we met in Oceanside. We're somewhere about 35 miles south of El Centro."

"That's Imperial County."

"Right. We broke in and freed Ruth and in the struggle, two men were killed. I've called the Imperial County Sheriff's office and they're on their way here now."

"Where's Pepe?"

"He went after Santos Villalobos last night. We found out Villalobos is holed up in a cabin in Rice Canyon."

"That's in San Diego County. We've got some jurisdiction now."

"Pepe took the only map but Santos Villalobos's girlfriend is here and knows where it is."

"Do you think she'll cooperate."

"She wants to protect Santos."

"I'll alert the Park Service and see if I can get some rangers out there ASAP."

"OK."

"You know this is a mess."

"Yeah, I do. But, we had to play it this way."

Rowe scratched his head, then took a deep breath.

"Look. Stay in touch with me. I gotta take an immediately whiz. But, I'll do everything I can for you on this."

~*~*~

Mano a mano
Casmiro's cabin, Rice Canyon, San Diego County, CA
Same day, 5:42 AM, Sunday

The green pines grew thick near the edge of the canyon, poking their tops out of shaggy bark trunks from the rocky soil into a still dark sky. The pre-dawn darkness obscured the splotched soil with patches of brown between the stands of trees. Brown pine needles lay strewn everywhere except on the barren edges of the gray rocks that jutted out over the canyon's edge.

Leaning forward, breathing hard, Santos plodded one foot in front of the other up the steep path among the pine trees. He had thrown on the heavy jacket because the morning had broken cold. The smooth leather soles of his loafers slipped on the pine needles, the loose rocks lining the path making his footing difficult, adding to his discomfort.

He paused, wiped at his sweated-dotted brow, then looked around.

At the crest of the path, he could see the stone retaining wall at the edge of the canyon. Blowing out a lung-full of air, Santos took a deep breath, started forward once more until he stood at the edge of the retaining wall.

Coming into the clearing rimmed by the low stone wall, he leaned on the lip of the stacked cemented rocks, then looked out over the edge at the straight two hundred yards drop.

Thrusting his hand into his coat pocket, he felt the cold steel of the automatic Nacho had given him. Running his fingers over the smooth metal of the receiver, he pricked the ball of his finger on the sharp point of the front sight.

Santos shivered, missing sounds, noises he knew. The crash of water from the rushing tributary of the Colorado below in the canyon disturbed him. The sound of a hawk screeching overhead annoyed him.

Impatient with the constant smell of the pines, the wheezing, rustling sounds of the wind through the pines, the cold morning breeze, he wished for a cigarette even though he had not smoked in years.

He ran his hand over his dark curly hair now starting to speck with more tiny flacks of gray, leaned over to look down the dark canyon once more.

"I'll just have to fucking wait," he said aloud to the empty world around him.

~*~*~

Pepe parked Cassie's Mercedes in the landing beside the cabin, slid out, walked to the side of the cabin, peeked in through a window seeing a stack of dirty dishes piled in the sink of the small kitchen.

Stepping around, Pepe peered through the window into an empty front room. He tried the door. It opened in his hand.

He slipped inside, looked around. Clothes thrown on the floor in the connecting bedroom, a disheveled bed that held sheets and blanket shoved in a pile– no Santos.

Pepe moved, looked toward the back of the bedroom at an open bathroom door. The house was deserted.

Stepping outside through the back door, Pepe noticed the car parked beside the house. Then he saw the path leading into the woods toward the canyon at the edge of the cabin. Without hesitating, he followed it.

About a 100 yards down the trail, he saw a fresh footprint in the dim dawning light. He quickened his pace.

The way became steeper, the footing more difficult, he was glad to be wearing the hiking boots that Jake had recommended. Moving in quick steps up the steep path for nearly a mile, he came to the clearing at the edge of the canyon.

There, leaning on the edge of a hand-stacked rock retaining wall was the man he was looking for. He called out,

"Santos!"

Santos jerked around at the sound of the voice.

"Who in the fuck are you?" he said.

"Pepe Ortega."

Santos blinked without recognition. Then, the name seemed to stir something in his brain. He jammed his hand in his pocket, fumbled out the pistol, thrust it out in front of him toward Pepe's face like a spear.

"I'm not sure who you are but you're bugging me."

Pepe did not move. In the red streaked morning light, he saw that Santos had not released the safety on the automatic.

"It's been a long trail, '*Mano*," he said. "And, now I've found you."

"You ain't gonna do shit. I got the gun and won't hesitate to blow your fucking face off."

Pepe sat the edge of his butt down on the edge of the retaining wall looking straight into Santos's eyes.

"Like you killed my brother?"

Santos's eyes went wide. The gun in his hand shook. He advanced a few more paces, the pistol still pointed in Pepe's face.

"Your brother?"

"The policeman in Mexico."

"That was an accident," he said. "I didn't mean to hurt that cop— he grabbed me, tried to stop me. I just swung that binder and it caught him in the throat."

Pepe did not react.

"So, you just left him there to choke to death. You could have called for help but you ran off to cover your stinking ass— all for a fucking piece of shit writing you stole from another man."

"I didn't mean to hurt him. God damn it, it just happened."

"I could forgive you for that but you stole Matt Spyner's thesis, passed it off as your own, then turned his work into a piece of literary crap that made you a fortune. And then you killed him— because you needed to cover your ass."

Santos came closer, thrust the pistol into Pepe's face.

"Shut up! Shut up, damn you. I'll shoot your fucking face off."

"It took Matt a long time to find out you'd ripped him off but he did, he came back after you. Then, when he confronted you, you killed him."

"Shut up, Damn you, I'll blow your eyes out."

Pepe crossed his arms, narrowed his eyes.

"Why'd you kill him, Santos? Did he ask for too big a payoff?"

"No," Santos screamed. "The stupid shit wouldn't take a payoff!"

Santos trembled, the pistol quaked in his hand.

"He wanted my blood," he said. "He wanted to out me and ruin the project."

"So, you bashed his brains to cover your ass and bank account."

"He was going to screw me over."

Santos shoved the gun forward in Pepe's face.

With one flash of motion, Pepe grabbed, twisted the pistol from Santos's hand, hurled it over the side of the canyon, then shoved Santos off his feet.

"Santos," Pepe said. "You're a lying, murdering piece of shit."

On his back, Santos tried to crawl away from the taller man leaning over him.

Pepe reached down, grabbed him by his jacket, jerked him to his feet, pushed into a sitting position on the retaining wall.

"You're going down, Santos," Pepe said. "You killed two people. You, your bitch girlfriend, her gangster brother and their killer pal have left a trail of bodies."

Santos seized a rock the size of his hand, slung it in Pepe's face.

Pepe rolled back from the impact, his hand went to the abrasion on his face.

Santos pushed off the wall, bolted down the path back toward the cabin. Pepe darted after him. Ahead of him, Santos glanced back over his shoulder, then tripped on an exposed tree root, sprawling forward on his hands and knees.

Pepe leapt on to him, grabbing him by the shoulders. Santos grabbed a handful of dirt, threw it in Pepe's face.

Shaking the dirt from his eyes, Pepe swung as he scrambled to his feet, hitting Santos on the shoulder. Santos staggered to one side, snatched up a broken tree limb, then chopped it at Pepe's head.

Pepe blocked the clubbing motion, the brittle pine limb shattered on his arm.

Santos turned to run. Pepe grabbed him, smashed in the face with a right hook.

Santos stumbled to a nearby tree trunk, stood there nose bleeding, glaring at Pepe. Santos waved his arm.

"I didn't want to hurt anyone."

Pepe moved in front of him, fists raised, spitting dirt out of his mouth.

"That doesn't wash it," he said.

"I was only trying to protect myself. I'da been disgraced. Everyone would have laughed me outta town."

"Shameful acts deserve disgrace."

Santos began to weep. He put hands to his face and sobbed.

"I can make you rich," Santos said.

"Fuck you and fuck your money," Pepe said.

Santos bellowed, charged forward knocking Pepe down, then took off in a run back up toward the canyon.

Rolling to his feet, Pepe sprinted after him back to the edge of the canyon. Santos scrambled up onto the retaining wall at the edge of the cliff, then turned to face Pepe.

"Come any closer," Santos screamed. "I swear to God I'll jump!"

Pepe gripped the lapels of Santos's jacket, pulled him close, stuck his face in his, then said in a growl,

"I don't fucking care."

With a quick shove, Pepe threw Santos backwards over the edge of the canyon.

Santos fell, waving his arms, screaming, bouncing off the jutting rocks until he came to a broken, jerked heap at the edge of the river below.

Pepe turned without a sound, then hurried down the path toward the cabin where he had parked the car.

PART SEVEN

The inquiry
FBI Offices, Federal Building, San Diego, CA
Six months later, 10:45 AM, Tuesday, July 15, 1975

Pepe opened the door for Ruth, then followed her into the glass-windowed conference room where a long, ovoid table with 12 chairs occupied the center of the office. A recording system with lines leading to several microphones at various stations crouched in the middle like a giant black and gray spider.

Jaime Morales came over, shook Pepe's hand, gave Ruth a hug, kissed her on the cheek.

"Don't I get a kiss?" Pepe said.

"No," Morales said. "You're too damn ugly."

"You've got good taste, Jaime," Ruth said.

"Pérez will be here at 11," Morales said. "I've got the files from the forensic investigation of the alleged kidnaping..."

"Alleged my ass!" Ruth said. "Those bastards grabbed me, taped me up..."

"No worries, Ruth," Pepe said. "Until it's proven in a court of law, it remains an allegation."

"Bullshit!"

"Yeah, it is," Morales said. "But, we do it anyway."

"That doesn't make it any less bullshit," Ruth said.

"This is a complicated criminal case– a stinking booby trap with trip wires strung out every which way," Morales said.

"More fun and games," Pepe said. "And, now we got the family shark to deal with."

"Cortez is damn sharp," Morales said. "He's got his fingers around Pepe and Jake's balls squeezing damn near as tight as our case against Lola."

"Jake said those barrio chicks are tough," Pepe said.

"Her ass is in deep," Morales said. "But we gotta get you and Jake outta this shit. This may require us to give some ground."

"What ground?" Ruth said.

"I dunno yet," Morales said.

"How'd you get stuck with this case anyway?" Ruth said.

"I was on the wire for the drug bust but got pulled back into this mess because my boss wants me to cover Pepe's ass," Morales said.

He looked from Pepe to Ruth, then went on,

"We've got tight-assed evidence to nail Lola's ass to the wall. That gives us a lot of maneuverability."

"Do you think she'll walk?" Pepe said.

" '*Mano*, I don't fucking know for sure," Morales said. "What I do know is that I'm authorized to cut a deal to get your and Jake's asses outta the line of fire– that's first in my book."

"That's damn unfair," Ruth said.

"Welcome to the world of law and order," Morales said.

"Cortez's here," Pepe said, looking through the window.

Casimiro Cortez opened the door and stepped in.

"Dr. Hall, Gentlemen," he said. "We all know why we're here. So, let's begin."

Cortez took a seat, looked across the table at Pepe with no expression.

Pepe stared back until Morales cleared his throat, then spoke,

"For the record, I'm Agent Jaime Morales, authorized agent of the FBI and a member of the State Bar of California. Today, we're conducting an inquiry into the alleged kidnapping of Dr. Ruth Hall by Ms. Dolores Santiago and others now deceased..."

Cortez raised his hand.

"Can we shut that goddam machine off and talk some business?" he said. "Or, do we have to play more legalese."

Pepe saw Morales push a button in front of him, then look up at Cortez.

"Your serve, Counselor," Morales said.

"No pun intended," Cortez said, "but we've got a Mexican standoff."

"Go on," Morales said.

"Ortega and Spyner abducted me by force, took me into the desert, stuck a rattlesnake down my pants, coerced confidential client information from me, stole my car and very likely murdered Santos Villalobos."

"May I point out to you, Counselor," Morales said, "We can place your client and her deceased brother at the site of abduction..."

"Alleged abduction," Cortez said.

"... and demonstrate that these two men you accuse are both registered and commissioned public safety officers, who rescued Dr. Hall from your clients' illegal and criminal restraint."

"Alleged criminal restraint," Cortez said. "Yeah. We know all that."

"So, what do you have in mind, Cortez?" Morales said.

"You drop all charges. We pursue no further action and everyone goes home bent but OK."

Ruth gasped. Pepe watched Morales stared at Cortez for a long moment.

"Wow," Morales said. "Do you want my house, car and children too, Counselor?"

"Can we cut the shit, Morales" Cortez said. "We've both got a gun stuck up each other's ass."

"And," Morales said, "this is your solution?"

Cortez leaned back in his chair, looked up at Pepe with a hard smile, then said,

"You guys aren't going to just drop the big turd on us and walk away. You broke the law four ways from Sunday and I'll be goddamned if I'm gonna let it slide by while my client takes the hard fall."

Ruth banged her fist on the table.

"You sonfabitch," she said. "You murdered my roommate, you fucking kidnaped me– all to protect a shithead who stole another man's work and made a fortune from it."

Cortez didn't blink.

"Dr. Hall," he said. "I did none of those things and while there may be circumstantial evidence linking the late Jorge Reyes to other crimes, there's no way you can prove that his actions were done at the behest of my client."

"Bullshit!" Ruth screamed, "She confessed it to us."

Cortez shrugged his shoulders, said, "Hearsay under coercion. Won't stand up."

"And, that fucking Santos stole Matt Spyner's thesis..."

"Where's the proof?"

"Hold it right there," Pepe said. "Santos himself admitted to me he took the thesis."

"No kidding?" Cortez snapped back. "Too bad he ain't here to affirm or deny that."

"OK, OK," Morales interrupted. "Let's get back to reality."

Pepe leaned back, put his hand to his mouth, looked over at Cortez sitting back in his chair.

"I ain't heard nothing real yet from you, Morales," Cortez said.

Morales leaned forward.

"I might get the DA and the Federal prosecutor to go along with conspiracy to abduct. Lola does some soft time and comes out with a few bruises– maybe three to five..."

"What?" Ruth said.

Cortez ignored her, didn't take his eye from at Morales, then said, "Go on,"

"In turn," Morales went on, "You forget any Ortega and Spyner involvement."

With a face showing no emotion, Cortez looked over at Pepe, then over at Morales.

"That might work," Cortez said.

"What about Matt Spyner's murder?" Ruth yelled out.

Cortez threw her a bored look. "What about it?"

"Santos Villalobos killed him stole his work, made a million or two off it and then killed him."

"So you say," Cortez said.

"We can go to the papers," Ruth said. "We'll have this in every journal and review..."

"No, you won't," Cortez said.

"What makes you think not, asshole?"

"As tempting as it is, you won't do it," Cortez said. "I'd slap lawsuits on you left and right and have this tied up for years. I'd drain every nickel you have before it finally comes to trial and gets thrown out. In the meantime, while you're going broke and getting in deep debt, we'll be selling books like cheap coke all over the world."

"You bastard!" Ruth shouted.

Cortez shook his head, then said, "Sticks and stones, Dr. Hall."

Pepe put his hand on Ruth's arm. She brushed it away, then flopped back in her chair, arms folded over her chest, muttering.

Pepe heard Morales speak over Ruth's mumbled string of obscenities,

"Do we have a deal, counselor?"

"I think we have something we can work with, Agent Morales," Cortez said.

Pepe looked over at Morales who winked at him.

"OK," Morales said. "Let me talk to my bosses and then I'll get back to you."

Cortez stood up, walked to the door, turned once more looked Pepe in the eye, gave Ruth a curt dip of his head, then said,

"Gentlemen, Dr. Hall."

Then he left, closing the door behind him.

~*~*~

Final confrontation
Zarzueta village, outside Mazatan, Sonora, Mexico
7:45 AM, Saturday, July 19, 1975

Cloaked in the pleasant warmth of the early morning sun, Lucero's nanny, Doña Luz clutched her brown and green covered basket as she picked her way through spread out serapes and mantas loaded with fruit, vegetables, chilies and other greens in the beehive busy marketplace. She fixed her gaze on a row of stalls at the back of the town square pitched next to a line of two storey buildings housing a cantina, a small dry goods store, a *velatorio* funeral parlor. The herbs she needed would be there.

Pursing her lips, she scolded herself for being so careless in overlooking the diminishing supply of herbs she needed for her everyday rituals.

It's been this way since my Señor Luchito disappeared over the border. I should have seen the signs.

When she came toward the stall, she saw Pedro, the herb seller raise his eyebrows, turn to his 12 year old daughter at his side, then heard him whisper,

"Unusual. *La Añeja*, the Ancient one, comes herself."

The girl raised her pigtailed head, gawked a second, then dropped her gaze before the transfixing green opal eyes of Doña Luz.

She placed her basket on the counter, then spoke to him in Nahuatl.

"What do you have for me, *Petzi-tzun?*"

"Whatever your needs might be, Doña Luz."

"Have you *xiitzo?*"

"Aplenty."

"I need *milahuahua* too."

"Yes."

"*Kanititla* too."

"Of course."

With quick, deliberate motions, Pedro uncovered clay pots, took out handfuls of the herbs, wrapped them in sheets torn from the pages of an old newspaper, rolled them into cones, twisted the ends, lifted the woven lid of the witch woman's basket, then dumped in the tubes of paper.

"How much?" she said, picking up the basket.

Pedro dropped his gaze, whispered, "One hundred ten pesos, if it pleases you, Doña Luz."

Doña Luz sat the basket on the ground, took two 100 peso notes, from her dress pocket, handed them to Pedro, who rifled for change in a which he kept under the counter.

Doña Luz frowned, shook her open hand.

"Give the change to the beggars," she said.

Pedro doffed his hat, dropped his head in a deep bow.

"It is done," he said.

When Doña Luz turned to pick up her basket, she noticed a big woman standing directly behind her. Taller, darker skinned than Doña Luz, she wore a bleached cotton muslin dress with a green, red and blue needle-point collar, her face showed large, dark brown eyes.

Doña Luz scowled into the woman's expressionless gaze, then growled in Spanish,

"Stand aside. You're in my way."

The woman didn't move. She stood, looking into Doña Luz's eyes. The woman's lips tightened into a slight smile, then spoke in Nahuatl in a low voice,

"I have words for you."

Doña Luz flinched. The woman spoke a different dialect but she understood every word.

"Who are you?" Doña Luz said.

"I'm called Ixcheli."

"I don't know you."

"But, I know you." Ixcheli poked a soft, quick touch to Doña Luz's right cheek below her eye.

"I've come a long way," Ixcheli said. "I wanted to behold the face of the one who brought pain and tears into my house."

Doña Luz opalescent eyes blazed, her lips formed into a snarl. Her hand flew to her face where she had been poked.

"How can that be?" she said. "My eyes have never held your face before this moment."

"Nor mine, yours. But still I know you."

"You gargle riddles."

"You killed my Señor Patrón."

Doña Luz drew a deep breath, stepped back, touched her face again.

"You babble madness."

"My Señor Patrón was Don Armando Ortega."

Dona Luz's heart skipped a beat, her bright hazel green eyes widened.

"How can you say that I had anything to do with his death?"

Ixcheli did not move. Her eyes showed no expression. Then, her lips molded into a small, sad smile.

"You came to his office," she said. "You brought what you said was tea for Don Armando's cough. You said it was from our Señora. He drank of it. The next day, he died from an attack on his heart."

Doña Luz's lips lost their color when she knotted them into a tight ball. Her eyes spat green fire.

"I was protecting my own," she said.

Ixcheli didn't blink.

"As I would have done," she said. "I can't hate you for that."

"Then, why come here to bother me?"

"I came to see the one who lured the shadow of death to my doorstep."

"You've seen. Now, stand from my way, or face harm," Doña Luz said.

Ixcheli's mouth lost the little smile. Her dark brown eyes turned cold. She stepped to one side.

"Pass," she said. "I am done."

Doña Luz tightened her hand on the basket bail, pushed past the bigger woman, strode to the edge of the market, then spun around to look back once more at the confronting figure.

The woman called Ixcheli was gone from the open marketplace.

~*~*~

Doña Luz pushed open the door to her room in the hacienda, strode to the cupboard where she kept her herbs, When she set the basket on the counter, it seemed to shimmer in her hand. She lifted the woven lid, peered in.

As soon as it saw the light, the snake struck her in the right eye. Doña Luz screamed, grabbed it by the throat. The twisting serpent twisted from her grasp, struck again– this time hooking its needle-sharp fangs into her throat, just under her jaw line.

Doña Luz tore the snake from her throat, grabbed a hard wooden pestle from the counter, then pounded at its shovel-shaped head against the counter top. The twisting reptile whipped its tail in a coil around her arm, sank its fangs into Doña Luz's hand. She brought the heavy pestle down on its head, the fangs still stuck onto her hand.

At the blow, the snake's head jerked loose from her hand. Doña Luz pounded it until its head was a bloody pulp. One eye popped out, hanging down from the smashed skull.

"Chato," Doña Luz screamed.

Some seconds later, a servant boy threw open the door, dashed into her room, then stopped, staring at the long, striped snake at his feet. It twitched on the floor, then lay still. Doña Luz slipped to her knees on the floor, her eye a bleeding patch, blood on her face and throat. She looked up at the boy.

"Go. Get Patli ," she gasped.

The teenage boy turned, ran out of the door screaming the woman's name. Three other women peered in, then went running to Doña Luz, stretched her out on the floor. One grabbed a towel and wiped the blood from her face.

An older woman, Patli followed the boy into the room. Coming over, she bent down to Doña Luz.

"The snake," Doña Luz gasped. "It was in my basket."

Patli rose, went to the dead snake, poked it with her toe, then turned it over.

Doña Luz's good eye was glazing over. She groaned, sought Patli's face, reached for her hand.

"What was it?" Doña Luz said.

"It's a *nauyaca*," Patli said. "The Gringos call it a '*fer de lance.*' It's not from around here."

Doña Luz was choking, her good eye was not focusing.

"What do we do?" she asked the older woman.

"We sing your death song, my sister," Patli said. "There's no cure from the bite of the *nauyaca*."

~*~*~

The Secret of Don Pedro Miguel
La Cueva Azteca Mexican Restaurant, San Diego, CA
1:47 PM, Saturday, September 27, 1975

The gold plastered walls of the restaurant were splashed with Aztec scenes taken from the artwork from old recovered codices. Pepe looked around at the decor, nodded with a smile, then spoke,

"Not a bad ambience, Jaime. Our ancestors would be proud."

Jaime Morales lifted a bottle of Modelo Especial to Pepe, then spoke in Nahuatl,

"May your heart soar like the eagle above the bloody corpses of your enemies."

Ruth snorted.

"What in the hell was that all about?" she said.

"Just an old Indio way of saying 'congratulations,' " Morales said.

"An interesting bit of news," Pepe said. "My old Ñaña wrote me a cryptic note a month or so ago."

"What'd she say?" Morales said.

"She wrote in Indio, saying 'the spirits of your beloved family rest peacefully now.' "

"Huh," Ruth said. "What does that mean."

"Just what it said," Morales said. "Us Indios don't intellectualize."

"Well," Ruth said. "Since I don't do mysteries, I'll just have to let that one go."

"So, Ruth," Morales said, "Do you feel better now that Lola's going to be a guest of the Federal government for at least the next 15 years?"

Ruth pursed her lips, wrinkled her face into a frown as she focused on the bottle of Corona in her hand.

"I feel kind of hollow," she said.

"I can relate to that," Pepe said.

"No one walks away from this kind of a mess completely clean," Morales said.

"How's the case going with Alban?" Pepe said.

"The federal judge threw out Rydell's petition to drop the case on the grounds of illegal seizure and it's scheduled for trial."

"Will he get out of it?" Ruth said.

"No way, Jose," Morales said. "With all that smack he and Drako were carrying, they're going down big time."

"It still pisses me off that Santos Villalobos's book is still on the market," Ruth said.

"We can let that one go too," Morales said.

"Look at it this way, Ruth," Pepe said. "You'll always have one supreme satisfaction that few people will share."

"What's that?" Ruth asked.

"You know *The Secrets of Don Pedro Miguel*." Pepe said.

ABOUT THE AUTHOR

Frank P. Araujo, , is an anthropologist and linguist with interests in structuralism, language and myth. Having lived in California for most of his life, the majority of his professional career was consulting on international economic development projects in developing Third World countries. He enjoys cooking, fencing, movies classical music and his grandchildren.

This is his second novel. His prior published work includes 4 children's picture books including several translations into English and Spanish.